"I don't mind you standing there," he added as he pushed aside the curtain and stepped from the tub, scrubbing his hair with the towel. "But you are somewhat to blame for this."

"I am?" she squeaked. Heavens, he was good-looking all wet and frumpled. His water-soaked T-shirt was plastered to his chest. Kate's tongue became the Sahara.

"*Mmm hmm*," he nodded. Now he was finger-combing his hair, a crooked grin making his face boyishly appealing as he dropped the towel on his toolbox. "I was thinking about you, you see—"

"You were?" Kate backed up against the sink, the small bathroom feeling suddenly much smaller. Dangerously small. As small as the pocket in her lungs still capable of holding air. "What were you thinking?"

He paused, his eyes dancing. "I'm thinking I ought to keep that to myself."

"Why?"

"I don't think we know each other well enough for me to tell you that."

Suddenly the flannel of her robe felt very hot on her skin. Kate sucked air through her nose and stared at his lips, that crooked smile teasing her, beckoning her.

"I want to know," she said, her voice barely a whisper...

If only life had a refresh button...

Luck of the Draw

Cheri Allan

~ Book One ~
A Betting on Romance Novel

Five Oaks Books

This is a work of fiction. Names, characters, places and incidents are either the product of the author's imagination or are used fictitiously, and any resemblance to actual persons, living or dead, business establishments, events or locales is entirely coincidental.

Luck of the Draw

Editing by Orchard Edits
Cover and logo images © Elena Elisseeva | Dreamstime.com

Publishing History
First Five Oaks Books Edition, 2014
Print ISBN: 978-0-9904815-1-5
Digital ISBN: 978-0-9904815-0-8

Published in the United States of America

Acknowledgements

I am eternally grateful to my dear husband, Alan, whom I love beyond words, for supporting me through successes and stumbles and for never once questioning our household's unusually high per capita consumption of chocolate.

I give thanks…

To my children for supporting me even though I've told them they can't read my books until they're older, because they, too, believe in following one's dreams…

To the beautiful, talented and inspirational ladies of NHRWA without whom I wouldn't be sane *or* published. The waiting room was lovely, but it was time to move on…

To old friends and new for asking me how it was going, reading, critiquing, and often simply wading through imperfect versions of this and other projects before I—finally—got it right…

And, to Charis, a true angel from above, for sending out her beacon of hope when I most needed it and lighting the way through countless e-mails and 'murky middles.' You are a critique partner extraordinaire.

I raise my bunny to the Plotbunnies (you know who you are) for your creativity and strength and open-minded support. May all your dreams come true!

And finally, I thank you, my readers, for taking a chance on me. Without you, I'd just be a crazy cat lady with a computer.

~ Cheri

For my husband,

Who believed in me long before I believed in myself
and gave me the gift of following my dreams.
You are my every hero. Love you madly!

~ Your Cookie

CHAPTER ONE

IT RAINED THE NIGHT RANDY DIED—scattered spring storms that left shimmering puddles on the pavement under the streetlight outside the house. They swirled with surreal, iridescent color as Kate opened the door with one hand and clutched her robe closed at her throat with the other.

There were two of them, their uniforms dark with rain, eyes dark with fatigue. They spoke with gently dispassionate voices as they delivered the news. *Single car accident... Only occupant...* They asked if she understood. *Yes*, she said. *Yes.* Was she alone? *No.* Would she like a drink of water? *No. No, thank you.* She didn't want them in her home, didn't want them searching for a clean cup in her kitchen, compassionately detached as they watched her and waited for her to fall apart.

After they left, she stared at the wet boot-prints on the living room carpet and wondered what she should do or whom she should call. Her limbs felt strangely heavy as she wandered through the house to her room, too stunned to cry, looking around for traces of *him*, but, of course, she'd already packed away the pictures and mementos of their life together. All that remained of their ten-year marriage sat in a small bowl on her dresser.

She picked up the ring, her breath held tight in her chest, and slid it back on her finger—as if, somehow, by putting it on, she might magically go back in time and make things turn out differently.

But the miracle never happened, and then Liam woke up. She assured him everything was all right—even though it wasn't—and curled up with him on his small bed, in the dark, trying not to hug him too tight.

She didn't sleep.

She didn't weep.

She simply stared at the plain gold band on her finger as the pre-dawn hours slid into day.

June 7
Time. They talk about it flying, as if it were a child's kite, but as I get ready for Liam's third birthday party today, it occurs to me that for every year of his life, I've lived TEN. That's not flying, that's careening. Just sayin'.

CHAPTER TWO

Seven weeks later...

"MY GOD, KATE—I THINK I'D *die* if I were you."

Kate Mitchell's hand froze in mid-air, a mini wiener inches from her lips as she tried to think of an appropriate reply. Granted, wieners weren't considered top-drawer fancy fare, but Liam loved them, and it was *his* day. She lowered her hand to her plate and forced a smile.

It was stunning how tactless people could be when expressing their condolences. Here they were, surrounded by streamers and giddy children, and yet Betsy's china-doll blue eyes blinked earnestly as if they were standing next to Randy's casket instead of eating finger foods at a three-year-old's birthday party.

Kate cleared her throat. "Yes, well, you know what they say about not being given more than you can handle."

"Still, you're so *brave*. I mean, how will you get by? I heard Randy didn't even have life insurance!" Betsy finished *sotto voce*, her china-blues blinking back compassionate tears.

"Well, under the circumstances..."

"I know," Betsy touched Kate's arm meaningfully. "I heard about the DUI."

She pronounced it 'dee-wee' as if it were some child's game and not a misdemeanor crime. Kate fought the urge to stuff her mini wiener up Betsy's pert, surgery-enhanced nose. She pasted what she hoped was a suitably neutral expression on her face. "Oh?"

Lord, she hated this. Hated, especially, feeling like she *still* had to defend Randy even though he'd been days away from being her *ex*-husband, even though—ironically—he hadn't actually been drinking the night he'd plowed his Lexus into a tree. No, it was enough he had the reputation of drinking and driving. It was enough he'd still, technically, been her husband.

Betsy gave her hand another pat. "I understand," she said.

Kate stifled a bubble of hysterical laughter. How could Betsy possibly understand something she couldn't understand herself? She couldn't explain why Randy had run off the road that night any more than she could explain the wild mood swings that had plagued her the last few weeks, her gut turning over itself like she'd eaten bad chicken salad or something. Grief, the counselor had told her. But, it didn't feel like grief. It felt like fear.

Kate glanced around for escape from Betsy's glistening eyeballs and spied Nana—dear Nana!—in the corner with elderly Mrs. Pemborly who lived next door at the end of their southern Connecticut cul-de-sac. It was a quiet neighborhood, picturesque, with forsythia bushes and mature trees shading small, well-tended yards. Just the place to raise a family. Or at least, that's what Nana had insisted nearly three years ago when she'd offered to rent the house to Kate and Randy after Poppy died. Nana had decided to move back to her hometown of Sugar Falls, New Hampshire. She'd said she didn't have the heart to sell the house in Connecticut but didn't want to rent to strangers, either.

It hadn't surprised Kate when Randy jumped at the chance to move out of the tiny second-floor apartment they'd rented since their wedding day. He'd always cursed the too-short shower and cramped kitchen. Made fun of the baby-blue walls.

But Kate hadn't hated it. Snippets of memories flooded her. The bouquets of wildflowers she used to put in mason jars on the windowsills. Liam asleep in his bassinet in the corner of their bedroom. How Randy had carried her up the narrow stairs and made love to her on the living room floor when they'd first moved in.

Lord, it all seemed a lifetime ago.

Another mother smiled and reached across Kate for a celery stick, her hand hovering momentarily as if assessing it for calories. The woman finally picked it up and nibbled delicately, her white linen pantsuit looking impossibly fresh and sophisticated next to Kate's khakis and plain blue tee. Kate stepped aside and nodded politely in case the woman gave into temptation and picked up a carrot.

Liam waved from across the room and smiled, his forehead sweaty, his hair sticking up adorably on the side. Kate waved back, her heart squeezing in her chest as a swift surge of love flooded her.

She watched the woman pick up another celery stick, and the surge of love turned to a wave of guilt. She should be taking better care of herself, for Liam's sake if not for her own. She should be reaching for carrots instead of loading her body with salt and nitrates. Hadn't she given Randy heck every time he'd brought mini wieners home? Of course, she'd never expected to *like* them. She'd never expected she'd be a thirty-one-year-old widow, either, for that matter. Kate stabbed another mini wiener and stuffed it in her mouth, resenting the celery-eating mom's self-restraint immensely.

"So," Celery Mom said. Kate couldn't for the life of her remember the woman's name, but she was pretty sure she'd come with the girl dressed entirely in Hanna Andersson who was currently jumping on the sofa. "Kate," she continued, her face creased in delicate sympathy, "have you made any plans?"

Plans? Kate looked around at the three-year-olds running rampant in her living room and wondered how these people could be so incredibly insensitive. How was this any of their business? "I don't know," she murmured, grasping for something to say besides the impolite retort that came to mind. "My grandmother suggested I meet with her financial planner—"

"Oh, honey, I don't mean *those* kind of plans." Celery Mom backed up a little. "I was just wondering if you had any plans, you know, for the summer. Vacation?"

"Oh! No. No plans," Kate said. "No plans whatsoever." Without a plan. *Planless...*

That wasn't precisely true, of course. Kate had lots of plans. Plans to get her life back on track. Plans to finally finish her art history degree and get a real job. Plans to prove to her parents once and for all she hadn't flushed her life down the toilet the day she married a smart-talking bad-boy from nowhere.

Unfortunately, Randy's accident had thrown all those plans up in the air like a messy game of *52 pick-up*. Without alimony or child support and, just as importantly, another adult to watch Liam, she wasn't sure how she would manage classes and tuition now. If she could convince Nancy to let her switch to a reduced schedule or even a four-day workweek, that'd save on daycare expenses. She might just be able to swing it.

Lord knew she didn't want to ask her parents for help. Her father took great pride in his self-made success and said hand-outs eroded character. Kate sighed—she could accept a little less character if it bought her some time. Maybe she should buy a Powerball ticket...

"You should come to Sugar Falls!" Nana piped up from behind as if reading her thoughts. Kate jumped in surprise, nearly dropping her mini wiener off her toothpick. Good Lord. For a woman pushing seventy, Nana was surprisingly quick on her feet.

"What? No. I couldn't." She'd love to, hadn't been to New Hampshire since she, Nana and Poppy had gone together that summer after high school, but now was so not the time.

"Nonsense," Nana insisted. She did a lot of insisting. "It'd do you good to get away for a while. Fresh air. Swimming. Fishing…"

"*Fishing?*" Liam exclaimed, bouncing over to join them. "I never fished! Can we go? Can we?"

"Not for a while," Kate hedged.

"Why not?" Nana and Liam asked in unison.

Kate gritted her teeth and tried to simultaneously smile at Celery Mom, shoo Liam away and give Nana the evil eye. "Please don't get Liam's hopes up," she whispered in Nana's ear. "I can't afford a vacation."

Nana dug a carrot into the veggie dip, popped it into her mouth and crunched loudly. "Nonsense. You could stay at Ruth Pearson's little house on the lake. She moved in with her kids last year after her knee surgeries. It's just sitting empty. I'm sure she wouldn't mind." Nana touched Kate's arm. "I'll call her."

"No! No. Work is… busy. Besides, I don't think any more upheaval would be good for Liam. He needs to be home."

"Home?" Nana sniffed, stuffing another dip-drenched carrot into her mouth. "I thought it was a memorial to Randy Mitchell what with all the pictures you've got lying around. He's here more now than he was when he was alive."

Kate gaped in disbelief before finding her tongue again. "Excuse us," she mumbled to Celery Mom. She grabbed Nana's elbow and steered her away from the snack table. Oh. My. Lord! She didn't have the strength for this conversation. Not on Liam's birthday of all days. "We've been through this, Nana. The psychologist said it would help Liam process Randy's… being gone." Not that Randy's death had had nearly the impact on Liam Kate had feared it might. She shouldn't be surprised. Randy had always been too busy… or drunk… to spend quality bonding time with his son.

"Anyway," muttered Nana with single-minded determination, "I don't see why you have to have a picture of him on the back of the *toilet*."

"It's Liam's favorite photo of his father. He likes to look at it when he's taking a bath. Can we drop this now? *Please?*"

Kate scanned the room. She should probably serve the cake at some point. Right after she gagged her meddling grandmother and stuffed her in a closet somewhere.

Nana, God bless her, had been poking around the edges of Kate's 'situation' ever since arriving from New Hampshire the day before. And when Nana got a hold of something, she was harder to shake loose than peanut butter from hair. Don't ask how she knew.

Hanna Andersson girl poured the last of the lemonade into her paper rocket-ship cup. Grateful for an excuse to escape, Kate grabbed the empty lemonade pitcher and pushed through the kitchen door. Unfortunately, Nana picked up a chip bowl and trailed behind.

"No, I won't drop it. The ladies and I are worried. What's happened to you, Katie? You were so determined to move on, to start fresh —"

"But he *died* first!" Kate cut in, pouring way too much pink lemonade powder into the empty pitcher. Oh, heck. Who cared? The kids were already plenty sugared up. Kate held the pitcher under the faucet with shaking hands. "He's *dead*. That kind of changes things, you know? I know he wasn't perfect, and—*yes*—we had our problems, but he was the only father Liam had. I have to respect that. For Liam's sake."

Nana raised an eyebrow and tugged open a bag of chips. "At what cost to you?"

Kate could feel the tears threaten as she searched the counter for her extra-long spoon. "Oh, Lord, Nana, I can't get into this with you, again. I'm fine. *We're* fine. Tell the ladies they don't need to worry."

"*Pfft*. Anyone can see you're not taking care of yourself. You're not eating right. You haven't had a haircut in months..." Nana motioned vaguely toward Kate's hair.

Kate stuffed a hunk behind her ear. Sure, it was a little longer than the shoulder-length page-boy she'd worn it as for so long, but she was still deciding what to do with it.

"Your problem is you've been so busy trying to preserve Randall's memory and pretend everything's okay you haven't given yourself time to be angry."

"Angry?" Kate pushed her hair out of her face again and tried to concentrate on Nana's words. She spied the spoon and began to stir the lemonade with more vigor than precisely necessary.

"Yes, angry. Why, for six months after your grandfather died I paced this house hurling insults at him. I was so mad at him for leaving me."

"I know how much you loved Poppy, but I hardly see how that's anything like—"

"He was my rock, true, but I don't think it matters. Love. Hate…" Nana waved the empty chip bag and crumbs sprinkled the floor. "They're really not that far apart. The point is I'd built my life around that man. I couldn't see how I could make it work without him. But, apparently, the Almighty could. 'Cause here I am." She flicked the bag toward Kate. "And here *you* are. So get angry and get on with your life. Take some time to figure out what you want to do."

"What I want to do," Kate shook her head and put the spoon in the sink, choosing to ignore the neon pink dribbles that spattered the counter, "is get through this damn party without discussing this anymore."

Nana pursed her lips. "*Well*. There's no need to swear. I get the hint. We'll talk later."

Kate rolled her eyes. "Nana, I know you want to help, but I don't—"

"Kate! There you are." Betsy pushed open the kitchen door and stepped forward. "Here. Let me get that. Thirsty crowd out there! Oh, and Cindy wants to know if the cake will be gluten-free, because she brought sorghum flour cookies to share just in case." She took the pitcher and disappeared back into the living room.

Kate wiped her hands briskly on a dishtowel, ignored Nana's pointed, questioning look and returned to the fray, letting the door swing closed behind her. She stepped over a girl crawling on all fours and nearly collided with the leggy, Nordic-looking nanny with the low-cut top and generous cleavage. The nanny apologized. Or at least Kate presumed she did, not actually recognizing the language being used. The nanny's smile was brilliant and white and could only be expensive and imported.

"Are vee having de kek soon?" nanny asked, blinding Kate again with her teeth. "Vee av an—ow do you say?—appoint-mont?"

"Cake! Yes! Yes. Good idea. I'll serve the cake now." Kate whirled back toward the kitchen where Nana was already ripping open a package of paper plates.

"All I'm saying," Nana continued, as if Kate had never left the room, "is it's better to be a widow when you're young and attractive than when you're old like me."

"*What?*" Kate gaped at Nana and reached to pull the cover off Liam's rocket ship cake. "Where is this even coming from?"

"I'm just saying if you were my age, you'd have to accept you're going to spend your remaining days alone."

"Surrounded by family who loves you." Or at least tolerates you. *Hmm.* Kate stuck the plastic astronaut figurine on the cake about where she figured the cockpit would be. The cake was a little lopsided and Kate had accidentally dumped the food coloring bottle into the exhaust-plume frosting, so it was *really* vivid, but Liam loved it. That's all that mattered. Liam *loved* orange.

"Maybe. But that's not the same as a warm man in your bed and you know it."

Kate forgot about the frosting for a moment as she sucked in a fortifying breath. She *so* didn't need a man in her bed. "I'm not ready, Nana."

"Come on, Katie. Don't waste your youth mourning him. You need to move on. He's been gone two months."

"*Seven. Weeks.* It's only been seven weeks."

Nana waved a dismissive hand. "Time enough," she muttered.

"Nana, it's more complicated than just getting on with life. I can't pretend Randy meant nothing to me. We had a child together!"

"Oh, for Pete's sake. Randy knocked you up. There's a world of difference." Nana held up a hand to stop Kate from interrupting and pulled open the package of candles. "I saw how things were... before things went down the tubes. Let me tell you, once you've got a few kids running around the house, it isn't sex that holds things together. At least, not the *only* thing."

Kate propped her hands on her hips to argue the point then instantly regretted the action. She scrubbed at the frosting smear on her pants with a dishtowel. And they were having this conversation now... *why??* "So now a wife's not supposed to be attracted to her own husband? Is that what you're saying?"

"Don't twist my words, young lady. Of course, she is. And Randy was a charmer, I'll grant you that. But there's got to be more to it. A marriage isn't all about the bedroom. What you need is to find a man who'll take care of you. One who'll take care of little Liam, too."

"They don't make superheroes anymore, Nana."

Nana pursed her lips and handed over the cup of plastic forks. "Not a superhero. Just one good man. That's all you need."

"What I *need* is way more complicated than any man can fix." Kate licked a blob of icing off her knuckle and began rummaging through the junk drawer. "*Aargh!* Where are the matches?"

Her grandmother carefully stuck three candles into the cake. "Maybe you could try one of those internet dating services. The ladies agree—"

"*No.*" Kate could only imagine what that personals ad would look like. "Definitely not. No way." She narrowed her eyes. "Oh God. You haven't done anything I should know about, have you? Tell me you haven't!"

Nana gave her a blankly innocent look. "Of course not." She reached around Kate and pulled a lighter from the drawer, lit the candles then picked up the cake. "Never mind. We'll talk more when you've calmed down. Time for cake. Can you get the door?"

They sang *Happy Birthday,* Liam blew out his candles, and Nana started doling out cake, the kids descending like locusts.

Kate knew Nana meant well, but there were times it seemed Nana was so intent on everyone being *happy* she couldn't let go if she thought there was something she could fix. Unfortunately, Kate's problems felt like the mess in Liam's *Cat in the Hat* book... so big... and so wide... she'd never clean it all up...

She absently stabbed another mini wiener and stuffed it in her mouth.

"Kate! There you are."

Kate chewed rapidly and gulped as her boss, Nancy, appeared beside her. Nancy's daughter and Liam were thick as thieves in music class, or Kate wouldn't have been guilted into inviting them.

She'd been avoiding Nancy for days—ever since Nancy had not-so-subtly hinted about wanting to talk, a look of pinched concern telling Kate it wouldn't be a fun conversation.

"I'm sorry to corner you like this, Kate. I've been hoping to speak with you, but I've been so busy finalizing the strategic plan with the new Board of Directors and taking care of last-minute details before we leave next week...." She shook her head on a wry smile as if to say, *Husbands! How are you going to tell them their surprise anniversary cruise is poor timing?* "Anyway, do you have a moment?"

"Now?" Kate forced a smile, the mini wiener lodging somewhere just short of her stomach. Nancy raised an elegant brow expectantly. Kate wondered where all these women found the time for personal grooming. She vowed to find her tweezers as soon as the party was over. "Um. Sure." She motioned for Nancy to follow her down the hall. "I'm sorry, Liam's room is a mess, and my grandmother is using the guest room during her visit. Maybe right he—"

"This is fine."

Kate scurried back down the hall as Nancy veered into the laundry room behind her.

A pair of dingy white panties hung from a clothespin above the washer like a limp, graying flag. Kate snatched them down and shoved them in a laundry basket.

Nancy pursed her lips. "I'll get right to the point. I know about your plans, Kate. I know... you're leaving."

"What?"

9

"I saw the college paperwork in your drawer. I wasn't snooping, but you'd left for the day, and, well, it doesn't matter now."

"Oh. *That*." Kate relaxed a little remembering the papers she'd brought to the office to copy. "I was going to tell you, er, talk about that, when you got back. You see, I'm not—"

Nancy held up a hand. "It's okay. You don't have to explain. I get it: you hate your job. It was too much to expect someone of your caliber to want to be my assistant forever. I just want you to know… I won't stand in your way."

Kate opened her mouth to protest, *hate* was such a strong word, really, but then… Nancy sighed.

Uh-oh.

Nancy's sighs were epic in intensity and length, expressing her disappointment, frustration and sympathy in excruciating slow-motion. Kate had timed one sigh at seventeen seconds. The student had gone blue by the time the last low, guttural syllables had passed over Nancy's lips.

Then she'd expelled him.

Eight... Nine... Ten...

Nancy inhaled. "Look, I know this has been a difficult time for you. It's perfectly understandable that you'd want to explore your options. Especially now." She paused and Kate sucked in a breath, bracing herself for who knew what. "I don't know how to say this, but I want you to know what I'm about to say... I'm not speaking only as your boss... but as your friend."

Kate nodded, the blood rushing from her head. "Am I being *fired?* "

"No! No. Of course not. It's... Look, I know Randy's death has been difficult. I understand. *I do.* But I think it's fair to say your heart hasn't been in your work for a while now."

Kate nodded. "I had so many things to take care of after Randy—"

"I'm not talking about Randy, Kate. I'm talking about *you*." Nancy laid a sympathetic hand on Kate's shoulder. "It's clear you're at a crossroads. I've read *Eat, Pray, Love.* I get it. The fact that you're applying to college again *proves* it. I want you to know… I support you. Go! Find out what's next for Kate Mitchell. Find your passion."

Kate blinked. "My what?"

"Your passion! Figure out what makes you happy. *Alive.* Figure out if being my assistant is enough or if you need something more in life."

Kate shook her head as Nancy's hand dropped away. Her gut clenched. "I don't need to—"

"I'm giving you a leave of absence," Nancy announced as if she were sending Kate on a cruise and not shoving her into choppy seas without a life preserver. "Take the summer. Explore! *Get away.* You can leave as soon as classes end. I can't pay you, but think of it as a gift of time—"

"I don't need time! I'm *fine!*"

"No, you're not. You're exhausted and lost." Nancy's head tilted compassionately. "Randy is gone, Kate. You're no longer in his shadow. But, I'm here to tell you that, come September, the strategic initiatives the board just approved will demand a renewed commitment from everyone, including you. As your employer, I need to know I'll be able to count on you to give me 110%. As your friend, I'm giving you time—*now*—to figure out whether that's want you want."

Kate let out an unsteady breath. "Do I have a choice?"

Nancy smiled. "No."

"I didn't think so."

A moment later, Kate stumbled back into the living room, her thoughts swirling, her summer opening up liking a gaping black hole before her. Some gift! How would she ever pay for tuition without a *job?* And, where would she find the time to attend classes and finish her degree if she gave Nancy the 110% she was asking for?

"Kate." Celery Mom lightly touched Kate's shoulder, and Kate dropped the carrot she didn't know she'd been holding. It rolled under the loveseat. "We were talking, Betsy and I, and we feel awful about all you're going through."

You have no idea.

Betsy nodded sympathetically. "I know it may sound crazy, but trust me. The best thing you can do right now is pamper yourself. Get a facial, a massage—*the works.* It'll do you a world of good!"

"A spa day always makes me feel so *refreshed*," Celery Mom agreed.

Kate watched as Betsy fished in her fancy designer bag. Her spirits lifted a little. A little me time did sound heavenly. While a spa day wouldn't fix her problems, it would go a long way toward smoothing the rough edges.

Betsy found what she was searching for and pulled it from her bag. "I just happen to have a business card for my massage therapist. Trust me—he's the *perfect* escape." She winked conspiratorially and pressed the little ivory card into Kate's palm. "It's clear this ordeal has left you drained," she whispered.

"And haggard," mouthed Celery mom.

Kate stared at the card. Drained? *Haggard?* She tried not to erupt in semi-hysterical laughter. When was she supposed to have gotten a manicure? After the funeral but before her bereavement leave was over?

She wanted to tell them all—Betsy, Nancy and especially Nana—to jump in the proverbial lake. Oh God. But they were right. She hadn't taken care of herself. And, while a gift certificate to said spa would have been a heck of a lot nicer than a measly business card, that had to change. Now.

She shoved the card in her pocket. "Actually, speaking of escapes, we *are* taking a vacation. Liam and I. Getting away for a bit. We're headed to New Hampshire, um, next week. So… no time for a spa day!"

"How lovely!" Betsy enthused. "My Evan's family has a cottage on Squam Lake. You know—*On Golden Pond*?" Seeing as Betsy referenced the decades-old Oscar-winning movie every time she mentioned the 'cottage,' Kate nodded.

"That is a lovely spot," Celery Mom interjected. "*Unspoiled.*"

By this, Kate assumed she meant there weren't too many pesky locals hanging about. "Yes, well, we're actually going to Whisper Lake. In Sugar Falls." Just as soon as she made arrangements.

"Sugar Falls? New Hampshire? I can't say I've heard of—"

"It's on the western border. Near Vermont. My grandmother grew up there."

Betsy's head tilted, her elegant, spa-shaped brows gently knitted. "Oh. Well. I'm sure it will be lovely there, too."

"Lovely," Celery Mom nodded in agreement.

Kate wasn't sure how lovely it would be once she was arrested on attempted-murder charges for poisoning these toxic women with lethal doses of Red Dye No. 3, but she figured she'd find out soon enough. She grabbed the lemonade pitcher's handle with a death grip and refilled each of their paper cups with neon-pink liquid.

The pink dot that happened to jump onto Celery Mom's white shirt was just a bonus.

AN HOUR AND A HALF LATER, Kate waved goodbye to the next to last guest with no small amount of relief. She put the slice of cake she'd wrapped up for Mrs. Pemborly in a plastic bag and handed it over. "Remember," she said, "you're not supposed to have too many sweets. So, this is for tomorrow."

Mrs. Pemborly pulled the bag's handles over her wrist, her pale blue eyes conveying what she thought of the admonition. "I'm ninety-three years old, Kate. There isn't much point in waiting to indulge in anything." She heaved a beleaguered sigh. "But I will. You can sleep with a clear conscience tonight.

"Liam!" the older woman barked, "Happy birthday, young man! Enjoy your loot!" Liam grinned and waved as Mrs. P. peered out the front window. "Oh, June, you're right. It's starting to rain again."

"I'll get my coat and walk you home," Kate offered.

Mrs. Pemborly rolled her eyes and opened the door. "I'm ninety-three years old. I think I know how to walk. Besides, you look spent." *Great*, thought Kate, *another unflattering adjective to add to the list.* Mrs. P. turned to Nana. "Just open my umbrella, would you, June? I have such a time with it. It's a little rusty, but at ninety-three, there doesn't seem much point in buying a new one."

Before the woman could announce she'd turned ninety-four, Kate tied Mrs. P.'s little plastic hood under her chin, Nana popped the umbrella and they both helped her down the front steps. Nana closed the door with a satisfied thump. "Well! That takes care of that!"

Yes. That it did. Kate blew out a breath and tried to ignore her frayed nerves as she surveyed the mess. Toys and wrapping paper lay in mounds on the loveseat under the window. Popcorn and chip crumbs littered the carpet like pale confetti. Half-eaten plates of cake sat on the mantel, the snack table, the floor. And, a single cup of pink lemonade balanced precariously on a windowsill. Kate wanted to go curl up in bed with a cup of hot tea, but this mess wasn't going away by itself. "You've been on your feet all day, Nana. Why don't you go rest for a bit? I'll clean up."

"Nonsense. I'll help. Mrs. P.'s right. You look exhausted!"

"Thanks for noticing." Kate picked up a trash bin and began loading it with half-eaten cake slices and the larger chip crumbs, her eyes welling with tears. She poured the lemonade into a potted plant and threw the cup in the trash. Nana didn't mean to be unkind, but the truth was, she *was* tired. And haggard. And out of a job! Kate swallowed. She wouldn't lose it now, not after holding it together all afternoon.

The doorbell rang and her eyes flew to Nana.

"I'll get it. Probably somebody left their jacket or something." Nana swung the door wide, and Kate's stomach rolled.

"Katherine. *Mother!* Thank God. I'm *so* worried about Sandy..." Kate's mother stood on the other side of the screen door, a giant golf umbrella sheltering the small pink animal crate in her hand. "She's been acting lethargic all day," her mother whispered.

Kate opened the screen door and took the dog crate as her mother shook the umbrella and set it next to the door. "My God! What happened here?"

"Liam's birthday party." Kate set the crate next to the umbrella.

"Oh, right. I couldn't make it. Sandy has been suffering so. I needed to be with her. You understand." Her mother frowned. "Honey, don't put her by the door. She'll catch a draft."

Kate dutifully picked up the crate again and carried it to the dining room.

"I hate to ask," her mother continued, "but I have an event this evening and Rosaria has gone home, and I don't like to leave Sandy alone when she's under the weather…"

"I'll watch her." Kate said, returning to the living room.

"Thank you. You know how she looks up to you."

Kate fought the urge to roll her eyes and accepted the designer pink backpack that included Sandy's leash, favorite toys, treats, organic food, stainless measuring scoop, pop-up dishes, biodegradable poo baggies, tick remover, hairbrush, and personal pillow with lambswool covering. Kate knew this because her mother itemized its contents as she passed it over. "And only *one* scoop of food. Don't let her beg for more. I know you'll want to give in to that sweet little face, but we can't have our little pooch getting poochy, can we?"

Kate glanced toward Nana—who *was* rolling her eyes.

"When will you be picking her up?"

Her mother shrugged gracefully. "A few hours? Four at most. I'll try not to linger."

"Of course."

"I have to use the little girls' room before I go. Be back in a sec." Kate's mother's kitten-heeled sandals made little *schtuck, schtuck* noises as she walked down the hall.

Liam pounded out a jar of Play-Doh onto the coffee table.

"There are times I cannot believe I gave birth to that woman," Nana muttered from the other side of the room.

"Nana!"

"Oh, please. I think the chemicals she uses in her hair have done something to her good sense."

Kate went back to picking up food debris. "She doesn't use anything but the natural dyes now."

"After thirty years of pickling her brain. But, she had you, so it's clear the commonsense genes made it through before she did too much damage."

Kate knew Nana was only trying to lift her spirits, but still. It hurt that a dog meant more to her mother than her own grandchild. Kate wondered if she had married one of the prep-school boys her parents approved of rather than the son of a factory worker whether Liam would

14

be more acceptable in her parents' eyes. She didn't have time to dwell on the thought, as a shriek rang down the hall.

"Katherine! Come quick! There are *feces* on your bathroom floor!"

Kate met Nana's eyes across the room. "Well, don't look at me," Nana said.

Kate hurried down the hall.

"*There*. On the rug. The corner was flipped over, and when I went to straighten it—you really should invest in those mats that stay in place—I found *that!*" Kate's mother shivered and pointed in horror at the bathmat. "Who *does* that?" she cried.

Kate sighed and carefully picked up the mat to shake the offense into the toilet. "Ma, there were a dozen three and four-year-olds here today. Obviously someone had an accident and didn't know what to do about it." She rolled up the mat. "There."

Her mother looked at the toilet dubiously. "Do you have any sanitizing wipes? I think it'd be a good idea to touch up... surfaces."

Kate pulled a package of wipes from under the sink and disinfected the sink, toilet handle and finally the toilet seat. Not that she could picture her mother actually sitting on the toilet seat. No doubt she'd hover like she'd always advised Kate to do in public restrooms. *You never know who's been there.* "I'll take this to the laundry."

Kate returned to the living room where Liam was now busy chopping Play-Doh into tiny bits that were quickly adhering to the carpet fibers under his knees. "Pumpkin, can you bring your Play-Doh to the kitchen? Nana will give you cookie cutters to use with it."

Nana ushered Liam toward the kitchen door and raised an eyebrow at the rolled bathmat. "Don't ask," said Kate.

Kate closed the laundry room door behind her, fighting back a bubble of hysterical laughter as she clutched the soiled bathmat in her hand. *Good God.* She unrolled the bathmat on top of the washer and stared at the little brown smudge in the corner, and suddenly... suddenly it seemed a commentary from the universe on the state of her whole life. Randy's death. Nancy's ultimatum. Ma's stupid dog. It all distilled down to this one, simple fact.

Her life was a poo-stained bathmat.

Kate's chest grew tight and her eyes blurred as she grabbed the pre-treater bottle off the shelf and aimed it at the smudge. She squirted blindly, blinking back tears. You'd think after all she'd cried over the last seven weeks, the source of them would have dried up already.

But they weren't tears of grief. They were tears of panic.

Nancy's words replayed in her head like a bad movie reel...

Go. Find out what's next for Kate Mitchell. Find your passion.

Kate pushed away from the washer, the mini wieners roiling in her gut. Find her passion? How in hell was she supposed to find anything when she was barely making it through the day? And, furthermore, who in their right mind would be passionate about being a secretary in a private school?

Fine. *Executive Assistant*. Whatever.

Kate blew out a shaky breath and shoved the bathmat into the washer. Her gaze bounced around the cluttered room. How was she supposed to find her passion in the middle of this chaos? She'd meant to clean it. Truly. But then Randy had gone and died, and that was the end of that.

Except it wasn't.

Her heart pounded as she closed the washer and fought against the small, nagging, paralyzing thought that had been poking at the edges of her sanity for days. She'd buried herself in preparations for Liam's birthday, Nana's visit, contacting the admissions office at the school, hoping against hope she would be saved from having to acknowledge the truth. But she couldn't hide from it any longer.

Randy had been gone for *seven weeks*.

And she hadn't gotten her period since.

She could barely breathe as her eyes fell on the small pile of clothes on the dryer. Randy's clothes. She'd washed them and set them aside, had meant to return to him. Now it was too late.

Her lips twisted as she picked up a T-shirt and rubbed the soft, faded fabric between her fingers. She concentrated on the sensation, trying to picture Randy in it, trying to remember how it felt with him beneath it, trying to remember how life felt before everything fell apart, but all she felt was... T-shirt.

Kate let her head sink to the washer, the metal cool and hard beneath her forehead as tears seeped through her lashes. She fumbled in her pocket for a tissue, her fingers instead finding a folded piece of paper that had already gone through the wash.

She peeled it open, recognizing the raised letterhead at the top, and her hands shook as she smoothed it out on top of the washer.

Dear Ms. Mitchell,
It is our pleasure to inform you that your application for admission to the Fine Arts Program has been accepted...

The words blurred. She'd carried the letter around in her pocket for days, rereading it, not quite believing how neatly life was working out.

And then she'd gone to drop off some things at Randy's apartment. She hadn't meant to say anything, but she had.

I'm happy for you, he'd said. *I know you'll do great. I always loved how you could do anything you set your mind to.*

She'd hugged him then, her spirits buoyed by his unexpected support. She never intended to kiss him. Never intended to let it go further. But as he'd pulled her tight against him, all she'd been able to hear were the words *...I'm happy...* and *...I always loved you...* even though neither was true.

"Katie, you still in there?" Nana knocked on the laundry room door, and Kate straightened and wiped her eyes. "Liam wants to know if he can watch Bob the Builder, your mother's left and I think Sandy needs to pee."

Kate cleared her throat. "Just a minute."

She picked up the letter, running her fingers over the softened folds, rereading it one last time. It seemed like yesterday she'd opened the envelope, her heart fluttering with excitement, her future unfolding like sweet promises and fresh starts.

She let out a long, shaky breath... then tore the letter into tiny, confetti-like pieces.

Sweeping it into the trash, she started the washer and opened the door.

CHAPTER THREE

FOR THREE YEARS THE SAME horrid poppies and sunflowers had blinded her. If cataracts didn't ruin her eyesight, those god-awful flowers would. June sipped her gin and tonic, held her cards close to her chest and squinted against the blinding riot of flowers on the vinyl tablecloth that Lydia *insisted* they use whenever poker night was at her house. At least the woman made good brownies. It was worth the stop in Sugar Falls before she left for the Quilt Show in Portland the next morning, just to have these brownies. June reached across and snagged another as her friend, Ruth Pearson, placed an edge-weary photograph on the growing pile in the middle of the table.

"All right, June," Ruth said. "I'll see your granddaughter with that darling great grandchild and raise you one eligible grandson who owns his own business."

June waited for Ruth to bite her cheek—it was one of her tells.

Ruth reached for a brownie instead.

Sugar. Ruth must have a good hand. She always reached for sweets when she was feeling victorious. June dropped her cards to the table. "I'm out of luck *and* relatives. I fold. What do you have, Ruth?"

"Read 'em and weep, ladies!" Ruth fanned her cards face-up in front of her.

June sloshed gin and tonic on the tablecloth. "Ruth Pearson, if you weren't chair of the Gifts for the Greater Good campaign, I'd swear you were cheating. You've won five hands in a row!"

"Oh, stop your belly-aching." Ruth gleefully pulled the pile of photographs toward her as if it were cold hard cash and not the winning pot in their own personal twist on poker. She'd only won the right to talk about anything she wanted for the evening—old stories or new—but it was exciting nonetheless. "Did you see my cards? Don't you know what that means?"

"A royal flush—?"

"In *hearts*!" Lydia chimed in meaningfully, her silver bangles jingling excitedly.

18

"They think it's a sign." Claire tapped the deck and slid the playing cards into their box.

June looked at her friends as if they were showing signs of early dementia, which was entirely possible given they were all well past menopause. "A sign of what?"

"That someone in the pot will get married!" Lydia tittered.

June snorted indelicately. "What kind of hooey is that?"

Ruth continued to sort photos. "Not hooey. Don't you remember? It happened before with Claire's son, Barry. Within three months of lying in the winning pot next to Lydia's niece... *married*."

"Oh, I can barely breathe!" said Lydia. "Who do you think it'll be this time?"

Ruth scanned the photographs in front of her. "Hmm. After I take out all the children and married men, I'm left with my grandson. But the only woman is your granddaughter, June, and she's in mourning, poor dear." She swept her small pile of photos into the box on her lap and sighed. "Oh, well."

"So much for fortune-telling cards." Claire muttered, wiping a brownie crumb off the front of her late husband's bowling shirt.

Lydia reached across and picked up the two pictures, her coral-polished fingertips shaking slightly as she looked at them through her bifocals. "Too bad, too. They would have made a handsome couple. See?"

June peered over Lydia's shoulder. "*Hmm.* I shouldn't be saying this, him being dead and all, but I wouldn't be disappointed to see Katie move on to someone more reliable than that deadbeat she was married to, may he rest in peace. She was planning to kick him out, you know. And none too soon, if you ask me."

Claire *tsk tsked*. "Young people take marriage too much for granted these days."

June downed the rest of her drink and resisted a third brownie. She had her waistline to consider, after all. "There was a time I would have agreed with you. But after seeing all my Katie did to make that marriage work, she needed to get him out of the house. If not for herself then for the sake of that precious little one."

June shook her short, silvered hair. "Oh for heaven's sake, now you've got me talking out of turn. Ruth, it's *your* turn. You won bragging rights. What do you want to talk about?"

June 13
Why is it that going on vacation with a toddler feels like preparing for a trip up Mt. Everest? Gone are the days when I could throw a few things in an overnight bag. I have to plan for food, water, wardrobe changes, entertainment, Acts of God and Calls of Nature. And that's just for the ride there. Wish me luck tomorrow. Here's hoping the Sherpas know where they're going!

CHAPTER FOUR

KATE STEPPED OUT OF HER car and took a deep breath, glad to be free of the hot, stuffy interior. She could think of plenty of things she'd rather do than drive five hours with a temperamental A/C and cranky toddler. Dental work came to mind. But her aging Corolla was all she could afford for the time being. Maybe ever.

She swiped a hand across her forehead and looked toward the cottage that would be their home for the summer.

Faded white clapboards, odd dormers and a slightly tilted front porch spoke of decades of renovations and occupants rather than any specific architectural vision. Grass and weeds speckled the gravel drive and fought with pink and purple lupine in neglected planting beds. A stand of white birch—all shimmering oval leaves and arching branches— cast dappled shade across the stone path. And reflecting it all were the glittering, dark waters of Sugar Falls' Whisper Lake.

Despite the band of sweat that had her T-shirt clinging to her back, Kate felt the tension flowing out of her in undulating waves. Given how life had gone lately, she'd braced herself for sleeping in the car. This at least looked habitable.

She turned just as Liam scrambled into the front seat and out the driver's door. "Whoa! What's the hurry?"

"I wanna swim!"

"Me, too, but I need to unload. We'll swim after I unpack and put away the groceries." Kate pulled a heavy suitcase out of the car and set it on the drive. *Two months.* Two months reprieve from all the sympathetic looks and probing personal questions.

Oof. Two months to figure out a decent reply.

"Liam! For heaven's sake—keep your clothes on. We are not swimming yet."

"But—"

"No buts. Keep your pants on, young man."

Liam squeezed his face into a mutinous frown, the expression so like his father's it made Kate wonder why it didn't make her cry. Shouldn't she be crying more? No, it was anger she was supposed to be feeling. At least according to Nana.

But she didn't feel mad either. She just felt... like she was waiting. To land. To take off. For the lottery commission to tell her she'd won. Maybe for life to stop feeling like it was a runaway train she couldn't get off... Yes, *that*.

"Wanna swim *now*," Liam said.

Kate stooped down and cupped her son's cheeks. His father's dark eyes flashed up at her. Like it or not, Randy Mitchell would always be a part of her life. Maybe they hadn't worked out, but hadn't they made a beautiful baby together?

Kate swallowed a sudden lump in her throat and stood up. "Do you want to see inside?"

"Yeah!" Liam ran toward the front door.

Kate hurried to keep up, stepping gingerly over a profusion of purple violas popping up through the flagstones, her suitcase banging against the worn porch steps. She grasped the doorknob. It felt warm in her palm like a friendly handshake. She turned it. Good Lord. It wasn't even *locked*.

Liam rocketed past. "Are there toys?"

Kate hauled the suitcase over the threshold. "Only the ones we brought. You can explore while I get the other bags. But *no touching*."

Liam disappeared down a hall.

Kate looked toward the living area. She wasn't sure what she'd expected. More furniture, maybe? The nearly empty space featured bead-board walls, a fieldstone fireplace, a large braid rug... and a single, hideous, gold-painted rocking chair with tasseled seat cushion. On the other side of the room under a picture window stood a small dining table and mismatched barstools.

Kate stepped toward the view of the lake as it sparkled in the late afternoon sun.

Well, it wasn't overly large. Or grand. Or awash with seating options. But it looked clean. And unlike her own parents' home, it was blessedly free of fragile knick-knacks and collectibles a rambunctious toddler tended to endanger simply by breathing.

Reassured Liam wouldn't immediately find anything to break, Kate swiveled around. She had a few more bags to bring in, groceries to unpack... Checking off her mental to-do list, she stepped over the threshold... and slammed gracelessly into the tall, lanky stranger on the porch.

Tall. Lanky. Yup, that was the sum total of what she discerned before the air whooshed out of her lungs and her face came into abrupt contact with a firm chest. Before she could react, she picked up the warm, faintly sweet scent of man. She inhaled—an involuntary action—and stepped back.

Oh. Lord. She'd almost forgotten how good a man could smell.

"Whoa." Strong fingertips briefly grasped her arms, steadying her. "Sorry about that," he said, letting go. "I didn't expect anyone until later."

Kate's gaze skimmed slowly up the damp vee of sweat on the man's T-shirt. A smile creased his lean, tanned face. She swallowed, her heart doing an odd somersault in her chest. "And you are...?"

"Jim Pearson. Ruth Pearson's grandson." He reached out his hand and Kate shook it numbly. It was warm. Firm. "I'm sorry. I'd come back another time, but Grams insisted I do this ASAP."

"She insisted?"

"I think her exact words were, 'get your butt over there before she grows desperate.' My guess is she thought you deserved something more, ah, reliable. So...?"

Kate stared at him, perplexed, but then his words finally sank in. She could feel the heat creeping up her neck. Oh. Dear. Lord. Did Ruth Pearson think she was so desperate for a man she needed one delivered to her doorstep the moment she arrived? Don't people normally send cookies or a batch of brownies? Quiche, maybe? But a *man*?

And if this man was sent as a sacrificial offering on the altar of her non-existent love life, what must Nana's friend have told him? What must he think of her? And how pathetic did that make her appear?

Good grief. Good-looking or not. Gracious or not. She wasn't some sorry charity case!

He gestured toward the door. "Can I come in?"

"Ah... you know..." Kate blocked the doorway, trying to ignore the lean, well-toned torso in front of her. How could she tell him he was wasting his time with a capital W? "I don't know what your grandmother told you, but... I'm really not interested."

"You're not?" He stared at her, nonplussed.

"It's nothing personal, but the thing of it is, I usually kind of like to choose my own—"

A furrow appeared in his brow. "You want to choose your own."

Kate nodded, wondering why this should be so surprising. "Exactly. I know your grandmother meant well, and I'm sure what you have to offer is very..." She swallowed again. "Nice. What I mean is—please, don't be offended—but I really don't see any reason for you to come in."

Despite what she felt was a crystal clear 'no-thank-you' he didn't make a move to leave.

"Um." He cleared his throat. "Do you want to look at it first? It's gotten good reviews. If you come over to my house, I'd be happy to show you—"

"*Show me?*"

He shifted his weight to his other boot. Cleared his throat again. "Ah, what are we talking about?"

Kate gulped, her gaze resting uneasily on his shirtfront. "Um... hooking up, er, dating?" she wheezed. "What are *you* talking about?"

He touched her chin, his long fingers urging her to meet his eyes. They were hazel. And incredibly sexy. The corners crinkled with humor.

"Toilets," he said evenly.

"*Toilets?*"

"Yes." He dropped his hand. "What made you think I was talking about... that other thing?"

"You're kind of cute. I thought..."

A grin creased his features as he touched the brim of his faded baseball cap. His eyes went dark. "Thanks."

She wanted to die, to dissolve into a puddle and seep through the floorboards.

As he watched her, he pulled off his cap and turned it in his hands. His hair was light brown, soft waves streaked with highlights from the sun. He tilted his head toward his pickup. "You still want to look at it, or should I just put it in?"

"Put it in?" *Aargh!* If she could stop ogling his hair, perhaps she could stop parroting him like some brainless twit! What was wrong with her?

"You've obviously just arrived, or you would have already seen there's no—"

"*Hey!*" Liam cried from inside. "Somebody took the potty!"

"—toilet," he finished. "Why don't I bring it in?"

"Good idea," she managed to croak around her mortification.

"I'm going to get my tools now," he said, putting on his cap, "and by that, I mean... *tools.*"

She nodded. "Got it."

He paused, and when he next spoke his voice had a low cadence that had Kate leaning toward him ever so slightly. "Just so we're even," he said, "I think you're kinda cute, too."

The breath stuck in her throat as she nodded. It had been so long since a man had flirted with her, she wasn't sure if she'd heard him right.

By the time she regained the ability to speak, he was halfway to his truck, his legs eating up the uneven ground in long, loping strides.

She hurried down the stairs to the car to get her other bags, the breeze doing nothing to cool her hot cheeks.

But she didn't care.

She'd take Jim Pearson over a quiche any day.

KATE FOLDED THE LAST grocery bag and set it on the kitchen counter. Thankfully, Liam had played contentedly with the toys from the bin she'd hauled into the corner of the living room while she brought in the rest of their suitcases and unpacked.

The front door slammed.

"Liam? Are you still inside?" Okay, she was a little panicky, but at home, large bodies of water had fences around them.

"It's just me!" Jim Pearson answered.

Kate stepped out of the little kitchen where, yes, she'd been hiding. "Oh. Thanks."

Jim nodded and headed down the hallway again, a white toilet tank in his arms.

Kate sucked up her courage and followed. She waited until he'd set the tank on the bath mat then cleared her throat and reached out her hand.

"I'm Kate, by the way. Kate Mitchell. June Hastings' granddaughter? She's a friend of your grandmother."

"Ah, right, one of 'the ladies.'" They shook hands awkwardly over the toilet tank. "When does she get here?" he asked.

"Who?"

"Your grandmother."

"Oh, Nana won't be back for a few days. She went to Portland for a quilt festival."

He nodded and turned to screw some things to the bottom of the tank.

Kate cleared her throat. "Um. About earlier..."

He glanced up.

She swallowed. "What I said... about being *cute*..." She mouthed the last word. "I didn't mean it. I mean, not that you *aren't*... but I don't want you to get the wrong idea. The truth is, I'm not in a place right now for, um, dating... and I just wanted to be clear I wasn't hitting on you. Or anything." She felt her face flame to her hairline and briefly considered high-tailing it back to Connecticut.

He set the tank on the back of the toilet. "That's good."

"Yes," she agreed, taken aback.

"Nothing personal, but I'm not into married women." He looked pointedly at her left hand.

"Oh, I'm not married. That is... not anymore." Kate twirled with the gold band on her finger. She'd worn it ever since the night Randy had died.

"Divorced?"

She dropped her hand. "That was the plan."

"Ah. Separated." His lips twisted humorlessly, and he shook his head. "*Definitely* not interested."

He bent over and fiddled with something inside the toilet.

Kate frowned. She didn't know why she didn't correct him and tell him she was a widow. Maybe it was because she didn't want his pity. Maybe it was because dating right now would be like inviting a guy to hop onto the sinking Titanic for a pleasure cruise. Or, maybe, it was because he was already rejecting her as if she'd offered herself on a silver platter. Which, for the record, she most certainly had not.

"Great," she said, forcing a smile—not that he was looking or anything. "We're on the same page, then." She picked up a little seashell from a shelf by the sink and set it down again. Damn, it was hard to make a grand exit when the offending party wasn't even looking at you. "Well, I guess I'll go, um, take care of some things."

"Sure," he grunted, folding himself into the space between the wall and the toilet.

Kate retreated to the barren living room. Liam ran over her toes with his toy car. "I'm going to start putting some things away upstairs," she announced. "You stay here, all right?"

"'kay."

But when Kate returned a few minutes later, Liam was gone.

"Liam? Liam!" Kate skidded to a halt outside the bathroom. "I thought I told you Mr. Pearson was working. Come on. Let's get your sunscreen on. I'm done unpacking."

Ruth's grandson searched in his toolbox and pulled something out. "It's Jim," he corrected. "And he's not bothering me. We were just getting acquainted. Weren't we, Bud?" Jim reached behind the tank to attach a thin hose.

Liam nodded earnestly.

"Well, I'll get him out of your hair so you can finish."

She made a grab for Liam, but he scooted over to the far side of Jim's legs, which were, at the moment, splayed across the bathroom floor. She tried not to stare as she pondered how to extricate her uncooperative son.

"I'm nearly finished. Don't worry about the sunscreen, by the way." Jim stood and fiddled with the floatie thing in the tank before setting the cover on. "This time of day, you need bug repellent more than sunscreen."

Kate turned toward the tiny window at the far end of the room. Crap. Now that he mentioned it, the sun wasn't as brilliant as it had been when they'd first arrived. "I'm sorry, Liam. I guess it took me longer to get organized than I thought it would. Maybe we can swim tomorrow."

"But you promised!"

"Why don't we have a special dinner instead? We can have pizza!" She turned to Jim. "I'm assuming there's a place nearby?"

"Right in town." He began collecting his tools. "All set."

"Great."

They stared at one another a moment before she briskly patted Liam on the shoulder. "Well, Pumpkin, we should go get that pizza, don't you think?"

"Can he eat with us?" Liam asked.

Jim tossed a wrench into his toolbox and avoided Kate's eyes. "Thanks for the invite, Buddy, but it's been a long day. Maybe another time."

"You're more than welcome to join us," Kate lied, stuffing a wad of unruly hair behind her ear. It slid out again, undeterred. "But we'd understand if you're too busy."

"I'm not busy," he assured Liam before looking up at Kate. "But I'll bet your mom is tired after her long drive."

"Not tired at all." Kate assured them. She eyed Jim again. "But maybe Mr. Pearson isn't hungry."

"I skipped lunch," he said.

"Really?" she challenged.

"Really."

She swallowed, the air inexplicably charged. She had no idea what was going on between them, but it didn't feel like disinterest.

"Well," she finally said, breaking eye contact, "I'll need to place our order and get directions. Things have changed so much since I was here ten years ago, I don't recognize—"

"I'll pick it up."

"You will?"

"Sure." A ghost of a smile played at his lips as he stepped abreast of her in the doorway. He ducked his head and whispered in her ear, "But it doesn't mean I want any."

Kate lifted an eyebrow, heat sizzling to her toes. "Who said I was offering?"

"A SALAD. I SHOULD MAKE A SALAD." Kate stared at the contents of the small refrigerator as if she hadn't just put away the groceries an hour earlier. As soon as Jim had driven away for the pizza, she'd dashed upstairs to change out of her sweaty travel clothes. "A salad doesn't make it a date or anything," she told herself. "It just makes it a well-rounded meal."

Retrieving assorted produce from the crisper, Kate set it on the counter. "Liam? Are you being good?" He'd walked by moments earlier with another box of construction vehicles.

"Liam?"

"Yup."

Kate smiled at the distinctive sound of make-believe engines. "Stay in the house, please."

"'kay."

Kate pulled a wooden cutting board from beside the sink and ran her hand over its rough surface. Marked and stained from years of use, it would have disgusted Randy, but to Kate it felt good, like countless meals prepared and enjoyed.

It was something Randy had never understood, her love of old things. She'd always been drawn to objects which held the mark of use, purpose, the patina of age. They told stories to her. Held secrets.

To Randy they were in need of replacement.

"That's how you and I differed," she mumbled. As if a love or disdain of antiques had been the ruin of their marriage.

She rummaged for a knife and began washing and chopping vegetables. Anyway, it seemed unfair to point out petty differences to a dead man. They'd had things in common, too. Hadn't they both liked the house just so?

Then she paused, the bright red pepper glossy under the cold water, remembering Randy's crushing words as if he'd said them yesterday.

"...you've let the house go, Kate. Hell, you've let yourself go. Who would have thought becoming a mother would make you less of a woman?"

27

Liam had been two months old then. He'd just begun to smile.

Kate stared at the red pepper in her hand, her fingers numb in the running water.

She pulled the seeds out in one hard yank and began to chop.

She'd been mistaken about Randy. While she embraced the natural order of things, Randy had striven to impose his own order on his surroundings. It took six months of therapy to learn that when he couldn't control his own weakness, he'd tried to control everything else.

Including her.

As if she'd been a *thing* to boss around.

Kate hurriedly tossed salad into bowls as she heard the sound of a man's footsteps on the front porch.

"I was never a thing," she murmured as she adjusted one of the placemats she'd found in a drawer, "I was your wife. And I was always," she put a hand over the fluttery hunger pangs in her stomach and turned toward the deep voice in the front hall, "a *woman*."

KATE STOOD JUST OUT OF sight as she heard Jim thank Liam.

A moment later, the screen door banged shut and Liam ran through the house yelling, "Dinner!"

Jim rounded the corner to the kitchen and held up the pizza boxes. "I'm back."

Kate made a pretense of wiping her hands on a dishtowel. Not that they were wet or anything. But she felt the need to think, and cleaning always helped her think. "That was fast." Long enough to make a tossed salad, change into fresh clothes, put in her favorite pink cubic zirconia studs, and mop her face with a cool washcloth but not long enough to shower. Or brush teeth. Don't ask her how she knew.

"It's not far." He tilted his chin toward the boxes in his hands. "Hope you don't mind, but I got one cheese and one everything."

"Anything's fine," she said. She bit her lip and attempted to relax. "Can I get you something to drink? Water? Iced tea?"

"Iced tea would be great."

She poured two glasses, acutely aware of Jim moving around as he set the pizza boxes on the short peninsula between the kitchen and dining area. She turned and handed him his tea. "So, would you like some pizza to go with this or were you just delivering?"

His lips tilted with humor. "*Hmm.* By pizza, I'm assuming you mean…"

"Pizza." She said, the breath light in her chest.

She swallowed, the words 'hooking up' floating across her consciousness, and for the first time ever she understood the power of the phrase. Its impact was more than a moment's shock value. Once spoken, the words couldn't be taken back. They were *out there*. Hovering between them. Coloring the most innocuous comments with sexual awareness.

Or maybe that was just her.

Jim sipped from his glass.

She sipped from hers.

A moment later Liam slammed into her legs with the full force of a three year-old. "Momma! Let's eat!"

"Okay. Okay. Go sit down." Iced tea splashed onto her arm and the floor, effectively putting an end to further flirtatious banter as Liam darted away again. It was just as well. She felt like the dorky kid at the school dance who'd just sloshed punch down her sleeve. Who knows what sort of things she'd be tempted to blurt out to the hunky guy standing way too near?

Besides, he was out of her league, totally gorgeous and so *not* what she needed to focus on right now.

Kate blotted up the spill on the floor and carried the salad and silverware to the table. She carefully set one knife, one fork and a folded napkin at each place setting. "Do we need spoons?"

"Spoons? It's pizza. I usually eat it right out of the box."

"What? Oh." Heat warmed her cheeks. "I guess I'm not feeling prepared to entertain yet."

"You're in luck. Pizza is the perfect dinner for the unprepared. It even comes on a convenient, disposable serving platter." He slid two slices of everything pizza onto a plate.

Kate cut a small slice of plain pizza for Liam. "Sorry. It's just that Randy—my husband—always insisted things be... just so."

"Even for pizza?"

"You have no idea."

Jim walked past her toward one of the mismatched barstools but then stopped. "Oh, almost forgot. Found this at the pizza place. Thought it might help you orient yourself in town." He pulled a rumpled map out of his back pocket and smoothed it on his thigh before handing it over. "It doesn't show everything, but it's got most of the local highlights including the new ice cream place. You should check it out. You won't regret it."

"Thank you. That was very thoughtful."

"And there goes my reputation." He grinned, a flash of dimples causing Kate's breath to catch.

She took the map. It was still warm from being in his pocket. A part of her wondered if it was wrong to notice that, to admire his dimples, to keep thinking about the phrase 'hooking up' or to feel strangely hopeful when he was near.

He's not interested, she reminded herself. *He's just being friendly.*

She set the map aside, put a slice of pizza onto a plate, and sat down. She busied herself picking carrots out of her salad for Liam who was idly rocking in the ugly gold rocker, his pizza sliding back and forth alarmingly.

"Oh, by the way, I should warn you the shower knob leaks a little." Jim took a bite of pizza. Kate watched his throat as he swallowed. She tried to think practical, hope-squelching thoughts. "I've got a new knob and head on order, but it's okay to use in the meantime. Should be able to switch them out in a couple days." He served up some salad. "So how long are you here for? Grams didn't say."

"Me? A couple months."

He gave a low whistle. "That's quite a vacation. What do you do you can take that much time off?"

"I'm a Headmaster's assistant at a small, private school."

"Must be nice to have your summers free. When do you start again? September?"

"End of August, actually. If I go back, I'd need to help prepare for the new term."

His eyes widened ever so slightly. "If?"

"It may not be practical to go back."

She concentrated on wiping a smear of pizza sauce off Liam's cheek then leapt to her feet. "Sorry. I forgot the salad dressing. Do you like Ranch or Italian?"

"Italian would be great."

"I'll be right back." Kate scurried to the kitchen, ineffectually tucking her hair behind her ear again—she so needed to get it cut!— before finding the dressing and setting it in front of Jim. She frowned at her son. "Liam, how many pieces does that make?"

"Two," Jim offered.

"Eat some carrots, young man."

"'kay."

"Speaking of eating," Jim said as he dug into his salad, "if you don't sit down, we'll be half-done before you even touch your food."

She perched on the edge of her barstool and stared at the slice of pizza on her plate. "It's all right. My appetite has been kind of sketchy lately."

"Stress?"

"You could say that."

"A nice cold beer usually cures that for me." He looked at her, his fork hovering over his food. "Did I say something wrong?"

"I don't drink."

"I see."

"I mean—"

"No, don't explain. I'm sorry if I said something—"

"You didn't say anything. It's just... my husband was an alcoholic, and I *used* to drink... I mean, *I'm* not an alcoholic. I used to drink it—alcohol, that is—but I don't... now."

Jim stared at her. Blinked.

She sighed. "I sound like a complete loon, don't I?"

"Is that a trick question?"

"Oh, Lord," she laughed then, what she prayed was a non-maniacal sound, "I do. I'm sorry." She picked up her fork and stabbed some lettuce in an effort to act normal. "My family's been driving me a little crazy lately, is all. Not that they're all bad, just—intrusive sometimes."

"I can relate to that."

"You're from a large family?"

"There were seven of us."

"Including parents?" She picked up her tea.

"Just kids."

She choked on her tea. "Ohmigod! I can't imagine giving birth seven times!"

"If it makes it any better, three of them are actually my cousins. They came to live with us after my aunt and uncle died in a fire."

She set the glass down with a thud. "How awful. I mean, I'm so sorry."

Jim shrugged. "I was eight, so it was a long time ago."

"Still, that's awfully young to deal with something like that."

"It's in the past." He motioned to his bowl. "Do you mind if I have more salad?"

She glanced at his empty bowl. Randy had hated vegetables. "Of course!" But before she could pass the serving bowl, a shrill tone filled the air.

Jim pulled something from his waistband, stared at it intently for a moment, then jumped from his seat. "I'll have to take a rain-check. I've gotta go."

"Go?"

He nodded, downing the last of his iced tea. "Fire call."

"But... your salad. And I haven't paid you for the pizza!"

"My treat," he said, striding to the door.

He turned abruptly. "But if you decide to buy me ice cream at the Lick N' Dip while you're in town, I might be persuaded. Their Kahlua fudge brownie is killer good."

"Yay!" cheered Liam from the dining room. "Ice cream!"

Kate was about to tell him ice cream hardly made up for a whole meal, but he wasn't listening, was already half-way to his truck. Which was okay.

If she were being perfectly honest, she liked ice cream. She liked ice cream a lot.

CHAPTER FIVE

"GRAMS SAID THERE'S A HOT young widow over at the cottage. Thought I might swing over and see if she needs a tour guide."

Jim stared as his cousin pulled a water bottle from his truck and downed it in one long draw. They were both filthy and sweaty, and the acrid smell of smoke hung in the air but Jim barely noticed as his cousin's words sank in.

Young. Widow.

He was an idiot for not figuring it out sooner. Kate Mitchell wasn't separated. Her husband was *dead*.

"So, whaddya think? Too soon after he's kicked the bucket for me to pop in and console her?"

Jim fished for his eye drops on his console. "You're some piece of work, Carter. I can't believe you're talking about this now. Reynolds here just lost his garage. He only finished it last summer. That John Deere he was restoring is toast. And there's no way Grams said she was 'hot.'"

"You're right. Her exact word was 'charming.' But that's better than 'sweet' or 'smart,' which we both know are code for ugly."

"And charming means?"

"At least pretty. And pretty's good enough for me."

"You amaze me. And I don't mean that in a good way." Jim squeezed drops into each eye. Bloody hell, if Carter smelled a woman, he wasn't one to waste time. But Kate wasn't interested. She'd made that perfectly, ego-bruisingly clear.

Not that his libido had been listening.

"Thought I'd drop by tomorrow before the cookout at Grams. Maybe invite her over if she looks good."

Jim threw the eye drops on the seat of his truck and slammed the door with more force than he intended. "Don't bother. She's not your type."

"She's breathing, isn't she?"

"Kate doesn't need you sniffing after her."

Carter's lips tilted at the corner in a way Jim knew made women fall at his feet. "Kate, huh? Well, why didn't you say you had first dibs? I'm cool with that."

"I don't have 'dibs.'"

"Then she's fair game?"

"She's not a hunk of beef for God's sake. Besides, she's got a kid."

"Ah. No wonder you're all hot and bothered."

"I'm not—" Jim let out a slow breath. He hated how Carter got under his skin sometimes. "I'm *not* hot and bothered. I don't have nor want dibs, and I think you should shut up."

"I'm just trying to be neighborly."

"Sure you are."

"Besides, I'm great with kids."

"Yeah. Everybody loves you."

"Speaking of which," Carter continued, undeterred, "guess who I ran into at Lucky's last night?"

Knowing he didn't want to know, Jim asked anyway, "Who?"

"Your ex."

He gripped the door handle more tightly. "You make it sound like we were married."

"Nearly were."

"But not." He considered getting more eye drops but decided a shower was preferable and swung open the truck door.

"She asked about you."

He drew a hard breath into his lungs. "Really?"

He wouldn't look at Carter, didn't want to be pulled back into those wasted years. It left a bitter taste in his mouth. Two long years he'd wanted. Waited. Two years he'd wondered if Justine would choose him or her cheating, asshole of a husband, only to find out she and her husband were meant for each other.

"Don't you even want to know what she said?"

"*No.*" Jim swung himself into the cab of his truck and slammed the door.

It was just after dark by the time he reached home, his tires crunching over the gravel drive. He pulled his pickup under the long shadows of the oak that marked the steps down to the lake, turned off the engine—and decided he wasn't ready to be inside after all.

He swore under his breath as he stared, unseeing, through the windshield.

It was easy blaming his foul mood on Carter, but it wasn't fair. Carter had nothing to do with it.

It was him. And he had the nerve to think this Kate woman had baggage? Lord, he was such a hypocrite.

As much as he'd tried to push it out of his mind, seeing Kate's little boy today had brought back all the memories he thought he'd excised from his mind. Sarah's beautiful smile. Her easy laugh. Her sheer, innocent joy in life.

As the girl he'd come to think of as his own daughter, Sarah had come to mean everything to him, then, overnight, she was gone. Ripped from his life like Justine had ripped his heart from his chest.

Before he knew what he was doing, he was sliding the sweaty, filthy T-shirt over his head and dropping it on the bench seat of his truck. As much as he'd like to deny it, he'd been a part of all the ugliness, been so wrapped up in wanting Justine, in picturing their future together, he hadn't thought what might happen to little Sarah if things didn't work out.

Until she was pulled out of his life like the pawn she was.

He swallowed the bitterness clogging his throat, flung open the driver's door and untied his boots. Throwing his boots and socks onto the passenger floor, he slid out of the truck, the stones of the driveway rough and familiar under his bare feet.

The lake was quiet now, boats at their docks, the muffled sounds of an early summer cookout carrying softly over the water as he made his way through the trees and down the steep stone path, drawn to the soothing rhythm of lapping waves.

He knew his way like the back of his hand and slid easily, noiselessly, through the shadows. The rock outcropping by the water was cool under his feet as he stood and stared blindly over the lake. He ran a distracted hand through his hair. It felt stiff under his fingers. More than anything, he wanted to swim, to dive in and wash away all the smoke and sweat—all the stupid mistakes he'd ever made.

He let out a frustrated breath, knowing the frustration was as much aimed at himself as anyone else. The water lapped almost silently against the dock.

Oh, hell. Who would even know? The only place close enough to see this part of the lake was Gram and Gramps old cottage and Kate and her son were bound to be asleep.

Tall pines cloaked him and the shoreline in darkness, but as he unbuttoned his jeans, he glanced toward the cottage anyway. It sat quiet, dark. *No one's around,* he chided himself. Before he gave himself time to reconsider, he tugged off his jeans and boxers, the softly scented summer breeze tightening his skin, and stood naked on the moss-covered stone.

He chuckled to himself without humor. He was thirty-four years old, but he could've been fourteen again standing in this very spot, seeing this place from this very vantage point, looking up at Grams and Gramps and wondering if they could see him skinny-dipping on a double dare.

His gaze slid to the porch of the cottage just barely visible through the trees. There was no light. There was no double dare.

Gramps was long gone.

And he wasn't fourteen anymore.

Jim took one long cleansing breath, stepped out onto the dock and dove into the water.

KATE SAT ON THE PORCH SWING and enjoyed the intermittent flicker of a campfire across the lake. She heard a distant, though not unpleasant, drone of a motorboat, then quiet. Saying a silent prayer of thanks for an exhausted toddler, she leaned back with a sigh.

Liam had gone down without a fight for once, leaving her to enjoy the luxury of a hot cup of tea and utter peace. She snuggled into the fleece blanket she'd brought out and let the cool, evening air brush her cheeks. The bulb in the porch light didn't seem to work, but it didn't matter. She didn't feel like reading. Or planning.

Oh God, she *hated* feeling like she had to be doing something every minute of every day. Like dating. Or finding her passion. Wasn't it enough to just... breathe?

Closing her eyes, she toed the swing into motion and tried to inhale a long, meditative breath. A breeze caught the wind chimes.

It would be so easy to get used to this, tea-sipping, porch-swinging life. Simpler. Without complications.

A blank page on which to start over.

She snorted indelicately and sipped her tea.

It wasn't as if she could ignore the realities that awaited her around every corner. She had responsibilities. Bills to pay. Children to care for. It was easy for Nancy to say, 'go find your passion.' It was a heck of a lot more difficult to put into practice.

Kate blew on her tea.

And yet, she could hardly sit around all summer doing *nothing*. I mean, this was her chance, her break if ever the universe and the planets and the fates were going to give her one. And they owed her, didn't they?

Big time.

Kate stared into her mug, the smooth warmth of it doing little to soothe the unease inside her.

Not that the universe was to blame for *all* her mistakes. She had only herself to blame for some of them. She let out a silent, humorless laugh. It wasn't like the universe had *made* her fall into bed with Randy that last time.

She'd only meant to drop off some things at his apartment, deliver the odd piece of mail from those who still didn't understand that even though they were still married, they no longer belonged together. But then he'd said something sweet, and she'd gone to give him a hug. It had felt familiar and awkward and sad all at the same time, and she'd turned, meaning to kiss him on the cheek—she *had* loved this man. Once. But then he'd captured her lips with his, and there was so much sadness and longing in that kiss, she wondered if she was making a mistake after all.

Which of course it had been, but she hadn't realized how much of one until after Randy drove into a tree two days later.

Kate took a gulp of tea. It was hot and her throat felt tight, but her eyes were dry as she stared out into the dark.

The question was—what now?

Even if she could have figured out a way to juggle her work for Nancy *and* finish her degree, would she have even been able to *find* a job? Realistically, what could she show she'd done over the last ten years that would indicate to potential employers she had a discriminating eye? It seemed logical at the time she'd left Randy, to try to pick up where she'd left off so long ago, but now…

Where did she go from here?

If she listened to Nana, she'd be signing up for on-line dating services, moving on and getting angry. But she was tired of being angry. And resentful. Or regretful. More than anything, she just wanted to start over.

If only life had a refresh button.

Maybe she *should* take Nancy's advice. Find out who Kate Mitchell was. There must be a new, purpose-filled woman deep inside waiting to be discovered. Isn't that what Oprah and those self-help books she'd been meaning to read always said? Inside she had a woman who wasn't afraid to take chances. A woman comfortable in her own skin. A woman who might have considered an adventurous, humanitarian life in the Peace Corps or something. Not *now*, of course, but a woman who once felt— and could feel again—like a woman?

Kate took another slug of tea, a wry, humorless laugh bubbling inside her. The only way to *really* feel like a woman was to… She shook her head as an image of her attractive neighbor popped to mind.

As if a summer romance would cure what ailed her!

A sudden gust of wind sent a shiver up her arm, and she hugged her blanket tighter, cupping her mug of tea. Her gaze traveled over the water. Wait—what was *that?*

Tea sloshed down her wrist a second time that day, and she bolted upright. Dimly, through the trees, down by the lapping shore, she could just make out a form in the water.

Images of the Loch Ness Monster sprang to mind, but of course here in the wild it was more likely a beaver or a bear or a… *man?*

Riveted, she watched him slide through the darkness, muscled arms cutting through the water. His body disappeared for one, two, three seconds then reemerged soundlessly, as he moved in the opposite direction, swimming rhythmically through the water near the shore.

It was so dark, she couldn't say how she knew it was a man, but the sudden tension warming her core seemed to know.

Kate held her breath and tried to merge into the slats of the porch swing as he pulled himself onto the dock, his toned form barely visible in the half-light of the crescent moon. The trees teased her with glimpses of him as he stepped ashore and retrieved something from the ground, then turned...

Kate clamped her lips shut and watched in stunned silence as Ruth Pearson's grandson climbed the path up the hill to his house, his clothes bundled in his fist, his hair slick with water, and his body as wondrously naked as the day he was born.

June 14
Ancient Greeks. Not only did they live in a moderate, Mediterranean climate with beautiful ocean views, they were comfortable in their own skin. Democracy, Socrates and baklava aside, I wish I could claim them in my family tree. Maybe some of that innate self-confidence would be in my genes, too.

CHAPTER SIX

"I'M WORRIED ABOUT SANDY."

Kate rolled over, spit out her night guard and berated herself for not letting the call go to voice mail. "Hi, Ma."

"She hasn't been herself lately."

Kate blinked at the clock on the nightstand and stifled a groan. "And you had to call me at 5:30 in the morning to tell me this?"

"Is it that early? I tell you, I've been doing this new yoga routine. It's amazing. It's called 'Awaken the Dawn.' I feel so refreshed! You should try it."

Kate flopped back onto her pillows. "I'll get right on it."

"Anyway, ever since she choked on that chicken bone over Memorial Day weekend, she hasn't been herself. I blame the caterers. Why would they leave a plate of chicken wings in plain sight knowing what a weakness it is of hers? You know she can't help herself. Plus the canapés were soggy, but don't get me started."

"Have you taken her to the vet?"

Her mother harrumphed through the telephone line. "They insist there's nothing wrong, but I can tell. A mother knows. Your father pooh-poohs it, but I think she had a near-death experience. She won't talk about it, though, even to the psychiatrist. I'm at my wit's end."

"They have psychiatrists for *dogs* now?"

"Bhardwaj doesn't call himself that. He's more of a shaman, dog-whisperer-type. My yoga instructor recommended him. He's very spiritual."

Kate lolled her head toward the window as the first rays of morning sun crept across the ceiling.

"Anyway, she's been listless for nearly a week. Do you think she could be depressed?"

"I don't know. Maybe it's something else."

"I thought of that. You know your father had his dressing room re-carpeted last week. I told him to specify formaldehyde-free, but did he listen? It smells awful. You don't think those fumes could be causing her nerve damage, do you?"

"It's unlikely."

"You're right. No sense taking chances. I'm calling the vet as soon as we hang up. Oh, but that's not why I called. I need your mailing address."

"What for?"

Her mother's voice grew hushed. "I picked up the remains yesterday, but Rosaria is throwing a fit about having them in the foyer, so I'm going to send them to you."

Kate tried to process what had her mother's housekeeper/cook so up in arms. "What?"

"You know. *The remains*," her mother whispered again.

Oh God. *Randy's ashes.*

"Anyway, I need to get them out of the house. Rosaria keeps mumbling the rosary and crossing herself and carrying on about how it isn't natural to have dead bodies sitting around in boxes in a person's foyer, and frankly, she's disturbing my chi with all of this. I mean, I have Sandy to worry about..."

Kate's mind scrambled to keep up. "But why do you have them?"

"Oh, the crematorium called your father's office when they couldn't reach you at home. It's been two months and they wanted to make sure you hadn't forgotten them, so I picked them up. What a rigmarole *that* was! They almost didn't give them to me. Anyway, they're here now, so I need your address. I'll have Jill FedEx them this afternoon."

Oh, Lord, is it even legal to FedEx something like that?

Kate didn't bother to point out that her father's secretary probably wouldn't appreciate having to handle her dead husband's remains any more than Rosaria. And there was no use suggesting they could stay in Connecticut until she returned home.

Promising to e-mail Jill her address, Kate said her goodbyes then let out a choked, semi-hysterical laugh.

Great. How was she supposed to find her passion with *dead Randy* sitting around in a box?

CHAPTER SEVEN

———————

"I HEAR YOU'VE GOT A HOT young widow living next door now."

Jim rolled his eyes and stared at his life-long friend, Alex Lamont. "You shouldn't socialize with Carter so much. It's bad for your health."

Alex shrugged. "I would have been socializing with you, but he warned me you were in a foul mood. You missed a good game last night."

Jim ignored him and grabbed a package of hamburger rolls off the shelf.

Alex pointed at the display. "Get some hotdog rolls, too. No, not the wheat. The good kind."

Jim grabbed a jumbo pack of hotdog rolls and pushed the grocery cart ahead of him.

"Tell me again why we're grocery shopping instead of, hell, anything else?" Alex pressed.

Staring at the jars of condiments, Jim blew out a breath. "I volunteered."

"Why?" Alex grabbed a jar of mustard off the shelf and held it out. "Is brown the same thing as Dijon? Susan said she wanted Dijon."

"I think I flashed the hot young widow next door."

"You *what?*" Alex fumbled the mustard jar then set it carefully in the cart.

Jim's voice was a low mumble, "I was skinny-dipping last night—"

"And you do this often?"

He gave his friend a hard look. "Do you want to hear or not?"

Alex absently threw a couple jars of relish in the cart. "Absolutely."

"Long story short—I felt like a swim and when I stopped by this morning so she could help me move an extra sofa into the cottage, she blushed. And maybe snickered. It was hard to tell."

"You go for an impromptu swim in the buff, and you think you've been caught because she looked flushed while hauling heavy furniture?"

"Yes."

Alex rolled his eyes and pushed the cart toward the ketchup and chili sauce. "Your conscience is working overtime. Did she say anything?"

41

"Of course not."

"Then we're really only going on speculation at this point."

"Alex, I think I know when I have or have not flashed a woman."

"That much experience, eh? I thought this was an infrequent thing."

"I'm getting the lettuce and tomatoes," Jim announced, pushing the cart purposefully down the aisle.

"Oh, no. You don't get to change the subject that easily. This sounds like a problem. Do your clothes fall off often? How did this happen? I don't think I'm the only one concerned about this…"

"Very funny. I had a fire call. I was hot and sweaty, and I thought I'd take a swim to cool off. Clean up. Enough said. But this morning, when I offered to lend her that extra couch from my basement—because Grams took most of the furniture when she moved out—we get onto the porch with it and her son yells, 'watch out' because we're knocking into the light fixture. And *she* says, 'Don't worry. *It doesn't work, anyway.*'" Jim stopped meaningfully.

"So?"

"So, I asked how she knew, and she said she'd come out last night to drink her tea on the porch after her son went to bed… She was on the porch, Alex. *After dark.*"

Alex stopped the cart with his foot. "Wait a minute. Are you *insane*? You're after another woman with a kid?"

"Out of everything I said *that's* what you focus on?" Jim pushed the cart forward. "And I'm not after anybody. She's my neighbor. I was being neighborly. I brought her a couch. *I* wasn't the one skulking around in the dark *spying* on people…"

"Technically, I think you're both guilty of skulking." Alex shook his head. "Why can't you hook up with a nice single woman with no strings attached? Just once?"

"I'm not hooking up. Or dating. I'm taking a break. I enjoy being a bachelor."

"Since when?"

Jim scowled at Alex's dubious expression. "I'm not Carter. I can live without a new woman around every corner. I have hobbies. Interests."

"Name one."

"I don't know. I used to carve. I could do that again."

"Like that'll last."

"Your point?"

"My point is you're a serial monogamist. You go from one, long, ill-fated relationship to another. Before Justine there was Megan. Before that, what was it? Leeann? Lee?"

"Leah."

"Right. And let's not forget Velcro Veronica."

"I wish you wouldn't call her that..."

"Did she ever let you out of her sight? Anyway, you can't *not* be involved with a woman. It's who you are. Trouble is you always pick the wrong ones. Women with issues. And baggage." He wheeled the cart toward the produce section. "You want my advice?"

"No."

"What you need is a woman who just wants to have fun. Skip the heavy stuff. And the needy ones. And definitely skip the ones with kids."

"You're a regular poster child for fatherhood. Does Suz know you talk this way?" Jim gave up trying to open the plastic produce bag he'd been struggling with and tossed a bunch of tomatoes loose in the cart. "Anyway, easier done if I avoid women altogether. Not so easy if they're at Grams' barbecue."

"It's your fault for inviting her."

"I didn't. Grams must've called her."

"Ah. So *she's* at your Gram's house and that's why we're here?"

Jim threw a head of iceberg into the cart. "Bingo."

Alex shook his head. "There's something wrong in the universe when a single, heterosexual male has to hide from women for his own safety."

"Tell me about it."

"That was a joke, man. Suck it up. I highly doubt she's going to jump your bones at your Grams' barbeque just because you flashed her. You're not that good looking."

"Thanks."

Alex grinned. "Anytime."

"CAN I HELP WITH ANYTHING?" Kate hovered near the kitchen door, assured for the hundredth time that Liam was perfectly fine playing in the sand box with his newfound friends, twins Jimmy and Alexi Lamont.

Ruth Pearson waved Kate in. "Please. My granddaughter is driving me crazy."

The granddaughter in question pushed an enviable mass of auburn hair over her shoulder and eyed a jumbo pack of ground beef with distaste. "I was just asking where everybody was. All my relatives seem to be conveniently late."

All her relatives? Great. Any hopes of avoiding Jim were quickly diminishing. As if this day hadn't been awkward enough with him delivering that couch and flexing tanned muscles all over the place while Kate pretended she hadn't seen him in all his glory. Lovely.

But Ruth had insisted she come, and seeing as Kate was staying at Ruth's cottage for free for the next couple months, it seemed rude to say no. Kate washed her hands. Nothing said she couldn't hide in the kitchen for as long as possible. "I can help make burgers if you'd like."

Ruth's granddaughter heaved a grateful sigh and pushed the package of ground beef forward. "*Thank you*. I cannot handle meat. By the way, I saw you drive in earlier. Your son's adorable. I'm Grace."

Kate smiled and nodded awkwardly, her hands already in the hamburger. "Thanks. I'm Kate."

"So, you're staying in Sugar Falls for the summer?"

"Yes. At least that's the plan for now. I'm on... leave."

"Like a sabbatical kind of thing?"

"Not exact—"

"Grace, before you embarrass yourself," Ruth cut in, "you should know—Kate is recently widowed. I've invited her to stay at the cottage to have some peace and quiet."

Grace's eyes grew huge. "Widowed? I am *so* sorry. How did it happen?"

"*Grace.*"

"It's okay," Kate assured them. "It was a car accident."

"Oh, no. What happened?"

"*Grace!*" Ruth hissed.

Kate stared at the raw beef in her hands, looked up. "The truth is, nobody knows. He was an alcoholic, but he hadn't been drinking. It was late at night. He was driving too fast to make the turn. They said there might have been fog or maybe an animal was in the road..." Kate trailed off. Who would ever know what happened that night? Although the animal theory never struck Kate as likely. Randy used to yell *ten points!* each time he accidentally hit something, as if they were playing some macabre video game and he hadn't just run over a living creature.

Grace didn't say a word, her mouth a silent 'oh.'

Kate went back to shaping hamburgers. "I'm sorry. That's probably more than you wanted to know."

Grace went to Kate then, throwing her arms around her, momentarily knocking the breath out of her. "Oh, God, *no!* I'm an idiot for prying. I'm so sorry I put you on the spot. How awful!" She gave Kate another squeeze, and when Kate pulled back, she saw tears pooling in Grace's eyes.

"Grace, enough already," Ruth chided from the other side of the island. "You're the only one crying, for heaven's sake."

"It's so tragic!"

"I'm really okay," Kate insisted, finding it somewhat surreal that she felt the need to comfort Grace.

"I'm sorry," Grace mumbled as she swiped at her nose. "Oh, God, I need a tissue." With that she pushed through the door into the next room.

Kate looked at Ruth.

"Before you ask, yes, she's always like that. A bull in an emotional china shop. You get used to it. Oh, where is that infernal colander? I swear, I've been here a year, and I still can't find where anything is in this kitchen. Good heavens, what is it doing in here?"

Ruth pulled the colander out of a cupboard next to the side door and brought it to the sink.

Kate shaped another burger. "One of my friends back home is a caterer. She showed me how to organize my kitchen for maximum efficiency. I'd be happy to come over some afternoon to see if we could use some of her strategies. If you like. I don't mean to intrude."

"Like? Oh, bless your heart, Kate. I'd love it! You'd think that moving from my tiny kitchen to this big one would make life easier, but it's been the opposite. What are some of her tricks?"

"Well, she took the doors off her upper cabinets, for one thing, but that's a little extreme for most people. Mostly, she said to think of the kitchen as different stations of activity and be sure it doesn't take more than two movements to reach anything you use often."

"We've got a church yard sale coming up. Maybe that would be a good time to go through everything. Not until you're settled, of course..."

"Just let me know when you need me."

"Aren't you a sweetheart? Ah, here are the boys! Right on schedule." Kate tried to appear nonchalant as the sound of car doors slamming met her ears. "Jim! Come here and grab that bowl for me, will you? Kate has her hands full."

Kate could feel the heat rise in her face as Jim set his grocery bags on the counter and brushed past her. He retrieved the bowl, his shirt pulling taut across his shoulders as he did so. Kate concentrated on her task and willed the wild butterflies in her stomach to quiet down already.

Ruth opened the grocery bags and inspected the tomatoes. "Where are the veggie burgers?"

Jim shrugged. "They weren't on the list."

"Weren't they? Oh, bother. Grace is counting on them, and there are none in the freezer. Would you mind running back to town and picking some up?"

"Why can't Grace do it?"

"She's helping your folks get the boat ready for later." Ruth pointed through the window toward the boat.

"I don't see her out there."

"Well, anyway, you can take Kate! It'd be good for someone to show her how to get to the stores. You know how confusing that new intersection can be. I'm sure Susan will be happy to watch Liam while you're gone."

Jim turned to Kate, his expression closed.

"You can point me in the right direction," Kate said as she washed her hands. "I can pick up the burgers. I'm sure I can find my way."

Jim simply adjusted his cap and pulled it low over his eyes. "I don't mind."

JIM HELD THE DOOR AS KATE slid onto the bench seat of his truck, her purple shorts pulling snug across her bottom as she shimmied onto the seat. He found it strangely erotic that she wore clothes the color of popsicles. Pulling his gaze from her thighs, he cleared his throat and shut the door.

He didn't consider himself overly modest, but the distinct possibility that this woman—correction, *mother*—had seen him in the buff was awkward as hell. He couldn't imagine what she must be thinking right now, stuck in a truck with an exhibitionist.

Jim started the engine, cleared his throat again and tried to concentrate on the road.

"Would you like a cough drop?"

Jim kept his eyes on the road. "No. Why?"

"That's the fourth time you've cleared your throat. I thought perhaps..."

He cleared it again. "Throat's dry is all."

"Oh."

He shifted down at the stop sign and made the mistake of glancing at Kate.

She sat quietly, her breasts rising and falling evenly under her white T-shirt, the material smooth and taut...

Jim began to clear his throat then decided to disguise it with a cough. Mistake. Now Kate was peering at him with open concern.

"Are you sure you're okay?"

"Fine. Too many fire calls lately. Always dries me out."

"So you're a fireman *and* a plumber?"

"No. A volunteer firefighter and a carpenter/general contractor."

"Sorry. I didn't mean to suggest you were just a plumber or anything—"

"It's all right. I've the highest respect for plumbers. I just don't happen to love the work. Water and I don't always get along."

He nearly choked again when he realized what he'd said. Kate was looking out the passenger window, but he could see her face flushing pink, her lips fighting a smile.

"Anyway," he said, heat flushing his own face, "I prefer carpentry. I just meant that water's often the cause of the problems I'm called in to fix."

"I see," she replied. "So, you enjoy carpentry more?"

Grateful they were finally at the grocery store—and on safe conversational ground—he pulled into the parking lot. "Yes."

"Rough or smooth?"

Jim whipped his head around. "Pardon me?"

"I mean, finish. Do you prefer rough or finish work?" A slight hint of a smile played around her lips. God they were lush. Like that actress, what's-her-name.

His gaze dropped to where her hands lay, loosely clasped between her thighs. "Smooth. Incredibly smooth."

"Pardon me?"

Did he just say that out loud? "I mean, finish," he said, yanking the truck into the nearest space and flinging the door wide. "I like finish work best."

He shut the driver's door, pocketed his keys and rounded the back of the truck to open her door. Good Lord. What the hell was wrong with him? The last time he'd acted like this around a female, his voice was still cracking, and back then the only thing on his mind was making it past second base.

Kate slid out of the truck, her purse strap running diagonally through her cleavage. Jim tore his eyes away with effort and turned toward the store.

Clearly nothing had changed.

"IS THERE ANYTHING ELSE I can help with?" Kate emptied the last bag of chips into a serving bowl and looked around the kitchen. Bowls of homemade potato and garden salads sat next to trays of burgers and hotdogs ready for the grill. A giant pot of water heated on the stove, awaiting a pile of shucked corn on the cob.

Ruth shook her head. "Thanks to you, I think we're all set in here. Can you hand me that ring by the sink?"

Kate picked up the delicate sapphire and diamond band. "It's lovely. Anniversary gift?"

Ruth clucked. "Engagement ring. Surprised he could even afford this, we were so young, but he was a sweetheart and wouldn't hear of saving the money." She pushed it on her finger and chuckled. "I should probably leave it in my jewelry box. One of these days my knuckles will be so swollen I won't be able to get it back off." She shrugged. "Comes with living so long. Anyway, while I wait for the water to boil, maybe you can find something patriotic in that corner cabinet to dress up the tables. I put out white tablecloths earlier, but they're looking rather plain. I don't know where all my holiday decorations disappeared to after the move."

Kate opened the cabinet. There were some mismatched linens, assorted napkin rings, the stubs of a few candles, cookbooks, a collection of seashells in mason jars and a pile of junk mail. Yes. A reorganization was definitely in order. "There's not much in the way of red, white and blue. How do you feel about a beach theme?"

"Why not?"

Kate grabbed the seashells, mason jars, and some assorted placemats in hues of blues and greens and turned, knocking a manila envelope to the floor. She set down her decorating supplies and bent to pick it up.

Ruth waved her hand. "Just set that on the counter. They're photos of Carter, my grandson." She leaned forward. "I'm working up my nerve to look at them. I'm afraid they might be a little spicy."

"Spicy?"

"He can be that way, you know, but it may work to our advantage."

"I don't understand."

"It's for one of our fundraisers. The Gifts for the Greater Good committee is raising money to fix up the food pantry and emergency shelter here in town. Oh, the roof had ice dams and there was all sorts of water damage. Anyway, James gave us an estimate on the work and when I brought it to the committee... Well, I don't know if you've noticed how handsome my grandsons are, but, I said to myself, 'Ruth, who wouldn't want to look on their handsome faces all year long?'"

Nonplussed, Kate felt heat rise up her throat. Was that a rhetorical question?

"So we decided to put together a calendar, and we're calling it 'Sweets of Sugar Falls!' At least, that's what Lydia wants to call it. I'm still not sure it sends the right message, though I admit it has a nice ring to it.

"Every month will be a new photo, see? One of our very own boys. Carter sent his photos over a couple days ago." Ruth motioned at Kate. "Open it. It'll be good to get a young lady's opinion."

Kate undid the envelope's clasp and pulled out a glossy eight-by-ten. A bare-chested man in faded jeans leaned on a shovel, one muscular forearm swiping the sweat from his brow as he smiled cockily at the camera. Self-confident, good-looking and dripping with sexuality—a *boy* he was not. "Wow."

"Well? Do you think it'll sell calendars?"

Kate slid the photo back into the envelope and suppressed a smile. "Most definitely."

Ruth beamed and nearly clapped her hands. "I'm so glad. I was a little nervous, to tell the truth. Carter can be a bit of a wild card sometimes." Kate gathered her supplies. "Of course I'm not sure what we'll do if we have more than twelve good entries. I don't want to hurt anyone's feelings. We're still working out the kinks, I'm afraid."

"You could always have people vote for their favorites." At Ruth's puzzled look, Kate continued. "If you had a website or social networking fan page, you could post the photos on-line for people to vote on. I did that for Spirit Week last year at the school I work for. The kids made school pride banners and then voted on their favorites. It really brought the kids together. Who knows, if you involve the community, it could build interest in the calendar."

"And boost sales! Oh, that's brilliant! We could announce the winners at the auction we're holding over Labor Day weekend, too. That may be just what we need to bring us over the top of our fundraising goals." Ruth grinned, the twinkle in her eyes taking decades off her face. "But who would do it? I wouldn't know the first thing about setting something like that up."

"I suppose I—"

"Oh, bless you! If you were willing to organize the entries and keep things respectable, it'd be *such* a help."

Kate licked her lips. "You want me to make your beefcake calendar web page respectable?"

Ruth nodded vigorously. "We wouldn't want it to appear unseemly."

"Of course not."

"It *is* for a worthy cause," she added.

"Absolutely."

Ruth rested a wrinkled hand on Kate's arm, her voice soft and comforting. "Normally, I wouldn't dream of imposing on you, what with your recent loss and all, but June *was* talking the other day about how worried she is about you. Maybe a little project like this will help take your mind off your troubles."

Kate's eyebrows shot up. Coordinating with dozens of local bachelors would take her mind off her troubles? Okay, well perhaps momentarily, but that's probably what Pandora thought as she approached the box. *How lovely! I wonder what I'll find in here to amuse me?*

"Um. I appreciate your thinking of my, um, troubles, but I don't know. What if someone got the wrong idea? I'm not ready..."

"Oh, honey, they don't have to know it's you! In fact, now that I think about it, it's probably best they don't. They might try to sway you otherwise. Nothing worse than a contest that seems rigged. We want it all on the up and up, don't we?"

"Of course. But—"

"We'll worry about the details later." Ruth patted her hand. "Will you at least think about it? Oh, it feels like fate that we had this talk today, doesn't it?"

It was feeling a wee bit like manipulation, actually, but it'd be selfish to say no. She was staying in this woman's cottage for free the entire summer! And, honestly, how much trouble would it be? Who knows, if she did a good job, it could be a resume builder. "Sure. I'll think about it. It might be fun."

Ruth beamed. "Good! Well, it looks like we're done in here for a bit. Do you need help with the tables?"

"I'm all set." Kate picked up her decorations and escaped through the patio door before she rashly committed to anything else. She had to do something about this impulsive streak she was developing.

Coordinating a beefcake calendar? Good grief.

Twenty minutes later, satisfied with her table decorations, Kate stepped off the deck. She bent to retie her shoe at the same moment someone rounded the corner of the house.

Kate peered through the daylilies. *Jim.* She watched as he stopped, kicked off his sneakers and closed his eyes for a moment, his bare feet sinking into the grass.

Kate's pulse kicked up a notch. There was something about watching Jim enjoy one of life's small pleasures that tugged at her.

She could feel it knotting in her stomach—a stab of jealousy or regret, she wasn't sure which. When had she last given in to the temptation to curl her bare toes in cool summer grass? When had she lost touch with the tactile, sensual side of herself? She glanced down at her practical Keds, neatly if not stylishly encasing her feet. Oh God, maybe Randy was right. Maybe motherhood *had* made her less of a woman.

Kate turned to slink away at the same time Jim stepped forward and spotted her.

His eyes registered surprise. "I didn't know you were out here."

She stood up and turned awkwardly. So much for slinking. "I came to check on Liam." She looked away, but her eyes were drawn to Jim's toes again. There was something strangely intimate about seeing his bare feet in the grass.

Jim flashed a charming, lop-sided grin and wiggled his toes. "Feels good after being in my boots all week. You should try it."

"Oh, I don't think—"

"Why not?"

Good question. By Connecticut standards, the lawn needed mowing and some weed killer. But it was tempting to sink her toes into the slightly long blades of grass. Besides, it wasn't a health violation. She was on a lake in rural New Hampshire, for cryin' out loud.

And Jim was waiting. She sat on the deck steps and pulled off her sneakers, neatly tucking her white Peds into each. She stood up.

"You've got to close your eyes, or you can't really feel it."

She half-laughed, enormously self-conscious now. "I think I can feel it just f—"

"Close your eyes," he insisted. As if he didn't believe she would comply, he reached up and brushed a feather-light thumb over each of her lids.

Kate closed her eyes, trying to tell herself that the sudden, tingling awareness that had her skin humming and her ears tuning into the soft rasp of his breathing and the faint hum of a nearby bee were because her world had gone black, not because it had sprung to riotous life at his touch.

"Feels good doesn't it," he whispered somewhere near her left ear.

Kate's body swayed involuntarily toward his voice. *Good?* Good didn't begin to describe what she felt. Cool, slightly damp, blades of grass tickled her toes, but it was a distant sensation to the heat curling its way through her body in a way that grass had never before affected her.

"*Mmm*," she said. "Good."

"I like your nail polish by the way."

Kate's eyes flew open. She looked at her feet. Purple glitter. Randy would've been horrified. "You don't have to say that," she said.

"I mean it. You're a colorful woman."

She flushed with pleasure. "That's the nicest thing anyone's said to me in a long time."

"You hang around with a tough crowd then."

"I'm trying to change that."

"You should." His hazel eyes swirled with the colors of the landscape, intense and mesmerizing. Kate swayed slightly toward them. Oh, my. Did he just move closer? She found herself staring into his eyes, lost in them, taking an unconscious step forward.

Shooting pain stabbed the ball of her foot, and she yelped and stumbled.

Jim's hand snaked out to grab her arm, steadying her. "You okay?"

"My foot— I think I got stung!" She spun around, hopping on her right foot, pulling her left one up to look at it.

"*Whoa*. Steady." Jim's hands clasped each of her arms from behind, his grip firm but soothing. "Let me take a—*Oof!*"

Suddenly, they were on the ground, Jim sprawled on the grass beneath her, the soft rasp of denim abrading the backs of her thighs. Dear Lord, she was sitting in the man's *lap!* "Ohmigod! I'm so sorry! I was—" She struggled to right herself and knocked them over again.

Jim's arm clamped around her. "Jesus! Hold still. *Watch your elbow.*"

Kate stilled and choked out an embarrassed laugh. "I'm trying to sit up so I can look..."

Jim pushed them upright again, shifting Kate to his left thigh. He grabbed her foot before she could scurry away. "Let me look."

"It's okay, I can..."

He glanced up. "Handle it yourself? If you handle it any more, we'll both end up in the ER. Just let me look." His fingers closed over her foot, warm and firm, as he bent his head to look more closely. Kate's face flamed. Not only was she sitting on his lap, leg twisted toward him, intertwined like they were testing some sort of Kama Sutra pose, she was *thinking* the words Kama Sutra.

"You're not allergic, are you?" He was rubbing the pad of his thumb lightly over the bottom of her foot. Kate shook her head. "Aha! Yup. I found the stinger. *Don't move.* I'll get it." He twisted, thrusting his hips toward her as he held her foot with one hand and fished for his wallet in a back pocket with the other. He flipped the wallet open and pulled a credit card out with his teeth.

Oh, Momma.

Kate caught her breath as he bent his head again to remove the stinger. She inhaled, the scents of sun and man making the world tilt and blood rush to parts of her body that had no business getting excited. She closed her eyes and concentrated on steady, consciousness-inducing breaths.

He let go of her foot. "All set."

"Thanks," she murmured.

She swallowed. The adrenaline was receding, replaced by the awkward knowledge that there was no graceful way to climb off the man's lap—especially when she'd rather stay right where she was.

"Do you think you can stand now?" he finally asked.

No. "Yes! Yes. I think so. Sorry."

"Don't be."

He spoke the words softly, but their effect was electric. Awareness sizzled through her, trapping the breath in her lungs as his gaze fell heavy and warm on her lips. She fought the urge to wet them with the tip of her tongue.

He wouldn't kiss her. She wasn't reading him right. She must be mistaking the signs—if she could even remember them after all this time.

But then her eyes flew to his, because there was no mistaking the sensation of a man pulsing against her thigh.

Kate swallowed again and flattened her palm against his chest.

Oh God, she wanted to kiss him. Here. *Now.* In the damp grass, in the late afternoon shadows, she wanted to sink her fingers into his hair and taste this man's lips. She wanted to be colorful inside and out. She wanted...

"...no hamburgers on the vegetarian side of the grill!"

A screen door slammed, and Kate shoved at Jim's chest, falling gracelessly off his lap, as a group of his relatives rounded the corner of the house.

She was down on all fours, one leg pinned under Jim's thigh, when Grace came to an abrupt halt, five others nearly plowing into her. Kate shimmied out and pushed herself upright off Jim's shoulder. "He was just... I was..."

"No need to explain," Grace said. "Women fall at Jim's feet all the time." She leaned closer. "We've told him to stop tripping them."

Kate pushed the hair out of her face. "Yes, well, I think I took him down this time."

"That would be something new." This from a tall, dark-haired man Kate guessed was the eldest brother.

"Is no one hungry around here?" Another man pushed through the pack of gawkers and extended his hand, flashing a devilishly charming smile. "Hi. I'm Carter. You must be Kate. Sorry about my klutzy cousin knocking you down—"

"I didn't knock anybody down." Jim said as he stood up.

"It's okay. You don't have to cover for him." Carter leaned closer to Kate to stage whisper, "He's always been a little awkward around pretty women."

"Shut up." Jim said, swiping at the grass and dirt that clung to his jeans.

Carter laughed. "While Jimmy here regains his dignity, Kate, why don't you and I head down to the grill. Grams said we should start dinner—"

"She's not grilling with you."

Carter cocked an eyebrow at Jim. "Maybe she wants to."

"She doesn't."

"I really did hurt my foot..." Kate said.

"Sorry to hear that." Carter glanced down then looked up again. He winked. "Nice toes."

Just then, little Alexis Lamont ran up the path from the lake and tugged at Carter's shirt. "Where you go? You promised me a piggy ride!"

"So I did! So I did! Well, duty calls." Carter scooped up the giggling toddler and swung her over his shoulder like a potato sack.

Kate mumbled pleasantries as the rest of the group followed the laughing pair toward the lake.

Jim ran a hand through his hair. "Sorry about that."

"About...?"

"Carter. He comes on a bit strong sometimes. He's harmless. Just... annoying."

Oh. *Right*. They were going to talk about his cousin, *not* the strange electric currents that nearly had them lip-locked in a tangled heap on the lawn. Nor, she supposed, were they going to talk about the tell-tale bulge near Jim's zipper.

No, they were going to stand in the grass in their bare toes and pretend they didn't want to jump each other's bones like two horny teenagers.

Correction. Kate would pretend that. She couldn't say what Jim was pretending, because he was already walking away.

CHAPTER EIGHT

"I'M WORRIED ABOUT RACHEL."

Jim fought the urge to roll his eyes as Grace scrutinized the distance between the veggie burgers and hamburgers on the grill. "Rachel is fine," he asserted, closing the lid so Grace would stop frowning. He didn't mind grill duty, precisely, as it kept him conveniently away from Kate for a few minutes, but he'd forgotten how Grace hovered. He'd hoped for a few minutes by himself.

Grace sipped her diet cola and pursed her lips. "Haven't you noticed how quiet she's been lately?"

"We've seen her twice since Christmas. Hardly a statistically meaningful sampling."

"Maybe they're still having problems."

"Rachel and Doug?" Jim choked on the words, the feel of them odd and foreign on his tongue. It was ludicrous, and yet even the thought made him feel edgy and unwell. Rachel and Doug had been in puppy love ever since senior year of high school. They'd married far too young and far too confidently for everyone's comfort, but ten years later, he couldn't imagine them as anything other than together. "Did Rach say they were on the rocks?"

Grace looked as shocked and horrified as Jim felt. "No! Has Doug said that to *you?*"

"No!"

"Then why would you even suggest it?"

"Me?" Jim flipped open the grill and started poking at the burgers, looking around to be sure they weren't overheard. "You're the one that said it."

"I never said they were having problems in their marriage! I said I think they're still having problems getting pregnant!"

"What?"

Grace motioned for him to flip her veggie burger with the meat-free spatula then heaved an exasperated sigh. "Like you didn't know they've been trying to get pregnant for ages?"

"In that tiny apartment?"

"I'm surprised Doug didn't tell you they had him tested last fall."

Jim closed his eyes. *Way too much information.* "Guys don't talk about that stuff."

"You're talking about it with me."

"Not willingly." Jim looked around the yard. *Where the hell were Ian and Alex?*

"Anyway, they've verified he's not shooting blanks, so they had Rachel tested and she's normal, too."

"If I say, 'sometimes these things take time,' can we end this conversation? Please?"

"This is your sister we're talking about. Aren't you at all concerned?"

"What am I supposed to do? Stage a fertility dance? We're only speculating, anyway."

"She was quiet at Easter, but today, she barely said hello before disappearing into the house. It kills me to see her so sad! Why do bad things have to happen to good people?"

Jim nodded. What was there to say?

"Do you think it's too soon for them to consider adoption? I have a friend who just adopted a baby girl from Guatemala. I could give them her number—"

"Grace, leave her alone. If she wants our help, she'll ask."

"Sure. But just in case she doesn't open up, see what you can get out of Doug."

"And how—?"

"*Ssh!* He's coming. Pretend we weren't talking about them!" Grace pasted an unnaturally bright smile on her face as Doug closed the breezeway door. "I was just headed out back to, ah, help. So, I'll be going now... in case you wanted to talk about anything, you know, guy stuff."

"O-kaaay." Doug gave Jim a look.

Jim shrugged and opened the grill.

"Don't even ask," Jim counseled.

"I wasn't planning on it."

The two men stood in silence, the smoky grill wafting downwind.

"Kate seems nice," said Doug.

Jim transferred the hotdogs to the warming shelf while the burgers finished cooking. "Grams invited her."

"Is that why you two were rolling in the clover together?"

"It wasn't what it looked like."

"Ah. So you weren't blushing like two kids caught necking behind the bleachers?"

Jim moved the veggie burgers to a plate as a chuckle rose in his chest. "Doug, I love you like a brother, but if you give me any more grief I'll personally disembowel you with these tongs."

"Huh. That would be too bad—my kid being born without a father and all."

It took him a minute to process, but as soon as it registered, Jim couldn't suppress a grin. "No kidding?"

Doug smiled a silly, happy grin of impending fatherhood. "No kidding."

"Congratulations."

Doug rocked on his heels, his hands stuffed in his pockets. "Thanks. But don't say anything yet. Rachel doesn't want to make it general knowledge for a few more weeks. Just in case."

"Sure." Jim opened the grill. "Though you might want to wipe that foolish grin off your face before you go back in or people might start asking questions."

"It's hard not to smile. We've planned for this for so long."

Jim chuckled and shook his head. "You guys will make great parents."

"Thanks."

Jim opened the grill and squinted against the sting of smoke as the breeze shifted. He was happy for them. Truly. If anybody deserved to be happy, it was those two.

After all, they'd done everything right.

CHAPTER NINE

"WHAT'S THIS?" JIM FINGERED the little seashell with his name on it.

"A place card. So people know where to sit." Grace rolled her eyes. "Grams' idea."

Grams reached forward and repositioned the seashell labeled 'Jim' in front of his paper plate. "I thought it looked nice with all the decorations Kate set up for us. Besides, you boys always hole up together and get rowdy. I thought spreading you out would make things more pleasant."

"I've never been rowdy," Jim protested. He grunted as Carter nudged him hard in the back.

"Hey, Jim. Taken any more spills? Might want to get your balance checked. All that late night swimming must be playing havoc with your inner ear."

Jim narrowed his eyes at Alex who was across the deck corralling the twins at a neighboring table. There were absolutely no secrets anymore. Ignoring Carter's teasing, Jim checked the names on the shells beside him. Rach was to his right and Alex was to his left. Fine. He could handle that. It would make it easier to silence Alex before he had a chance to run at the mouth again.

Jim grabbed a fistful of chips. He watched Kate settle Liam next to Susan, his mom and the twins at the smaller table. Kate's honey-blonde hair kept falling across her face, and he couldn't help but remember how good it had smelled when she'd fallen in his lap. Christ. He glanced around, feeling like he was sixteen again and waiting outside his locker for the cute girl to notice him. He turned away and sat down.

A moment later, Kate stood across the table from him, reading a little seashell and flashing those long smooth legs as she stepped over the bench to settle in the only seat left. Directly across from Jim. He popped a chip in his mouth and fought the urge to roll his eyes. Grams was anything but subtle.

"Hi," she said, as if she hadn't just seen him five minutes ago. Or been sitting in his lap for that matter.

"Hi," he said. The potato chips were making his throat constrict. He stood up again. "I'm gonna get a drink," he announced to no one in particular.

"Grab me a water?" Grace asked.

"Sure." He wasn't particularly thirsty, but he needed air. Or something.

"I'd love a water, too. If you don't mind," Kate said.

Jim nodded, scraped his chair back and ducked down the deck steps toward the breezeway. He grabbed two bottled waters from the case and a beer from the cooler.

He slid back into his chair, nearly knocking over a mason jar jammed with wildflowers as he handed a water bottle to Kate.

Grams made a little speech about patriotism and sacrifice, they had a moment's silence and then little Alexis burped and announced her root beer needed refilling. Nice.

Jim passed the tray of hamburgers.

"So, Kate," Grace began as other dishes made their way down the table, "do you enjoy swimming?"

"Yes, but I haven't been for quite a while."

Jim narrowed his eyes at Grace who focused intently on spooning out her potato salad.

Carter leaned across his sister and grabbed the ketchup. "Now that you're living next door to Jim, maybe you'll get more opportunities to enjoy the water. He's practically a fish, you know."

Kate looked at Jim. "Is he?"

Jim tried to ignore the heat swirling in his gut as Kate's gaze rested on him. He'd kill them all with his plastic butter knife if they brought up the skinny-dipping.

"Oh, yeah. Swim team all through school."

"No kidding?" Kate's eyes were bright with interest now.

"It was no big deal," Jim objected.

"No big deal?" cut in his sister, Rachel. "You made it to the Championships senior year! Made front page of the local paper, too."

"He used to practice all the time, even at night," his mother added loudly from the other table. "Why was that, anyway?"

"It was cooler at night," he said, glancing up long enough to catch a faint twist to Kate's full lips. For some reason, knowing she was watching him, seeing the soft fullness of her lips as she fought a smile, brought a fullness to his groin that didn't make sitting under the scrutiny of his entire family any more comfortable. He twisted in his seat and took another slug of beer. "Great potato salad, Grams."

"I seem to remember you swimming off the dock near our cottage," his grandmother mused. "You'd go back and forth in the water for ages. Reminded me of myself at that age. You should have seen him, Kate. He was beautiful to watch."

Jim squirmed in his seat again as Kate choked on her bite of food. She quickly washed it down with a healthy drink of water. "Sorry," she wheezed, her cheeks blazing, "went down the wrong way."

"Grams was just saying Jim swam over near your cottage all the time and he was beautiful to watch," Grace helpfully repeated, forking potato salad into her mouth as she grinned at him innocently. The imp.

All eyes focused on Kate. "I'm sure he was... beautiful, that is."

She glanced up at the same time as Jim, and just for a moment, their eyes met. He sucked in a breath at the unadulterated look of awareness that flashed in her eyes. But she said nothing as she ducked her head and took another drink. He licked his lips, wishing he were anywhere but sitting at this damn folding table with his family all around.

"Jim's right," Susan commented from the kids' table. "This is terrific potato salad, Mrs. Pearson."

I love you, Susan, even though your husband is a blabbermouth.

"Thank you. The bacon bits are the key."

"There's *bacon* in this?" cried Grace. "Does no one around here know what being vegetarian means?"

"Just pick it out," said Carter. "It's easy to spot."

"Would you pick around a bunch of bugs in your food just because they were easy to spot? That's disgusting!"

"Extra protein," Carter added.

"I've lost my appetite." Grace pushed her plate away.

"Here," Kate took the offending plate piled with potato salad. "I'll get you a garden burger."

"*Thank you.*" Grace waited for Kate to walk away then swung toward Jim. "She seems nice," she said meaningfully. "Don't you think?"

"Yeah. Sure." He waited for her to look away. She didn't. "What?"

"Well? Don't you think maybe, *you know*, you might ask her out? She's all alone. She'll be here the whole summer... You broke up with Justine months ago…"

"Oh, for cryin— "

"I made sure it hadn't touched any of the other meats," Kate announced as she approached the table. She set the garden burger in front of Grace.

"I'm thinking after dinner Jim should show Kate some of his moves," Carter suggested. Jim shot Carter the evil eye. "In the water, I mean."

"That's an excellent idea!" Grams enthused from the end of the table. "I'd love a dip after this warm day. We can go right after the boat ride."

Jim stabbed another chunk of potato. "Kate might not be in the mood for a swim."

"Actually, I'd love to go," she said.

He glanced up. She gave him a shy smile, her eyes crinkling softly at the corners.

Ah, hell.

AFTER DINNER, JIM'S PARENTS shooed Kate away and told her to run and get her swimsuit. Assured Liam was happily playing with his new friends, Kate made the short drive around the lake to the cottage.

Was it foolhardy to entertain the excited butterflies in her belly at the thought of swimming? She couldn't help herself. The Pearsons were loud, chaotic, unpredictable, and unapologetically themselves. With her own parents too enmeshed in their isolated social circle to do much more than "give her space" and a grandmother who thought giving advice was a full contact sport, she found the Pearsons' light-hearted family dynamic refreshing.

Kate parked and walked to the door, her feet feeling unusually light. It was odd not having Liam in tow. Odd not having him chattering at her elbow or pulling on her arm.

Kate hurried to her room and laid out the swimsuits she'd packed on the bed. There was the navy tankini—practical for nursing when Liam was an infant, but showing its age. A little stretched out. A lot faded. Kate fingered her coral print bikini and wondered if she could still get away with baring her stomach. She hadn't expected anyone to see her other than Liam, so it hadn't seemed practical to buy something new. On the plus side, she hadn't been eating well the last couple months and had dropped a few pounds. She'd have to change that, of course, but for now... heck, she'd bring both and decide when she got there.

When she arrived back at the house, Kate followed the sound of voices to the dock. Liam sat perched next to Mr. Pearson at the Captain's seat of a large pontoon 'party' boat. The rear canopy shaded Jim's mom and grandmother, his friends, Susan and Alex, and their twins. At the front sat Rachel, her husband, Grace, Ian and Carter. "Sorry I kept you waiting." Kate stepped onto the softly swaying boat and slid onto the seat next to Rachel. She looked around. "Jim's not coming?"

"He didn't think there'd be room," Rachel said. "He said he'd sit this one out."

"Oh." Kate's disappointment seemed disproportionate even to her. But, as they got underway, a cool breeze refreshed her heated skin, and she gave herself over to the relaxing movement of the boat and golden sun on the water.

"Liam seems to be enjoying himself." Rachel pointed as Liam grinned ear to ear with the opportunity to 'steer' the boat.

Kate nodded. "He's really taken to your dad."

"Dad's great with kids. He'll be great when he has grandkids. I think they invite Alex and Susan every year as much because they're good friends as to see the twins."

Kate's heart felt tight as she watched the happy interplay. "Liam doesn't have a lot of contact with his real grandfathers."

"Do they live far away?"

Kate shrugged. "My dad is busy with his business and... other things." *Like the golf game that kept him from attending his only grandson's birthday party.*

"What about your late husband's father?"

Kate watched a pair of kayakers on the far shore as they bobbed like orange and yellow buoys in the water. "He isn't in the best of health."

"I'm sorry."

"It is what it is." Kate glanced again at Liam, honking the boat's horn and waving exuberantly as they passed a family barbecuing on shore. *Isn't this the kind of experience every kid should have?*

Why had she let Randy talk her into moving to southern Connecticut anyway? Sure, they were near pools and gyms and lots of conveniences, but there weren't big sloping lawns that rambled into lakes or quiet, peaceful back roads that went on for miles.

But Randy had jumped at the chance to move into Nana's house. *We'll never be able to afford to move there otherwise, Kate...and you know that's where all the good customers are. Just think! If I get a job at a Lexus or Jaguar dealership... do you know what the commissions are on those babies? Do you have any idea? With my sales skills, we'll have it made!*

"Are you okay?" Rachel peered at Kate, concern creasing her brow.

"Just thinking." The wind blew soft on her face, the hum of the pontoon's motor washing over the murmur of other conversation. Kate gave herself a mental shake and forced a wry smile. "I suppose it's finally occurring to me that for the first time in my life my future is entirely up to me."

Rachel gave her arm a reassuring squeeze. "That's not a bad thing, is it? Think of the possibilities."

"I am, and it frightens the hell out of me."

Rachel laughed, and Kate clasped her hand to her mouth. "I'm sorry! That just came out!"

"It's okay!" Rachel brushed the hair from her face. "I feel exactly the same way!" She leaned close and smiled—a warm, friendly grin. "I like your honesty. It's very refreshing.

"You know, I know you're only here for the summer, but Doug will be interviewing in the area over the next few weeks—we're hoping to move closer to Sugar Falls—and I was thinking it'd be fun to get together now and again. We can hang out. Grace. Susan. Whomever's around. Just us girls. What do you say?"

Kate paused. She didn't know what to say.

Oh, sure, she'd been social enough these last few years. She'd gotten together with neighbors… coworkers… people who invited her to their Martha Stewart-inspired Fourth of July barbecues and wine and cheese buffets. But, since having Liam and moving to southern Connecticut, she'd lost touch with all her old friends. Nowadays, get-togethers seemed less about enjoying herself and more about making an impression on someone for her parents' sake or for Randy's.

Rachel's relaxed invitation to 'just hang out' was a breath of fresh air in a life that was closing in on her.

Just us girls.

Kate grinned. "I'd like that very much."

AFTER THE BOAT RIDE, SUSAN took the three kids to make s'mores, and Kate followed Grace and Rachel to the house to change. She tried to duck into the hallway bathroom, but it was occupied.

Grace held open the door of the spare bedroom. "Aren't you coming?"

Kate hesitated for a moment before following Grace into the bedroom. Grace shut the door. As the two cousins chatted and stripped to their underwear, Kate slid her shorts and tee off and dug in her tote for her things. Not having grown up with sisters, she felt the old disquiet of the high school locker room, wondering what the others would think of her plain, practical briefs and tired old bra. She really needed some new things.

"You're not wearing that, are you?" Kate glanced up and was relieved Grace was speaking to Rachel, clad in a sporty maillot, and not about her underwear.

"What's wrong with it?" Rachel countered.

"It's *navy*."

"So?"

Grace glanced around and leaned toward her cousin, "It just seems... *Oh, Rach*, I hate to think... you're giving up. There's always hope..."

Kate pretended to look for something in her tote as Rachel stared at her cousin.

"Giving up?" Rachel asked, but then her face broke into a coy grin. "It just so happens, Doug loves this suit on me. And for the record, it hasn't hurt my fertility either."

Kate held her breath as she watched the cousins from across the bed.

Grace's eyes widened. "*No!*"

"*Yes!*" Rachel beamed.

"Oh. My. *God!*" Grace blinked then turned and yanked a fistful of tissues out of a box before flinging herself bodily at her cousin. "I'm *so* relieved! I thought there was something awful happening. You weren't talking to me... Then Jim made this *stupid* comment—" She blew her nose heartily, still clenching her cousin tightly to her. "Pregnant? Really?"

Kate's hand went to her own stomach.

"I know!" Rachel beamed. "I've been popping with the news all night, but I wasn't sure how to tell you. If you'd be okay with it..."

"Are you crazy? I'm so happy for you!"

"No one else knows," she said. She turned to include Kate. "And I don't want to make it public until I'm further along, so if you guys could just keep it between us?"

Grace pretended to zip her lips and drop the key. "I can't believe it!" she burst out in a whisper. "When?"

"February, we think, but I totally stopped charting in December because it was stressing me out, so we're a little sketchy on the date of conception. It's ballpark until I go for my ultrasound next week."

"An ultrasound!" Grace enthused.

Kate dropped her hand and eyed Rachel in her swimsuit, her blonde hair and petite figure set off beautifully by the classic lines and deep color. Kate looked at her own tankini, as the cousins quietly chatted about the good news, and quickly stuffed it back in her tote. Baby belly or not, there was no way she was wearing a stretched-out runner-up of a navy swimsuit. Rachel was *glowing*.

Kate pulled out her coral, tropical print bikini and tugged it on before she could chicken out.

Thankful for the waning light, she pulled her towel snug around her and followed Rachel and Grace to the dock. The mother in her noted Liam with Dick Pearson at the outdoor fireplace toasting marshmallows. The woman in her quickly saw the men at the water's edge, laughing and jostling each other like teenagers. Carter was threatening to throw Doug off the dock. Ian was trying to block his escape, and Jim was standing to the side, laughing, an easy, light-hearted sound that rolled through the air and sent warm shivers up her bare arms.

Each was good-looking in his own way. Ian and Carter, clearly brothers, with their dark hair and broad shoulders. Doug, lean and golden-haired like his wife.

But it was Jim who drew and held her attention. Slightly taller than the others, his body all fluid muscle and masculine beauty, a soft thatch of hair on his tanned chest. He wore khaki swim trunks, and Kate's mouth went dry as he absently adjusted the waistband.

Ruth Pearson, or Grams as everyone called her, waved them to the dock. "Took you girls long enough. I thought we might start with some races."

Kate gulped. No one had said anything about... "Races?"

Rachel leaned in. "Grams is a hotshot swimmer. She was quite the competitor in her day. Even after her knee replacements last summer, she's hard to beat."

"I'm not sure..."

"Only if you want to," Grams allowed. "I enjoy a brisk swim, limbers up the old bones, but you can sit this one out if you like."

Kate sighed with relief even as Rachel challenged her husband to a race. Grace quickly decided she could beat Carter, and Jim's grandmother paired off against Ian.

This was clearly not the first race of its kind. Rachel explained the rules to Kate. "We swim to the Bellevieu's dock, rock the buoy to show you've made it that far, then be the first to grab the ladder at the end of our dock."

"Ready, set... *go!*" Grace yelled. With that, Rachel and Doug dove into the water. Rachel took a decisive lead. The far buoy wiggled once, then twice, then the pair swam back, Doug calling out for mercy.

Rachel grabbed the ladder in triumph as Grams dove over her like a member of an Olympic relay team. Ian quickly followed.

"Go, Grams! Go!" Grace yelled as Ian began to catch up.

"Can't you beat your own grandmother?" Carter bellowed. "Get the lead out!"

"You're still ahead!" yelled Rachel.

Grams lost a little momentum on the return trip, but was still ahead by a whisper when Grace dove in with Carter in hot pursuit.

Kate wished she felt like a strong enough swimmer to take part, but there was no way she'd pit herself against the likes of Jim. Not with his reputation!

Grace cut through the water with single-minded determination, Carter pounding his strokes inches behind.

"Go, Gracie!" Rachel yelled. "He's right behind you!"

Kate clapped with excitement as Grace jiggled the buoy and flipped around in one smooth turn. Moments later, Grace gave a yelp of surprise and disappeared under water. She came up howling as Carter roared past her.

He was nearly a body length ahead when he choked out a bark of surprise himself, then Grace surged forward, grabbed the ladder and thrust a fist in the air. "The women are the victors!"

Carter slicked his hand over his face. "At least the losers still have their pants on."

"Where are they, anyway?" Grace demanded. "Don't you know when you pants somebody you're not supposed to rip them completely off?"

"Serves you right for buying a swimsuit so cheap it falls apart with one yank." Carter climbed onto the dock and tossed the scrap of material onto the decking.

"You better not have torn my new bikini, or you'll be buying me a new one!" Grace grabbed her swimsuit.

"It's shocking, I know," Jim said from behind Kate's shoulder.

"What?"

"This unsportsmanlike behavior. I can see you're shocked. As well you should be. Pants-ing is strictly forbidden. Automatic disqualification. Now we'll never know the victors."

Grace pointed at Carter. "He started it."

"Regardless, there's just one way to finish it," said Grams. "Jim and Kate will have to compete."

Kate felt herself pale. "Oh, no. I don't think so. I'm no match for Jim."

"Nonsense. You're a perfect match for Jim! We'll just level the playing field. Ian, fetch the chicken raft."

Rachel clapped her hands. "Perfect! All you have to do is stay on the raft, Kate. You can't touch each other,　but whomever stays on the raft the longest is the winner."

Ian soon returned with a bright red plastic raft about six or so feet long by three or four feet wide. He dropped it in the water by the dock. It bobbed reassuringly.

"Okay," said Grace, fully clothed again. "Paddle out so nobody falls into the dock and gets hurt. When you're both standing, we'll start."

Jim stood holding the tow line on the raft so it stayed near the dock. Self-conscious now with all eyes on her, Kate dropped her towel.

"It looks stable enough," she said, eyeing the raft.

Jim's eyes were downcast, his expression blank. So much for the tropical print bikini catching his eye. "Kneel on it for now. We'll stand once we're away from the dock," he instructed.

Kate climbed on.

Soft waves and Jim's paddle strokes carried them thirty or forty feet from shore, making the once benign raft feel markedly less secure. Kate knelt awkwardly on the hard plastic, trying to simultaneously relax and suck in her stomach, wondering if she'd remember how to swim if she fell overboard.

"Just out of curiosity," she asked as much to break the awkward silence as anything else, "how deep is the water here?"

Jim glanced somewhere over her left shoulder. "I don't know. Fifteen? Twenty feet?"

Kate nodded. They were fairly close to shore, and she was a reasonably good swimmer last time she'd been in water deeper than the kiddie pool.

"Do you want to go back in?"

She looked up. He was incredibly close, so close she could see a soft sheen of sweat on his cheekbones. He swallowed then, his sinewy neck working, and Kate's mouth filled with something that might have been desire. "No. No. Just wondering. I'm more used to pools with depth markers."

Jim stared over her shoulder again, his hazel eyes turning a mysterious green like the water around them. "It's probably easiest if I get up first. I won't start until you're ready, okay?"

He stood with an easy grace, and Kate's heart sank. There was no way she'd be able to stand on this thing much less knock him off when he was such a natural. She mentally rehearsed the rudiments of swimming as he extended his hand and pulled her up in front of him.

"Bend your knees a little. Loosen your hips. It'll help."

Kate nodded and tried to emulate his relaxed posture. But how could she relax when she was in a ridiculous little bikini over water that looked like it might disgorge the Loch Ness Monster at any moment? Okay. Forget mythical monsters. When she fell off she would just have to remember to close her mouth and let herself bob to the surface. Then, she could grab one of the raft's hand-holds and kick toward shore. Theoretically speaking.

"Ready?" he asked.

"Ready," she lied.

Just then, Grace yelled from the dock. "On your mark. Get set... *Go!*"

Jim rolled his shoulders and cleared his throat. His tongue darted out to moisten his lips, like an athlete about to race, and in the next heartbeat, he looked up.

"I like your bikini," he said, his voice a virtual caress.

Kate swallowed. Her hands felt sweaty, and her bee sting itched on the hard plastic. "Th-thanks." She adjusted her left foot and tried to loosen her hips some more, waiting for Jim to start rocking the boat.

Instead, he just smiled, albeit a sensual, lazy, bedroom-eyed smile that had her bent knees buckling for one brief moment.

"I, ah, like your suit, too," she said.

"The color sets off your eyes," he continued, as if she'd never said a thing. "Makes your skin glow."

"Thanks. I almost wore my navy tankini."

"I definitely like this one." He winked. "It goes with your toes."

For some reason, having Jim stare at her toes again made her flush all the way to her hair line. If he kept it up, she'd be completely flustered.

Unless... *Wait a minute.*

"Are you trying to throw me off balance?"

His eyes crinkled slightly at the corners. "Is it working?"

"Maybe." Her lips tilted, little shivers of excitement rippling through her. Okay, who was she kidding? It was definitely working. With a wickedly boyish grin on his face and nervous butterflies fluttering in her belly, chicken raft just got a whole lot more interesting. *Besides,* she thought, as an uncharacteristic boldness blew in on the cool breeze, she knew something Jim Pearson didn't.

Kate had a competitive streak.

"You have a nice tan for so early in the season," she said.

"I work outdoors a lot."

"Bare-chested?" she asked with wide-eyed innocence.

"Sometimes. It's cooler."

"I've thought about gardening bare-chested for that same reason. Do you think I should?"

The raft jerked in response. "You catch on quickly," he said.

"Thanks."

Kate could hear Carter urging Jim not to go easy on her just because she was a girl. Grace yelled, wondering if either of them was going to make a move.

"They want us to make a move," Kate said.

"Go ahead," Jim said. "Make a move."

Her body swayed easily with the raft now, the motion more familiar and natural. An electric tingle raced through her. She sucked in a deep breath and let it out as her eyes traveled down his torso. *Make a move.* "Okay. I really do like your swim trunks, they... um... suit you."

"I like your bikini," he replied, his gaze sliding over her skin in a way that had her insides melting. He looked up again. "But I like topless beaches more."

Kate swallowed the rush of awareness that flooded her mouth. Her pulse quickened. "I might... um... go topless. Under the right circumstances."

"Really?" He sounded genuinely surprised.

"Really," she said, wishing for all the world she seemed more the topless sort. Just once. She took a breath and assumed her most self-confident air. "You might not think this about me, but not only might I go topless, say on the French Riviera, I've always wondered what it would be like to swim... *in the nude.*"

His harsh intake of breath was all Kate needed to know she'd hit the mark. "Have you now?"

"Yes." Was that *her* throaty voice? Just go with it! "Ever since I saw someone skinny-dipping one night, I've thought about it... with him. NO. Not— I mean, skinny dipping!" Kate's cheeks burned. Oh, dear Lord! She hadn't meant to say it like that! Hadn't meant to imply anything other than *swimming*, but her subconscious clearly had other plans.

"Have you now?" Jim whispered, clearly having caught her double entendre.

Their eyes locked, the raft going unnaturally calm. Kate could hear his breathing, quick and shallow, not unlike her own. If she weren't forbidden to touch him, if his family wasn't standing—*watching*—she'd probably push him off the raft, throw herself at him bodily and happily let him perform mouth-to-mouth. As it was, she had a competition to win.

"Yes," she whispered, not sure where she found the nerve to speak, but in for a penny in for a pound. She'd be darned if she'd lose this game *now*. "I have. And if your family weren't watching, I… um… might untie my bikini top and dive in right now."

"You would?" Jim's voice was barely recognizable, his gaze riveted to her chest as she slid a single finger beneath the thin strap at her shoulder just to be sure it was still in place; although, his look said he was perhaps hoping something else.

Oh Lord! She was enjoying this game way too much—enjoyed being this bold, sensual woman who could flirt with a virtual stranger. Maybe it was because she felt a million miles from reality out here on the water with this man, but she couldn't seem to stop the words from tumbling out now. "I might even take my bikini off completely… but only if I weren't alone."

She smiled at the answering whoosh of air Jim expelled.

"You wouldn't have to be alone."

Kate met his eyes, a nervous tremor running through her. His eyes had gone dark, his body still and tense. Serious. "Are we still playing a game?"

Jim blinked and shook his head as if to clear it, an uneasy smile flashing across his face. "No. *Yes!*" The smile was full and genuine now. "And you're definitely winning."

Kate bit her lip. Maybe she'd gone too far. "Maybe we should go back to swimsuits."

"I'm pretty sure getting naked would be more fun," he murmured.

It was Kate's turn to gasp, a soft excited intake of breath that had them giggling and reaching to steady each other as the raft tipped again.

She caught and held his gaze.

He was aroused.

She was aroused.

And the game was far from over.

"Like you were the other night?" she asked.

In an instant, Jim's smile disappeared, replaced by an intense, feral look that had her purple-tipped toes curling. She hadn't meant to say anything, had never intended to confirm that she'd been there that night. But now… she was acutely aware of the sound of the water lapping on the shore, the cool breeze on her bare skin, his heated gaze on her body and suddenly she felt all the power and possibility of being a woman.

"You saw me," he said. It was a statement, not a question.

"Yes."

Then they were silent, the raft virtually still, their eyes locked in a look so smoldering Kate was surprised they didn't spontaneously ignite. Every nerve ending pulsed with anticipation. Awareness. *Need.*

Then Jim's eyes creased with humor, his lips tilting in that easy lopsided grin she was finding all too dangerously attractive.

"You win," he said. Then he dove into the dark waters of the lake leaving Kate rocking uncertainly in his wake.

CHAPTER TEN

———————————

JIM SWAM AWAY, THE SOUNDS of his family hollering from the dock ringing in his ears. There was no way he'd return to shore now, not until the bulge in his swim trunks receded.

He treaded water, a perverse stab of jealousy heating his gut, as Carter reeled in the raft and helped Kate onto the dock. Happy laughter floated over the water to him as she stooped to grab her towel and wrap it around herself. She needn't cover up on his account. The image of her in that bikini had permanently etched itself onto his corneas.

Then she turned, bit her lip almost shyly, and waved.

Jim nodded and returned with a mock salute. Then his relatives swept her toward the house as they fled the cooling air and fading light.

He was tempted to join them but then slid onto his back and stared at the sky. Perhaps floating in the cold water would help him return to reality.

Hot young widow. Good Lord, it didn't even come close to describing how he'd seen her, standing on the raft in front of him, all luscious curves in that candy-store bikini. He'd never in his life felt such an intense, immediate attraction to a woman. Not even Justine, with her confidence and striking beauty, could compare.

Kate was different. There was something deeply appealing about her bold words and shy looks, as if she were testing the feel of them on her tongue for the first time. He'd wanted to grab her and taste them right along with her.

And she'd looked like she'd wanted the same.

God! He was an idiot for thinking about her this way. Kate in no way resembled the single, carefree woman he should be dating. She was a widow. And a mother.

What had just happened was only a game.

The thought tasted sour on his tongue, but it was there nonetheless. What did he really know about this Kate, anyway? She was the shy, blushing widow one moment, but she'd turned into a sultry seductress in the blink of an eye.

Shit.

Fact was he didn't know if he was coming or going when she was around, which meant she was way more complicated than he had any business getting involved with.

With considerably less enthusiasm, Jim headed for shore.

Carter met him on the beach. "You *dove* in?"

Jim grabbed his towel off a rock. "She won."

"No. You threw the match. Now Grace is carrying on about how women are superior and crap like that. So what gives? The hot young widow get the best of you?"

"Would you stop calling her that?"

"In that bikini, what would you call her? My God, if that isn't hot, I don't know what is."

What could he say? It was true.

Carter dogged him up the steps toward the house. "So?"

"So, what?"

"Are you kidding me? This is the first woman you've looked at since Justine dumped you. Why aren't you up there right now asking her out?"

"Justine didn't dump me. I left her."

"Right." They both glanced at the deck, gaily lit with citronella torches and landscape lights. Kate was holding Liam now, saying her thank-yous and goodbyes. "Women like that don't drop into Sugar Falls every day."

"I don't even know her." And what he'd learned out on the lake wasn't anything he'd tell Carter.

"What's to know? She's pretty, single, living next door and, most importantly, she likes you."

"She said that?"

Carter cuffed Jim on the side of the head. "Idiot. It's written all over her face every time she looks at you. It's embarrassing. Go on. Ask her out. You can't tell me you're not interested. You get a woody every time she walks in the room."

"Shut up."

Carter chuckled, unperturbed. "Idiot."

Jim walked toward his truck. "Runs in the family."

June 15
*Vacation: To get away and leave your old life behind. I could get used to this. The locals are friendly. The views are stunning. I'm eating way too much pizza and reading way too many novels. If only this life bore any resemblance to reality. *Sigh**

CHAPTER ELEVEN

"WOULD YOU STOP FROWNING? It's not attractive."

Jim frowned at his cousin. "The sun's in my eyes."

Grace let out a long-suffering sigh and let the camera sling around her neck as she walked over and repositioned his arm. "You're not making an effort," she chided.

"We've been at this for nearly an hour. I'd call that an effort."

"*Jim*, you've got to relax. You're too tense and stern. This isn't going to sell calendars." She put the camera up to her eye again. "Okay. Let's try it again. Look at me and think sexy thoughts."

Jim pulled his foot off the sawhorse they'd been using as a prop and unclasped his toolbelt. "Forget it. This is not working. I can't look at my cousin *and* think sexy thoughts. It's physically impossible."

"Oh, come on! That last one would have been good if you hadn't kept frowning at me."

"I was *squinting*."

"Frowning," Grace insisted.

"What ya doin'?"

Jim turned and nodded at little Liam as he pushed through the lilacs. His shirt was streaked with dirt, his hands and the toy car he held covered in more dirt. He couldn't have looked happier.

"Wasting time," Jim said, swiping the sweat off his brow. Stupid calendar. How the hell did he get himself roped into these things?

"Can I watch?" Liam wanted to know.

Jim laughed despite his frustration and sat on the sawhorse. "Be my guest, but there's nothing to see. Grace is leaving soon. And I've got a job to get to."

"Not until we finish this," she said.

"Forget it, Grace. I'm not calendar material."

"Liam? *Liam!*" Kate's voice cut across the yard, followed by her footsteps.

"He's over here!" Grace called back. "Just visiting!"

Kate shoved through the opening in the lilacs a moment later, her face lightly flushed from the heat of the day, her T-shirt and shorts, like her son's, lightly smeared with dirt. She looked all lush curves and warm sun, and for some perverse reason, Jim couldn't get her bare-chested gardening comment from the day before out of his head.

"Liam, you need to stay where you can see mommy. That's the rule." Kate brushed a strand of hair from her cheek, leaving a smudge of dirt behind. Jim swallowed, fighting the traitorous urge to wipe it off. "I'm sorry if he bothered you."

"No bother," Grace assured her. "But if you're not busy, we could use your help."

"No, not busy," Kate replied, avoiding Jim's gaze. "Just weeding. What do you need?" She tried again to tuck the strand of hair into her ponytail. It brushed her cheek instead. Right near the smudge of dirt. Jim's gut twisted.

Grace flipped around her digital camera and began scrolling through the shots they'd taken. "Can you look at these? We need a good picture for Grams' fundraising calendar, you know?" Kate nodded in understanding. "I say we don't have a good shot yet. He says we're done. What do you say?"

"I don't think Kate—" Jim began.

"I'd love to help," Kate assured them. "I studied art in college. Maybe I can give some tips on composition?" She wiped her hands on her hips and moved past him to get a better view of the camera. Jim busied himself inspecting a frayed loop on his toolbelt while the women discussed the relative attractiveness of each pose.

"*Mmm.* That one's not bad," Kate murmured. "This one's a good pose, but he's kind of frowning..."

"*Squinting,*" he muttered in his own defense, "I was squinting. The sun was in my eyes."

"This one's nice," Kate continued, pointing at the view screen as if he'd never spoken. "Definitely a possibility..."

"I thought so, too," Grace said. "But it's missing something. That spark, you know?"

Kate nodded, which didn't do great things for Jim's self-confidence. He lacked spark? Since when? "Why don't you try some with him standing in the water?" she asked.

"Okay." Jim pushed himself off the sawhorse. "I think we're done. I'm *not* doing some cheesy swimsuit photo."

Kate looked up from the camera, her head at an angle, her baby blues brilliant in the sunlight. "It doesn't have to be cheesy."

"You're right," Grace agreed, ignoring him entirely. "I hadn't thought about doing any water poses, but it could make for a really nice background if we can avoid glare. Plus, it has that sensual appeal the others were lacking. Definitely worth a shot." She started down the path to the lake then turned abruptly toward Jim. "Well? Aren't you coming?"

Minutes later, he stood on the small, rocky beach in his bare feet, waiting for the two women to decide where to position themselves and feeling like a fool. How the hell was he supposed to look sexy for a photo when his cousin was barking orders and a three year-old was making construction noises with his miniature backhoe in the sand?

Then there was *Kate*. She kept biting her lip in that shy, nervous way of hers and bowing her head toward Grace's behind the camera. Murmuring in hushed tones. Before he knew what was happening, he'd been told to step into the water up to his hips—but not too high, mind you—and to look at them with 'bedroom eyes.'

Grace snapped a couple pictures and the women huddled around the camera again.

"I feel ridiculous," he groused to no one in particular.

"Only because you're not cooperating," Grace said. "Put your right hand on the dock. No, not like that. More... relaxed. Like you're casually leaning on it."

"While standing in water wearing my jeans? Did I casually fall in, too?"

"You're frowning again," Grace chided from behind the camera.

Jim tried to smooth his features. He knew the sooner he made the women happy the sooner he could be done with the whole charade. If he was lucky, no one would vote for his photo and he wouldn't be included in the damn calendar.

"I'm thirsty." Jim watched as Liam tugged at his mother's shirt hem.

A deer fly buzzed low over Jim's head and landed in his hair. He smacked it hard and scowled at his cousin. "Are we almost done?"

"No. Stand still..."

"I'm *really* thirsty," Liam whined.

"Just a minute, Pumpkin," Kate soothed.

"I think that thing bit me," Jim mumbled, fishing in his hair.

"Oh, for Pete's sake!" Grace yanked the camera strap over her head and shoved it at Kate. "*Here*. Maybe you can get him to behave. I'm taking Liam in for a drink." And with that, she took the three year-old's hand and marched back up the path toward the cottage.

Kate watched them go then turned toward him. "I'm sorry. I truly was trying to help."

"It's not your fault. She needed a break."

Kate nodded. Bit her lip. Fingered the camera strap. "We can wait. For Grace. If you like."

Jim picked the dead fly from his hair and chuckled in wry amusement as he flung it over the dock. Nothing sexy about this photo-shoot *at all*. "I don't think waiting for her will make this any less a supreme waste of time. But thanks." He took a step toward shore. Could anything feel worse than wet jeans?

"I'd be happy to try," she was saying, "taking some shots, that is... if you wanted. Maybe it would be easier—you know—with fewer people watching."

He stopped short, the water lapping around his thighs. For some reason her tentative question, the way she nibbled her bottom lip, the sound of the water, brought back the memory of when she'd first stood to face him on the chicken raft. His gut tightened. He *had* to get out more. "You don't have to," he said.

She smiled, a shy smile, the same one that hinted at a less shy Kate lurking somewhere underneath. He remembered that Kate, too. "I don't mind."

He shrugged. "Okay."

She focused on familiarizing herself with the camera settings.

His lips twisted as he watched her, intensely aware of her. That they were alone. "I'm sorry, by the way."

She glanced up. "Sorry?"

He winced, embarrassment knotting his stomach. Cleared his throat. "For the other night. I'd just come back from a fire call and I was filthy. I didn't think anybody would be out here. I don't normally—"

"*Oh*," she said, a blush creeping up her nape. "It was so dark, I didn't see much. I wasn't even sure—"

"I just don't want you to think I'm some exhibitionist. I don't usually—"

"It's okay," she said just as quickly. "I'd practically forgotten about it. Really. Think nothing of it."

He nodded. "Great."

"Great." She stared at him for one awkward, aware moment then seemed to remember the camera looped around her neck.

"So, why don't we get started?" she asked, raising the camera. The shutter clicked. "Can you, ah, move back to where you were a minute ago?" *Click.* "Right there is good." *Click.*

"You're taking a lot of pictures."

"Habit. I have a three year-old, remember? I'm used to a moving target. You've gotta play the odds." *Click.* "Now how about if we try it again with your hand on the dock, but maybe you could splay your fingers a little this time?" *Click.* "Nice." *Click.* "Can you face me more?"

"Like this?"

Click. "Right, but not too... *yes.*" *Click.* "Now lower your chin—not too much!—just a little..." *Click.* "But don't frown."

"I'm not frowning." He frowned.

"Then don't squint." Her smile curved behind the camera. He could see her lips, plump, slightly parted. "*Ooh,*" they said, making a small 'o' shape. *Click.* "Very nice. Now hook your thumbs through your belt loops. There you go..."

He felt his own lips curve and did as instructed. She was getting bolder as time went on. He liked that. It was chicken raft all over again. Strangely intimate with her behind the camera giving commands in that soft voice. "Nice, eh?" he asked. *Click.*

"Don't get cocky." Her face peeked out to the side a moment. "And don't talk."

He laughed as she disappeared behind the camera again. *Click.* "I'm not getting cocky."

Her lush lips curved again. They really were fantastic lips. "Yes, you are. And you're *still* talking." *Click.*

He mimed locking his lips and throwing away the key. *Click.*

"By the way, I had fun yesterday," she said. *Click.* "I didn't mean for you to lose." *Click.* "But when you think about it, you started it."

Jim pointed to his own chest as if to say *me?*

"Yes! You did. And as they say, all's fair, right? So..." *Click.* "...no hard feelings?"

He watched her, waiting, until she slid out from behind the camera again, then he shook his head. Smiled. *Click.* She retreated behind the camera. "Good." Her lips smiled her relief. "You bring out the worst in me, Jim Pearson."

"That depends on your perspective."

"No talking," she admonished softly, but he knew there was no heat in the reprimand. The camera clicked a few more times.

"Thanks for helping with this," he said.

"You're talking." Her lips smiled. *Click.*

"Sorry." *Click.*

"I'm happy to help," she said.

"Why? Because I'm kinda cute?"

He watched as her cheeks flushed pink behind the camera. "You're not going to let me forget that, are you?"

He considered a moment. "Nope."

"That's not very noble of you, holding that over a girl's head. Turn to the right a little."

He turned. *Click.* "What makes you think I'm noble?"

"I'd like to think I was a good judge of character."

"But you're not?"

Her easy smile faded. "Not a very good track record. You?" *Click.*

"Hit or miss. But I think I've got you figured out now."

"Have you?" The amused smile was back. "Square your shoulders more. *Mmm...*" *Click.*

"Yeah. I thought at first you might be trolling."

"Trolling?"

"You know, fishing... for a man."

The camera dropped. "That's hardly flattering."

"True, but it happens."

"I think you're getting cocky again. I distinctly remember telling you I wasn't interested." Kate disappeared behind the camera. *Click.* "And just for the record, I'm *not* trolling."

"I know. You don't have it in you. You blush too easily when you flirt."

"I'm out of practice," she blushed.

He grinned. "That was the other hint."

The camera clicked a few more times, then Kate paused, her bottom lip caught between her teeth as she repositioned herself on the bank. *Damn.* Out of practice or not, she had a sweet sensuality that was making it hard for him to remember he was keeping his distance.

Relationships were difficult enough when both parties wanted to make things work. But Kate had a son, and she'd lost her husband. Hell, she was still wearing her wedding ring. Despite her light flirtations, it'd be hard to overlook those obstacles. Jim knew she wasn't in a place for a casual anything, and he wasn't interested in anything else. Not after Justine.

"Okay," Kate's lips moved and his gaze zeroed in on them. "I'm *not* trolling, but do you think you'd like to try a few shots... without the T-shirt?"

He knew his eyebrows rose ever so briefly, knew she was hiding behind the camera, but as he watched the tell-tale flush creep up her neck and tint her cheeks again, a flood of arousal coursed through him, and he felt himself respond to her despite his better judgment. She was more dangerous than any troller, he realized. She was sexy without even knowing it.

Click.

"I suppose it is all for a good cause." Then he grabbed the hem of his shirt and yanked it over his head.

June 16
Flirtation. Some call it harmless. Some call it scandalous. Some call it a
lost art. I don't know what to call it except... wow! ☺

CHAPTER TWELVE

KATE WOKE THE NEXT morning to the shrill ring of the phone on her
nightstand.

"Hello?"

"Kate, it's your grandmother."

"Nana? What's...? It's only," she peered at the clock, "seven a.m."

"I'm sorry. Were you not awake?"

Kate spit out her night guard, pushed the hair out of her eyes and
slumped against her pillows. "Yes. No. I... Liam's sleeping in. We made
s'mores on the beach last night with... Anyway, we were up pretty late.
What's up?"

"I'm coming home early. Today, as a matter of fact. Turns out if
you've seen one quilt, you've seen them all. I'm calling to see when I can
stop in and see my favorite little boy. I miss him. I know it's only
Tuesday, but I was hoping to catch you and see if we can get together
later this week. I thought I'd better check with you now so you could fit
me into your plans."

"We have no plans, Nana. We're still getting settled."

"Good! Then maybe we'll see each other in a couple days. How's
dinner and ice cream sound? There's a new playground near the ice
cream place. You think Liam would like that?"

Kate chuckled. "I think we'd all like that."

"I'll pop in tomorrow, then, and set something up. Oh, but not
Friday. I'm getting together with the ladies Friday."

"Right. Speaking of the ladies, I think I sort of volunteered to help
Ruth Pearson with her beefcake calendar."

"Oh! Wonderful! Sounds like the perfect job to take your mind off
everything."

"That's the problem. I think it might be a bigger job than I'd
thought, and I don't have a lot of spare time to spend on something like
that. I—" Wait. It's not like she could admit she'd been sent on leave by

81

Nancy to find her passion. Nana would have a field day with that one! "Besides. I don't think it's appropriate," she said instead.

"Well, you won't sign up for a dating service. You never go out. Think of this as an opportunity to preview the eligible men in the area. What harm is there in that? No one has to even know it's you. You can set up an e-mail account, assume a name. It'll be completely anonymous."

"Right. I'll just call myself Desperate in Dallas."

"Now, you're being cheeky. It doesn't become you. Just pick a character from your favorite book or something. Come on, Katie. It'll do you good to see what's out there."

"Nan—"

"And, it's for a good cause..."

"So I've heard. Still—"

"I'm sorry. I have to get going if I'm to make good time. Why don't we talk when I get back?"

"Nan—"

The phone went dead. Kate slumped against the headboard. If she hadn't had so much fun with Jim yesterday snapping pictures at the dock, she might actually feel more resentment over Nana's heavy-handed interference in her personal life. God bless her.

No sooner had Kate set the phone on the hook when it rang again. She picked it up. "Nana, it's not polite to hang up on people when—"

"Kate? It's Jim. Jim Pearson."

"Jim!" Kate sat up straighter and ran a hand through her hair. "I thought— what's up?"

"I'm sorry to call so early, but..." He cleared his throat. "Can I come in?"

"Come in?"

"Yeah. I'm out front."

"You're *here?*" Okay, when she'd fantasized about seeing him again, she hadn't intended for it to be at the crack of dawn before she'd even showered! Kate scurried out of bed and peered through the curtain. Sure enough, there he stood on the front path.

"I, uh... why are you here?" she asked, hastily stepping away from the window.

"I have the new shower head and knob I mentioned the other day. I was hoping to switch out the old one before heading to my first job if that's okay. It'll only take a few minutes. You won't even know I'm here."

"Sure. Hang on a minute. I'll let you in."

Shower knob? Images of Jim, wet and sexy, and standing in the lake flashed into her consciousness. Kate frantically searched for her robe and threw it over the faded oversized T-shirt she'd worn to bed, pulling the sash tight. She couldn't remember, precisely, whether she'd remembered to lock the front door or not, but she'd be damned if Jim—heck *any* man—would occupy the only bathroom in the house if she'd yet to even brush teeth.

A few minutes later, her hair hastily finger-combed, her teeth brushed and a lightning fast coat of lip gloss on her lips, Kate opened the door with as much aplomb as she could muster.

"Good morning," she said brightly as she ushered him in. "Sorry it took so long. I, ah, was just checking on Liam. He's still asleep."

"He is?" Jim stepped in, some shiny shower thingy in one hand and a toolbox in the other. "Aren't kids usually up at the crack of dawn?"

"Last night was pretty exciting. Wore him out, I think."

"I hope he had fun."

"We did. I mean, he did. We both did."

Kate's mouth went dry. Jim stood silently, casually gorgeous in a plain navy tee and tan pants. He smelled fresh and clean like Ivory soap. Kate tried to inhale without being obvious.

Jim nodded, his eyes skimming over her quickly. "I'd better get to work if I'm gonna make it to my job at nine."

"Of course." Kate chewed the inside of her cheek as she followed him down the hall. "I, ah, was going to start some coffee. Can I bring you a cup when it's done?" Best to act casual. Friendly. Like sexy, flirty games of chicken raft and shirtless photo shoots were par for the course.

"That'd be great. I take it black." Jim was already setting down his toolbox and stepping behind the shower curtain, his apparent indifference not doing great things for Kate's self-confidence.

"Okay."

"And Kate?"

She paused, a shiver of breathless anticipation coursing up her spine at being called back. "Yes?"

"Better do it before I shut off the water."

She nodded, deflated. "Sure."

For heaven's sake, what did she expect? Here she was in a tired old bathrobe, her hair a mess, no make-up... Did she really expect him to pin her with his eyes, press her against the bathroom wall, and have his hungry way with her?

She pulled out mugs and started the coffee. Dear Lord, if she were this bad over one eligible man in her vicinity, what kind of disaster would the charity calendar prove to be? Did the ladies even know what a fragile state she was in? Was this even *normal?*

No. Nothing was normal. Her life was one big raucous roller coaster, and it was heading for the big dark TUNNEL with a capital T.

Bedsides, mooning after her good-looking neighbor probably wasn't what Nancy had meant when she'd told Kate to 'find her passion.' Not that he was an unpleasant diversion. Thinking about him kept her mind off worrying about REAL LIFE.

Damn. The capital letters were back. That couldn't be a good sign.

"*Ow!*" A loud clatter of something falling into the tub was quickly followed by a colorful curse and the distinct sound of water spraying.

"Everything all right?" Kate hovered near the bathroom door, a masculine-sized mug of coffee in hand.

More frantic fumbling, more mumbled curses, and more water spraying sounds emerged from behind the shower curtain.

"Jim?" Afraid to interfere but also intensely curious about what was going on, Kate peered around the far end of the curtain. "*Oh, my.*"

Jim stood like a dog caught in the rain, giant water splotches soaking his front, water dribbling from his hair and nose. And the new shower thingy was on the floor of the tub.

"What happened?" Really, she was making every effort not to laugh. A supreme effort.

Jim wiped his dripping brow with his forearm. "Forgot to turn off the water."

"I see." Kate could feel the corners of her mouth twisting up, could feel the bursts of laughter trying to sneak out of her lungs, her nose. "I, ah, brought your coffee," she said, holding out the mug.

He took it with as much dignity as possible under the circumstances. "Thanks."

"You're welcome." Letting the curtain fall back into place, she allowed a single hiccup of laughter to escape. "It could happen to anyone."

He sighed, a long-suffering good-natured sound that had her snorting indelicately and covering her mouth with her hand. "Thank you," he said. "Could you hand me something to dry off with?"

Kate hurried to the linen closet and grabbed a towel. She thrust it behind the curtain.

"Thanks."

"You're welcome."

She stood outside the tub as he set his coffee on the edge to dry himself.

"You know," he said, "you really don't have to stand there."

"Oh. Right. Sorry."

"I don't mind you standing there," he added as he pushed aside the curtain and stepped from the tub, scrubbing his hair with the towel. "But you are somewhat to blame for this."

"I am?" she squeaked. Heavens, he was good-looking all wet and frumpled. His water-soaked T-shirt was plastered to his chest. Kate's tongue became the Sahara.

"*Mmm hmm,*" he nodded. Now he was finger-combing his hair, a crooked grin making his face boyishly appealing as he dropped the towel on his toolbox. "I was thinking about you, you see—"

"You were?" Kate backed up against the sink, the small bathroom feeling suddenly much smaller. Dangerously small. As small as the pocket in her lungs still capable of holding air. "What were you thinking?"

He paused, his eyes dancing. "I'm thinking I ought to keep that to myself."

"Why?"

"I don't think we know each other well enough for me to tell you that."

Suddenly the flannel of her robe felt very hot on her skin. Kate sucked air through her nose and stared at his lips, that crooked smile teasing her, beckoning her. "I want to know," she said, her voice barely a whisper.

He wasn't touching her, was still nearly two feet away, but every nerve cell in her body registered his presence. Her skin tingled with the need to make contact. Her fingers itched to press themselves against his damp skin. He took a step forward and she almost moaned.

He said nothing, simply stared at her, his eyes dark, his face taut. His smile had disappeared, replaced by a look so smoldering Kate nearly pooled at his feet.

"*I don't want—*" he began.

"*I know—*" she agreed.

And then his lips were on hers, hard, scorching, stealing the remaining air from her lungs.

Dear Lord, she thought, *if I suffocate because this kiss never ends, this is exactly how I want to go.*

He pulled back, blinking at her, shaking his head in confusion. "I don't... want..." he began again.

"I don't care," she said. Then she grabbed his face in her palms and yanked him back to her, fusing their lips once more.

She *did* moan this time as his hands held her shoulders almost desperately, his fingers squeezing her flesh as he plundered her mouth, those beautiful, skillful lips lighting a fire in her that burned all the way to her toes.

He might have said something more, but having finally tasted this man—this man she had already seen naked—she couldn't get enough of him. She pressed him back, eager, hungry, pinning the door closed behind him as his hands—*Lord, those hands!*—splayed across her back, kneading the fabric, her flesh.

He groaned, a deep masculine sound of surrender before spinning her around and pinning her to the door in his place.

There was no thinking. No rationale. No analysis of what was happening. For the first time in her life, Kate was acting on instinct alone.

And it felt incredible!

Her hands ran down his sides, over the rough fabric on his hips and pulled him hard to her. He grunted against her lips, a light sound of surprise and then issued a moan as his erection pulsed against her.

Her robe was halfway down her back, his hands hot through her tee, when he pulled back, gulping air. "Kate?"

"Please don't talk," she insisted, pulling his lips back to hers.

She didn't want to talk. Didn't want to think. Didn't want to analyze what in the world she was doing with this man in this place at this time...

Didn't want to admit that it was wrong for more reasons than she could ever count.

She inhaled deeply.

She had to stop smelling him. Had to stop *kissing* him.

With a heavy sigh—because, Lord, it was painful to do so—she pulled away, her breathing as labored as his. "I think... we... should stop," she managed to say—pushing the words through her lips—lips that were still tantalizingly close to his.

He nodded, his chest heaving. He stepped back. "Yes," he agreed. His tongue moistened his lips. "Good idea."

Kate ran a shaky hand through her hair. "I don't know—"

"Me either."

They nodded, eyeing each other as if the other might try to finish what neither wanted to leave off.

"Liam will probably be up soon."

He nodded again, let out a cleansing breath. "I, ah, should go turn off the water now."

"Right."

They stared at each other, the air thick with the smell of desire.

"I'll need to leave the room to do that," he said.

Kate scurried to the side so he could open the door. "Right. Of course."

Jim shimmied by her. They avoided eye contact.

"I should start breakfast," she said, righting her robe and heading for the kitchen.

"Good idea," he said, clearing his throat and heading for the basement.

In the kitchen, Kate clutched the edge of the sink, her legs like noodles.

What was she thinking?

She was a sensible woman. A rational woman. A—dare she say it?—*practical* woman.

Practical, sensible, rational women did not go making hot and heavy with virtual strangers just because they were sexy and wet in their bathrooms.

Of course, she knew that. She knew that! It wasn't as if her subconscious needed to tell her. She was perfectly aware that giving in to her desperate housewife alter-ego would have ramifications. She was a sensible woman. Sensible women knew these things.

Kate knew these things.

JIM LEANED AGAINST THE basement wall and sucked in long, cleansing lungfuls of air. He wet his lips again, lips that still held the taste of the woman who even now was probably pouring cereal into a bowl like it was any old day of the week.

Instead of the day Jim Pearson had lost his mind.

Okay, so maybe that was exaggerating, but how to explain the scene that had just played out—in his grandparents' bathroom no less? He'd never be able to step foot in that room again without thinking about it. Without thinking about *her*.

Thinking. Yes. Good idea.

He should *think* instead of follow the front of his pants everywhere like some pornographic divining rod. She was a widow... with a *kid*, for Christ's sake!

He had to stop swearing. He was going to hell. For swearing and lusting after a widow with a kid, he was going to hell.

Jim began to pace, his leather work boots scuffing the old floor.

If he could only think what triggered the, ah, incident, he might be able to prevent it from happening again.

Why the hell would I want to do that?

Good question. No, not a good question! Of course he wanted to prevent it! They hardly knew each other! She was in mourning, or on the rebound, or... well, whatever vulnerable state one is in after a loss like that.

But vulnerable didn't seem to describe Kate at all. Passionate. Gorgeous. Uninhibited. Sexy as no woman had a right to be looking all tumbled and warm first thing in the morning. *That* was Kate.

An image of her, panting, flushed, pushing him against the door, her lips soft and urgent against his, flashed to mind.

"I'm going to hell," he muttered, ducking to avoid the joists overhead. "This can't be healthy either. This kind of... *reaction* to a woman. Can't be good."

As if in agreement, his erection surged against his fly.

"Shut up," he mumbled to his crotch. "You're half my problem."

Jesus. He was talking to his dick. This *was* a bad porno movie. Except...

He didn't feel sleazy at all. He felt...

Confused. That's what that feeling was. The stale, damp basement air was just making it hard to think this through. Kate was obviously missing male company and he'd been too long—okay a few months— without female companionship. It was only natural they'd jump each other at the first opportunity. Right?

Right. So, if he just kept his distance, she'd realize the same thing, that this was a one-time mistake, and all would be well.

They'd simply avoid each other.

Yes. Avoidance. Always a winning strategy.

Kate would move to the next stage of her, ah, grief and he'd forget it ever happened.

He'd simply wait for the tent in his pants to disappear and he could start his avoidance plan in earnest.

June 17
Don't you love surprises? I'm not talking about dog poo or stomach
bugs. I'm talking about the good ones. Like one last chocolate when you
thought the box was empty. A happy ending when all seems lost. Or,
especially, discovering something—or someone—wonderful, when you
least expect it...

CHAPTER THIRTEEN

HE ARRIVED THE NEXT MORNING.

Kate signed for the FedEx and carried the small square box into the
cottage. It was heavier than she thought it would be.

She set Randy on the mantel and stared at him.

"When can we open it?" Liam demanded at her side.

"It's not for opening. This is a special box that stays just as it is."

Until I figure out what the hell to do with it.

Nana, of course, was no help whatsoever.

"I don't see why you didn't just bury him," she said later that day as
they stood staring at the FedEx box on the mantel. "That's what you're
supposed to do with dead people."

Kate closed her eyes. "He was claustrophobic, Nana. He hated small
spaces. I couldn't do that to him."

They stared at the box.

"Seems to me it's not all that roomy in there either."

"I know that," Kate said. Nana looked at her expectantly. "I just
need some time to figure out what to do with them, that's all."

"You could make him into soap."

"Nana!"

"Oh, lighten up. I'm kidding. But don't let this fester. You need to
take care of this and move on. Randy is a part of the past for you. You
can't let him keep popping up like this. It's not good for you."

Kate felt light-headed. If Nana only knew how wrong she was.

"What am I supposed to do? He hasn't spoken to his dad in years.
And since his mom died... It's up to me now." She laid a hand on her
forehead. It felt clammy. "I'll think of a place to scatter them, okay? I just
don't know right now where that should be." Kate looked around the

89

tired old living room. She stared at the gold rocker with the colonial-print fabric. If it had any bright ideas, it wasn't sharing.

"Well," said Nana, "I'd love to stand around and brainstorm some more, but I've got to run. My friend Lydia's got some silly idea of holding a benefit sale at her consignment shop in a few weeks, and she's swamped with donations. She has no idea what she's gotten herself into."

"Sounds good. Going to town, I mean. I need to buy some paint. And if you could watch Liam for a bit, there's something I have to do."

"What?"

Kate blew out a cleansing breath and grabbed her purse. "Get a haircut."

CHAPTER FOURTEEN

———————————

IT WAS FRIDAY POKER NIGHT again, and as much fun as the quilt show had been, June Hastings was glad to be home. She stepped onto Lydia's screened porch, set her gin and tonic on the table and selected a riotously floral seat cushion to perch on. What Lydia lacked in ability to grow actual flowers, she made up for in her choice of upholstery fabrics. But that didn't matter. They had some grandchildren to discuss. June plopped her box of family photos onto the table in front of her and turned to Ruth Pearson. "How was the barbecue last week?"

Ruth pursed her lips and reached for the veggie platter. "Good. I think. It was hard to tell."

Claire sniffed, dropping a glob of dip onto the front of her late husband's bowling shirt. "Probably not meant to be, then."

Lydia pushed open the screen door. "What's not meant to be?"

"June and Ruth's grandkids. They're not setting off sparks."

"I didn't say that," Ruth said. "I think there's definite interest, but they're both skittish."

"Kate's always been shy," June concurred then her eyes narrowed. "Lydia, *what* is in your drink?"

"A marshmallow. Claire ate all my cherries again. Besides I thought it might be fun to experiment with something new." She began to deal the cards, her silver bangles sing-songing on her wrist. "Maybe they just need a nudge," she suggested.

Ruth sipped her cocktail and nodded. "I thought of that, but the problem is, and don't take this the wrong way, June, there isn't a lot of opportunity for romance with the little one around."

June picked up her cards and fanned them thoughtfully. "I know. She uses him like a shield. Just an excuse not to get back in the swing of things. She's hardly stepped foot out of that cottage since she arrived last week. Puttering around. *Weeding...*" She pursed her lips and rearranged her cards. "It's not healthy, if you ask me. Grown-ups need grown-up time."

"That's for sure," Claire said, sorting through her photos to decide what she'd ante up with. "If the grown-ups aren't... *enjoying themselves,*" she said with a meaningful look, "the kids suffer, too. Then no one's happy. We all figured that out pretty quick, didn't we?"

Lydia gasped softly and June cast Claire a quelling look.

"What?" Claire asked. "*Oh.* Lydia, I'm sorry..."

Lydia waved her marshmallow breezily in the air. "It's okay. Stu and I sure enjoyed our grown-up time, if you know what I mean. If we *could* have had kids... well, we would have ended up with more than we could handle!" With that she popped the marshmallow through her bright pink lips and bravely chewed.

Ruth glared at Claire. "Very tactful. Can we play now?"

Lydia blinked back a tear. "I bid one fourteen-foot Christmas tree," she said, tossing a Christmas picture into the center of the table.

"A Christmas tree? It's nearly July!" Claire said. At June's look, she shrugged and reached for the veggie platter again.

June pulled a photo from her own box and added to the pot. "Okay. I'm in with one perfect purple crocus on a frosty April morning taken with my new digital camera." She shook her head. "The thing is, she's stuck. She doesn't cry. She doesn't swear. I'm worried that by the time she remembers what it's like to feel young and carefree, what it's like to be a woman, it'll be too late."

Lydia sighed and stared at June's crocus. "My Stu always made me feel like a woman."

June took a sip from her drink. "I'm thinking of setting her up on a date. Something casual. Without Liam. What do you think?"

Ruth nodded distractedly over her cards. "Good idea. I'll help. By the way, nice crocus, but I'm raising the stakes now. Lydia, I see your giant Christmas tree with my award-winning jack-o-lantern display and raise you one cherubic grandson with his first fish."

Lydia smiled and dug through the fabric-covered shoebox she held on her lap. "Very nice fish, Ruth, I grant you that, and I've always loved that picture of little Jim at the fishing derby, but... I raise you again with one incredibly handsome, nicely tanned, bare-chested man, *in his underwear.*" Lydia reverently laid the photo on the table, a soft, happy sigh escaping from her fluorescent lips.

Claire scowled. "Lydia, that's from a magazine! You can't use him!"

"And why not? I'd love to talk about him. Isn't he juicy? Look at that six pack..."

June frowned. "*Juicy?* Nobody uses that anymore. Come to think of it, I don't think they ever did."

Ruth picked up the male model in question and brought it closer for inspection. "If Lydia wants to talk about the new Calvin Klein model, I don't see why we should object."

"I wasn't objecting," June was quick to point out, peering over Ruth's arm at the picture, "Claire was."

"Oh, never mind," Lydia relented. "I just like to spice things up sometimes." She retrieved her magazine clipping and pulled an edge-weary photograph from the box. "Here's Stu and me at the Grand Canyon. *Again...*"

June 20
I'm well aware that running in circles does not get me far. Don't judge
me. At least I'm moving forward.

CHAPTER FIFTEEN

THE NEXT AFTERNOON, Kate tucked Liam into bed for his nap, the air in the bedroom heavy and still as a distant clap of thunder rolled down the valley over the lake.

"Hug you," Liam slurred sleepily.

Kate leaned forward and pressed a kiss to his forehead. "Love you, too, Pumpkin." She repositioned the fan on the dresser to face him then tip-toed from the room and down the stairs.

The living room was quiet and smelled pleasantly of fresh paint and window cleaner. Kate looked around. It was amazing what a couple quarts of paint, a few hours and a little imagination could do. She'd given the old rocker a coat of sky-blue paint and slipped a pair of vintage lace pillowcases she'd found at the local thrift shop over the hideous gold cushions. An old wedding quilt lay across the sofa in lieu of a slipcover, and the detached mirror from an upstairs dresser she'd discovered stuffed in a closet now rested atop the mantel. Kate walked to the kitchen table where she'd replaced the barstools with a mix of wooden chairs she'd found in the basement and wished the weather had held a bit longer. She had a can of soft pear-green paint set aside for them.

Not that she was procrastinating or anything.

The box with Randy's ashes still sat on a corner of the mantel.

Kate's chest felt heavy. She blew out a long breath and walked to the screen door.

The lake grew choppy as the wind kicked up. Kate told herself she should make use of the rainy weather to sit and read the book she had upstairs, but somehow discovering the color of her parachute seemed pointless now, seeing as she'd spent the better part of the night dreaming of being shoved from a plane, her parachute left behind, and hurtling through the air toward certain disaster.

She should move the book from her nightstand at the very least.

Kate pushed at her hair, a restless, frustrated movement. She'd been in New Hampshire more than a week but was no closer to figuring out what she wanted to do with the rest of her life than she had while crying over her washing machine in Connecticut. Hell, what she *could* do with it. It wasn't as if she were swimming in options.

The most obvious choice was to go back to Nancy and the academy. She'd have health insurance, which was good, especially now.

Oh God...

The sky outside grew darker, the air electric.

Kicking off her sandals, Kate pushed open the screen door and stepped onto the porch. The wind slammed the door shut behind her. Chimes clanged together, and a gust of wind rushed through the trees and lifted her hair. Kate stood at the porch railing and closed her eyes as the first heavy drops of rain spattered the ground and the skies opened up.

She reached a hand out and let the rain pound into her palm as it cascaded from the roof. Water droplets splashed onto her shirt and danced off her wedding ring.

She pulled her hand back as memories flooded her of the night Randy died.

Her chest ached with chaotic emotion—of feeling hollow and scared and stunned—the weight of events closing in, bearing down on her, like a tsunami roaring ashore.

She remembered grasping for something to hold onto, gasping for breath and equilibrium as she tried to absorb what it meant, how it changed things, as she'd moved through the silent house that night. And yet, it had felt almost peaceful, the in-between time, as she lay next to Liam on his bed, in the dark.

But the stillness and quiet of night had given way to the grim reality of taking stock of the damage. Cleaning up. Moving on.

Funeral arrangements. Clearing out Randy's apartment. Making it through each day. Then the next...

Pretending life went on as normal, because there was no other choice.

Kate shoved the memories away as lightning sizzled in the sky above the cottage.

She held her breath, watching the rain bounce off the ground, as she twirled the ring around her finger. More than anything she wished she could erase the numbness that had followed that night, the unnerving sense of having been shoved out into the unknown, the rushing air taking away her ability to breathe, like she'd been pushed from a plane without a parachute.

She twirled the ring again, and without consciously trying, it slipped off her finger and into her right hand. She looked at it, surprised, and for a moment had an overwhelming urge to hurl it long and hard into the dark, choppy waters of the lake, to let the power of the storm swallow the hurt, the mistakes and the unfilled promises the tiny circle of gold represented.

But she couldn't.

She'd made promises, too.

Kate let out the breath she'd been holding. Throwing the ring away wouldn't change anything. But Nana was right. *Something* had to change.

There had to come a point where she hit rock bottom, where the air stopped rushing by her, where she could stop cringing and start picking up the pieces. And maybe it was foolish, even selfish, to wish for that moment, to pray for the impact. But, surely, nothing could be worse than this not feeling at all.

A new wave of rain sheeted across the lake toward the cottage as if daring her not to be moved by its power.

Kate dropped the ring into her shorts pocket.

Then she stepped off the porch and lifted her face to the sky.

CHAPTER SIXTEEN

JIM CONSIDERED HIMSELF a smart man.

Smart men avoided complications.

And so, he had successfully avoided Kate for nearly a week. Considering she and Liam had spent countless hours puttering and playing around outside the cottage next door, this was no small feat.

But he knew he was caught—hell, his truck was sitting in the drive—when he heard the distinctive rap of knuckles on the door.

"Oh! Hi." Kate smiled as he yanked open the door, her hand still poised to knock again. She pulled her hand back to tuck her hair behind her ear in a familiar gesture then lowered it to her side. "I'm sorry to bother you, I probably should have caught you over the weekend, but I saw your truck and I've been meaning to ask... would it be okay if I spruced up a couple things you brought to the cottage? I picked up some paint at the hardware store, and I thought I'd refinish some of the old furniture. Just a couple things..."

Jim frowned, trying to concentrate on her words. She had on a little skirty thing in a bright, tropical blue with a matching print tee. She looked sweet. Tasty. Like one of those fruity cocktails with the little umbrellas.

"Your grandmother said I could do what I like, but I remembered you had brought over that little side table and that floor lamp with the brown shade, and I—"

"You got your hair cut," he said, interrupting her.

"Oh! Yes." She smoothed a hand down one side and her hair shifted and swirled by her chin. It made her neck look sexy and long. His fingers itched to reach out and play with it.

He stared at her. She bit her lip. "About the table..." she said.

"Oh, right. Sure. Paint away."

"Thanks. I just thought I'd brighten the place up a bit. You know. While I'm here." She swallowed. "Anyway, I'm sorry to bother you. I'm sure you have places to be."

He met her eyes. "No bother."

She nodded and turned to go.

"Wait."

She paused and looked at him expectantly.

"It looks good. Your hair. It looks good."

Her lips curved in a smile. "Thank you."

She lingered, and some obtuse, idiotic part of him wanted her to find a reason to linger longer.

"Oh, I almost forgot," she said, "that new shower head seems to be leaking a little. Not all the time, but I thought you'd want to know."

"I can stop by after work and look at it."

"Great." She bobbed her head and smiled again, her tongue darting out to her lips.

"See you tonight, then." He forced a smile in return, which probably came across as more of a grimace, then shut the door and leaned against it.

Good God. What the hell was wrong with him? Sure, Kate had the whole shy-sexy thing going on, but that was irrelevant. She couldn't undo being a mother or a widow any more than he could undo his tendency to get involved with women who needed way more help than he was qualified to give.

Alex was right. He needed to find himself a nice, uncomplicated woman with no baggage—*and no kids*—with whom to have a casual, no-strings fling.

He pushed away from the door.

And failing that, he could get to work.

WHEN JIM GOT HOME LATER that afternoon, he waited until he saw Kate and Liam walk down toward the water before heading over with his toolbox—denial being the tool he intended to use first.

"Hey," he waved. "Okay if I let myself in?"

Kate waved back and nodded. For a moment she looked like she would head back up the bank toward him again, but he took the porch steps in one long, purposeful stride and pretended not to notice her hesitate.

The fix was easy, just needed a little tightening, and he was done without incident—carnal or otherwise.

Jim slid the wrench back into his toolbox and was congratulating himself on successfully avoiding contact when Liam blocked him at the front door.

"Can you fish?" the boy demanded.

Jim blinked. "Can I fish? Well, yes, I—"

"Yay!" Liam squealed, then turned and thumped down the porch steps toward his mother. "*He* fish with me!"

Kate strode toward the cottage, a child's fishing pole in hand. "Are you sure?" she asked, looking sweet and grateful all at the same time. "He saw this in town and insisted we get it, but it turns out fishing is harder than I thought. We've mostly been spending time being bug-bait."

Jim looked from Kate's flushed, pretty face to Liam's hopeful, excited one.

"What are you using for bait?" he asked.

"Um, this thingy?" Kate pointed to a little bit of feather on the end of the line.

"No worms?"

"I was hoping we wouldn't have to get into that."

"Were you hoping to actually catch fish?"

A dimple flashed in one cheek. "Truthfully?"

At her guilty expression he couldn't not laugh. "What if by some miracle you did catch a fish with this?"

"I was counting on that not happening," she whispered.

Liam looked up at him earnestly, a bright, little yellow tackle box in hand, and Jim couldn't help but remember the fishing derby when he'd caught his first fish. A six inch perch. They must've thrown it back, but he remembered Gramps cooking *something* up back at the house and serving it to him for dinner with great ceremony.

Jim crouched down in front of Liam. "Tell you what, Buddy—you go get a hat and some bug spray on, and I'll get my own pole and meet you back here in a few minutes. Then your mom can cook some dinner..." He looked up and got a spectacular view of Kate's legs. "Ah, just in case the fish aren't biting tonight. Deal?"

"Deal!"

Liam scrambled up the steps and into the house, leaving Kate to smile shyly at him. "Thank you."

Jim nodded, tugging at the brim of his cap. "Good to see you, again," he said, backing up toward the trees that separated the driveways. "Shower's fixed, by the way."

"Thanks."

He nodded, tried to smile in a casual, neighborly, non-leering kind of way, and swung around toward home before he said or did something stupid. Like kiss her again.

Back at his house, he pulled the little Styrofoam container of worms out of his fridge, retrieved his pole from the basement, and headed toward the door.

Liam was waiting on the other side.

Kate stood a few steps behind. "Do you, ah, need me to come?"

"No! No. We'll be fine. I'll show him the joys of worms." Jim held up the container of worms and jiggled it between them.

Kate backed away. "In that case… I'll start dinner."

Jim watched her rapid retreat toward the cottage and blew out a slow breath before he realized Liam was tugging on his shirt hem. "We fish now?"

"Right. We fish now." Jim led the way down the path toward his dock.

Liam scrambled after him, all little boy enthusiasm and exuberance as he tromped down the boards of the dock—despite the fact that Jim had told him to walk quietly so as not to scare the fish.

"Are those worms?" Liam asked in the loudest whisper Jim had ever heard.

"They sure are. You want to get one out?"

Liam excitedly grabbed the container and pried open the top… then dropped it onto the dock like a hot potato as a worm broke the surface of the dirt. He looked at Jim in horror.

Jim scooped the clump of dirt and worms back into the container and swished his hand in the water to clean it. "By the way, they're alive."

Jim held the container toward Liam a second time.

"You do it," Liam said, making a face.

Jim chuckled and pulled out a worm, stuck it on the hook on Liam's line then proceeded to do the same on his own. He showed Liam how to cast. Or, in his case, drop his line into the water, and then they settled down to wait.

Jim set his pole beside him and pulled off his boots to dangle his legs over the side of the dock into the water. Liam followed suit, and before long they were sitting amiably next to one another, feet cooling in the water, lines drifting. No way were they catching any fish, but it wasn't a bad way to relax at the end of the day.

Jim watched his line float and let his mind wander.

After a while, he showed Liam how to gently tug every so often to keep the worm moving, but Liam ended up slapping the water with his pole more than anything. No matter. They were having fun. Liam turned and beamed at Jim, and Jim felt a tug of something other than his fishing line.

Maybe if Doug and Rach had a son, he and his nephew could go fishing like this sometimes.

Jim pursed his lips and squinted over the lake.

Just as likely Doug would take his own son fishing. And swimming. And show him stuff like how to replace rotten boards in the dock or grill a steak just right.

Things dads do with their sons.

Jim bobbed his line as the sun dipped toward the horizon, the water turning dark with streaks of burnished gold. He noticed that shadows were forming where trees overhung the shore. They should probably hang it up soon. Just as well.

He startled as Liam scootched closer toward him on the dock, Liam's little face sweaty, dirt-streaked... and unbearably hopeful.

"We catch fish soon?" he breathed.

Jim tugged the brim of Liam's floppy-style fishing hat and tried hard to ignore the knot in his gut. "Not sure they're biting tonight, Buddy. How about we try another time?"

"Tomorrow?"

Jim swallowed and looked back toward the cottage. Christ. A woman with a kid? Had he learned nothing from Justine? But then he looked back at Liam's hopeful expression, and something in him answered hopefully in return.

What harm was there in a little fishing? And who else was going to teach the little guy? "Tell you what... if you see me out here fishing, you can join me if your mom says it's okay. Deal?"

"Deal!" Liam said, scrambling to his feet.

"Whoa!" Jim pointed to Liam's pole. "If the fish aren't going to swallow it, who's going to take care of the worm on your hook?"

Liam looked out at his line, and his face scrunched up. "Do *I* hafta eat it?"

Jim barked out a laugh as he, too, rose to his feet. "Not unless you've got an older brother that says you do." Liam shook his head, wide eyed. "Then I guess you're safe." Jim reeled in his line and set his pole on the dock. "Here, you give it to me, and I'll take care of it. This time."

Liam passed over his pole just as Kate appeared at the porch railing of the cottage to announce dinner was ready. "See you 'morrow!" Liam called, running up the dock toward his mother.

Jim watched from below the brim of his hat... not the boy bounding up the path toward the cottage... but at Kate as she stood waiting at the top of the steps, the breeze forming her skirt to her thighs. A perverse side of him wished it would pick up the hem, just a little, because he clearly hadn't tortured himself enough for one day.

And then Liam's pole jerked in his hand as Kate turned away... and Jim pulled a six-inch perch from the water.

June 25
You don't need to tell me I make unhealthy choices. I *know* fish is good
for you, but try as I might, I've never been able to choke it down. I always
end up craving the bad-for-you foods. Onion rings and juicy burgers
dripping with cheese. The foods you know will come back to bite you, tell
you you're fat and make you miserable in the long run.
It's so hot today, I'm craving ice cream. Ugh. See? What did I tell you?

CHAPTER SEVENTEEN

"THANKS FOR HANGING OUT with me on such short notice." Rachel swung her legs under the outdoor picnic table and licked her ice cream. It was a steamy June day, and the *Lick-n-Dip* ice cream stand was hopping. Dang if it wasn't as good as Jim had said. "I'd just be twiddling my thumbs at Grace's apartment or window-shopping for things I shouldn't buy otherwise, and I can't go to Mom and Dad's. Doug and I aren't ready to say anything to them quite yet about the baby, and I know I'd end up blabbing."

"It's our secret," said Kate as she slid into the opposite side of the table.

She'd been pleasantly surprised when Rachel had called and invited her to get together for an hour or two. The day had turned out hot and humid, and crouching in the sun weeding the perennial beds back at the cottage and stressing about her future held a lot less appeal to sitting in the shade, eating ice cream and people-watching. With more thunderstorms predicted for later in the day, the barometric pressure had Kate feeling antsy anyway.

It had nothing to do with her feelings for her sexy neighbor.

"I hope Doug's interview goes well," she said.

"Thanks. He's meeting the head of QC, General Manager and one of the techs today, so it's a good sign things are moving in the right direction." Rachel sighed and licked another dribble from the side of her cone. "It feels surreal, though. A month ago we were just a couple in a tiny apartment in Methuen... Now, we're expecting a baby, and Doug gets this lead for a job in Sugar Falls..." She licked her cone again and stared down the sidewalk at the midday spattering of people going about their business. "Don't get me wrong, it's wonderful! Just... surreal."

Kate nodded. She understood surreal all too well.

The nearby playground had proved too big a temptation to put off, so Liam was running his matchbox cards over the jungle gym bars while Kate and Rachel enjoyed their cones. Kate scooped some of Liam's overly-melted ice cream from his dish and popped it in her mouth.

"*Rachel?*" Kate dove across the table and saved Rachel's cone a second before it hit the top of the picnic table. She grabbed the spare dish she'd asked for 'just in case' and shoved it under Rachel's cone. "Are you all right? You just turned white as a ghost."

"The ghost of mistakes past," Rachel mumbled, grabbing a napkin and wiping the ice cream that'd dribbled onto her wrist. She laughed shakily and waved off Kate's concern. "I'm okay. I'm okay. Just surprised."

"And not in a good way."

Rachel shook her head and stared at her cone, now melting in the dish despite their shady cover. "It shouldn't be a surprise. I mean, I should have expected it." She ran a hand over her brow and met Kate's eyes. "I'm sorry."

"Don't be," said Kate, still concerned.

Rachel poked at her upturned cone with her index finger. "Can I ask you a question?"

"Of course."

"I know we don't really know each other, and I hope you don't think I'm one of those people that blurts out all her troubles on somebody she just met. As a rule, I'm not. But I don't want to talk to Grace—she *cannot* keep a secret—and I don't know who else..."

"What is it?" Kate prompted.

Rachel grimaced, looked back down the sidewalk then back to Kate. "The truth is...I just saw someone."

"Someone? I'm not sure what your question—"

Rachel winced. "An ex-boyfriend. Lover, actually."

Kate's eyebrows shot up momentarily before she could rein them back in. "Um... how ex, ah, lover are we talking?"

Rachel sighed, picked up a spoon and took a small bite of ice cream. "High school." She winced. Swallowed. "Doug had gone to college. It was my senior year. I was feeling left behind and questioning everything, and long story short...it happened."

"Happened," Kate echoed.

"I had a fling," Rachel said *sotto voce.* "Well, not really a *fling* fling, more of a one-night stand. But then it ended. Over. I—*we*—broke it off, and we've never talked since. At least... until last week."

"Wait. You *talked* to this ex—?"

"I called him. I knew I'd be coming to town and I wanted to set some ground rules, you know? In case we ran into each other..." she gave another shaky laugh. "Kate, he wants to see me and I don't know what to do!"

"Does Doug know anything about this?"

"No! I called while I was at work."

"No, about your fling—stand— *thing.* Did you ever tell him?"

Rachel blanched. "No! It would crush him! Doug was my—he likes to say he was my first and last... I could never tell him. Ever."

"Then I guess you have your answer."

Rachel stared down at her dish. "I know. It just feels so awkward. The way things ended between us... this guy... and me... I wasn't very gracious. I blamed him for something that was both of our faults. Don't I owe him an explanation?"

"Owe him? It's been years. I'm sure he's fine by now."

"He said he just wants to get coffee. There's no harm in that, is there?"

"Is he single?"

"Yes."

Oh Lord. "I guess the question is why do you want to have coffee with him?"

"What if we move back to Sugar Falls? That's what Doug is hoping. That's what *I'm* hoping. But what then? It's a small town, Kate. What if Doug runs into him? What if this guy says something?"

Rachel licked her finger and rubbed at a sticky smear on her forearm. "He sent me a friend request."

"Ignore it," Kate told her. "You're a married woman, Rachel. A *pregnant*, married woman."

"I know. I know! I just wonder sometimes what my life would have been like... if things had gone differently." She swallowed and forced a smile. "I mean, don't get me wrong, I love my husband. I do! But don't you ever wonder if you've made the right choices? If you'd chosen a different path, would things have ended the same way?"

Kate must have made a face, because Rachel reached across and grasped her arm. "Oh God! I'm sorry! I didn't mean... What choice did you have with your husband's accident?" Rachel let go and let out a soft sigh as they watched Liam on the slide. "But that's what I mean, I guess.

We never know what's going to happen in life, and this guy—he was intense and *exciting*. He drove a motorcycle and had this eagle tattoo right here..." She pointed to a point just below her left shoulder. She shivered and hugged herself despite the heat. "But then..."

"You had regrets."

Rachel's eyes flew to Kate's. "Regrets? No. Never. I mean, yes, it was a mistake, but then I was at college and with Doug, and I never looked back. Never gave this guy another thought."

"Until now?"

Rachel shook her head and then glanced at the sky overhead, tears glistening. "I always knew we weren't meant to be together, always knew he belonged to someone else, but I couldn't bring myself to turn down the opportunity to be with him. I knew it was wrong, but I *needed* it. I needed to experience that intensity, be that wild, just once in my life before settling down, you know? Doug is wonderful. He's responsible and sweet and hard-working. But he doesn't do impulsive. And he certainly wouldn't do half the stuff—" She cut herself off and dabbed at her eyes with her napkin. "But it couldn't last." She laughed without humor. "Actions *always* have consequences."

Kate nodded and licked her ice cream, her thoughts tumbling over each other. Randy had been her fling guy. Her dangerous, intense, wild guy. With him, she'd felt everything her carefully choreographed upbringing had protected her from. Excitement. Daring. Disorder. Randy had pulled her outside the stifling, country-club bubble her parents had raised her in, and it had been intoxicating. But instead of having her fling and returning home to marry a nice, stable, reliable guy like Doug, she'd married Randy. And look where *that* had gotten her.

Kate licked her ice cream with considerably less enthusiasm.

Who could blame Rachel for a fling that happened years ago? If only Kate had had the good sense to end things with Randy when things went downhill—when it became clear the Technicolor excitement of 'us against the world' had faded to a dull, unbreachable distance between them. But no. She'd thought she could fix it, this problem they had, like she'd bailed them out so many times before. A baby would surely bring them closer, right? But, after Liam was born, the silent divide in their marriage only grew wider, and Kate had cared for Liam alone—as Randy sat around watching NASCAR and drinking himself into oblivion. She knew she'd been grasping at straws, praying there was some way to bring back what they'd once had, but she knew better now.

Some problems are simply un-fixable.

Kate watched as Liam tumbled onto the ground at the bottom of the slide, giggling to himself. He stood dazedly and grinned at her, and Kate's heart squeezed hard in return.

Maybe Randy hadn't been a great husband or father, but she would never regret he'd made her a mother. And, maybe, like Rachel said, her life would have been different if she'd chosen a different path. Maybe *she* would be different. But, it was the past now. Any chance of choosing the sensible path was behind her. She'd chosen Randy, and now it was her job to be the responsible, reliable one. She had a son to raise, a job to do, a future to prepare for...

Rachel smiled wryly and pushed away her ice cream. "Well, I see I *have* become that overly new acquaintance that shares way too much personal information for comfort and now you don't know what to say."

Kate shook off her reverie. "No! Not at all. I'm glad you feel comfortable confiding in me. I just don't know how I can help."

Rachel shrugged. "I suppose I just needed to tell someone. Get it off my chest. I'll figure it out."

"What will you do?"

"I don't know. Did I mention he's *really* good looking?"

Kate raised an eyebrow.

"Not that I'd act on it! That was a joke..." Rachel trailed off.

"There was a reason you broke things off. And you said yourself—Doug's a good guy."

"I know. I know," she sighed. "He is. But he's no eagle tattoo."

CHAPTER EIGHTEEN

"*NO*," SAID JIM.

"Don't be stubborn." His grandmother pursed her lips. "It's not a date—"

"Of course, it's a date!" Jim countered. "You said it yourself: *Double. Date.*"

"It's just a phrase, James, not a marriage contract."

"I'm still not going."

"Why not?"

"It's a bad idea, that's all."

"She's in mourning," Grams argued.

"I'm well aware of that."

"She's been holed up in that cottage since she arrived. Don't you think she'd like something to look forward to?"

He pushed his hand through his hair and eyed the potential exits. "Why the big push, huh, Grams? Why can't you let it be?"

"Because you're being stubborn. It's not healthy. You *need* this. Get out with other young people once in a while. Ever since things fell apart with that woman, you've been sitting around night after night waiting for that fool beeper thing to go off."

"You know why I volunteer. If there'd been more responders that night..." He didn't have to finish the sentence. They both knew what he was referring to. Twenty years later, the tragic fire that had taken his aunt and uncle was still too fresh to speak of.

Grams nodded, her eyes glistening. "That doesn't mean they'd want you to sacrifice yourself to their memory. You have a life, James. You need to live it."

"I *am* living it." At that moment, the 'fool beeper' Grams had just complained about went off. "I gotta go."

"You're going on that double date, James. It'll be good for you."

"I'm not." He grabbed his cap off the hat rack and opened the screen door. "Kate doesn't need this."

"I *SO* NEEDED THIS," KATE SIGHED as she slid into the vinyl booth at the local diner. "Thanks for inviting me."

Jim shrugged. He pulled his cap off and set it on the hook at the end of the booth, then slid in next to her. Rachel and Doug settled in the opposite side.

"It was Gram's suggestion," Rachel said, her hands fluttering like birds as she passed the menus from the end of the booth. "Doug had a final interview today, so we were already in town."

"Who knows, if we're lucky, we might be moving back to Sugar Falls sooner than later," said Doug. "I'm keeping my fingers crossed."

Kate watched as Rachel refolded her paper napkin on the table and straightened the tines of her fork. "When do you think you'll hear?"

"They hope to make a decision in the next couple weeks."

Rachel glanced a brilliant smile at her husband. "We're so excited."

Kate nodded encouragingly and pretended to peruse the menu. Aside from taking Liam fishing a couple times, Jim had avoided her ever since the shower incident nearly two weeks ago.

And then he'd stopped by at noon to ask if she were busy tonight— *nothing fancy, just casual*—and she'd hoped he wasn't avoiding her after all. It seemed a sign of rare good fortune when Nana had invited Liam to come for a sleepover, just for fun.

Now here she was. Sitting in a 1950's diner, in her prettiest floral sundress, her toenails painted a delicate pale blue, with a date who refused to even make eye contact.

She sipped her water and nibbled her bottom lip.

Jim set his menu on the table and smoothed his hand down his thigh as if he were trying to press himself down in his seat.

"What do you suggest?" Kate asked, hoping he'd at least look at her if she asked him a direct question.

"It's all good," he answered, reaching for his soda.

"They have *great* onion rings," Rachel enthused.

"Mmm." Kate nodded. At least Rachel wasn't giving her the silent treatment.

"Lots of people like the turkey dinner platter," Doug suggested. "That's what I'm getting."

"What are you getting?" Kate asked, leveling her gaze on Jim. She'd make him talk if she had to pull his lips apart herself.

Jim stared at something beyond her right shoulder. "Bacon burger."

"I only like burgers if they're thick and juicy. Are they thick and juicy?"

His eyes skittered over her face, bouncing off her lips, before he put all his concentration into repositioning his silverware. "Ah, yeah. Yeah. They're good."

"Sold!" she announced, closing her menu. She reached across to stack it with the others. She couldn't care less what she ordered. Her mouth was watering—but not for hamburgers. Her entire right side was burning with awareness for the man who was so incredibly close... but apparently making a superhuman effort not to touch her.

After the waitress took their orders, they talked more about Doug's potential job. Rachel chattered over-brightly and Jim continued to sip his soda, contributing to the conversation only when spoken to.

"Where will you live if you move back to Sugar Falls?" Kate asked.

Doug shrugged. "I don't know. The housing market is kind of tight here, but nothing could be worse than our current place. It's on the second floor, only one bedroom—"

"But it's been home since we were married," Rachel added.

"Sounds like Randy and me. My husband," Kate explained. "We had a place just like that for years."

For the first time, Jim looked up, his expression tight.

"We'll have to move anyway," Rachel was saying. "Our apartment will be too small for a baby."

"We moved, too, right after Liam was born. Randy hated tripping over a crib in the bedroom."

Jim looked away again, his body rigid beside her.

Smooth move, Kate admonished herself. *Way to go, bringing up the dead husband. Twice.* She sighed, deflated.

"Do you miss him terribly?" Rachel asked softly, her taut smile replaced by a look of genuine sympathy.

Kate glanced up. "What?"

"Do you miss him terribly, your husband, that is?"

"I, ah..."

"You were so quiet just now. I thought maybe it was hard to talk about him."

Kate glanced around the table. Rachel and Doug's earnest, sympathetic faces. Jim's blank look and distant demeanor. *How to explain she'd been thinking something entirely different?*

"It's okay," Rachel assured her, "we're all friends here."

Kate bit her lip. "The thing is, Randy and I... we'd separated before his accident. In a way, I think I'd already mourned him before he died. I'm fine now. Really."

Rachel reached across the table and squeezed Kate's arm. "*Wow.* I had no idea. You're a brave woman. Most people don't have the guts to be that honest, with themselves or anyone else."

"It's the truth."

"What happened? In your marriage?"

"Rachel!" Doug admonished, but his wife ignored him.

Kate shrugged. "It's okay. He was an alcoholic. We married young. Lots of reasons." She shrugged again. "Sorry. I don't want to make everyone uncomfortable, but I'd rather you not be thinking you need to tiptoe around me."

Kate looked to the side. Jim was still playing with his utensils. When she looked up again, she caught Rachel's curious glance.

"That's two bacon burgers. Medium. A turkey platter. Garden salad with chicken and onion rings. Did I miss anything?" The waitress set down their plates. "Drink refills?"

"I'll have another decaf tea," Rachel said, pushing forward her empty glass. "Plus I need to use the little girls' room," she said into her husband's ear. When Doug shuffled out, Rachel grabbed his arm. "Why don't you come, too, dear?"

He looked at her a moment, then mumbled. "I'm going to go, ah... wash hands."

When they were gone, Kate watched out of the corner of her eye as Jim opened his burger for a generous dollop of ketchup then set the bun back on top. He took a bite.

"I'm sorry if I made you uncomfortable," Kate said.

"What makes you think I'm uncomfortable?" he asked, reaching for his soda.

"You're very quiet."

"I'm a man of action, not words." The moment he spoke, his eyes shot to hers, and she knew he regretted saying them. His eyes darted away.

They both knew what kind of action he was capable of.

Kate fought the nervous giggle that threatened to erupt.

He took another bite.

"Anyway, I—"

"Try the onion rings," he ordered.

"What?"

"The onion rings. Try them."

"Okay." Kate reached out to pick up an onion ring, not entirely sure why it was so critical she try them *at that moment.*

Jim grabbed one, too, then stuffed it in his mouth as if he could speed eat and be done with it.

"Oh, I see. You're uncomfortable because of what happened the other day." Okay, so the onion rings *were* good. Still...

"Of course not. I'm fine. Just fine. Try your burger."

Kate pressed her lips together. "Oh, for Pete's sake... Rachel and Doug aren't here. You can say it. Something happened the other day, something... *wild*... and we can't explain it."

His eyes flashed to hers. "I can. It's wrong. Whatever wild thing that happened between us is wrong, pure and simple."

"Why?" she demanded more out of curiosity than anything else.

"Because I can't control it," he nearly hissed through his teeth

Okay, she'd admit it. That annoyed her. Good, rational, practical arguments she'd listen to, but this? It was a sorry excuse if she'd ever heard one. "Wrong and imprudent are two different things," she said. "But I won't say I'm sorry it happened."

He stared at her then. Really stared at her. Kate fought the urge to touch her head to be sure she hadn't grown horns.

"Are *you* sorry it happened?" she asked.

"Yes. No. I don't know."

"Then why did you ask me here tonight?" she asked, throwing up her hands.

"I said it was casual," he grumbled.

Right. Her mistake. Her mistake for making more of it than it really was. Her mistake for hoping for just once things would turn out the way she wished them to, rather than how life always seemed to turn out.

Kate's face burned with humiliation as Rachel and Doug scooted back into the booth. She stared at her burger, the smell of which had been so enticing a few minutes before was now nauseating.

"Everything okay?" Rachel asked.

Kate faked a smile, sipped her water. "Why do you ask?"

"Probably because you still both look like you'd rather be anywhere but here. If you guys aren't up to this, we could do this another night."

Kate snuck a peek at Jim through her lashes as he heaved a sigh and stood up from the booth. "Could you excuse us?" he said.

He reached his hand out to help Kate from the booth then dropped it like a hot potato as soon as she was up. He strode to the door, her trailing behind.

"We need to talk," is all he muttered once they were outside. Someone bumped them on the sidewalk, and he ran a hand through his hair. "But not here." He looked up and down the busy main street then

111

gestured toward a path by the side of the diner leading toward the river. Jim led the way, grim-faced.

He stopped in the shade of a nearby bridge and threw up his hands in a helpless gesture.

"What is it about you?" he asked, as if she had any idea whatsoever what he was talking about. He closed his eyes for a moment. "I'm sorry. That didn't come out right. I'm just trying to figure out... make *sense*..." He shoved his hand in his hair again and took a couple steps forward then stopped as if thinking better of getting too close. "What I can't figure out is what is it about you that every time we're in the same room, I can't think of anything but— "

"Kissing me?" she ventured.

His lips became a grim line. *"Among other things."*

She stared up at him, at the soft clump of hair that stuck out where he'd shoved his fingers into it. She already knew how it would feel. "Maybe it's pheromones."

"Pheromones."

"Yeah. You know, like hormones for the olfactory senses. I read about it in a magazine once."

"Pheromones," he repeated.

"Apparently you don't really smell them, more your body senses them and reacts. It happens completely without our being aware of it."

He nodded, stepping closer. "That would explain why I can't explain it. I just have this really out-of-proportion attraction to you, and it's driving me nuts. I haven't been able to figure out what happened that day... why we—"

"Collided in the bathroom?"

"Yeah."

She nodded. "It took me by surprise, too." She looked at him then—at the way a little shock of hair curled adorably over his forehead, at the way his eyes crinkled at the corners—and got all tingly inside. "So, um...what now?"

He stared at her, clearly not understanding the question.

"What do we do now... about this, um, out-of-proportion attraction thing?"

"You're not bothered by it?"

"Should I be?"

"You're a widow!" he cried.

Kate closed her eyes. "So everyone keeps reminding me."

"Isn't this," he made a rapid motion back and forth between them, "I don't know... *inappropriate*?"

"Inappropriate?" she cried, the warm fuzzy feeling zipping away. "Do you realize this is the first time I've been out—*alone*—like a real grown-up since Randy died? Do you think I want to stand here in my best sundress debating whether I've gone through an appropriate mourning period? What does that even mean?

"I was looking forward to just one night where I could be me, okay? A night I could relax, have a good time, laugh a little, maybe get lucky..." *Get lucky?* What was she saying? Never mind, she was on a roll!

"So, don't talk to me about what's appropriate," she said, practically stabbing him in the chest with her index finger, "or I'm liable to do something really inappropriate just to spite you!"

He stared at her, the silence stretching out between them. "You were hoping to get lucky?"

CHAPTER NINETEEN

———————————

KATE STARED AT JIM. Okay, more precisely, his mouth. "Maybe," she said.

He glanced up the hill to the diner. "Would it be really inappropriate to suggest we ditch Doug and Rachel and go somewhere... alone?"

Kate absorbed his words, a warm tingle swirling deep in her belly. "Probably." His face fell. "But I'd like that anyway."

"You would?"

She smiled. "Do you want me to change my mind?"

"No! No, don't do that. We'll—let's go." With that, he grabbed her hand, his fingers warm and firm on her own, as they stumbled up the embankment to the diner.

"Go where?" she asked.

He paused in front of the diner. "My place?"

Kate felt another swirl of heat in her belly. She nodded.

Eager excitement flashed across Jim's face, as he pushed at the diner door. "I'll handle this," he said as he handed her his truck keys.

A few minutes later he slid into the pickup, a plastic bag of take-out containers in hand. "Thought you might want it later," he murmured as he grabbed the truck key and crammed it into the ignition.

They rode in silence, the anticipation palpable. Kate thought she could feel it, pressing on her skin, her own excited energy pushing out.

She licked her lips and glanced out the window. It was a short drive to the lake. A few minutes. Not nearly enough time to entertain second-thoughts.

Which was just as well, because if she allowed herself to wonder what she was doing, whether it was fair to Jim, to Liam, to... Dear God, she'd probably run back to the safe familiarity of Connecticut at the first opportunity.

Fact was, though, it was July second. Randy had been gone over two months now.

She closed her eyes and resolutely closed the lid on her emotions.

She wasn't thinking about that tonight. She wasn't thinking about the past or mistakes, who she was or what the future held. Tonight was about living. Here. Now.

The pickup lurched to a stop in Jim's driveway. He cut the engine, silence filling the cab, his hands resting on the steering wheel. Finally, he looked at her.

"It's not too late to change your mind," he said.

She swallowed any remaining uncertainty. "I wouldn't be sitting here if I wasn't sure."

He nodded, tugging at the brim of his cap thoughtfully before pulling it off and setting it on the dash. He grabbed the take-out bag then jogged around to open her door. Kate slid out, her sandals crunching on the gravel drive.

He stood so close she could see the sweat glisten on his brow, a muscle twitch in his cheek. He wet his lips and took a step away. She watched his throat shift as he swallowed.

Jim unlocked the back door to his house, and Kate preceded him into the small hallway of his walk-out basement. Pegs on the wall overflowed with coats and clutter. Jim hurriedly relieved a peg of its cargo and stuffed it over another. "Maybe we should have gone around front. I wasn't expecting company."

She assured him it was fine and hung her purse and sweater on the hook then followed him upstairs. The house had a simple layout with the kitchen/dining area to the left and living area to the right. And while it was clearly a bachelor's home, it was homey; and, aside from a toppling pile of *Fine Homebuilding* magazines by the lone couch and a partially-dissected power tool on the dining room table, it was neat.

Jim indicated Kate should make herself at home in the living room while he put away the food. "Can I get you something to drink?" he called from the kitchen. "Lemonade?"

"Sounds perfect." Kate picked up a small but exquisitely crafted wooden decoy from a shelf in the living room and turned it over in her hands. She set it back and picked up another.

"Gramps carved that one."

She jumped at Jim's voice and nearly bobbled the decoy before placing it back on the shelf. "They're lovely. Did he make them all?"

"No. Just those two. The rest are mine."

"*You* made these?"

He shrugged.

"They're beautiful!"

"Thanks." He bit his lower lip. "Here's your lemonade."

Kate thanked him for the drink and took a sip. He was staring at her again. Clearly she was going to need to get the ball rolling or they'd be talking about wooden birds and drinking lemonade all night.

"What did you say to Rachel and Doug?"

He took a sip of his drink. "I, ah, told Doug we had to go."

"Didn't he want to know why?"

Jim cleared his throat. "I think it was obvious." He looked away, his cheeks tinged pink under his tan.

He was staring at her now, the easy smile that had become so familiar in the brief time she'd known him replaced with a tense, watchful demeanor.

Her skin tingled and she looked for a place to set down her drink. Spying a coaster, she set her glass on a side table. Jim leaned over and put his drink next to hers. He didn't bother with a coaster.

She could hear their breathing in the quiet room, the air a bit close from the heat of the day. She smiled.

He grimaced.

"Kate, I—"

She put her finger to his lips. "Please, don't. I know this must seem crazy. We hardly know each other, but… I don't want to analyze it. Not now."

She didn't want to talk. Didn't want to admit her behavior was so far removed from her usual comfort zone it was like observing someone else. But Jim made her feel safe in a way she couldn't put her finger on. Safe… and alive. No, that wasn't right. He made her feel… hopeful. There was something about his eyes. So gentle, so kind. When she looked into his eyes, all the sad, lonely years melted away, and her heart felt light again, like a butterfly in her breast. She hadn't felt that feeling in so very, very long. She couldn't bear to turn it away. Not now. Not yet.

He nodded, his gaze boring into hers as he grasped her hand and pressed a kiss to her palm. His thumb brushed over her fingers as he looked at her hand. "You took off your ring," he whispered.

She nodded, and he brought her hand to his lips again, looked her in the eyes. "Tell me what you want," he said.

"For you," she managed a shaky breath, "to do that again."

He grinned against her wrist.

Kate watched, mesmerized, as his lips brushed her skin again, tracing a heated trail up her arm, his afternoon stubble lightly abrading as he worked his way to her shoulder.

Her mouth opened on a silent sigh as he trailed kisses up her neck, his tongue a silken tickle behind her ear. Her heart was pounding in her chest, an excited drum beat, and he hadn't even kissed her on the lips.

"Are you sure about this?" His voice was low, his breath an uneven staccato on her cheek.

She closed her eyes. She could smell the light, sweet scent of arousal on his skin. "Yes."

She slid her hands to his shoulders, her fingers digging in as he teased her with feather-light kisses, always a breath away but never quite touching his lips to hers.

This is what she wanted. To lose herself in the moment. To live in the moment. To forget everything else. Everyone else.

To feel happy and hopeful and, dare she say it, desirable for just a little while.

His body tensed under her fingertips, muscles bunching as she held onto him, her own balance compromised by his tender assault. She slid her hand instinctively down his rib cage, to the side of his hip. Forward.

"Kate," he warned, his hand holding hers at bay. "I'm trying to take this slow."

She grasped his face in her palms and made him look at her, a shiver of excitement sliding up her spine. "I never asked you to."

He stood, motionless, his breath coming in short bursts, his hair lightly mussed, eyes dark.

She could hear the hum of the refrigerator in the kitchen, the ticking of a clock somewhere in the room and the pounding of her own pulse in her ears.

She couldn't say who made the first move. All she knew is one moment they were staring at each other—still as the air around them—the next moment their mouths were fused, bodies crushed together in inelegant, urgent need.

His T-shirt went first, yanked over his head while trying to avoid separating their lips for any longer than necessary.

Kate appreciated this effort. As he toed off his sneakers, she kicked off her sandals and guided his hands to the button on her halter dress, sighing against his lips as he cupped her breasts in his palms as soon as the light fabric slid away.

She dug her fists into his hair, plastering their lips together, then pulled away to gasp for breath before diving back for more.

They made their way across the living room, fumbling with clothes, exploring, tasting, tugging. Then Jim stumbled on the trousers that had pooled at his ankles and pulled them both, sprawling, onto the couch.

Kate giggled against his lips, his muffled *oof!* swallowed by her mouth as she let her hands roam over his bare skin, enjoying the fact that he was pinned beneath her. It gave her a sense of power. Control. Except she didn't need or want control over this. Wanted it to consume her. Invited it to.

Jim groaned against her mouth then pushed up and over in an effort to roll her beneath him.

They slid unceremoniously to the floor, narrowly missing the edge of the coffee table, tangled in their remaining clothes. Jim slumped his head against her bare shoulder.

"Before we kill each other," he gasped, "why don't we take this upstairs?"

Kate nodded earnestly, unable to form a single word, much less a whole sentence.

He kicked off his trousers and stood, cotton boxers the only clothes he had left on, as he helped her to her feet. Kate swallowed hard when he slid his hands down her body, taking her dress to the floor, leaving her in nothing but a pair of hot pink bikini underwear.

She held her breath as he stared at her nearly naked body. It had been a decade since anyone but her husband and gynecologist had seen this body. His gaze swept over her breasts, hips and thighs.

"I was right," he finally said, his voice low and husky. "You're *not* pretty." As her heart all but slammed to a stop in her chest, his old smile returned, teasing and unbearably sexy. "You, Kate, are unbelievably... *hot.*"

She grinned with relief. "The feeling is mutual."

Without another word, he grabbed her hand and pulled her up the stairs. She felt like giggling, as if she were a teenager sneaking away to do something terribly wicked.

Nervous shivers shot up her spine, made her flesh tingle with awareness. The air upstairs was cooler, a window left open, and she could hear a wind chime somewhere in the fading light of the day.

She smiled to herself. She'd never done anything like this before. But she didn't want to be practical or responsible. She didn't want to think about the future. She wanted to be in the arms of a man who thought she was hot. And, conveniently, he was right in front of her.

Jim impatiently tugged her to him, his hands like fire on her skin, his lips firm and moist on her mouth.

She slid his boxers down his thighs, her fingers delighting in the soft rasp of hair on his legs. She stared at his naked body with awe. He was glorious. Lean. Muscular. Ready.

Perfect.

She pressed against him, and he moaned, his mouth hungry on hers, then he was urging her back against the edge of the bed. She held onto him greedily as his arms braced her, his body hard and pulsing against her as they fell to the mattress.

He dragged his mouth from hers and lowered it to her breast, his lips teasing her nipple, sending electric heat rippling through her. She arched on a moan, her hips seeking his, her hands reaching for him.

When his fingers found the edge of her panties, she wiggled her hips, letting him slide them down her thighs as his mouth worked its magic elsewhere.

Then he found her center with his hand and she arched against him. *Yes.*

He pulled away.

She tugged him back. "Don't go..."

"I'm just getting protection," he murmured as he rummaged, one-handed, in the nightstand.

Desire was nearly a fever pitch in her. She wanted—no *needed*—the feel of him. *Right now.* "Don't worry," she gasped as she felt him pulse against her belly, felt an answering surge deep inside her. "You don't need any."

"You're covered?" he asked.

"Yeah," she said.

He nodded—then on a groan, entered her.

Kate let her head fall back against the sheets, glorying in the feel of his body moving over her, in her, as he began an urgent rhythm they both craved. She groaned and gripped him to her.

It wasn't really a big lie, she reassured herself as she surged toward climax. There was no risk of Jim making her pregnant.

At least it would be some trick if he did.

Seeing as she already was.

CHAPTER TWENTY

"WOW."

Kate turned her head to look at Jim as he lay sprawled on top of the bedclothes next to her.

"That was incredible," he breathed.

Her body was slick with sweat, her breathing still returning to normal as she lay, boneless, on the sheets. *Incredible* was a good word for it.

She'd hoped for a fun, remember-it-fondly frolic. What she'd gotten was one of the most intense orgasms of her life.

"Was it good for you?" He grimaced. "I sound like a teenager. You're just so quiet."

"Good," she said as she laid a weak hand over her brow. "Very good."

He nodded, his face relaxing with relief. "I thought maybe I'd been too... we were so..." He trailed off and rolled to his side to face her, his finger coming to draw little circles on her bare shoulder. "I'm not normally like that."

"I'm sorry to hear that."

He chuckled and pressed a kiss to her lips. "That's not to say I didn't enjoy it. Which I did. Very much." He tilted his head and studied her. "But I also like to take my time. Enjoy the journey not just the destination." He replaced his finger on her shoulder with his lips. Soft, sensual lips. Kate closed her eyes as his mouth trailed slowly along her collar bone, rekindling a fire that still smoldered inside her.

"Maybe, if you don't object," he said, "we could try it again. Savor it this time."

She shivered under his touch, whether from regret or excitement she wasn't sure. A bittersweet longing squeezed her heart. *Oh God, there shouldn't be a 'next time,'* she counseled herself. *Shouldn't have been a 'this time.'* But her mouth was already saying something else.

"I'd like that," she said, knowing she should put some distance between them, but unable to concentrate with Jim's lips tantalizingly close to her breast. "But, maybe we should, ah, eat first?"

He raised his head, hazel eyes smoldering, hair in sexy, tousled disarray. "Good idea. Sustenance. I'll start reheating dinner."

She nodded. "I'll go, ah, freshen up. If that's okay."

He pointed her to the bathroom then headed downstairs, completely nude. The guy certainly didn't have a problem with excessive modesty. Not that it bothered her. He could parade around in front of her all he wanted.

Sighing, she sat up and looked for her sundress, then realized it was somewhere on the living room floor. She picked up a T-shirt from atop Jim's dresser and hoped he wouldn't mind if she borrowed it. Sliding it over her head, she padded across the hall and closed the door.

Then she shut her eyes and leaned her head against it.

Oh. Lord. What was she *doing?*

More to the point, what had she *done?*

She turned from the door and walked to the sink, staring at herself in the mirror.

She barely recognized the woman staring back at her. Hair a tangled mess, eyes unusually bright, cheeks flushed. She turned on the tap and splashed cold water on her face, her wrists.

She'd made a mistake.

She'd thought she could indulge in this out-of-proportion attraction thing, as Jim called it, get it out of her system, and go back to her messed up life.

Only she'd known the moment he rolled over and said *wow* that things weren't going according to plan. She'd already been thinking once wasn't enough, not nearly enough.

Maybe it was the hormones.

Or maybe it was the feel of him real and naked inside her.

She closed her eyes. *That* had felt particularly good. For never-again mistake sex, it had felt very, very good.

Kate sighed and opened her eyes. Even the last time with Randy, she'd insisted he use a condom.

She grimaced at her reflection. What were the odds of getting pregnant by your dead husband's sperm *after* the separation *while* using birth control? If she were a gambler, she'd be laughed off the track for betting on odds like that.

She squeezed her eyes shut against the hot sensation gathering there.

But here she was, with the jackpot.

CHAPTER TWENTY-ONE

IT WAS AFTER ELEVEN O'CLOCK that night by the time Jim pulled back into his drive after the ill-timed fire call.

What a night.

As exhausted as he was, he still couldn't wipe the goofy smile from his face. And it was all because of one woman. One amazingly sexy, spontaneous, incredible woman.

Kate.

He glanced at the cottage through the trees, wondering if she were still up. No lights. He sighed lightly into the cool night air. She'd probably gone to bed.

If only he'd known her longer. If only this hadn't been their first night, he'd feel more confident about going over, knocking on her door... or just letting himself in.

Jim swallowed as he felt a stirring in his groin. Better not think about that right now, or he'd be suffering the rest of the night. Although, it would be really hard *not* to think about it. Especially now that he was so close to the woman who'd amazed the hell out of him just a few hours ago.

He knew he needed a shower. Knew also, he really wanted to see her again. Which was why, when he walked in the door, his pulse quickened. There were three messages on his answering machine. He pressed the 'play' button.

The first was Doug, ribbing him about bailing on them at the diner.

The second was Rachel, apologizing for Doug ribbing him about bailing on them at the diner.

The third was Kate.

Jim turned up the volume as Kate's voice filled his kitchen.

Hi, Jim. It's Kate. I just wanted to say thanks for... tonight. Dinner was great and... I put your food in the fridge after you left. Sorry you didn't get to finish.

Well, it's nearly eleven now, so I guess I'm headed to bed. Have a good night. Bye.

He stared at the phone. *Nearly eleven?* The kitchen clock read 11:17. Maybe it wasn't too late to call after all.

Before he knew what his fingers were up to, her line was ringing. He should let her sleep. Probably it made him look desperate to call like this, but then she answered, and he didn't care how it seemed, he was so pleased she'd picked up.

"Kate? It's Jim."

"Jim? Oh. Hi. I didn't expect to hear from you... tonight."

"I just got back." She was quiet. "I'm sorry. Is it too late to call? I thought I saw your light on..." Okay, so he hadn't, but...

"No, it's fine. I... It just feels silly to talk on the phone knowing you're right next door."

He grinned and looked through the window toward the cottage. "We could change that."

"I'm not sure that's a good idea," she said, although he could tell by the tone of her voice she was at least entertaining the notion.

"I could come over for a nightcap."

"A nightcap, huh?"

"Yeah, you know, we could have a drink. Sit on the porch. Relax."

"Relaxing isn't how I'd describe time spent with you so far." She was teasing him. That was a good sign.

"Yeah, well, I'm open to suggestions." She was quiet again, but she hadn't said no, so he pressed his advantage. "How about we give it half an hour? If you're not feeling... relaxed... in that time, we call it a night? Okay?"

She laughed lightly, and the sound sent warm tingles over his skin. "Okay. You win. Just give me a couple minutes."

"How about ten? I need to shower."

"Ten minutes," she agreed.

TEN MINUTES!

Kate scrambled from under the covers and quickly pulled them back into place, straightening the pillows and stuffing her night guard in a drawer—just in case. She raced downstairs to put in her contacts and brush her teeth.

Eight minutes.

She stared at her reflection, fluffed her hair with her fingertips and rummaged quickly for her tinted lip gloss.

I'll shoot for natural beauty, she thought, as she swiped the gloss over her lips. *Hmm.* Okay, so she'd grab the eyelash curler and pretend she had naturally curling eyelashes, too. But, no mascara! It would only smear and look awful by morning if Jim spent the night.

Spent the night?

Four minutes.

Okay. Focus.

Kate glanced down at the oversized tee she had on and dashed toward the stairs. She *could not* let him see her in the same saggy T-shirt she'd had on on Monday!

Five minutes later, there was a light knock on the front door. Kate poked her arms into a long-sleeved pink cotton shirt and hurried back down the stairs as Jim called from the entry. "Hello? Kate?"

She checked to be sure she'd actually remembered to pull on the capris she'd decided on and stepped off the bottom stair. "I'm here."

He stepped over the threshold and shut the door. "Hi."

"Hi."

She licked her suddenly dry lips and smiled shyly at him, feeling awkward and unsure after all they'd done earlier that night. Had she really stood naked in front of this man just three hours ago? If so, why did she feel so self-conscious now?"

"Sorry about dinner," he said.

"It's okay. I put the rest of your burger in your fridge."

"I saw." He licked his own lips. "I brought us something." He held up a bottle. "Sparkling apple juice. Leftover from a birthday party. I hope it's okay it's not chilled."

Kate smiled more easily and stepped forward to take the bottle. "It's perfect." *He* was perfect. Standing there in his bare feet wearing that soft, lopsided smile, he was just what she would have asked for if she were at the man-bar ordering up something delicious and refreshing.

He followed her into the kitchen. She knew this because every sense was acutely aware of him behind her. The soft shuffle of his feet on the bare wood floor. The fresh scent of his soap. She reached up for glasses and nearly dropped the bottle on the floor when he pressed his body against hers and began to nuzzle the back of her neck.

"Kate..." he murmured into her hair, his lips doing dizzying things to her already jumbled brain. Thankfully, he grabbed the bottle and set it on the counter, as Kate could do little more than hold herself upright, her knees threatening to buckle.

She couldn't say how long they stood like that, him driving her dizzy with tantalizing kisses, before he finally pulled away. "Turn around," he ordered thickly.

Slowly, she turned, her pulse thundering in her ears.

"Kate," he said again.

Oh Lord, she thought unsteadily as she stared back at him. His hair was still damp from his shower, his jaw shadowed with the day's stubble. He wore a plain tee and an old pair of jeans, and she was quite sure that if he said 'Kate' in that low, sexy voice again, she'd dissolve into liquid heat right before his eyes.

"I've been thinking about you all night," he said as he dipped his lips to her nape again. How did he know that was the one place that drove her crazy?

"You have?" she squeaked.

"Mmm," he murmured against her cheek, her closed eyelid. "I've been thinking about taking it slow this time."

"I thought you wanted to come for a... a nightcap?" She gripped the edge of the counter as she felt herself slumping toward the floor.

"Is that what you want?"

"What I want?" Thank heaven he'd slid an arm around her, because this verticality issue she had when he was near was definitely becoming a problem.

"Mmm," he murmured.

His mouth was now so close to her own, she felt her lips plumping up on their own accord just to make contact with his. *Just a little closer. A little more*, they seemed to say. "I want... I want...," she stuttered.

And then his lips were on hers, saving her the effort of finishing her sentence, because he was giving her exactly what she wanted.

A long sigh escaped her lips as he traced his tongue down her nape, then up to nip lightly on her earlobe. "I'm glad you're still up," he said.

"Me... too," she breathed as his hands moved slowly on her back, stroking rhythmically down to her hips. Then he pulled her against him and held her hips against his so she could feel his response to her.

He kissed her again, softly, slowly, then more firmly. Teasing. Tempting. "I don't normally do this," he said, pulling back just enough to separate their lips. "I want you to know. I'm not that kind of guy—this kind of guy—normally."

At least, that's what she thought he said. She was having trouble listening to him, what with her blood pounding in her ears.

"Me either," she said as his mouth went south again at the same time his hands went north—under her shirt, that is. "But, I, ah... didn't see that it did any harm earlier to... *indulge*." This last word came out in a burst as his fingers undid the front clasp of her bra, setting her breasts free a scant moment before he cupped them in his palms.

"I like you," he sucked in a breath as she fumbled with the zipper to his jeans. "It's not just about the sex."

"I like you, too," she replied as his jeans slid down his thighs, exposing the strong, sexy contents therein. She looked up. "And it's totally about the sex."

He nodded, his eyes rolling back under his closing lids as she began to stroke him through his boxers. "Maybe... now... it... is..." He grabbed her hand and opened his eyes. "But, it doesn't have to stop there. Just so you know."

"I know," she said as she wet her lips and slid to her knees, watching as his eyes grew wide. "But it's okay if it does."

CHAPTER TWENTY-TWO

"I DON'T UNDERSTAND," Carter said later that Friday morning. He uncoiled the hose and began to spray down Sugar Falls' Engine No. 2, just one task in a host of preparations for the town's Fourth of July Parade the next day. "How could we possibly be related—even remotely—if you aren't totally psyched about this?"

"First of all, I've always had my doubts about our being related. And second of all, I was talking to Doug." Jim followed Carter around the engine with a long scrub brush and a bucket of detergent.

"Sorry, I just came by to see how things went after you left last night. Didn't mean to start anything." Doug leaned against the wall of the fire station. He didn't look particularly sorry to Jim, not after hearing a highly-edited synopsis of the previous evening's events.

"So just to review what we know so far: You're saying you actually slept with the hot widow next door and she says that's all she wants from you?" Carter said.

Jim put all his concentration on eradicating a particularly sticky bug smear. "Basically."

He scowled at the bug guts, trying to sort through his emotions. He was relieved, certainly, that Kate wasn't looking for a serious relationship. Hadn't he just gotten out of one?

"You have so got it made," Carter laughed. "Where is *my* hot young widow who wants to get laid?"

"Would you keep your voice down? I don't want the other guys to hear."

Carter stopped, water spraying all over. "Why the hell not?"

"Because," Doug said, "if things do happen to work out with her, he doesn't want the whole town thinking she's a... well, *easy*."

"*Exactly*," Jim agreed. Wait a minute. *Was* that why he didn't want the other guys to hear? Sure, it sounded better than Carter's take on it, but maybe Carter's attitude just hit too close to home. Maybe he just didn't want the other guys to know *another* woman had already deemed him unsuitable for anything serious. Kate hadn't even asked if *he* wanted a relationship!

Which he didn't. Most certainly not. He was done saving women. Especially widows and orphans for Christ's sake.

"But she already told you she just wanted sex and wasn't looking for anything long term," Carter said.

"That's what she *said*, yes," Doug agreed. "That's what Rachel said at one point, too."

"*What?*" Carter and Jim turned as one.

Doug took a step back. "But it all turned out for the best in the end, right? I'm just saying, maybe Kate's afraid of getting too attached in case you don't turn out to be the kind of guy that wants to hook up with a woman who has a kid."

"You know I'm not like that," Jim said.

"But *she* doesn't. Maybe she thinks if she convinces you both there's nothing expected, then if something's meant to happen it will happen."

Carter turned to Jim with baleful eyes. "Oh. My. God. Rachel's turned him into a girl."

Doug frowned. "Maybe she doesn't want him to feel trapped. She's giving him an out. It doesn't mean she wants him to take it."

Carter shook his head and went back to spraying. "I will never understand women."

"Just be careful," Doug said to Jim, ignoring Carter completely now. "It might be more complicated with Kate than it seems."

Jim dumped the brush into the bucket of detergent. "I think it already is."

AFTER SETTLING LIAM DOWN for his nap, Kate took a quick shower to wash away the heat and sweat of the day then logged onto the Internet. Once she'd called Jim's grandmother and agreed to help organize the Sweets of Sugar Falls calendar, she'd gotten in contact with the Gifts for Greater Good web manager and given him her new e-mail address. Now it was on the web site inviting men to submit their photos and bios to Kate, er, Liz Bennet, for review. Eek!

She felt a little foolish for picking such a well-known romantic heroine as her alter-ego, but Ruth Pearson had assured her it was perfect... a classic character would make it harder for someone to guess Kate's true identity, she'd said. Which suited Kate just fine. Certainly there were enough complications in her life without littering it with a bunch of men.

Kate signed into her e-mail account.

There were a handful of new messages. She popped them open to read. Most included small candid shots to download.

Okay. She could admit it. There were worse jobs than having to sort through the pictures of a bunch of eligible men. Troy looked kind of cute in an academic way. And Brent was definitely in the running. If only she were ten years younger. Or even five.

Ten minutes later, her chat window popped up asking if she would accept messages from Jim Pearson. She clicked yes and a moment later had an instant message.

Jim: *Hi. Is anybody there? I have a question.*

Kate stared at the screen, biting her lip. *He doesn't know it's me.*

She watched the blinking cursor in the chat message awaiting her reply. She couldn't ignore him, could she? Couldn't he *see* she was logged on?

She hesitated only a moment before her fingers tapped on the keys then hit *send* and watched her message appear on the screen.

Liz: *I'm here.*

His reply came quickly.

Jim: *Nice to meet you.*

Liz: *You, too.*

Jim: *I've got some photos but not sure which I should upload for the calendar. Can you help with that—or is asking advice against the rules?*

Liz: *I can help with that.*

Jim: *Should I e-mail them to you? They're pretty big files...*

Liz: *You can, or if there are a lot, you can just tell me what you've got. Describe them for me. Like, what are you wearing, that sort of thing.*

Jim: *Okaaaaay.*

Liz: *Sorry! That wasn't meant to sound... untoward. :)*

Jim: *LOL Untoward? Isn't that Old English? Is this the REAL Liz Bennet from Pride & Prejudice I'm chatting with?*

Kate smiled as her fingers tapped a reply. *Send.*

Liz: *Ah, I see you've heard of me.*

Jim: *Heard of you? We KNOW each other!*

Kate swallowed, her heart slamming in her chest as she typed.

Liz: *We do?*

Jim: *Sure. Don't you remember? You and me? AP English? Senior year? I'm shocked you don't remember. You were a part of my formative years, Liz. I could never forget you.*

Liz: *Formative years, huh? In what way?*

Jim: *Okay, let's not get untoward or anything. For all I know I'm talking to my grandmother.*

Liz: *LOL. I'm definitely not your grandmother.*
Jim: *...or one of her friends she plays cards with.*
Liz: *Or one of her friends she plays cards with.*
Jim: *Is this Estelle from the Senior Center?*
Liz: *No, it's not. Now, Jim, if I didn't know better, I'd think you were fishing for my identity, which we both know is against the rules.*

JIM SMILED AT HIS MONITOR and typed a reply.
Jim: *That's me. A rule breaker.*
Liz: *You are, are you?*
Jim: *Oh, yeah. Me and rules... we don't get along. Quick— what's your name?*
Liz: *Liz. Nice try, Mr. Rule Breaker.*
Jim: *Fine. We'll play it your way. I'm just saying it might be more fun if we didn't...*
Liz: *Don't be naughty or I'll have to put you in a time-out.*

Jim blinked as her words appeared on the screen. *Time-out?* He chuckled out loud. Flirting with Kate was more fun than he'd imagined. At least, he was pretty sure it was Kate. Who else would Grams have roped into doing this? It made perfect sense… only the mother of a three-year-old would use words like 'naughty' and 'time-out' in the same sentence.

Liz: *I don't know what made me just say that, or press SEND for that matter, but *please* ignore any untoward remarks I might blather from now on.*
Jim: *Are you kidding? No way. Your true colors are shining through. Are you SURE I don't know you? Quick—who shot JR?*
Liz: *You mean from the TV show Dallas? I don't know.*
Jim: *That's okay. Neither do I. A little before my time. But I'm signing off anyway. For all I know you're sixteen. Or married. Or a guy... (Alex? Please tell me it's not you.)*
Liz: *I'm not Alex. And before you sign off... why would you ask me a question you didn't know the answer to?*
Jim: *You mean about Dallas? I figured if you knew the answer it would date you. If you didn't even know who JR was, it would date you in the other direction. See?*
Liz: *Tricky. Now you know I'm over 20 and under 40. If it makes you feel any better, I AM female, single and, just for the record, NOT related to you.*
Jim: *Cross your heart?*

Liz: *And hope to die.*

Jim: *Okay, Susan, I'm telling Alex you're posing as a single woman to score points with all these calendar guys. Tsk! Tsk (What's a time-out, anyway? Sounds naughty.)*

Liz: *Stop. I said I was sorry about the time-out comment. (I'm not Susan.)*

Jim: *Hey, I'm not the one that brought it up. Don't point fingers at me. I was just asking for advice... You'd think after all we've been through together, Beth, you'd be nicer to me.*

Liz: *I'm not Beth either.*

Jim: *Are you sure?*

Liz: *Pretty sure. How would I know? A secret mole? Tattoo?*

Jim: *Hey, I'm not telling.*

Liz: *Neither am I.*

Jim: *Fair enough. Can you tell me if you're going to the fireworks tomorrow night?*

Liz: *And that will narrow it down... how?*

Jim: *I can rule out any blind women I know.*

Liz: *You're hopeless.*

Jim: *Not entirely. I'm hoping we chat again soon.*

Liz: *Why?*

Jim: *You're funny?*

Liz: *Is that a question?*

Jim: *Only if you don't return the sentiment.*

Liz: *LOL. You're charming, Jim Pearson.*

Jim: *So are you, Lizzie.*

CHAPTER TWENTY-THREE

――――――――――

"FLOOF IT A LITTLE MORE," Ruth Pearson instructed, eyeing the red, white and blue swag critically.

"*Floof?* Grams, that isn't even a word! It looks fine." Grace pushed her hair petulantly off her face. "Can we be done? It's hot."

Ruth frowned. If she were a few years younger, she'd be balancing on the ladder herself. *Then* it would be floofed properly. As it was, she had to depend on the reluctant help of her granddaughter.

"Fine. Come down. But if anyone comments on the limp and sorry state of that swag, I'll point them to you."

Grace descended the stepladder and wiped her brow. "The only limp and sorry thing they'll be commenting on will be the float riders. What is it with this heat?"

Ruth fanned herself lightly with her parade schedule. Fine, it was a *tad* hot and humid. It was to be expected. It was July. Young people weren't nearly as hardy as they were in her day. "Get yourself a cool drink and freshen up," Ruth offered charitably. "You have twenty minutes. Don't forget to change!"

Ruth pressed her lips together as Grace disappeared into the crowd milling around the athletic fields waiting for the parade to start. The average person would see chaos. To Ruth it was a well-synchronized, if not well-oiled, machine. She'd been in charge of organizing the town's parade for twenty years.

"Grams! Sorry we're late." Rachel jogged over.

Ruth smiled with satisfaction as she spied Rachel with Kate a few steps behind. "Right on time. So glad you could come, Kate. I always think it's more interesting to have a float with *people* on it. Don't you?"

Rachel hoisted herself onto the back of the pickup. "Kate's never ridden a float before."

Ruth looked to Kate. "You haven't? Oh, you'll have fun. Besides, a float promoting Gifts for the Greater Good will get a whole lot more attention with three attractive young ladies waving from it!"

Ruth noticed Kate's cheeks flush prettily against the navy tank and skirt she wore. Rachel looked fresh and lovely in an all-white tennis outfit.

A few minutes later, Ruth pursed her lips as Grace strode through the crowd in a red tank and a matching pair of shorts. "Young lady, just what is the inseam on those shorts?"

Grace looked down and shrugged. "I dunno."

"Well, maybe next year you'll wear something a little more modest. No time to change now."

Grace leapt onto the tailgate of the pickup. "I thought the whole point was to draw people's attention."

"The right kind of attention, young lady."

Grace rolled her eyes as she made room for Kate and Rachel on the bench beside her. She hooked her thumb toward Kate. "How'd you rope her into this?"

"Kate," Ruth said—wondering if she should reposition Grace to a lower seat to make her long thighs less, um, obvious—"was gracious enough to be the blue in my women of red, white and blue."

"This is so sexist," Grace harrumphed.

"Then why are you doing it?" Rachel popped one of the candies they had for the parade-goers into her mouth.

"If I weren't getting fifty bucks, I wouldn't."

"Grams is paying you fifty bucks?"

Grace frowned and lowered her voice. Thankfully, Ruth's hearing was better than anyone suspected, as she was able to just hear Grace's whispered reply. "Hell, no. Jeff Dayton is. He said he'd pay me fifty bucks if I wiggled my booty and blew him a kiss on our way past the police station."

Rachel coughed and swallowed her candy in a gulp. "And you think *Grams* is sexist?"

Grace shrugged. "If I'm gonna do something I dislike, I might as well get paid for it." She looked around the athletic field. "So where's that little cutie of yours, Kate? I don't see him."

Kate looked at Rachel who'd turned a little pale despite the heat. "Ah, Doug and Jim offered to take care of him during the parade."

Rachel looked at Kate then her cousin. "Right. I thought it'd be good practice for Doug to take care of a toddler. But then, Grams thought maybe it would be better to have two men responsible, their being inexperienced and all."

"Yeah. *That's* why Grams suggested it," said Grace.

"Why I suggested what?" Ruth piped in, knowing full well what the conversation was about. As if she was deaf as a doornail.

133

"Oh, nothing," Grace said.

"How much time until we get going?" asked Rachel. "I forgot my sunscreen and this sun is sweltering."

Ruth checked her watch. "Only a couple minutes. I have to gather the antique car contingent now. They'll be next to last."

"Who's the unlucky sucker to go *last*?" Grace asked as she swiped the sweat from her brow again

"Why, you, my dear," Ruth replied airily. Then she strolled over to the assembly of vintage cars.

Jeff Dayton would be viewing a very wilted wallflower by the time Grace got to him.

Fifty dollars, indeed!

"NOW HERE'S THE DEAL." Jim squatted as close to three year-old level as he could get. The sun was high in the sky and blisteringly hot. "In about five minutes, the parade will start coming down Main Street. I don't know how they do it where you come from, but here, because you're a little guy, people will throw you candy."

"They will?" Now *that* got Liam's attention, Jim noted.

"Yeah. And we're near the end, so that means, whatever they have left, they'll be looking to unload. So unless they've run out, you're liable to score big."

"Wow." Liam's voice was all humble reverence for this wonder of rural life.

"The thing is—and this is really important—you *cannot* run into the road to get the candy. That's Doug's job. You just collect what falls here on the sidewalk. Okay?"

"Okay." Liam looked down the road eagerly.

"And one more thing." Liam's brown eyes shot up again. Jim took off his baseball cap. "We collect it all in here until your mom says you can have some."

Clearly this was an unwelcome caveat, but Liam agreed.

Jim shaded his eyes as he looked down the street. He knew from experience, the first car would be the ambulance or a fire and rescue vehicle, the last a police cruiser. The high school band, local tow trucks, Miss Bessy and the 'Riders' all on their Harley Davidson motorcycles—not a one of them a day under seventy—Frank Reynolds on one of his antique tractors and a motley assortment of floats would fill in between. Most, of course, were simply pickup trucks or convertibles with simple homemade banners for various businesses, civic clubs and causes. The prom king and queen would be riding in Hank Russell's hay wagon with their "court."

As the first vehicle—an ambulance this year—approached with its lights going and occasional toots of its siren, Jim looked down at Liam and laughed.

The kid was jumping up and down on the curb, clapping his hands as if he'd never seen anything so exciting or wonderful in all his life. Jim didn't have the heart to tell him the whole spectacle would last all of fifteen minutes. Instead, he turned to look down Main Street himself, watching with his own degree of eagerness for the float that would carry the woman who'd knocked his socks off in more ways than one.

Members of the local ski club, wearing hats and scarves, waved limply from a float decked out in tinsel and tin-foil snow-flakes. *Poor kids. They must be frying in this heat.*

"Jim? Jim!"

Jim closed his eyes, knowing that particularly husky female voice all too well.

"I should have known we'd run into you here. You always were a civic pride sort of guy."

"Hi, Justine." Jim forced himself to turn and face his ex-girlfriend, knowing before he saw her she'd be cool and pulled together. Her demeanor had always struck him as mysterious, composed. He knew now it was simply indifference. "Didn't expect to see you," he said. *Didn't want to,* was more accurate.

"You know how Sarah loves this kind of stuff. Truthfully, I'd forgotten it was going on, but I'd just finished getting my nails done and what do you know?—there's a parade outside!"

Jim waved a hello to little Sarah, but she was too busy grappling for candy to notice.

She'd grown since he'd last seen her. And her hair was longer. She pushed it off her shoulder impatiently, and Jim tried not to think of the time he'd attempted to braid it—because she'd asked him to. He'd been all thumbs, and the results had been less than impressive, but when he'd finished, she'd given him a hug and smiled...

He swallowed the tightness in his throat and grabbed the back of Liam's shirt a second before the boy could scramble off the curb toward a pile of candy. "Whoa. No going in the street. Remember?"

"'kay."

"Oh, Dan! I didn't see you there." Justine waved dismissively at Doug, oblivious to the fact that she'd gotten his name wrong, then turned back to scan the crowd as if looking for someone of more interest. She'd always had a habit of doing that. Funny it hadn't struck Jim as blatantly rude until now. She motioned toward Liam. "Is that your son?"

"No," Doug said. "My kid's not this old."

"Oh. Right," Justine replied, as if she'd met Doug's offspring at some other occasion, which would be a pretty neat trick seeing as his kid wasn't born yet. She turned toward Jim. "Guess who I ran into the other day?"

Jim picked a Tootsie Roll off the curb and stuffed it in his hat. "I give up."

"Your cousin. Carter." She watched passively as little Sarah collected candy off the street.

Jim couldn't bite his tongue any longer. "Hey, Sarah, honey, why don't you let Doug get that for you?"

"So, tell me," Justine continued. "Is he available?"

"*What?* Christ, Justine. You have a husband. Or have you forgotten again?"

"Not for *me!*" She glanced around as if shocked by such an outrageous idea. "I have a friend who's single... I just thought they might—"

"*No.*"

"Oh, for heaven's sake, why not?"

He turned to look at her then. Her long dark hair pulled into a chic silver clip at her nape. Her too-thin model's frame in beaded halter top, white shorts and silver thongs. "Because we don't run in your circles."

"Run in our—? *Jim.*" She said his name as if it was some sultry reprimand. The naughty pool-boy that needed to be reminded who was boss.

"Justine, you treat people like things. I don't see how your friends would be any different."

She looked upset now, the petulant pout he'd once thought so alluring now simply looked childish. "Don't be mean, Jim. I don't bear any ill-will toward you. Water under the bridge and all that." She leaned closer, her lips a whisper from his ear. "You know I'll always love you, Jimmy."

He gritted his teeth, swallowing the traitorous reply that nearly spilled from his tongue. *Love.* As if Justine even knew what the word meant. As if he did.

He stared at her, a nerve throbbing in his forehead, and wondered how he could ever have said those words to this woman. He'd never say them now. And there was nothing more he cared to say to her. It was difficult for two years worth of wasted personal investment to flow smoothly under any bridge—fictional or not.

"Anyway, I'm glad I ran into you," she went on blithely. "I have news. Derek took a job in New York. We're moving the end of the month. So, I guess it's good we ran into each other today, so we have a chance to say goodbye."

Jim stared at Justine. Stared, then, at the little girl stuffing chocolate into her mouth, the little girl that not long ago had decorated his refrigerator with three-fingered princesses.

The little girl he'd once thought might one day call him *Daddy*.

She was looking down Main Street, oblivious to anyone but the hay wagon loaded with teenagers in their prom formals. He realized then she still hadn't said hello to him. Her eyes had skimmed over him with the same detachment her mother had perfected long ago.

And then it hit him.

Even though he'd once envisioned a future with this child in it, to her he was probably just another face in a long line of her mother's 'friends.' No one particularly special or momentous. Just another adult. And hadn't he played a part in that? Hadn't he allowed Justine to set the rules? Whether he'd enjoyed the game wasn't the point. The point was, he was no longer playing. Hadn't been for nearly five months.

It was better, then, that Sarah not remember him as anyone special. For her sake, he rationalized, forgetting him was for the best.

"I think we've already said our goodbyes," he said at last.

"Well, then, fine. Maybe we'll see you sometime. When we visit or something."

"Right." He knew he'd never see her again.

She turned away from him then, briskly impatient. "Come on, Sarah, that's enough. Let's get going."

"But, mama!" the little girl protested, albeit weakly, as if already knowing her voice wouldn't be heard.

"No buts. If we don't leave now, we'll have to wait for the traffic to clear after the parade is over." With that, Justine turned on her heel and strode away.

Jim watched as Sarah heaved a sigh of resignation, grabbed a few more pieces of candy off the sidewalk and hurried after her mother without a backward glance.

As if they'd never meant anything to each other.

"Can't see! Can't see!" Jim looked down as Liam tugged at his elbow. "Can't see!" he protested.

Jim realized a family had stepped in front of them while he'd been speaking with Justine. "All right, Bud. I hear you. How'd you like to sit up on my shoulders for a bit? We can let Uncle Doug collect the candy."

Liam's face lit up. "Sure!"

Jim passed the hat stuffed with candy to Doug and hoisted Liam atop his shoulders. Liam laughed and bobbed excitedly as he remarked on the view from up high.

Jim's lips twisted wryly.

A week ago he'd been anguished over the trauma little Sarah must have experienced when Justine had ended their relationship.

How ironic to realize the only one traumatized by it was him.

"You're NOT GOING THROUGH with it, are you?" Rachel asked as their float made its languid progress down Main Street.

Grace didn't pretend to misunderstand. "Fifty bucks is fifty bucks." She smiled serenely at the crowd and gave a beauty-pageant wave as Kate tossed candy to a group of kids clustered by the road.

The pickup stopped again, and the three women suppressed a groan. They were nearly to the end now, but the high school band was doing another number, and they'd have another couple minutes in the broiling heat.

"Oh look, Kate!" Rachel said. "There's your little guy up ahead. See? In front of the police station."

Kate scanned the crowd and then stopped short when she spied Liam atop Jim's shoulders. She blinked and then blindly dipped her hand in the candy bucket again, threw another handful at the same kids she had a moment before.

As she watched her son bouncing and smiling on Jim's shoulders, leaning down to giggle in his ear, it struck Kate that life could be unbelievably cruel. If she didn't know better, she would guess she was witnessing the easy exchange between a father and his son. A family. And if things were different—less complicated and unbelievably screwed up—maybe that wouldn't be such a stretch.

But reality was a far cry from appearances.

"Where's Doug?" asked Grace.

"I don't know," replied Rachel. "Oh, wait! Look! He's picking up candy. Isn't that sweet? He's going to be such a good dad."

"Yeah," Grace agreed as the pickup lurched into blessed motion again, "and your sex life will be dead."

"Oh, stop teasing. Look at you! You're wiggling your booty for bucks."

Grace grinned and tossed some candy, clearly not offended by the gentle ribbing. "You're not such a goodie-two-shoes as you like to pretend. You just haven't had the right kind of offer."

"Right. You've got me pegged. I'm a pole-dancer looking for my big break."

"I dare you," Grace said laughingly.

"Dare me what?" Rachel asked as she threw out the last of her candy.

"I dare you both!" Grace said, looking at Kate now, too. "When we get to the police station, I dare you both to wiggle your booties and blow kisses with me. Come on! It'll be a hoot!"

"Oh, I don't—" began Kate.

"What do we get if we do?" Rachel asked.

"I'll split the fifty bucks three ways."

Rachel turned to Kate. "I don't know. Not a lot of incentive. What do you think?"

"I…" They were nearly at the police station now. Liam was waving maniacally at her, Jim was grinning, looking more the picture of happy fatherhood than Randy ever had.

Kate stared at them on the sidewalk, the heat shimmering in waves over her vision, and suddenly it all struck her as cruelly unfair.

She couldn't say what, exactly, was unfair. Was it the vague sense of spending three decades of her life being the goodie-two-shoes Grace had just made fun of and still ending up empty-handed? Where was *her* adoring husband collecting candy? Where was *her* sexy admirer daring her to do something slightly naughty?

As if from a distance, Rachel and Grace turned, smiling, waving, egging her on. She stared at Jim and Liam and tried to absorb the unfairness of timing and fate.

Her pulse quickened, the heat rolling over her, making her dizzy. Emotion, dark and unfamiliar, swarmed her, a solar flare, blistering in intensity, robbing her of air and reason.

"Damn you," she breathed, the capriciousness of fate crashing over her in a wave. *Damn you, Randy Mitchell! Damn you for not being the father Liam deserved. Damn you for not being the husband I deserved. And damn you for being so RECKLESS, SELF-CENTERED and STUPID that you ran yourself into a Goddamn tree!!*

Rachel caught Kate's eye, her brows knitted in confusion and concern, but Kate felt strangely numb, set apart, the strumming, red-hot anger blocking everything out. Blanketing everything.

Till there was nothing.

No horns or sirens. No cheering, milling crowds. No parade. Nothing. Not even anger.

She spun around again, her heart racing, frantic, her hand gripping the stiff fabric of her skort as they inched closer...

And there he was. *Jim.* He stood on the sidewalk, watching her with laughing hazel eyes. And she wanted what they promised with every fiber of her being.

And at the last moment she leaned forward, brought her hand to her lips... smiled brilliantly... and blew him a kiss.

Like a dreamer bursting through to a world of sound and color, Kate watched the answering grin on Jim's face, heard her own laughter bubble up in the shimmering heat.

Nana was right.

Kate didn't want a superhero.

All she really wanted was one good man.

CHAPTER TWENTY-FOUR

KATE'S TANK TOP STUCK to her back in the heat. She tugged at the hem of her skort and trailed Grace and Rachel up the sidewalk toward the men, fighting the urge to bolt. Jim stood, watching as she approached, and even though he'd seen her with far fewer clothes on, she suddenly felt over-exposed. True, she hadn't actually wiggled anything, booty or otherwise, but she'd been as subtle as Marilyn Monroe holding her skirt down over an air vent.

"Ah, our saucy women of red, white and blue." Doug bent to kiss his wife. "Now, how come you didn't blow *me* a kiss?"

Flustered, Kate turned in time to see Grace elbow Jim in the side. "Don't look so disappointed," she said. "Doug didn't even get a kiss from his own wife."

"I didn't say a thing," Jim murmured, though he caught Kate's eye again, his look searching and a little confused. Her face grew warmer, if that were possible. No wonder he was confused! One minute she was telling him no more sex and the next minute she was blowing kisses? What guy *wouldn't* be confused?

He held out his cap. "Here's Liam's haul. Thought you'd want to decide what he could eat. You can return the hat later." He thrust it toward her until she took it.

Oh God. She felt like an idiot. Here he was collecting candy like a grown-up and she—

"Now what was *that* all about, young lady?"

"Nana!" Kate whirled, embarrassment raising the temperature in her face another few degrees.

Nana raised an eyebrow. "Looks like you kids could use a cool down. Why don't I take the little guy here around the corner for some ice cream or lemonade? Lucky's has air conditioning…"

Kate turned to look through the front window of the local pub. A patron in the front table pulled a cardigan over her shoulders. Grace sighed longingly.

"I wouldn't turn away a cold beer." Doug said.

"They do make fabulous fried ice cream," Rachel added.

"I'm not sure." Kate glanced at Jim, wondering if he wanted her to join them or not after her flagrant public flirtation. She'd wanted to keep things light and casual between them, but she feared she was being the Queen of Mixed Signals.

His eyes never left her face. "I could go for something sweet," he finally said.

"Me, too," Grace added. She waved and winked briefly to a police officer as he directed the last of the parade traffic then opened the door to the pub.

Inside, their hostess led them to two corner tables. Kate took a seat and blotted her forehead with a napkin. Jim was still standing, hovering, when the police officer they'd seen outside strode toward them.

"Tsk. Tsk. You disappoint me, Grace." The officer wore a teasing grin despite holding his body with the rigid control of his profession.

"I know," Grace sighed, "but if I'd come through, you probably would have brought me in for indecent exposure. Damned if I do. Damned if I don't."

"Jeff, you joining us?" Jim asked.

"No. Still on duty. Just came to cool off for a minute. Say hi." His eyes never left Grace as she draped languidly over her chair.

"How's that working for you?" she asked.

"Not well." He watched her another long moment, gave an odd look toward Rachel, then mumbled something about getting back to work before turning on his heel and heading for the door.

"What was that all about?" Jim asked.

Grace shrugged. "He said he'd give me fifty bucks if I blew him a kiss and wiggled my booty."

Jim's eyebrows shot to his hairline. "I'm not even going to ask how you came to that agreement."

"It's no big deal."

"Tell that to Jeff."

"When are you going to stop teasing him?" Rachel asked. "He's a good guy. It's not fair to lead him on like that."

Grace grabbed the dessert menu and began fanning herself with it. "You know why."

"Why?" Jim asked. "Jeff's a decent guy. Plus, he has a job. That's better than your last boyfriend."

Grace rolled her eyes. "You wouldn't understand. Jeff Dayton doesn't 'date.' Not like a normal person."

"What are you talking about? He's dating someone new every time I turn around." Jim pulled up a chair next to Kate.

"Maybe he's only happy on the hunt," said Doug. "As soon as things get serious, he loses interest. Some guys are like that. They don't stick around."

"He never struck me as being like that," said Jim.

Rachel twirled her wedding ring then set her hands in her lap. "Maybe there's someone in his past no one else can compare to."

"I don't think he even remembers when we were together," said Grace. "Anyway, it's all ancient history now."

Grace and Jeff dated? Kate looked toward Rachel who was rummaging for something in her purse. Doug abruptly excused himself to wash hands.

Kate scooted her chair over to let Doug out as the waitress arrived to take their drink orders. Jim also adjusted his seat, his knee brushing hers lightly and sending electric shocks up her thigh. Kate scooted her chair a respectable distance away again.

A moment later, Jim leaned toward her ear. "So why didn't *you*, um, flip your skirt and wiggle your booty?"

Kate pressed her lips together, the heat rising in her face—along with other parts of her body. Jim's hazel eyes were dark and playful and reminded her of how he'd looked when he'd arrived at the cottage after the fire call the night before last. "It's only a skort. And maybe I didn't feel like it."

"*Hmm*. But, as a float promoting the Gifts for the Greater Good, I would think you'd want to spread goodwill any way you could."

She couldn't suppress a smile. "Goodwill, huh? I suppose I do feel strongly about supporting charities."

"Indeed."

"And, it *is* important to bring attention to a worthy cause."

"You'd get my attention."

She hid another smile in her napkin then paused as their drinks arrived and they placed their dessert orders.

Jim leaned in again until his mouth was a hairs-breadth from her ear. "So, just to clarify, is a skort one of those skirt-short things?"

She knew her face was more than pink now but didn't care. Flirting with him felt too good. Easy. This was light and casual, right? "Yes. Why?"

He shrugged and slanted a sly grin at her as he pulled the wrapper off his straw. "Just curious."

"Do you think I'm the kind of woman who'd consider doing that if I *weren't* wearing a skort?" she whispered.

His knee slid against her thigh again. She didn't move away this time. "Well, considering some certain comments about the French Riviera you've made in the past, I have to say it does bring it into question..."

"All's fair in love and war," she murmured.

"Not that I'm complaining."

She met his eyes. "You're not, are you?"

"No way. You can wiggle your booty in my direction anytime you feel like it."

"Good to know." She sipped her drink and leaned into him. The hair at his temple was damp with sweat and very sexy. "Just to clarify, is that with a skort... or without?"

He choked on his iced tea, and Kate patted his back, a wicked part of her enjoying his discomfiture more than she could say.

"Whatever feels right," he finally managed.

"Would you two stop whispering down there?" Grace demanded. "I can't hear a thing you're saying over the A/C."

"I think that's the point," Doug said dryly as he took his seat again.

The waitress arrived with desserts for those who'd ordered them and the conversation moved to more neutral ground. Jim sipped his tea and dug into his fried ice cream with gusto. "Want a bite?" he invited.

Kate shook her head, too aware of his thigh against her knee to think about eating. It felt strangely intimate to be touching under the table, their hands and words perfectly poised and presentable above-board. Intimate. And confusing.

Wasn't she the one who'd given him the whole speech on just being friends? So what was she doing flirting and touching his knee under the table? Not that he seemed to mind, precisely, but...

"Guess who we ran into at the parade?" Doug asked, stealing a spoonful of Rachel's dessert.

"*Doug—*" Jim warned.

"Justine. She's moving. Out of town."

"Good riddance," Grace muttered.

"It's for the best," Rachel agreed.

"Who's Justine?" Kate asked.

"Jim's ex," Rachel said, *sotto voce.*

"I'm right here, Rach."

Kate glanced toward him. "I'm sorry."

"Nothing to be sorry about," he insisted.

"You're better off without her," Rachel assured him.

"Didn't have much choice," Grace murmured.

"Had you been together long?" Kate asked.

Jim sipped his tea. Toyed with his straw. "Two years."

"She reunited with her husband over Valentine's Day," Rachel informed Kate in a healthy whisper. "Jim was devastated."

"I wasn't devastated," he asserted, still toying with his straw.

"She was married?" Kate asked.

Jim winced.

"They were separated," Doug interjected.

"He was a jerk," Grace added. She looked around the table. "I mean her husband! A friend of mine worked for him once. He was always leaving the office at the drop of a hat leaving everyone else to pick up the slack. Totally self-absorbed."

Jim rubbed his temple as if fighting off a headache.

"Why would she go back with him if he was such a jerk?" Rachel wondered aloud.

Jim dropped his spoon into his bowl with a clatter. "Maybe she loved him. Who the hell knows? I'm done talking about it. Anyone else done?"

Rachel pursed her lips and nodded. "We're done."

Jim shoved another spoonful of dessert into his mouth with considerably less enthusiasm than before.

A married woman? It settled oddly in Kate's gut to think about Jim with anyone, much less a married woman. Not that she had any claim to him. Not after yesterday morning's speech. But didn't this prove how wrong any further involvement would be? She obviously didn't know a thing about him. Crud, she'd chosen toilet paper with greater care.

Though she didn't blame him for not wanting to talk about it. Who would want to have their failed relationships paraded around for discussion? Families meant well, but sometimes they didn't get it.

Besides, knowing his track record in the love department was no better than hers was perversely satisfying. She had been beginning to feel as if he was too good to be true. Poor guy.

She set a tentative hand on his arm. He glanced up.

"I'm sorry," she mouthed.

He shook his head. "It's in the past. Over. Enough said." She let her hand slip away as he stood up. "You know, I hate to break up the party, but I've got some stuff to take care of this afternoon before the lumberyard closes. If anyone wants the rest of my ice cream... I think I'll head out."

Grace reached forward. "I'll take it!"

"Jim," Rachel pleaded, "we didn't mean—"

He shook his head as he fished some bills out of his wallet for the tab. "Don't, Rach. I'm fine. Just done." He started to leave then turned back again. "Kate? Eight-thirty still okay with you? Fireworks start at nine."

She watched him, wondering whether any of this was a good idea, figured it probably wasn't, then nodded anyway. "Eight-thirty is fine."

"THEY HAD BALLOONS! AND aminals! And trucks!" Liam said excitedly as he zipped around the cottage's living room, his dark hair plastered with sweat to his forehead. "An' I gots ice cream with splinkles!"

Kate narrowly avoided getting knocked over by the whirling dervish that resembled her son and dumped the contents of Jim's cap onto the kitchen counter. Nana unwrapped a chocolate chew and popped it in her mouth.

"Can I have one, too?" asked Liam.

Kate shooed him away. "You've had enough sugar to last you a few more hours. Go run around while I get things cleaned up."

She pulled out a heat-softened candy from Jim's hat and snuck it into the trash. "This chocolate will be impossible to clean out."

"It's on the inside," Nana said breezily, "I wouldn't worry about it.

"I know, but Jim was nice enough to collect it and not just let Liam stuff his face with whatever he could fit in it." Kate eyed her grandmother. "I thought you were only going for ice cream. How did Liam end up with twelve candy wrappers in his pocket?"

Nana snitched another candy and shrugged. "I told him not to overdo."

"Right. Like a three year-old is going to exhibit self-control. Nana. Admit it. You're hopelessly indulgent with him."

"I'm the only great-grandparent he's got. Lord knows I won't be here forever. He ought to enjoy me while he has me."

Kate ran a sponge under the faucet. "You're lucky he didn't throw up on your shoes."

"Like when Randy was supposedly watching him on Easter?"

Too true. And Kate would have been left to clean up—again. Randy had always treated her like his personal hazmat team. Whatever mess he made, he expected her to swoop in and clean it up. Mend fences. Wipe her brush of vanilla paint over all his garish mistakes and make them right again.

The problem was, somewhere along the line, she'd taken that same vanilla brush and run right over herself.

Kate stopped scrubbing Jim's cap and looked at the blur of brown on the inside rim. Deliberately squeezing out the sponge, she set the hopelessly stained cap on the dish drainer to dry.

She wasn't going to make herself Jim's hazmat crew.

She wasn't going to be *that* Kate ever again.

"Don't eat too much candy. I'm going to see if I can settle Liam for his nap."

AFTER NANA LEFT AND LIAM was settled, Kate took a quick, cooling shower, then logged onto the Internet. She checked her e-mail, shot off a couple quick answers to questions posed by other calendar candidates and laughed when she saw Jeff Dayton's photo. She'd have to tactfully suggest he have someone take a shot that was a tad less... intimidating.

Her chat window popped up.

Jim: *Hey! Long time no chat.*

Kate paused, her pulse leaping, then typed a reply.

Liz: *Busy. Busy. So many men, so little time... :)*

Jim: *Something tells me you can handle it.*

Liz: *Oh, yeah. I'm a regular Liz-of-all-trades.*

Jim: *Nothing wrong with an independent woman.*

Liz: *And here I thought men liked saving damsels in distress.*

Jim: *Only in the movies. In real life? Not so much so.*

Liz: *You mean I've been marketing myself wrong all these years? Just kidding. What's up?*

Jim: *Wondering if you had a chance to look at the photos I sent you?*

Liz: *Not yet. Sorry. I wasn't kidding about the other men in my life. LOL*

Jim: *You're involved with other men? I'm shocked. And here I thought I was the only one... I'm leaning toward the first one, the one where I've got one foot on the sawhorse. You?*

Liz: *Okay, looking at photos now...*

Kate opened up the photos and looked at each.

Liz: *I like that one, too. Nice smile. I'm also partial to the one with you in the lake.*

Jim: *Which one?*

Liz: *The second. The one where your hand is on the dock. I like your expression.*

Jim: *I'm still wearing a T-shirt. You sure the bare-chested one isn't better?*

Kate looked at the photos. The bare-chested one made her drool. Then she thought of other women drooling over Jim. Ex-girlfriends. Potential girlfriends. Not that she had any hold on him, but the idea made her stomach queasy.

Liz: *Leave a little something to the imagination. The second one is good.*

Jim: *My ego will pretend it's not bruised. Okay, one vote for T-shirt by dock. You sure it's better than the sawhorse one?*

Liz: *I like them both, and the sawhorse one definitely has your profession coming into play, which I like, but...*

Jim: *But?*

Liz: *The lake one looks more relaxed. It's not so cocky looking, just—can I say this?—naturally good looking.*

And sexy as hell, she thought, but at least she had the presence of mind not to type *that.*

Jim: *Okay. I'll let you say that.*

Liz: *Sorry. Not trying to be untoward!*

Jim: *No offense. Soothes my bruised ego.*

Liz: *Would hate to inflict damage to your ego. Can I also say you're awfully chatty for a guy and you type fast, too?*

The seconds ticked by. Kate bit her lip. It felt somewhat surreal flirting with Jim this way. At least 'Liz' got to be friends with him. After the ways things had gone at Lucky's, she knew friendship would be much more complicated in real life.

Jim: *Like you said once. I need to get out more. As for the typing, no girls in school thought I was cute enough to type my papers for me. Plenty of practice.*

Liz: *Nice try, but I don't believe that for a minute. I've seen your pictures.* ☺

Jim: *I'll take that as a compliment. And may I say, whomever you are, you're easy to talk to. (And surprisingly well-versed in modern technology for a gal in her 70's.)*

Liz: *I'm not nearly that old!*

Jim: *So why are you doing this calendar thing?*

Because I was guilted into it by your grandmother, and I'd rather do this than contemplate my apparent lack of passion and purpose? Right.

Like she'd tell him *that*. Kate's fingers fidgeted on the keyboard. What would Liz Bennet say?

Liz: *I like balls?*

Kate stared in horror at the screen. ACK! *I like balls??* Where was the delete key??

Liz: *I mean DANCING balls!*

She stared at the screen again. Oh God! Could this get any worse? What must he be thinking?

Liz: *Like Liz Bennet? You know, THOSE kind of dancing... dances? Oh, just shoot me now!*

Jim: *When I'm done laughing.* ☺

July 4
Mr. Darcy. Is there a woman on earth who wouldn't throw herself at this man's shoes? And yet, what do we really know about him? Okay, yes, he's good looking and noble and unbelievably rich, but forgive me for saying, he's also a bit of a starched shirt. Give me laughter and fireworks over stiff nobility any day of the week.

CHAPTER TWENTY-FIVE

"LIAM, *PLEASE*. IT'LL BE FUN!"

"No wanna go!" Kate watched with dismay as Liam balled his little hands into fists by his sides and jutted out his bottom lip. Jim would be by any minute to pick them up, and Liam was throwing a first-rate tantrum. "No go!" he reiterated, as if she didn't already get the idea.

"Why not? We saw the fireworks last year. Remember when we went with Nana and Mrs. Pemborly?"

"No go!" he cried again, his little lip wavering now.

Kate sat back on her heels and blew out an exasperated breath. Just what she needed. She'd spent Liam's entire nap selecting just the right outfit, had washed and restyled her hair, then applied fresh toenail polish—candy pink this time. The last thing she'd expected was for Liam to object, for crying out loud.

"Liam—" she began, but the knock on the door cut into what she'd planned to say. "Look. Jim is here to take us to the show. He'll be disappointed if we don't go."

"No go!" Liam grunted at her back as she opened the door.

"Hi." Jim greeted her with an easy smile and a wave for Liam. "Ready?"

Kate pressed her lips together. "We may not be going after all."

"Why not?" Jim stepped into the room and glanced around for the cause of the problem.

"Liam doesn't want to go."

"How come, Bud?"

"Don't wanna," came the gruff reply.

Jim knelt in front of Liam. "Have you ever seen the fireworks?" Liam nodded. "Did you not like them?" Jim asked softly.

"Too loud," Liam whispered back, his dark eyes troubled.

"Ah," Jim nodded sagely. "That's because you're young and have sensitive hearing. Rock and roll will fix that in time. You like the way the fireworks light up the sky, though, right?"

Liam nodded again.

"Fine. No problem. How about I loan you my hearing protectors, just for tonight?" At Liam's frown, Jim chuckled. "They go over your ears so noises don't sound so loud. Big boys wear them for when we use power tools."

"Like chainsaws?"

"Exactly."

"All right!" Liam whooped as he raced for the door. "I get to chain saw!"

Jim glanced at Kate in surprise.

"It's okay," she laughed as she collected the cardigan she'd chosen in case it got cool, "we can explain it to him on the way there."

They rode in relative silence, Liam chattering periodically about chain saws and big boy tools. Kate was content to watch the passing scenery with an occasional furtive glance at Jim's profile.

She hid a smile as she remembered the steamy looks Jim had given her over his ice cream this afternoon at Lucky's, the shivers of awareness coursing through her at each innocent contact.

And then, the pickup brought her back to the present as it thumped across the field by the high school.

"They set the fireworks off over the river," Jim informed her. "The riverbank is a great place to view them, but it can get a little rowdy down there with the teenagers. Probably better for Liam if we watch from here."

Kate nodded. A handful of cars and pickups were already scattered over the field as people arrived for the show. The sound of crickets chirping and children running and laughing in the twilight lent a festive air to the evening. She slid out of the cab.

"We're not meeting your family?" She glanced around, surprised not to see a familiar face.

"Oh. They'll be here. Here and there. I didn't know you were hoping to see—"

"Oh. No. I just thought we might—"

"Yeah."

"Yeah."

Jim cleared his throat. "I think Liam will enjoy watching from the truck bed. I brought some blankets and stuff to make it more comfortable."

Kate looked over as Jim let down the tailgate then unrolled a sleeping bag for padding. He unrolled another and laid it next to the first, then glanced over his shoulder at Kate as if seeking her approval.

Oh, yes. It looked very accommodating. She'd been on less padded surfaces with this man without complaint.

Something of her thoughts must have shown in her expression, because Jim's grin grew warm and intimate. He glanced at the sky, then his watch. "I think they'll be starting soon. We should probably get Liam set so he doesn't freak out on us."

Kate nodded and tried not to think about Jim and sleeping bags and padded surfaces as he retrieved the hearing protectors and set them over Liam's ears.

Liam wiggled his head and grinned. "I look like a big boy?"

"Absolutely," Jim agreed as he helped Liam onto the tailgate. "Why don't you scootch back so I can help your mom up?"

Liam scrambled into the truck. Jim turned to Kate.

"I think I can manage," she said with a soft laugh.

"I think I'd really like to help," he said just as softly.

She caught her lip with her teeth as his hands came to rest on her waist. His warmth seeped through the light cotton top she wore as he picked her up and set her on the tailgate. Then he nudged her knees apart, leaned in and brushed his lips lightly over hers.

For a moment she returned the kiss then realized where they were and what they were doing. "Liam," she whispered urgently against Jim's lips, trying to pull away.

"—isn't even looking," Jim said, pulling back. "Relax. I wasn't going to jump you right here on the athletic field."

She felt heat creep into her cheeks and tried not to feel hurt by his tone. "It's just—"

"You don't want to do anything in front of Liam. I get it. Been down this road before." Jim stepped into the back of the pickup, leaving Kate to scramble up after him.

"I'm sorry." She fumbled for the right words even as they stuck in her throat. "I've never... He's never seen... I hadn't thought how I'd react."

Jim busied himself rearranging the blankets he'd brought into a makeshift pillow for Liam and her. "I get it, Kate."

She reached out and grasped his arm. How could he get what she couldn't explain to herself? "Jim, you caught me off guard. I just need to think about how to handle you."

He gave a hard little laugh. "I didn't realize I was out of control. I'll try to keep my hands off you from now on."

"You're not," she said, fighting exasperation. "That's not what I meant."

"No?"

"No. What happened Thursday night... I'm not good at this. I've never done this before."

"What? Blown hot and cold on a guy?"

"I guess I deserve that. " Kate glanced uneasily at Liam. Thankfully the hearing protectors made him oblivious to their exchange.

Jim ran a weary hand over his face. "I'm sorry. That was probably out of line." He shook his head, sat down and linked his hands around his knees.

Kate took her seat next to him. "Look. I can't pretend there's nothing going on between us. I don't *want* to pretend that. But, I don't understand it either. This whole thing with you—it's taken me by surprise."

Jim nodded and stared off toward the river.

"If I can't explain it to myself, I don't know how I'd explain it to Liam if he were to ask questions." She pressed her lips together and stared at the river, too, the warm night air unaccountably chill. "I have no regrets, though," she finally whispered. "I can't make any promises, but I have no regrets."

"Just for fun, is that it?" Jim turned to her now, his eyes implacable.

"Yes. *No!* I don't know. My life is so complicated right now..."

"And you don't need me to be another complication," he finished for her, turning away again.

Kate sighed and wished things could be different. Knew there was no way they could be.

"You're not a complication," she lied, wishing it were true. "You're just... a surprise I haven't figured out how to handle yet."

He looked at her now, his eyes registering some emotion she didn't want to acknowledge. "It we're nothing serious, then there's nothing to figure out, is there?"

She sat back without answering and waited for the show, wishing she could go back in time, kiss him and not worry about anything else. But she couldn't. She couldn't *not* kiss this man when he was intent on kissing her any more than she could *not* be pregnant with another man's child.

It was better they put some distance between them. Whether Jim knew it or not.

A wistful ache squeezed her heart. "I like you, you know."

He pressed his lips together, and she wished she could kiss away the twinge of regret she saw there. "I like you, too, Kate."

"I'm not trying to be difficult."

He ran a hand through his hair. "Neither am I."

"I don't mean to be a tease. I've never been that kind of person, but I need to figure some things out before we go any further." He let a raised eyebrow talk for him. "Fine. I know. They've gone plenty far. Farther than I ever intended—and I don't regret it, but I'm not looking for a relationship right now. I *can't* get into a relationship right now." She tried to ignore how good he felt beside her, how much her fingers ached to brush the hair at his temple and make all the awkwardness between them fade away. "Friends?"

He looked at her, wordlessly, as the fireworks began to burst overhead. She held her breath as he leaned in and pressed a single kiss to her hair, then pulled back. "Let's watch the show," he said.

Kate nodded and swallowed over the tightness in her throat.

Lying back, she watched the vibrant display, listened as the *boom! boom!* of the fireworks echoed down the river, and wished she were three again like Liam whose problems could be solved by a simple pair of earmuffs.

After a while, Jim leaned toward her. "Can I ask you a personal question?" His lips brushed her hair as he spoke, his breath warm on her nape. She shivered. In a good way.

"Sure," she said, though she wasn't sure about anything anymore.

"How come your toenails are always so glitzed up, but you never paint your fingernails?"

Kate looked down at her hands in the dark. She knew what they'd look like: short, practical, plain. "Randy didn't like my taste in nail polish. He said the colors were unsophisticated." She shrugged. "People don't usually see my toes."

"*Huh,*" was all he said.

She looked at the sky. *Boom. Boom.*

"Kind of an idiot, wasn't he?"

She turned then, startled, and stared at Jim's profile. He was watching the show overhead. He didn't look like he expected her to be angry. Didn't look like he expected any reply at all. It was as if he'd stated some irrefutable, unremarkable fact that didn't bear comment.

She turned and looked at the sky, too, letting the colors wash over her. "No," she finally said, even though she was sure he couldn't hear her over the fireworks. "I was."

July 13
Blessing in disguise. I've always wondered about that phrase. I mean,
truly, who wants a blessing to disguise itself? What if you don't recognize
it and somehow miss it—or throw it away? Seems to me, blessings should
shout from the rooftops all their considerable charms so we can take full
advantage of them. Miracles, too. Just saying...

CHAPTER TWENTY-SIX

BEING PREGNANT HAD ITS advantages. No need to stock up on
tampons. No wild PMS-y mood swings. No need for romance-killing
protection while having erotic fling with sexy neighbor...

Kate fought back tears and smoothed the quilt over her bed. How
could she have been so stupid? Good question. About so many things.
But second-guessing her judgment didn't change the fact that here she
was, more than two months after the blessed event/scene of the crime,
and still no visit from Aunt Flo.

She was so royally screwed.

She'd have to schedule a prenatal exam. But September, when she
was back in Connecticut, was soon enough for that. She knew enough to
take her vitamins and eat right in the meantime.

"Why did you have to be so damn fertile?" she demanded of the
square box sitting on her dresser. She'd moved it from the mantel after
Nana had threatened to fertilize her roses with it. "Huh? Couldn't your
drinking have pickled that, too?"

Randy's ashes didn't answer; they just sat in all their neatly-
contained finality.

In total opposition to her life.

As if mocking her sense of internal chaos, the phone rang at the
same moment someone knocked at the front door. Kate briskly swiped at
the tears on her face and peered out the window. *What?* She picked her
phone off the dresser. "Hello?"

"Kate! Thank God you're there."

"Hi, Mom."

"I need advice. Would you say you'd tend toward Eastern or
Western medicine as a rule?"

"I don't know. Depends. Ma, there's someone at the door..."

"If they conflicted, that is. Your father, as you might expect, is siding with the doctor, but you know how I feel about those chemicals they call modern medicines. Ahmed says that if we purge our aura that might help dissolve the crystals."

"What crystals? Who's Ahmed? Are we talking about your dog again?"

"Uric acid. My yoga instructor. And no, I am not talking about Sandy."

"Then what are we talking about?"

"Your father's gout."

"Dad has gout? Since when?" Kate hurried down the stairs toward the front door. "Actually, Ma, don't answer that. I can't talk right now. Someone's at the door."

Kate pulled the door open, covering her phone with her hand. "Can I help you?"

Jeff Dayton stood on her porch and nodded briefly. "I'm Jeff Dayton from the Sugar Falls Police Department..."

Kate's heart thudded with dread in her chest as she stared at the shiny, dangerous things strapped to his person. "Yes. Yes, I know. Is something wrong?" *Was it Nana?*

"...it's incredibly painful, dear, he's been hobbling around the house and complaining for days..." her mother droned on in her ear.

"Ma! Not now!" Kate hissed.

"No. No. This is a personal call." Jeff winced slightly and avoided her gaze. "The thing is, I need to get some pictures taken for this fundraising calendar Gifts for the Greater Good is putting together. Jim told me you'd helped him out, had a photography degree or something, and I wondered..."

"You'd think he'd been kicked in the family jewels or something the way he's been carrying on. Of course, it *is* swollen to three times its normal size..."

Kate nearly dropped her phone. "You want me to take your picture?"

Jeff nodded.

"Oh, I don't think you want to see it, honey. Truly. It is *not* pretty," said her mother.

"Uh..." said Kate.

"Yeah. I know," Jeff said. "We don't know each other, but I thought maybe that'd make it easier. One of the guys down at the station took the last one, but the calendar organizer didn't think it was appropriate. Jim said you were really good."

"He did?"

"A natural."

Kate worried her lip. Is that all he said? How close *were* these guys? "I don't know..."

"I'd pay you for your time." She chewed her lip. Money was always good, but... "Hey, I understand. It was a long shot. I just thought... I'm sorry to bother you."

He turned to step off the porch. Oh, crud. It was Ruth's calendar. How hard could it be to take a few lousy pictures of the guy? It *was* for a good cause. Kate stepped toward him. "How much? I mean... wait." He faced her again. He was actually pretty attractive now that she looked. Not that she *was* looking. "I suppose... I suppose I could try. I make no promises, though. I'm no professional. I only studied art..."

He smiled then. A genuinely gorgeous smile. "Thanks. I appreciate it. I'll catch up with you later to set up a time?"

After exchanging phone numbers and waving goodbye, Kate tuned back in to her mother. Obviously she'd missed a little something.

"... so we're coming for a visit. A long weekend, actually. Rosaria won't watch Sandy longer than that, and you know how she hates the Doggy Inn."

Visit? Kate sucked in a panicked breath and looked around. Nope, she was not in her bedroom. At least then she might have convinced herself she was having a nightmare—and not a conversation with the woman who'd brought her into the world.

"I'm worried about you," her mother continued. "You haven't said boo to anyone down here since you left for that godforsaken place."

"Sugar Falls has a name, Ma. It's part of the United States even, so it's really not so much a backwater as you seem to think."

"You know what I mean. New Hampshire is a fine place to visit, but it's not a place a person *lives*. I don't know what possessed your grandmother to move there."

"She grew up here. It's home to her."

"Anyway, we'll be there a week from Thursday," her mother blithely continued, not bothering to wait for an actual invitation. "Your father insists on beating the rush hour traffic through Hartford—the early bird gets the worm, as they say. We should arrive mid-afternoon the twenty-third."

"You're staying *here*?" Kate croaked into the phone.

"No, heavens no. A hotel. I understand the cottage you're staying at is more rustic than your father or I would like."

Kate heaved a sigh of relief even as she glanced around the room. Soft blue bead-board walls, white trim, and weathered wood floors surrounded her in comfort and reassuring simplicity. "Rustic? Who said it was rustic?"

"I heard Ruth Pearson was having her grandson do a number of repairs on it, now that she's moved in with his parents. I just assumed..."

"He updated some fixtures in the bathroom. Nothing major."

"Yes, well, we'll find a hotel just the same. I know you wouldn't want us to crowd you."

Right. And that was why they were driving nearly five hours to rural New Hampshire? So they wouldn't crowd her?

"See if you can find a nice restaurant, would you? We'd love to take you out for your birthday while we're there."

"My birthday isn't until next month."

"True, but we won't be able to make it back up there in August. We still haven't celebrated Liam's birthday, either. Dinner together will kill two birds with one stone."

"I already threw him a party."

"He's three. I'm sure he hardly remembers."

Kate's jaw began to ache from the strain of not grinding her teeth. "Right. Well, we'll see you next Thursday. Should I make reservations for that Friday night?"

"That would be lovely. I hate to make you go through all this trouble for your own birthday, but we really don't know where would be appropriate."

"No problem. Really. See you next week."

As she disconnected, Kate blew out a breath and shook her head. *Lovely. Simply lovely.* Here she'd purposefully gone to a place a half day's travel from her family to get away from them, and they were coming to visit?

True, she was near Nana, but Nana had had the good sense to retire *to* New Hampshire instead of Florida or New Mexico like so many of her parent's friends. Nana clearly knew a good thing when she saw it—and this *place* felt so much more honest, vibrant, to her than anywhere else Kate had ever been.

She stepped over the threshold and stood on the front porch. There were no sandy beaches or waving palms. No giant cacti, rugged rock formations or sunsets that engulfed the horizon in picture-postcard beauty.

What she saw was much simpler. Quieter. Trees hugged the shoreline, the surrounding hills intermittently broken by a roof, or small, irregular lawn. The water, a deep shadowy green at the shore, moved in shimmering, blinding ripples further out. Native stone dotted the lake's edge and formed walls, fireplaces, and the occasional garden border.

As far as she was concerned, it was more than a place to visit. If you were lucky, it was a place you could call home.

Kate listened as the wind chimes sang softly in the breeze.

But her home was in Connecticut. Wasn't it?

CHAPTER TWENTY-SEVEN

JIM TOLD HIMSELF HE WASN'T mooning around Kate. Sure, they'd had sex once upon a time, but that didn't go away just because they called themselves "friends" now. This infatuation he had for her wasn't going away by avoiding her, either. Not that he'd done *that* particularly well.

Jim stopped to admire the flower beds on his way in, neatly ordered and brought back to life through Kate's tending. To the right was the little rock garden wall he'd helped her rebuild last Sunday. He'd been thinking about the fireworks the night before when he'd seen her struggling to move the heavy stones. It only seemed polite to offer his back and pry-bar for a couple hours. Liam had pretended the empty spaces between the stones were caves for his matchbox cars until Kate had planted them with fresh little pink and purple blooms.

Oh, hell. They *were* neighbors. Would be for the whole summer. Bringing her dinner on Monday Madness two-for-one pizza night was just being neighborly. Like taking Liam fishing the last few days had been neighborly. And going with them to see the concert on the town common yesterday afternoon with Grams and his folks...

At the sudden scream from inside, Jim dropped the pizzas on the porch swing and burst through Kate's front door.

"Liam, stay where you are! Don't come in—" Kate's voice came from upstairs until another screech cut off her distant warning. Jim took the stairs two at a time.

"Kill it, Mommy! Kill it!" Liam yelled as Jim skidded to a stop outside the bedroom.

"*Jim!*" Kate gasped. "Don't block my exit!"

"Wh—?" But he didn't have time to finish the thought, as Kate screeched again and squirted a can of something at a buzzing noise near the window.

"Here let me—" he said, attempting to relieve her of the can of insecticide.

"No! I've got it!" She inched toward the window. "They've built a nest in the eave, I think," she panted, eyes wide as she warily pulled back the curtain. "There was one in here yesterday and I vacuumed it up. Today there's—" she shuddered and her eyes grew huge as a black and yellow insect buzzed across the ceiling toward him.

She turned as one with the can of insecticide and Jim reacted as anyone would—faced with a phobic woman armed with poison—he swung his arm to knock the can from her hands before she could do him any harm. It was only dumb luck he angered the stinging insect in the process.

"*Sh—!*" Jim cut himself short as he slapped dead the cause of his sudden pain. The can clattered to the floor, Kate squealed again and Liam stared at the whole spectacle from the doorway in avid, wide-eyed excitement.

"Ohmigod! Did you get stung? You got stung! Where's the bug spray? I'll get it." Kate was already re-arming herself as Jim shook off the surprise of getting stung—on the upper lip, no less.

"It's dead, Kate. I killed it. Save the spray, and I'll take care of the nest after dark."

"You'd do that?"

"Yeah. Though if you've got any ice, I wouldn't mind. My lip is going numb."

"Oh, no. Is that where it got you? I can't believe all the bees around here."

"Technically that was a hornet."

He would have shrugged off her concern except she was even now touching his face with the lightest brush of her fingertips. They were soft and tender and took his mind off being nearly blinded with bug killer and taking a hit in the process. "Here," he said, pointing to his upper lip.

"Mommy, kiss it! Her make it better!" Liam suggested helpfully.

"True. You could kiss it and make it better," He teased.

Kate stared at his lips. "I, ah..."

"I wouldn't refuse."

"I, um..."

"Mommy, he hurt!" cried Liam.

"It's okay, Bud. I think your mommy's not sure it will help."

"It will!"

"It really does hurt." Like a son-of-a-bitch, but he wasn't going to make a big deal of it. She looked miserable.

Which was about how he felt.

"Mom!" Liam all but yelled.

If he weren't in so much discomfort, he would have found Liam's concern for his welfare amusing.

Giving in to Liam's insistence, Kate leaned toward Jim, her apology in her eyes, and brushed her lips over his.

"That's not where it hurts," he whispered against her lips.

He had to fight a laugh as her eyes shot open. "It's not?"

"*Uh-uh.* You have to go deeper to reach the hurt spot." He had no idea what made him tease her this way. But with her lips so close, her eyes so blue... he knew how good she'd taste. What harm was in a kiss?

She bit her lip. "I don't want to hurt you."

"You wouldn't." Then he realized, too late, she wasn't talking about the hornet sting anymore.

"I already have," she whispered miserably as she pulled away.

"Don't." He grabbed her elbow before she could retreat entirely. "I'm a big boy, Kate. I don't need you to protect me." His lips tilted. "I think I can handle a kiss. Bug spray in the eye, that's another story."

Her lips curved, the tension sighing out of her body. Her skin was warm under his fingers. Soft. He fought the urge to rub his thumb over it. He couldn't think of a reason to keep holding her arm, so he reluctantly let it go and went to inspect the scene of the crime. Two black and yellow hornets lay on the floor in pools of insecticide. Poor devils.

"I don't like bees," she said.

"Hornets, actually," he mumbled, trying to see... oh, yeah, just outside the window. He could take it out after dark. He stepped back and turned toward Kate again. "And I'm not feeling too warm and fuzzy toward them either." At least that's what he tried to say. It came out more like *I'm naw feewing too wam an futhy towar them eitha.*

"Oh God, are you swelling?" Kate touched his lip gingerly, staring at his mouth in a clinical, non-sensual way. He much preferred the look she'd given him a few moments before. "Are you allergic? Let me get you some antihistamine just the same. Are you feeling okay? Light-headed? Do you think we should take you to the ER?"

He shook his head and touched his lip, surprised at how tender it had grown in such a short time. But he'd never had a reaction to any sting before. He'd never been stung in the face before, either.

She chewed her own sweetly full lip and shooed Liam out the door ahead of them. "Come with me. Before it gets any worse."

Before long, he found himself on the couch clutching a bag of ice to his face. Kate brought him a bottle of antihistamine and a glass of water. "It says one to two every four hours." She peered worriedly over the top of the bottle at him. "Better take two."

He took the little pink pills, washed them down, and handed back the glass. "Bedda in no time," he predicted. Half his face felt numb and a bit stiff. He attempted a smile with the other half.

Liam sidled up beside him and peered intently at his face with all the subtlety of a three year-old. "Mommy's kiss not work?"

Despite his condition, Jim laughed and ruffled Liam's hair. "She ca thwy agin waher," he suggested, giving Kate what he hoped was a friendly, albeit suggestive, leer.

Kate shook her head. "Incorrigible," she murmured, although Jim saw her eyes crinkle with humor.

"What's incorrbigible?" Liam wanted to know.

"Unable to be corrbidged," Kate replied. "I'm sorry. I shouldn't make fun of you."

"I wath twyin to hep," Jim said hoping for brownie points for being cutely pathetic. "Oh! Almoth forgot. Pitha on the porth."

Kate stared at him blankly for a few moments before comprehension dawned.

He rested his head on the bank of the couch and closed his eyes. Not being a hero was tough on a guy.

"YOU ALIVE?"

Jim blinked at the face peering over the back of the couch and wrestled himself into a sitting position. The room was dim, the windows dark beyond the curtains. He rubbed his eyes and ran a hand through his hair.

"He's alive!"

How long had that antihistamine knocked him out for? A decade? Jim yawned widely. "I'm what?"

"Liam, hush! Jim's resting." Kate hurried down the stairs, grabbed her son, and told him he needed to go brush teeth before Jim could ask again what the kid had said. "I'm sorry. I was on the phone or I would have kept him out of here. Was he bothering you?"

"No." Jim yawned again. "No. He—" He shook his head to clear away the cobwebs, ran a hand over his face. "How long was I out?"

"A couple hours."

"A couple—?" He peered at his watch. "Those little pills pack a big wallop, don't they?"

"The good news is—the swelling's gone."

He touched his lip tentatively. "You're right." He tested a half smile. "Guess that kiss did the trick after all."

163

Kate's cheeks grew pink as she perched on the end of the sofa. She picked at the fringe on an afghan that lay over the back of the couch.

He ran another hand over his face and swung his legs to the floor. "I can't believe I fell asleep on your couch."

"It's okay. You were injured in the line of duty. Now that you're awake, would you like some pizza?"

"Pizza? Oh, yeah. Sure."

"I'll get it started then I've got to get Liam to bed. He was waiting for you to wake up. He's been worried about you."

Jim turned toward Liam's giant eyes. The kid hadn't even been gone long enough to wet his toothbrush, but his concern was touching nonetheless. "I'm okay, Bud. Takes more than a hornet and a couple pink pills to keep me down."

"You just like Snow White," Liam said gravely.

"Snow White, eh?"

"He likes the dwarves," Kate said.

Jim pushed his hand through his hair. "I don't know how much I'm like Snow White. I got knocked out, but a kiss didn't wake me, now did it?"

"Yes, it did!" Liam said.

Confused, Jim looked to Kate for clarification.

She stood abruptly, her cheeks blazing. "I'll get that pizza warming," she said before shooing Liam out of the room to get into his pajamas.

Jim watched her retreat, a not unpleasant heat warming his own cheeks. Had Liam said what he thought he said?

Shaking off the residual grogginess, Jim went in search of the can of bug spray and a certain hornet's nest he had a score to settle with.

By the time he was done, Kate had Liam down for the night. They met in the living room.

"I didn't know if you'd want any, but I made some tea," she said.

A plate and mug waited for Jim on the coffee table. "Sounds great. The hornet's nest is taken care of."

"Thank you." Kate tucked her hair behind her ear, something she always seemed to do when she was uncertain. Funny how he already knew that about her.

"Hey, it's the least I could do for passing out on your couch for two hours." He sat down by the plate she'd set for him.

"It's fine." She sat down, too, and curled her feet under her on the opposite side of the couch, a mug of her own in hand. "Would you mind if I turned on the TV?"

"Go ahead." He picked up his pizza for a bite. It felt strange, but pleasantly domestic, to be eating and watching TV with Kate. Nice. "Anything good on?"

She glanced at the clock over the fireplace. "Nine o'clock? I'll see." She made a face. "Some cops show. A documentary..." She flipped the channel again. "Oh! *Happily Ever After*. Do you mind?"

A smiling bachelor and a dozen glamorous women flashed by in the opening scenes of the popular reality matchmaking show.

Jim looked at her. "Seriously? This is what you want to watch?"

"You don't?"

"Never seen it, to be honest, though Grams and Carter watch it religiously."

"They do?"

He took another bite of pizza. "He watches for all the good-looking women, and she's a hopeless romantic. Question is: why do you like it?"

"Who says I do?" she hedged.

He couldn't help but smile. "Please. Liam's in bed in under ten minutes flat? If you didn't feel guilt-ridden to feed me, I'm guessing I'd be out the door, too."

Her cheeks grew rosy as she sipped her tea. "Okay. Fine. I like it. I'm allowed one vice, aren't I?"

He chuckled. "As vices go, I think it ranks pretty low. Still, I don't see the draw. It's not like you're watching for the women unless you've forgotten to tell me something."

She smiled shyly and shook her head, pulled her knees to her chest. "I don't know. I guess I enjoy watching the dance of it all, you know? The thrill of getting to know someone new... the first time they say 'I love you.' I figure I can experience it vicariously through them." She gave a little shrug. "Pathetic, huh?"

"No. Surprising."

"I don't see why. I mean, it's not like it's going to happen to me again. I've had my chance. So, now I watch other people fall in love."

"You think that's what's going on? Who could possibly fall in love in such a short time?"

"You don't believe it could happen?"

He shook his head. "The words are easy to say. Actually feeling it? I don't buy it."

Her head tilted. "You're awfully young to be so jaded."

"And you're awfully young to feel your chances are all used up."

She went silent, then, drank her tea.

"I'm not being jaded," he said, not knowing why he felt the need to elaborate, but feeling a need to explain nonetheless, "just realistic. I've been in relationships that lasted a whole lot longer than a spring TV series, and I can say from experience, it's easy to say the words. Meaning them is something entirely different."

She muted the TV and set the remote between them. "When did you know you meant them?"

He chewed his pizza thoughtfully, knowing he was on the spot, then shrugged. "I don't know if I ever did."

She nodded. They silently stared at the characters on the screen for a few minutes.

"The thing is," he found himself saying, "she said it first and it was just automatic to say it back. I didn't give it much thought." He let out a sigh. "They seem meaningless now. I don't know if I could say them again."

Kate frowned, her knees held tight to her chest, as she worried her lower lip between her teeth. "I don't remember who said it first with Randy and me. After a while, he never said the words. It was always, 'you know I love you,' which—now that I think about it—isn't the same at all."

She shrugged and dropped her feet to the floor. "Any surprise I like to lose myself in the non-reality of a reality show? Sometimes reality is *too* real."

"There's honesty for you."

Her lips tilted wryly. "I suppose so." He watched as she let out a long, soft exhale and turned to him. "So, speaking of honesty, tell me... what are you doing? Here, I mean."

"Watching TV."

"Honestly?"

He set his plate on the coffee table. "Honestly? I haven't a clue. Maybe I'm hoping to get lucky again." At her shocked expression, he continued. "Can you blame me?"

"No." Her expression grew pensive as she glanced away, her cheeks tinting pink. "I suppose not."

"So you've thought about it, too?" She met his gaze. "Was this before or after you kissed me while I was asleep?"

Her face flamed, but he had to give her credit. She didn't look away this time. "It was a medicinal kiss."

"I've heard that before."

She laughed and he felt himself returning her smile. "I just wanted to, okay? I thought Liam was in the kitchen, and you were so incredibly..."

"Yes?"

"...good looking."

"Wow. Last time I checked I was only cute."

She laughed. "Yes, well, we've known each other nearly three episodes now. I've had time to reevaluate."

"Very clever. If I scoff at you about your show now, my ego will have to admit you haven't had time to judge my good looks either."

She chuckled, but when she met his eyes, her smile faded.

"Hey," he said, "I was only joking."

"I know."

"Why the frown?"

She let out a soft sigh. "Because I'm enjoying your company more than I should."

"So we're back to that."

"Jim, you've just gotten out of a bad relationship—"

"Five months ago."

"Still. You don't want to get involved with—"

"Would you let me decide what I want?" He pushed a frustrated hand into his hair.

Kate pressed her lips together. Christ, he even found *that* sexy. "You deserve someone... uncomplicated. Someone who doesn't have enough baggage to sink the Titanic without the iceberg."

He stood up. "You mean I deserve someone who knows what she wants and doesn't push me away with one hand and pull me toward her with the other?"

"Yes," she said quietly. "That's exactly what I mean."

CHAPTER TWENTY-EIGHT

———————————

"SO, WERE YOU THINKING something more serious or, um, relaxed?"

Two days later, Kate gripped her camera like a shield before her. What had she been thinking? Jeff Dayton—a guy she barely knew—was standing on her porch this very moment expecting—what? How had she become the local boudoir photographer anyway?

And, somehow, seeing Jeff in casual clothes instead of his usual uniform only stressed how little she knew about him. He wore a pair of old jeans, sneakers and a concert T-shirt from a heavy metal band you couldn't pay her to see. Sure, he seemed more approachable now, but somehow more dangerous, like the clean-cut hitchhiker you aren't supposed to pick up that turns into a serial killer. Maybe she shouldn't have sent Liam off with Nana. It would have been nice to have backup. Or witnesses.

"Not sure," he said in answer to her question. He shrugged. Wow. Those were broad shoulders. He could probably bury her in the back yard in under an hour with shoulders like that.

"Maybe we should just start with a few poses to get a feel for what might work," she said, stepping away from the door.

He trailed her down the steps into the yard. Stopped. She glanced around. What next? "Why don't we start here on the steps? The light's good for now, and we can see what might work."

"You want me to stand or sit?"

"Whatever feels comfortable."

He sat on the top step, hands clasped between his knees. Kate snapped a couple pictures.

"So, how are you liking Sugar Falls?" he asked.

"It's beautiful. Very relaxing. And everyone's been so welcoming."

He nodded and turned, presumably to give her another angle. *Click. Click.* "The Pearsons are good people," he said.

"They've been very generous to me." Kate stepped a little to her right and snapped another picture.

"I heard Rachel and Doug are thinking of moving back to town," he said.

Kate winced as he crossed his arms across his chest. It was a look that would rattle a witness, but it wouldn't sell many calendars. "Yes. They're very excited."

"Did she say that?" He grimaced. Kate made a mental note to delete that picture.

"I'm guessing she's happy they'll be closer to family and all once the baby is born. You heard she was expecting, right?" she asked.

"Yeah. Jim told me. Great news. She deserves to be happy. Both of them do."

"How about we try some with you standing now?" Jeff rose to his feet and a hanging planter knocked him in the head. "Maybe you could stand near the bottom step for these."

He brushed a couple flower petals from his hair. "Good idea." He turned and posed, his chin tucked down, smile taut.

Kate reluctantly took the picture.

"Have you been friends with the Pearsons for long?" she asked.

"Went to school with Jim." His mouth turned up at the corner slightly. "Dated Grace for a while, but that's ancient history."

"I guess I'd heard that." Kate took another couple shots just so he'd think they were getting somewhere, but knowing none were worth keeping. She needed to get him to lighten up. But how? "Okay, enough on the porch. Let's switch gears."

He stood again, casual, relaxed, hands in pockets. She snapped a quick pic even though he wasn't looking at her but longingly out over the water. "Let's think of a different background. Do you like to swim? Go boating?"

"Not really. I fish."

"Oh! Maybe we can work with that. Do have any poles or gear we could add to the shot?"

"In my truck."

"Great." This was turning out to be harder than she thought. She sighed with relief when another car pulled into the drive.

Rachel hopped out. "Hey, I was just killing some time while Doug was—oh. *Oh*, I'm sorry. I didn't realize you had company." Her eyes darted between Jeff and Kate.

"I'm helping Jeff do his picture for the calendar."

Jeff waved with the tackle box he'd just pulled from his truck. "Hi, Rach."

She nodded stiffly. "Jeff."

"You're welcome to—" Kate began, but Rachel was already backing toward her car.

"No, it's okay. I don't want to get in the way. I'll swing by another time."

Kate's cell phone rang. She pulled it out of her pocket. "Hello?"

"Kate? It's Doug. I'm looking for Rachel. Is she there?"

"Yes, as a matter of fact..." Kate paused as Rachel mouthed something and wildly waved her palms back and forth. "She *was* here, but she left."

Rachel nodded vigorously.

"You want me down by the lake?" Jeff asked at Kate's elbow.

"Who's that?" Doug demanded.

"Jeff Dayton. I'm taking his—"

"Jeff's there?"

Isn't that what she'd just said? "Yes. I'm taking his calendar photo for—"

Doug blew out a long breath that whistled over the line. "*If* you see Rach, can you let her know I'm done early? She can pick me up any time."

"Sure. If I see her, I'll tell her."

"Thanks. And Kate?"

"Yes?"

Another heavy sigh rattled over the line. "Can you tell her I love her?"

Kate bit her lip. "Sure."

She slid her phone back in her pocket. "Your husband is done and wants to be picked up."

"See?" Rachel chirped. "Can't stay!"

"He also sends his love."

Rachel stopped, her hand on the top of the car door. "He did?" She paused, her gaze traveling down to where Jeff stood by the shore. "If he calls again. Can you let him know I'll be there in five minutes?"

"Anything else?"

Rachel's eyes skittered back to Kate. "Yeah. Send him my love, too."

"Sure thing."

After Rachel pulled out, Kate walked down to shore to join Jeff. He cast out his line. Kate took a quick shot. Frowned. Wow. It actually looked good. Natural. Sexy, even, if she said so herself.

"I think this may work, but I hate to say, the T-shirt has to go. Whatever that thing is, it's scary."

He glanced down at his chest and genuinely smiled for the first time since arriving. "Scary? We drove all the way to Augusta in a snowstorm to see these guys."

He set his pole down. "It was Grace's first concert." He smiled again, wider this time. "She had the lead singer sign her..." He paused to pull the faded shirt over his head, hiding his face for a moment. "...but I think that's her story to tell." He picked up his rod again and turned toward Kate.

Kate bit her lip and raised her camera. "Perfect. Now, cast again. That was a good pose before." *Click.* "Okay, gently reel in. Yes. *Yes.* Like that." *Click.* "By the way... nice tattoo."

CHAPTER TWENTY-NINE

———————————————

JIM LOOKED AT THE MOLDING samples he'd laid on his client's front yard and heaved a sigh of relief. It'd been a long, hot Thursday, and this was his last stop of the day. He'd get a go-ahead from this client, run by the lumber yard in the morning and be at work first thing. It was a nice, easy job, too, replacing all the millwork in the home from crown moldings to door and window casings. The owner had gutted the place when she'd bought it and had been restoring it from the ground up ever since. While he wasn't general contractor on the job, he was fine with straight-forward carpentry. The owner had even hinted at wanting a custom inglenook in the library.

Jim smiled and hooked a thumb over his shoulder as the door opened. "Ms. Murdock? Hi. Jim Pearson. I have those door casing mock-ups we talked about on the phone. Whenever you're—"

"Please! God, no! Ms. Murdock is what people call my mother. Call me Cathy."

Jim's client stepped out the side door, her glossy brown hair just brushing the straps of a white tank top. She wore denim cut-offs, but he would bet his new laser level the shirt was silk. Everything the woman had done to restore the 150-year-old lakeside property had been top drawer, right down to the tumbled-granite pavers under their feet. "Then Cathy it is."

Her left hand briefly covered his as they shook hands, then slid to her side. She walked to where he'd laid out the three molding patterns he'd worked up for her.

"Is this the mahogany?" she asked. She had a throaty, 1940 starlet's voice and cat-like green eyes rimmed with thick, dark lashes that made her seem like she was flirting shamelessly even when she wasn't.

"No. That's the red oak. It's a native species like you asked about over the phone. It would have been available at the time the cottage was built. Looks nice when given a coat of sheer varnish, but it will darken with age so you might want to keep that in mind." She stroked a ringless hand over the next choice. "That, ah, that there is the mahogany. A popular choice for molding. Very stable. Resistant to rot and insects. But, it's a tropical species. That last design I did in poplar just so you could see the profile."

"Is that native, too?"

"Yes, but it's not as hard as the first two. Paints up well. Has a nice, ah, smooth grain."

She ran her hand along the grain of the wood again. Her eyes were closed.

"You're right. It *is* smooth." Her eyes slid open. "But I like the idea of something hard and solid. Something that will last. Something... local."

There was a sultry, flirty curve to the corner of her mouth as she said that last word. Jim cleared his throat and stood abruptly from where they'd been crouched, sure he'd misconstrued her meaning.

"Anyway, if you let me know which of these you like, I can get the material and start first thing. The rosette, I know is a little more formal, but you don't have to—"

"Would you like a drink?" she interrupted. "I'm feeling awfully warm out here all of a sudden."

He nodded. "Ah, sure. If you want something. Anything is—"

"Come and see what you'd like." She waved for him to follow as she turned and walked down the drive toward the rear porch. A tiny diamond ring sparkled on her pinky toe as she padded up the steps ahead of him. He thought of Kate's purple toenails. "I'm sure we'll find something that appeals to you. Wilson's good about keeping the fridge stocked," she said.

Wilson? Oh, right. Ms. Murdock's—that is, Cathy's— assistant. Usually Jim dealt with Wilson—whether that was a first or last name, he had no idea. Neither did he know what Cathy did for a living, if anything. He got the impression she enjoyed a healthy trust fund.

Minutes later, Jim found himself perched on a barstool beside her new granite island sipping a Sam Adams as she leaned against the sink. They chatted companionably for a time, the cold beer making a nice cap to a long, hot summer day.

"It's a shame we haven't had a chance to meet face-to-face until now." She smiled warmly.

"You've done a wonderful job on the place."

"Thank you. I've enjoyed it. I'm only sorry I didn't realize you were a general contractor earlier in the process. I could have saved myself some headaches."

"You've done admirably on your own."

"Thank you." She smiled again. Her green eyes sparkled excitedly. "Speaking of which, have you seen the beautiful stonework my mason did? He just finished Monday." She led Jim to an adjoining room. "They're all native stones taken directly from the property. See this? The lichen and moss are *still on it.*" Her hand brushed over a stone lightly. Her eyes closed again. "Come feel it. It's fabulous."

"Ah..." Jim stepped forward, the beer bottle beginning to sweat in his palm as she grasped his other hand and held it under hers against the stone. He could smell her scent, sharp and spicy, could feel her breast heaving softly against his forearm each time she took a breath. He tried not to yank his arm away and appear rude. Carter would have a field day if he knew Jim was trying to get *away* from a woman's breast. "Yeah. Wow. That's something," he said.

She released his hand. "Isn't it? I prefer to work with native materials whenever I can. Like the Vermont granite on the island and the maple counters. It gives a connection, an *authenticity* to a place, don't you think?"

"Absolutely." Jim wiped his damp palm on his thigh. My God, the woman wasn't even wearing a bra. Where the hell was Wilson?

"It feels honest, and I admire honesty," she continued.

Jim nodded.

She tilted her head. Let out a soft sigh. "That's why I have to be perfectly honest with you."

"Of course."

"I'm not sure I can work with you."

Jim blinked. "You're not? Didn't you like the profiles? If you tell me what you'd rather—"

"It's not that. I like profile number two. In oak. Varnished. No, it's the fact that I've just met an incredibly attractive man, and I'd really like to ask him out, but it's probably unethical of me to go out with someone who's working for me. So, you see, I find myself on the horns of a dilemma..."

"Oh. *Oh.* Well, I..."

Her lips tilted with a confident smile. "This is where you tell me you're fine with dating a client and technically Wilson hired you, so you don't see a problem."

Jim cleared his throat. So, this is what a deer felt like staring into the headlights.

Cathy was watching him. Waiting. She swung her dark hair over her shoulder and all Jim could picture was the sweet, uncertain gesture of honey-blonde hair being tucked behind an ear only to fall out again. His gut twisted. What the hell was he doing to himself? Isn't this what everyone kept telling him to do? Alex? Carter? *Kate even?* Wasn't he supposed to find a nice, single, *uncomplicated* woman? Cathy appeared to be all that and financially independent on top of it all.

"Unless you're already involved with someone..." she added.

Involved. A memory popped into his head, the feel of Kate nestled against him in the back of his truck as they watched fireworks together. Crap. Were they involved? He didn't know what to think anymore. At what point did friends—who had sex once and flirted shamelessly in public—get redefined as a relationship?

Christ. It was hard enough to make things work when both people *wanted* a relationship—impossible when only one of you wanted it. Justine had proven that. As much as he'd like to start something with Kate, she'd made it perfectly clear she wasn't ready. He had to respect that. At least she had the decency and honesty to be upfront about it instead of stringing him along. He swallowed over the lump in his throat.

"No," he finally said, hating that it was true. "Nothing serious. You? No boyfriend? Husband?"

She laughed and shook her head, raised a questioning brow.

"Okay." He made himself return her smile. Who knew? Maybe he and Cathy here would hit it off. It was just one date. "Then I'm fine with dating a client, and technically Wilson hired me, so I don't see a problem. Good?"

Her grin widened. "Very good."

Jim nodded, tipped up his beer and drained it.

July 18
Regret. Don't you hate that word? It's all tied up in missed opportunities and wish-I-hads. Or, worse, wish-I-hadn'ts. Personally, I'd like to be done with regret. Maybe my life choices aren't perfect, but I've made them, and no amount of regret can change them anyway. So, I'm thinking I should replace 'regret' in my life. Maybe you should, too. Any suggestions?

CHAPTER THIRTY

IT WAS LATE SATURDAY morning and Kate was dressed to earn her keep. Ruth Pearson had announced a plan to 'spring clean'—to reorganize her kitchen like Kate had suggested she do the night of the barbecue and clear out and set aside items for a church yard sale. Mucking out excess belongings from attics and garages sounded better to Kate than trying to figure out what color her parachute was... not that she knew what that meant seeing as she had yet to read past the title of the book the librarian had assured her was a classic for aimless people trying to find their true calling in life.

She'd moved it and a handful of other self-help books to the coffee table in the living room where Liam had made a Matchbox mountain out of them all.

Kate entered the Pearson's garage and watched as Jim yanked something large and dark from the wall. Her heart skipped an excited beat. "Is that what I think it is?"

"If you're asking if this is the same ice chest we dragged out of Gram and Gramps basement ten years ago. Yes. And it still weighs a ton." Jim wiped his brow and began unloading an assortment of tools and half-used quarts of oil from the top into a box.

"It's wonderful!"

She leaned down to smear a decade's worth of greasy dust from the latch in order to open it. The latch was weighty and stiff from disuse, and Kate wondered what life was like in simpler times when blocks of ice were delivered to your door. Aside from lack of electricity, it sounded heavenly. "Was it originally your grandparents'?" she asked.

"It's been in the basement of the cottage as long as I can remember. I'm sure Grams would be able to tell you more."

"It's beautiful! Why is it here in the garage?"

"Mom never got around to refinishing it."

Kate grabbed an old rag and began wiping off the dirty layer neglect had allowed to collect on it. The warm luster of old oak came into view. "I don't think it needs refinishing, just a little TLC. It has so much character and patina just as it is."

"You find anything worth heaving?" Jim's dad hovered in the doorway.

"I'm almost done clearing out the ice box like you asked," Jim replied.

"Good. Takes up too much space in here."

Kate gasped. *"You're not getting rid of it?"*

"Well, we're not going to shoot it and throw it off the nearest bridge, but yes," Jim said.

His dad rolled his eyes. "Now you sound like my wife. It's been sitting here waiting for her to do something with it for years."

Kate turned to Jim and leveled a finger at his chest. "Don't do anything more with it until I talk to your mother."

"I—"

"Don't."

"Mrs. Pearson!" Kate said, as she reached the kitchen where Grams and Jim's mother were emptying cupboards. "You can't let them get rid of it!"

"It's not Wilbur the pig," Jim mumbled behind her.

"Rid of what?" Jim's mother wanted to know.

"The old ice chest! You've got to save it!"

"Oh, *that*." His mom set down a collection of glasses. "I've always loved that chest, but I've never made time to refinish it. Plus, I wasn't sure what to do with it if I did."

Kate paced toward the dining room then back again. For some reason she couldn't explain, it was very important to save the chest. How many people had that sort of link to the past? Everything her parents had was the newest, latest, most cutting edge... but an ice chest was a piece of history. "You could put it here," she said, "on the way to the dining room... use it as a pantry for things like onions and potatoes. See this space here? It's like it was made for it. And I don't think you'd need to refinish it, just clean it up some. It has such wonderful character."

"It would fit nicely there, now that you mention it." Jim's mother nodded appraisingly. "I always thought it a shame not to find a use for it. But I don't know if I have the ambition to clean—"

"I'll do it! Please? I know you've been talking about how cramped things are combining two households. You might find it gives you some nice extra storage space."

"If it means that much to you, be my guest." Jim's mother laughed and handed Jim a box of glasses. "Get rid of these, would you?"

"*Jim.*" Kate grabbed his elbow. "I need some mild wood cleaning detergent, like liquid oil soap, and a pile of rags."

Kate hovered near the dining room while waiting for Jim to gather her supplies.

His Grams passed a small stack of plates to his mother. "Joan, these plates can go to the yard sale, too."

Kate watched his mother sigh as she set the plates in a box. "You served dessert on these the first time Dick brought me to your house for dinner. Remember?"

"Did I?" Grams asked from her step stool. "They are pretty, and I've always liked them, but they don't match anything else."

"I know. And you're right that we need to clear the cupboards. They're too crowded."

As Kate took the cleaning supplies from Jim's hands she got a good look into the box.

"Those are gorgeous!" she enthused.

"You can have them," his mom offered. "We don't have room for them anymore."

"Oh, no. I couldn't. You have to keep them."

Grams pursed her lips. "We can't keep everything, dear. I thought that was the point of cleaning out the cupboards."

"I know. But these have sentimental value to both of you, and I know the perfect place for them."

"Let me guess," Jim said dryly. "In the ice box?"

"No." Kate frowned at him then grabbed his mother's elbow, leading her to the hall by the dining room. "*Above* the ice box. You can hang them here, as a wall display. Wouldn't that look lovely?"

His mother's expression went all soft and mushy. "Oh, Kate, what a wonderful idea. Jim! Put those plates aside. I have plans for them."

Jim set the plates aside and lifted the box under one arm to bring to the driveway. Kate nodded her thanks as he held the door for her.

They met Grace and Liam outside. "How are things going in there?" Grace asked.

Jim nodded toward the house. "Kate's repurposing so much stuff, I think we may not have much left for the yard sale."

Kate ignored the gentle ribbing as she watched Jim reach out and absently ruffle Liam's hair, his fingers dark tan against Liam's darker hair.

Jim seemed to notice her watching and abruptly pulled his hand back to his side. He turned to his cousin. "So how'd you get roped into watching this guy anyway?"

"I didn't get roped into anything. I offered." Grace ruffled the boy's hair just as Jim had. Grace pushed Liam forward. "You ask your mom, and I'll try and butter up Uncle Jim."

"I'm not his uncle, Grace."

"It's just an expression."

"Can I go?" Liam demanded of Kate.

"Go where?"

"Kayaking. I told him I'd be happy to show him, but maybe Uncle Jim would like a break from inside work?"

"Oh! It's okay with me either way," said Kate.

Jim glanced at his watch and avoided Kate's eyes. "I can't."

Grace nodded and gave Jim a look as she ruffled Liam's hair again. "Let's get you a lifejacket, Liam, and I'll take you. Okay?"

"*Yay!*" Liam shouted. He ran around the garage to the backyard.

As Grace also disappeared from view, a tight, hollow sensation settled in Kate's gut. She decided to cut through the breezeway to watch the kayaking. Jim trailed behind.

"It's not that I don't like him," he said.

"What?" she asked, even though that's exactly what she'd been thinking.

"Liam. It's not that I don't like him. I just think it confuses kids when people start calling guys who aren't related 'uncle.'"

The breezeway door slammed behind them as they stepped into the backyard. "Did your ex-girlfriend do that?" Jim stopped abruptly, and Kate shook her head. It was none of her business. "Never mind. Don't answer that."

It shouldn't matter to her whether Jim liked Liam. At the end of the summer, this idyllic time would come to an end and she'd have to face the rest of her life on her own. But there were moments, like when she watched Jim and Liam fishing on the dock, that a part of her couldn't help but imagine what life would be like if it were real—if Jim fell in love with her and Liam and they made a family.

Her hand crept to her belly for a brief, bittersweet moment before dropping to her side. God, she was a fool.

They watched from the deck as Grace helped Liam into his life jacket and then into the boat. Liam appeared to be chattering excitedly as

Grace stepped into the kayak with him and pushed off the beach. Jim was silent, and there was nothing Kate could say to make it less awkward between them. "I wish I could go with them," she said, letting out a small laugh. "I'd probably capsize the boat, though, as I've never kayaked in my life."

Jim spoke but didn't look at her. "They're more stable than they appear. I can take you out sometime. You'll see."

"Would you? I'd love that." She smiled genuinely now, like the fool she was, until the sound of a vehicle out front brought her back to reality. "Oh! That's probably Carter. Let me get the ice chest cleaned and you and he can move it back into the house. But maybe after that? Do you think you'd be up for taking out the kayaks later?"

Jim avoided her eyes and she instantly regretted taking him so seriously. Clearly it was an off-handed offer, nothing more. "I can't," he said. "Not this afternoon. I'm going to the Artisan's Fair."

"You are? I love that fair! I haven't been in years. Would you mind if we tag along? Grace needs a gift for a bridal shower she's going to, and I think I should be done here by..." She looked at her watch.

"Actually, Kate, I'm going with a... friend."

"Oh." Her heart slammed down into her gut. "*Oh.* Well, then..."

"But I'd be happy to take you another time."

"Take her where?" Carter asked from behind as he stepped from the house.

"Kayaking," Kate said, trying to keep her voice from breaking. "Jim was offering to show me how to kayak sometime, that's all."

"I can take you if you want," Carter offered.

"I'm sure I'll get to it," Jim assured them.

"It's okay," Kate said. "I can go with Carter."

"Let me know what you decide," Carter called as he walked toward the garage. "Grams promised spaghetti if I throw some stuff out."

Jim waited till his cousin was out of earshot. "I'm happy to take you, you know. I just can't. Not today."

Kate watched Grace and Liam bob gaily in the water. "It's better if I go with Carter."

"I said I—"

"Because I *want* to go with you," she finished, turning toward him.

"You say that like it's a bad thing."

"Jim," she said, "we're... friends. And friends want each other to be happy." She placed a hand on his chest. She could feel the steady thump of his heart through the thin fabric. "I want *you* to be happy," she whispered. Her own heart clenched tight in her chest as she said the words. This beautiful, generous man deserved so much better than she had to offer. It wouldn't be fair to get in his way if he could be with someone else.

He sighed. "I just—"

"*Jim.*"

"You're right." His hand closed over her own for one sweet moment, then he pulled them both from his chest and stepped away. "Go with Carter."

Cheri Allan

CHAPTER THIRTY-ONE

"JIM!"

Jim nodded and closed the door of his pickup as Cathy waved a greeting, guilt creeping up his spine with every step she took toward him. He wasn't cut out for this. Carter? Sure. Him? No way. He'd repeated Kate's 'just friends' speech ever since agreeing to the date with Cathy two days ago, yet he still felt like a two-timing jerk.

But that had to stop, and it stopped just as soon as he got over this *thing* he had for Kate that she clearly didn't want to pursue.

He watched as Cathy wove her way through the parked cars. She had on a white, sleeveless dress, and her hair was pinned into a high, loose bun, a few free tendrils dancing around her face in the hot breeze. More than one male head turned to look at her. "You're here! I was beginning to think you were going to leave me high and dry."

"I'm sorry. I got held up. I was helping my parents clean out for a yard sale this morning. My grandmother moved in with them after her knee replacement last year. It's made things a little cramped."

"Oh, my. I suppose I can't fault you for being late now. I feel petty for even mentioning it." She flashed a smile. "Buy you a cool drink to make amends? I think they have an old-fashioned lemonade booth over with the food vendors according to the map. Shall we start there?"

"Sure. Sounds great."

She smiled again, a relaxed, breezy grin and linked her elbow with his to lead him through the crowds. She had on a wide, gold bracelet that winked in the sunlight, blinding him. She seemed like a nice woman. It wasn't fair not to give her a fair chance. Hadn't he agreed to be here? Swallowing his feelings for Kate, he forced himself to smile in return.

Two hours later, he found himself leaning against a tent pole and laughing at the most hideous handicrafts known to man. "Seriously? You've got to be kidding."

"You don't like it?" Cathy seemed genuinely surprised. "But it's handmade right here—"

"By color-blind craftsmen?"

"That's the beauty of it! It says right here on the tag. They use scraps of wool that would otherwise go to waste. No two are alike."

"Yup. They've got butt-ugly in every shade you could want."

Cathy frowned at the item in question. "You truly don't like it?"

"I truly don't like it. Think about it. They're cleaning out their yarn bins *and* charging top dollar to unsuspecting out-of-staters. Trust me. Go with the blue one. The blue one is nice. And it's still handmade right here in Sugar Falls."

She picked up the blue. "You're right. What was I thinking? But did you feel it? The wool is so soft." She grinned. "Even on the butt-ugly one."

"But given the choice, which would you choose?"

Her lips tilted provocatively as she brushed the hair at his temple with her fingertips. "Hmm. I see your point." Then she turned to make her purchase.

With yet another bag swinging from her arm, she met him at the edge of the tent. He eyed the darkening sky overhead.

"I hate to rush you, but that's the third clap of thunder I've heard in the last ten minutes. I think we're building up to a storm."

"I know. I know. I just want to make it to the wrought-iron demonstration before we leave. All I want is to pick up a business card and then we can be on our way. I promise."

"Fine."

She smiled and linked her elbow with his again. "You're being an awfully good sport about this."

"I haven't been here for a few years. I've enjoyed myself."

"Really?" For once the cool, confident demeanor slipped just a little and Jim found himself wishing again for the confidant woman who wouldn't be hurt when he begged off and went home.

"Really," he said instead.

She grinned. "Me, too."

Cathy had just finished talking with the blacksmith about options for a small garden gate when the skies opened up. They dashed toward the parking lot with other fair-goers, their feet splashing in the quickly forming puddles.

They reached her car first. The lights flashed as she beeped open the locks. "Get in! Quickly!" she laughed as she threw her purchases into the trunk and dove into the front seat. She pushed open the passenger door from inside. "Come on! You're getting soaked!"

"But your seats are leather..."

She grabbed Jim's hand and tugged, and he sank into the interior of her Porsche and closed the door. "Cathy, your seats..."

"They'll dry. But I didn't want you to melt."

"I don't think that's likely." He shook his head, instantly regretting the movement, as it sent water droplets spattering across the dash. "Shoot. I'm sorry." He swiped across the water droplets with his hand and only ended up smearing them with more water from his palm.

She laughed then, a rich, throaty sound that filled the warm interior of the car. "Look at us! We're soaked!"

"I know. I'm..." He turned and for the first time noticed the effect of the rain on her white sundress. Good Lord. Did this woman even *own* a bra? He swallowed and met her eyes.

"Wet," she finished for him.

His pulse thudded in his ears as the smile slid from her face to be replaced by a look he couldn't fail to recognize. She leaned forward, reached behind him and pulled a beach towel from the floor in the back seat. She tossed it onto his lap. "I should apologize. If I hadn't insisted on going to one last exhibit we would have been on our way by now."

He cleared his throat. "It's okay. I grew up on the lake. I'm used to... getting wet." The rain pounded the outside of the car.

Her lips tilted. "Even so..." Her hand rose and wiped his cheek. It was a casual, yet intimate, caress. "I owe you. Maybe if we go back to my place, dry off, I can think of something to make it up to you?"

Before he could think of an answer, she'd put a key in the ignition and the car into gear.

There was no reason not to go to her place. He wasn't in a relationship. Kate had made *that* perfectly clear. And here was Cathy—a real, living, breathing, attractive female. And she wanted him.

So the problem was?

The automatic door opener lifted as they turned down her drive, and soon he was stepping into the dry, dim interior of her well-appointed garage. He was silent as he followed Cathy through a cobble-paved covered entry to her back porch. She smiled almost shyly as she pushed the door open and held it for him to enter.

He ran a hand through his damp hair and forced a smile to his face as he watched her kick off the strappy little sandals she'd worn to the fair and toss them on the floor by the door.

"I'll get you a towel."

She was gone again before he could utter a reply, but seeing as he didn't know what to say to the woman, it was probably for the best. He listened to the steady beat of rain on the roof. And waited.

She soon returned, a fat white towel in hand. She passed it to him as she swiped a hand through her own hair. A droplet of water slid around her neck and over her collarbone. He watched as it hovered a moment on the surface of her skin before sinking in. She smiled and turned away.

"Can I get you a drink? Or, are you wet enough?"

"A drink would be great. Anything."

She pulled two bottles out of the fridge and pushed the door closed with her hip. Her skin glistened. She opened the bottles and passed one to him.

"Seeing as we're already wet, how'd you like to christen the hot tub? They haven't finished all the tile-work around it, but I happen to know the spa is up and running..."

"I don't have a..."

At one knowingly raised brow, he let his words trail off. *Duh.* She knew that.

He watched her raise the brown bottle to her lips. Watched her slim throat work as she swallowed. She was beautiful. Stunning, even. Warm. Intelligent. Uninhibited.

So why didn't he feel more?

He took a long swallow from his own bottle and set it on the island. Screw it. He had to stop thinking about Kate. Kate wasn't happening. He was a fool if he didn't accept the open invitation of the woman right in front of him.

His hand hovered at the hem of his shirt. "Do you mind? It's soaked through."

She grinned. "By all means. I want you to be comfortable."

He sucked in a breath and let it out as he yanked the shirt over his head. It felt hot and clammy in his fist. He set it over a barstool to dry.

Cathy stared at him with open admiration. "Well don't stop there."

He took a mental step back. Was he supposed to strip naked in front of her on their first date? He dipped his head. "Ladies first."

She smiled then, a slow, feline grin and reached behind her to unzip her dress. She had to tug a little at each shoulder for the damp fabric to give up its hold on her flesh, but it was soon a puddle at her feet as she stood before him in nothing more than a wisp of white satin panties.

She had no tan lines.

She licked her lips and stepped forward to stand toe-to-toe with him, then reached up and brushed the hair from his temple. "You have the most beautiful eyes," she whispered.

"Thanks."

Her lips curved seductively as her gaze dropped to his mouth. "I've wanted to kiss you from the first moment I opened my front door."

"Did you?"

"*Mmm.* Does that surprise you?"

"Not much surprises me anymore."

She chuckled, the warm, throaty sound filling the room. "That can be fixed." She stood on tip-toe, her eyes holding his gaze as she leaned forward and feather-touched her lips to his.

She watched as she did it, which should have been sexy as hell.

She tugged at his hand. "Come," she urged, trying to pull him toward wherever the spa was.

He stooped to pull off a water-logged sneaker and stopped as his beeper dug into his side. He unclipped it from his waistband and held it in his palm.

"What's that?" she asked.

"My beeper. I'm on call—Fire Department."

"Good to know. I sense things are beginning to heat up." Her hand closed over his. "But don't you think we could leave it here? I'd hate to be interrupted."

She turned, and that's when he realized she wasn't wearing panties. The thin strap of her thong disappeared between two perfectly golden orbs.

No tan lines. No tan lines at all.

He sighed, knowing what he was about to do was probably going to make life difficult down the line, but screw it. To hell with what other people said he should or shouldn't do.

He clipped the beeper back onto his waistband and reached for his shirt.

July 24
Goals. The simple ones are the easiest to accomplish. Get up. Brush teeth. Clean the kitchen. It's the major goals I have trouble with. I have so many unfinished projects littering my past, I sometimes wonder why I start anything. I know life will interrupt. It ALWAYS does. And then what? So I ask you: Is drifting through life such a horrible, terrible thing?

CHAPTER THIRTY-TWO

KATE SAT BACK ON HER heels and assessed the growing mound of weeds beside her. She'd slowly made her way around the cottage, weeding the old perennial beds, resetting the stone borders. It was tiresome work, but therapeutic. It felt good to put some order back into something lovely and neglected. At least, in one small way, she could make something right. Plus, it had the added benefit of allowing her to feel productive while ignoring the wall of terror that threatened to wash over her every time she thought about her future.

"Jim gave me a job!" Liam suddenly announced, running up the front path toward Kate.

"A job?" She stood and stretched from her crouch near her weeding bucket. The last she'd seen of Liam, he'd followed Jim to the tool shed, a small black cat trailing behind them. "What kind of job?"

"I feed Mudge!"

"What's a mudge?"

"The cat. Smudge," Jim clarified, strolling up behind Liam.

"Jim paid you for feeding his cat today?" she asked. "Wow. That was awfully nice of him."

Liam shook his head. "No. Evewy day! I feed Mudge evewy day!"

Something of her confusion must have shown in her face, because Jim shrugged. "It's fine with me. He knows where I keep the food bin in the shed. Smudge will appreciate the extra attention."

"Wow," Kate said, as much to Jim as Liam. "Are you sure? That's a big responsibility."

Liam nodded. "Jim says we should take care of wittle thins can't take care of 'emselves. An' he give me money!"

"That's nice, but I'm not sure Jim wants to pay you every day, honey..."

"We haven't discussed terms," Jim said. "But he seemed to want to help out with the family finances."

Heat warmed Kate's cheeks. It was true she'd told Liam they had to watch their pennies now, but she hoped he hadn't given Jim the impression they were in need of a Widows and Orphans fund. "I see." She crouched in front of her son. "Honey, you don't have to earn money. It's wonderful that you want to help take care of Smudge, but maybe we could do it as a favor to Jim. That's what friends and neighbors do for one another. They help each other out."

Liam's face fell. "He not give me money?"

Jim crouched next to Liam. "Tell you what. How about you go wash up inside and I'll talk to your mom in private for a minute or two. She and I will negotiate your contract, okay?"

Liam clearly didn't know what that meant, but it must have sounded important given Jim's tone, because he nodded and ran inside the house without further argument.

"You don't have to—"

"I know I don't," Jim said, standing again, "but that's what friends and neighbors do. They help each other out. I'll give him a nickel a day."

"You don't have to pay him—"

"Okay, ten cents."

"Jim, he's only three. He doesn't—"

"Fine. You've worn me down. A quarter a day, and that's my final offer."

She couldn't help but match his smile. "What's he going to spend it on?"

"He's only three. He'll earn seventy-five cents, tops, before he loses interest. He can buy another toy car." Of course, he was right. But being right only made him more charming.

"You don't have to do this."

"Maybe I want to help him support the family. So what's this I hear about you needing a job?"

She waved a hand dismissively and pretended to focus her entire attention on eradicating a dandelion. So that's what this was about. "He must have misunderstood something he overheard."

Jim held up a hand. "It's okay. You don't have to get into it if you don't want to."

"No, it's not—" She blew out a breath and stood up. "I'm not trying to hide anything. I just... I haven't figured out my next step." She gave a half-hearted chuckle as she dumped her weeding implements into a bucket. She glanced at the pile of books on the table near the porch swing. "That would require my knowing what I want to do with my life."

Jim followed her gaze and she cursed the clearly visible spines. *What's Your True Calling? Beyond Hobbies. Design Your Future. Careers, Jobs and Internships. Work as Play.*

"Looks like you're going through a bit of an identity crisis. You're Kate, by the way."

"That part I knew."

He gestured towards the books. "That's quite the stack. I mean, I understand you're at something of a turning point in your life, but it seems like a heavy load—literally—to carry around at this point. Why don't you give yourself a break?"

"I wish I could, but for reasons I'd rather not get into, I feel it's the right time to be assessing my options."

He raised one eyebrow.

"I know, out loud it sounds like mumbo-jumbo. I'm sure it was a first chapter in one of those books, but they have a point. I'm thir— Let's just say I find myself at a certain age where I should know what I want to do when I grow up, don't you think?"

"People change. I don't know that I thought about doing what I do now when I was younger. But I enjoy it. It just evolved. Sometimes you just have to let things happen."

"But you're still doing what you were always passionate about. You loved to make beautiful things out of wood when you were younger—and you still do. I— I don't know *what* my passion is. Do you have any idea how inadequate that makes me feel?"

"Inadequate? How can you— All you have to do is look around you to see the positive impact you've made on this place in the short time you've been here."

"Anybody can pull weeds. Even Liam can."

"That's not what I'm talking about. It's like you have a way of seeing what other people overlook. You have a vision of how things could be in your mind's eye, and then you work your magic, and— poof!—it's something new. I've seen what you did with the ice chest, Gram's kitchen. And *here*." His arm swept around the front yard. "I can't believe you feel inadequate. You have a gift."

"For cleaning up? Thanks." She swiped the sweat from her brow. "But weeding doesn't pay the bills."

"Have you thought about going back to school? You said you were only a few credits shy of finishing your degree."

She chuckled humorously. "Yeah. That's not going to happen."

"Don't cut yourself short. You could always apply…"

"I have."

"Oh, I'm sorry." His face registered sympathy. "I'm sure there are other schools…"

"I was accepted."

His brow furrowed. "I don't understand. That's good news, isn't it?"

Kate shook her head. "I thought so. At the time. But going back to school hinges on so many things falling into place… there's no way it can happen now. And, really, if I'm honest with myself, how impractical is an art history degree? I'm a widowed mother who has worked as a secretary for ten years. Who's going to want me running their gallery or acquiring pieces for their collection? When I think about how naive and frivolous I was to have chosen *that* as my major, it makes me sick to my stomach.

"I don't even know why I chose it. I could have been an accountant or computer programmer. Something *practical*."

"Why did you choose it?"

Kate shrugged and looked out over the lake. Good question. *Because I was sheltered and privileged? Because my mother insisted it made me sound cultured? Because there was a time I didn't know what it was to worry about money, because, like her, I had a husband to do that for me?*

She turned to Jim. "Because I never thought I'd have to depend on myself."

"You make it sound like you're alone."

"It's the truth. No sense lying to myself about it."

He stepped closer. "Maybe you wouldn't be so alone if you stopped pushing people away."

She stepped back. "I'm not— I need to stand on my own two feet."

"By throwing away the chance to go back to school? Sounds more like you're intent on shooting yourself in the foot."

"It's not like that."

"No? It's a chance to get a degree so you can open up your options. You say your major is frivolous, but how frivolous is it to throw away a chance to finish what you started? How many people would kill to have a college degree to fall back on? And here you are throwing it away without even trying to see if it'll work."

"I don't even know what I want yet—"

"*Christ!*" He made a sudden, impatient movement. "Maybe you should stop wringing your hands and worrying about your passion and just try moving forward for a change. All you do is throw up your hands and say how much things will never work!"

She stepped back in surprise at his outburst. "I don't see how they can."

"Newsflash, Kate, none of us has a crystal ball. That's *life*. Just because things haven't worked out in the past doesn't mean you should stop trying."

"Says the man who can't say he loves a woman."

His lips compressed. "This isn't about me."

"That's where you're wrong." She grabbed her weeding bucket off the walkway. "If you'll excuse me, I have to go get cleaned up. I'm having dinner with my parents—who also enjoy second-guessing my every decision in life. Thanks for the pep talk."

He ran a weary hand through his hair. "I wasn't second—"

"You were," she said. "But I'm done with people telling me what do to."

"Kate…"

"*No.*" She shook his hand off her arm. "I'm not having this conversation with you. You don't get it. *Nobody* gets it. Don't you see? I'm *terrified* of moving forward. Terrified that I'm doomed to keep making the same impulsive, stupid choices in life.

"But when I think about going back… to a job I know is safe and secure… I can't breathe." She felt her arms grow cold despite the sunshine. "It's like my future is closing in and there's no way out. And the more I think about it, the more I realize that going back would mean I'm giving up hoping for something better. And… and I can't bring myself to give up on me quite yet."

She stared at him in the silence that followed, her chest rising and falling, feeling brittle and defiant all at once.

But then he took the bucket, set it down and tugged her hand until she sat beside him on the porch steps. He blew out a breath. "No one's asking you to give up on yourself."

"*You* think I'm giving up," she said. "But I'm not. I'm not throwing my hands up in despair. I'm not trying to quit. I'm trying to let go of the handlebars to see if I can do this without help."

"I don't understand what that—"

"I'm saying I know you mean well, but you've got to let me figure this out on my own."

After a long moment, he nodded. "Okay," he said, and he turned, the corners of his eyes crinkling in that warm, lovely way that always turned Kate's insides to jelly. "You may not believe it, but I do believe there's something better waiting for you."

"You're talking to a practically unemployed widow," she sighed. "It'd be hard *not* to go uphill from here."

Cheri Allan

"I'LL HAVE DECAF TEA and a small milk for my son." Liam was designing a rocket with his bread plate and butter knife. Kate hoped dinner arrived before he launched them into space. She could sense her mother's disapproval even without making eye contact.

"Tea? When will you get over the fact it wasn't *you* who had the drinking problem? Have a glass of wine. Enjoy today. You never know when your time may come. Besides, the flavinoids and antioxidants are extremely beneficial to your health. You're looking wan."

Kate concentrated on repositioning Liam's napkin on his lap. "I happen to like tea. And I'm driving home after this."

"Fine. Fine. I was just making a point. No need to be snippy."

Kate rolled her eyes then let out a sigh of relief when she spied Nana approaching the table.

"Sorry I'm late." Nana winked at Kate. "Happy early birthday."

"Thanks."

"Hello, Mom," murmured Kate's mother.

"June," her father acknowledged crisply.

Just like one big happy family. Kate took another sip of water. She half-listened as her parents filled Nana in on a recent fundraiser her mother had attended, the new décor at her father's office...

"Mommy. Mommy!" Liam tugged at her sleeve and Kate felt a jolt of annoyance, not at her son, but at the fact that no one was actually talking to either one of them by this point.

"Mommy!" Liam demanded again.

"What?"

"Happy buthday!"

Closing her eyes—in part to blot out her father's frown at being interrupted but mostly to hold onto the sweetness of the moment a few seconds longer—Kate let her mouth curve into a smile. It didn't matter that he was a few weeks early. It didn't matter that he was currently squeezing a butter pat in his little fist just to feel it squish. What mattered was the heartfelt sincerity stuffed into those two words.

Kate wrapped her arm around his shoulders and gave him an affectionate squeeze. "Thank you, Pumpkin. I'm sure it *will* be a happy birthday. You know why?"

He shook his head then turned enthralled attention to the yellow ooze in his palm.

Kate kissed his head. "Because I have you." She pulled a roll from the bread basket and pried it open. "Here, let's make good use of that butter."

Liam proceeded to smear his palm enthusiastically over the soft bread, took a bite and grinned.

Her mother frowned but not so much—Kate was sure to note—to cause permanent wrinkles. "Perhaps you ought to take Liam to wash before he gets grease stains on the linens."

Kate let Liam finish his roll then took him to the bathroom.

As she lathered Liam's hands in the ladies' room and watched him try to pop the tiny bubbles floating in the air, it struck her that her parents never seemed truly happy. Her mother was always fretting, her father, seemed simply... resigned.

Have I been just like them? she wondered with no small bit of alarm. *Have I moved through life trying to smooth the highs and lows into the same familiar blandness? Is that why Randy's unpredictable, firebrand personality was so attractive?*

Dad complained about his staff, Ma seemed ceaselessly taxed by 'crises' and yet neither seemed willing nor able to break free of it... to do what? What *would* they do? What was their passion?

What's mine?

If Randy had moved up to sales manager, if we had stayed together, stayed in Connecticut, in thirty years would I have looked just like them?

Kate shuddered and bustled Liam out the door.

"Kate, I was just saying I ran into Rita Smith last week." Her mother sipped her Bordeaux as Kate tried desperately to picture the woman in question. "She said if you wanted to retain a position for Liam at ABC Learning Center next fall, you'll need to act fast."

"You mean the Nazi Preschool?" Kate blurted, aghast.

Her mother pursed her lips. "Rita's daughter has already retained positions for the twins."

"What's this 'retained a position' garbage?" Nana asked, buttering a roll. "Are these kids joining a law firm or entering preschool?"

"It's very prestigious. I put Liam on the waitlist as soon as he was born. "

"I told you I think they're too rigid," said Kate.

"That's not what Randy thought," her mother said. "He thought it an excellent idea."

"Right. And he always exercised good judgment," Nana sniffed. "Sorry, Katie."

"It's okay, Nana."

"Anyway," her mother continued, "I told her I'd pass the word."

"Consider your duty fulfilled," Kate replied, pretending to focus on dunking her teabag. They couldn't help who they were. They couldn't change it.

But she could.

"I've been thinking," Kate said, setting down her spoon. Her heart felt light in her chest, but not in a bad way. "I think we should move."

Conversation came to an abrupt halt as everyone turned toward her. Liam slurped his milk.

"Liam and I. I don't know where we'll live or what I'll do, but I think it's time to leave Connecticut."

"*Leave Connecticut?*" her mother cried, as if Kate had just declared she planned to rocket to the moon/have a sex change/shave her head and live with the gypsies. Her mother took a fortifying sip of her wine. "*Why?*"

"We—I—need to start fresh somewhere new," Kate said.

"What about your job at Spencer Academy?"

Kate set her tea in its saucer, feeling slightly light-headed. "I'm quitting."

"You're what? Edward, talk to her!"

"Don't make any rash decisions," her father advised. "You're still in mourning."

"I know it sounds rash, but there's nothing keeping me there. It's time."

"What about your family?" her mother asked, her injured tone causing Kate pangs of guilt. "Sandy already misses playing with Liam. What will she do if you move?"

"I'd still be near family if I moved to Sugar Falls."

"Move *here?* You can't be serious."

"And why not?" Nana asked, coming to Kate's defense. "I think it an excellent idea. I planned to sell the house in Connecticut, anyway."

"Since when? You haven't mentioned it before," Kate's mother demanded.

"Since this evening." Nana patted Kate's arm. "Not out from under you, Katie. But soon. You're right. It's time. I wasn't ready to give it up right after your grandfather died. But now... my home is here. And if you don't need it anymore..."

"This is all well and good, Katherine," her father began, "but where will you live here? More importantly, how will you get by? You have a career in Connecticut, or have you forgotten?"

A *career?* Kate tried not to laugh. Her father had always minimized the importance of her 'job' in the past. Now, suddenly it was a career she couldn't leave?

"Your father's right. What will you do?" her mother gasped in dismay, as if Kate had just announced she were pregnant or something.

Hmm. Better save that bit of news for another time.

"Maybe Mrs. Pearson will rent the cottage for a while. I'll figure it out. But it's time I took the next step in life. It's time I found my passion."

"Your what?"

"Her passion, Anne. Her passion," Nana reiterated. "Something you'd know precious little about."

"You're making a mistake," her father prophesized grandly. "You have responsibilities, Katherine. A son to consider. We'd never let you starve, but..."

But, if you had to bail me out, it would be on your terms, not mine, she finished silently. Was she crazy to think she could pull together an income, a home *and* be independent and happy? Maybe she was. But as she looked at her mother and father, as she pictured what her life would be like in ten or twenty years if she stayed with the status quo, she knew she couldn't *not* try.

Kate met Nana's gaze over Liam's head, gratefully absorbed the encouraging smile she met there. "Maybe I am making a mistake," she finally agreed. "But I don't think so."

CHAPTER THIRTY-THREE

"OFFER HER A JOB," Ruth Pearson ordered as she set the plate of spaghetti and meatballs in front of her grandson. It was his favorite, or at least, one of his favorites. God bless him, Jim had never been a picky eater.

"A what?"

"A job. Employment. You must have *something* she can do. Filing? Typing? Cleaning?" Ruth smiled as she spooned sauce over another heaping plate. She and the ladies had quickly decided that if Kate were to move to town, she'd need an income, and what more happy situation than if she were working—day in and day out—next to her future husband?

Okay. Fine. It wasn't a *given* Jim and Kate would get together, but it was *possible,* wasn't it? Plus, there'd been the sign in the cards. And other signs as well. Maybe her eyesight wasn't what it used to be, but Ruth could spot goo-goo eyes in young people a mile away.

Call her heavy-handed and interfering, but she was too old to wait around for opportunity to knock without holding the door open a wee bit.

"Why would I offer Kate a job?" Jim wanted to know.

"She needs to work, doesn't she?"

"Doesn't she have a job?" This from Carter as he helped himself to more meatballs and sauce and relieved Ruth of the plate.

"In Connecticut, yes. But she's moving, and I thought—"

"Watch out," mumbled Carter around a mouthful of meatball.

Ruth sent him a withering glance, "—she'll need an income."

"Kate's moving where? To Sugar Falls?" Jim asked.

Ruth pursed her lips. "Perhaps it's not my place to say. I thought she might have mentioned it to you already."

"Why would you think that?"

Jim was eyeing her suspiciously. Lord, she wasn't good at this whole *subtle* thing. "Didn't you go to the fireworks together?"

Jim spoke to his plate. "Not a great opportunity for conversation what with all the explosives overhead, Grams."

"Well, now you know. So, do you have anything for her, or not?"

"I don't think she'd appreciate a hand-out. What is she even qualified to do?"

"*Qualified?*" Okay, now he was annoying her.

"Is she organized?" Carter asked. "Because we could use help in the office. It wouldn't be full-time, but it would be something."

"Great," Jim said. "Problem solved. She can work for Carter and Dad."

Ruth paled. This was not at all what she and the ladies had planned. "Work for *you?*" she said as she watched Carter mound more meatballs on his plate.

"Sure. You know I hate dealing with paperwork, and now that Pops wants to reduce his hours, he'd prefer not to be stuck inside either. If she needs a job, I bet we could work something out. Should I ask her?"

"Oh, well..."

"Sounds like a good solution," Jim cut in helpfully, if a bit sullenly.

"Yes, well..."

"Terrific. I'll give her a call," said Carter.

"Sorry I'm late. I got hung up." Grace breezed in the side door and peered into a saucepan. "*Ugh.* Grams, didn't you make any sauce without dead cow in it?"

"It's in the fridge. You were so late, I thought you weren't coming."

"And miss your homemade sauce? Not a chance." Grace kissed her on the cheek and waved at the boys. "Did I miss anything?"

"Grams is helping Kate get a job," said Carter.

"Really? Why?"

"That's what I'd like to know," grumbled Jim into his spaghetti. "Has anyone bothered to ask Kate about this?"

Ruth pursed her lips and busied herself pouring sauce into a pan to reheat it. "I would think you'd want to help her."

"Sure. If she *wanted* help."

"Trouble in paradise?" Grace cooed as she spooned salad into a bowl. She peered at the dressing label intently—as if they'd puree dead animals and stuff them in Italian dressing for heaven's sake.

Jim pushed his chair back with a hard scrape. "Back off, Grace."

"Aw, come on, you know I'm just ribbing you."

"I know what you're doing. You're all trying to set me up. Well, it's not going to work, so butt out."

"Don't you like her?" asked Ruth.

"Of course I like her!" Jim snapped. "You might want to first find out if she feels the same way!"

"Oh, for heaven's sake—" Ruth began.

"Thanks for dinner, Grams." Jim brought his plate of food to the sink, half-eaten. "I gotta go."

"Jim—" Grace tried.

The screen door slammed behind him.

"I think you've got him on the line, Grams," chuckled Carter. "Just reel him in, nice and slow."

"Very funny." Ruth frowned at the door. "But now's not the time for jokes. Jim's clearly upset."

"I don't know why."

"Don't you?" Grace demanded.

"Maybe, but I don't think present company would allow me to repeat it."

"Like you ever worried about that before!"

"Pot calling the kettle black," he replied.

"This is getting us nowhere." Ruth poured sauce over some spaghetti and placed it in front of her granddaughter. "Something is bothering Jim, and it's our duty as his family to figure out what it is. Carter, if you have information that may help us, you need to share it!"

Carter raised one dark eyebrow and set down his fork. "All right. Kate only wants to get laid and Mr. Commitment wants more. Is that enough information for you two?"

"*Oh my...*" breathed Ruth, but she was sure neither heard her as her granddaughter spewed salad across the table.

Heavens. They had the table manners of baboons.

"I am *so* hanging with Kate more often!" Grace laughed. At Ruth's frown she quickly straightened in her seat. "Not that we have anything in common."

Ruth looked to her grandson. "That's a serious accusation. Do you have any proof or are you simply making trouble?"

"Would I make trouble?"

"Yes. Yes, you would."

"Well, then," he went on good-naturedly, "I guess you guys are on your own figuring this one out."

"You mean it's not true?" Grace demanded, looking far too disappointed for Ruth's liking.

Carter shrugged, a smile toying about his lips.

Infuriating. All around infuriating, thought Ruth.

True or not true, there *was* trouble in paradise!

CHAPTER THIRTY-FOUR

"I HEAR YOU'RE MOVING to Sugar Falls." Jim infused the comment with all the casual indifference he could muster—somewhat difficult to achieve seeing as he'd just dashed down the stairs and out the back door so he could pretend to leave his house the same time she was.

Kate's hand paused on the roof of her car. She had on a knee-length flowered skirt today and her hair was pulled into a swingy ponytail. She looked the picture of girl-next-door wholesomeness.

"Yes. Thinking about it, at least," she called back.

He nodded, not having thought ahead to where he was taking the conversation, having only just spied her through his kitchen window thirty seconds ago. "It's a nice town," he replied conversationally.

"Yes. I really like it here."

"Well, I won't keep you." He turned toward his pickup, realizing, belatedly, he hadn't even thought to grab his car keys.

"Jim, wait!"

He heard her tell Liam to stay in the car and then the telltale sound of footsteps as she hurried over.

Jim closed his eyes. Waited.

Her hand touched his arm first—soft and tentative on his bare skin—a moment before the fresh-berry scent of her shampoo caught up. "Jim, I... I imagine this all seems sort of impulsive of me."

He shook his head in denial even though it did.

"Well." Her ponytail swung to the side gently as she cocked her head with a wry grin. "It *feels* impulsive. But, you were right. It's time for me to move forward, and I'm ready for a fresh start. Ready to move away from the old memories. Sugar Falls seemed as good a place to start as any."

"Right."

"I just hope..." She worried her bottom lip with her teeth. "I just hope it doesn't—you know—give you the wrong idea."

"The wrong idea?"

"You know. About me. *Us.*"

"I didn't think there was an 'us.'"

"Right." She smiled nervously, glancing over at her car. "Right. That's right. I guess I'll see you around, then?"

"Yeah."

She was watching him now, as if she wanted to say more but didn't know how to broach the subject, then she stepped away as if to leave.

"I suppose that means you'll be looking for a job here in town?" he blurted.

She nodded, a relieved look on her face. "Yes. Although I may have a lead already. Carter called yesterday about helping him and your dad with some office work. I'm on my way there now to talk to him about it."

"Oh. Right. That's terrific."

She smiled a warm happy smile he wished he could catch and keep, one he wished were meant for him.

"I suppose it's true what they say about things falling into place when they're meant to be." She glanced at her watch. "Well, I should go. I'm glad you're okay with this."

"Why would I not be okay with it? It's great. I hope it works out."

THIS IS NEVER GOING to work out.

Kate stared in disbelief at the piles of paper and debris littering the small room Carter referred to as his 'office.'

"I know it's a little messy..." he said, his voice trailing off.

A little? It would take heavy equipment to clear this disaster!

"—but I was kind of hoping you'd be willing to start in here."

Kate made a concerted effort to reclaim her sagging jaw before it hit the floor. "In here?"

"Yeah. You know. Sort things out. And stuff."

"Right." She reached for the light switch. Maybe some illumination would make things look better...

"I've never been really good at paperwork. I'd rather be outdoors."

"It's not everybody's thing," she said charitably.

"Anyway, I've got a job I'd better get back to. You think you'll be all right here for a while?"

"I'm sure I'll find plenty to keep me busy."

He grinned with relief. "Great. I was kind of worried you might have second thoughts. Once you saw it and all."

Kate wondered if there were a chair buried somewhere behind the desk. "Oh, no. Don't give it a second thought. I'll dig in and see what I can do."

"Thanks. You're an angel," he said with a charming smile.

As Carter drove away, Kate sagged against the door. *Good heavens!* But, it was a job. It was a start. And, she had four hours to roll up her sleeves and dig her way to the floor before Nana would be back with Liam.

Sometime later she heard a familiar voice float down the hallway.

"Hellooooo! Anybody home?" Grace's head popped around the door frame. "Where's Carter?"

Kate uncurled from her position on the floor and shook out her stiff legs. She wasn't done, but she'd made significant progress. A large box by the door held trash. Laundry baskets and cardboard boxes of papers to be further sorted and filed lined the wall. Plus, she'd finally found the chair.

"He's at a job," Kate replied. "I'm sorry but he didn't say where."

"Crap. I'm doomed."

"What's the problem?"

"Grams just dumped some charity rummage sale in my lap, but I need someone to take over, because I've got my hands full planning a Naughty Nightie party to celebrate Rachel getting *el prego*—by the way, you're invited. Friday night. Seven o'clock. Sorry for the short notice."

"When's the rummage sale?"

Grace rolled her eyes. "Friday. Grams convinced Lydia to let them hold a charity sale at her shop—you know, that little vintage and consignment shop down in the old woolen mill? Anyway, Grams thought Claire was doing the promotion side of things and Claire thought Grams was doing it and, long story short, Lydia is out of town with her brother in Ohio who just had emergency gallbladder surgery, and her shop is full of a bunch of old clothes for a sale nobody knows about and nobody's organizing and Grams is freaking out."

"Friday is only a couple days away. Why don't they reschedule?"

Grace threw up her hands. "That's what I suggested. But Grams is having a conniption saying Lydia expects the store to be 'back to normal' by the weekend of the Blueberry Festival, and what will they do with all the clothes? If I can't get somebody to run the sale and customers to buy stuff, I'm screwed."

Kate tried to process this flood of information. "What's a Naughty Nightie party?"

"You've never heard of them? It's sexy lingerie and sleepwear, that sort of thing. My friend, Belinda, sells it. Anyway, she does house-parties, and I thought it would be a fun way to celebrate Rachel's good news. Sort of a last hurrah, you know? Plus, with Belinda's eldest starting

201

college in September, they need all the extra cash they can get. You'll come, right?"

"I don't know. I'd need to find a sitter…"

"No problem. My parents are sitting for Susan's twins. I'm sure they'd be happy to watch Liam, too."

"Oh, I couldn't impose…"

Grace waved away her objection. "They love kids. That's not the problem. The problem is figuring out how to clone myself so I can be two places at once."

Kate contemplated the calendar on the desktop. "This may seem an odd question, but how many people have you invited to this party for Rachel?"

"*Hmm.* Twenty? I had to limit myself. Fire regulations and all. Jim has a cow when I cram too many people into my apartment. He insists it's a safety hazard." She rolled her eyes. "Which is ridiculous. It's not like I'm serving bananas flambé at these things."

Thoughts of Jim and flaming desserts sprang to Kate's mind. For some reason he was wearing a red bow tie in her imaginary world. And no shirt. She shook her head and pushed away from the desk. "I may have an idea that'll fix both your problems, but feel free to tell me if you don't like it."

Grace clapped her hands. "I *love* it!*"*

"You haven't heard it."

"I heard 'fix both your problems' which totally works for me. What's the idea?"

"What if you somehow *combined* the Naughty Nightie party and the rummage sale? You could hold a Swap and Shop event where your friends donate clothes they no longer want and then they can shop for new outfits with the proceeds going to your grandmother's charity. It would be like a rummage sale that helps them clean out their closets, too. If you hold it at Lydia's shop instead of your apartment I'll bet you'll have room for a lot more women."

"But what about the Naughty Nightie party? I've already booked Belinda."

"There's no reason you can't make that part of the evening. We could make it a 'Day to Night' fashion show where women model the outfits they've gotten from the Swap and Shop while Belinda sets up for her Naughty Nightie thing. If we get some music and lights, some glitzy decorations, it'll make it seem like a night on the town with your girlfriends.

"My mother has dragged me to a million events like this. If we don't get too ambitious, I don't think it'll be hard to pull together. What do you think?"

Grace launched herself at Kate and wrapped her in a hug.

"Ohmigod! You're *brilliant!* Are you sure you can do it?"

Kate gulped and looked up at Grace's hopeful face. It'd mean organizing dozens of garments as they came in, having at least a couple style-savvy volunteers to help women pull together outfits, someone to arrange for music and decorations to make the evening special. Maybe a caterer friend willing to donate finger foods in exchange for free advertising... Oof. Two days wasn't much time!

Then again, she'd been attending fundraisers in one form or another her whole life. As long as there was entertainment and food, people would overlook almost anything. If there was one thing Kate knew, it was how to whip things into shape.

She raised her chin. "Yes. But I'll need you to recruit some volunteers for me... and invite a *lot* more women."

"Done! Oh, this is going to be a hoot!"

"We haven't pulled it off yet."

Grace motioned to the orderly piles around the room. "I have no worries. If the way you've cleaned up this mess is any indication, we'll be fine. Should we have a margaritas mix station? My friend, Susan, came up with this recipe—"

"No alcohol. We'd have to get a permit to sell alcohol, and, besides, who needs the liability? I have a simple, white grape juice mocktail recipe that'll be perfect. They served it at a neighbor's bar mitzvah last year. You'll love it."

Grace looked slightly skeptical then glanced at her watch. "*Ack!* I've gotta go. I'll call you later so we can discuss details. Oh, this is going to be F-U-N, fun!" she said as she waved goodbye.

Kate stared at the empty doorway. She had to stop committing to things like this and focus on getting on with life.

But Grace was right. It did sound like fun.

July 31
I've lived a very sheltered existence. For instance, I only discovered last
year what they put in hummus. (Who knew?) And I've never been further
west than the Mississippi. (Though I have been to Canada. Twice.) It's
not that I'm afraid of new experiences, but so far they've been few and
far between. Hmm. I wonder what that says about me?

CHAPTER THIRTY-FIVE

THE SANDWICH BOARD outside Lydia's shop read:

Speakeasy Shop & Swap Event
~ plus ~
Naughty Nightie Party!

Friday, July 31
Doors open at 6:00; Show begins 8:00 PM
Must be 21 or over to enter
Refreshments! Prizes!!
Music by: Sugar Falls Jazz Ensemble
All proceeds to benefit the Gifts for the Greater Good
Renovation Fund

"They're not coming." Nana pulled aside the café curtain at the front window of Lydia's shop and shook her head. "Oh, Kate, after all the work you've put into this, too. I suppose it was worth a try."

Kate smoothed a hand down her beaded skirt and adjusted the feather in her headband as Nana let the curtain fall back into place. Little white lights glittered along the ceiling in the darkened shop as the four elderly musicians Ruth Pearson had lined up and dubbed the "Sugar Falls Jazz Ensemble" tuned their instruments. "It's only 6:25. Give them time." Kate swallowed and nodded encouragingly at Mr. Larson, the trumpet player. He'd had a coughing fit earlier while demonstrating his technique. She made a mental note to bring him some bottled water.

Ruth stepped out of the back room and surveyed the rows of empty folding chairs lining the center aisle. She adjusted the long strands of fake pearls around her neck. "Everything looks lovely, dear. It's just as I imagine a twenties speakeasy would look if it were a fashion runway. Truly."

"Thank you. Are Claire and Grace here yet with the refreshments?"

"They're loading the trays like you asked. But they wanted to know if you really think we need so many?"

Kate swallowed the doubt in her throat. "Absolutely." Just then, a knock sounded at the door. Kate cracked it open.

"It's me," Rachel said a little breathlessly, pulling a garment rack through the door, "and the last of the vintage clothes, cleaned and pressed. I would have been here earlier, but I couldn't figure out what would match that 1950's bustier top, so I just stuck it with a prairie skirt."

"It doesn't have to be perfect. I just wanted to give the women some ideas on how to incorporate the vintage pieces with current styles. Thanks for taking care of this last bit."

"It's amazing what fabric refresher and an iron will do. Should I put this out back with the others or do you want these displayed over there?"

Kate motioned to the spot she'd reserved for the sample outfits.

Rachel pushed the rack forward. "Love the black and white decorations Susan whipped up. Very retro. By the way, I think your first group will be arriving soon. I saw a bunch of women coming around the corner."

Kate smoothed her skirt again, the beads tickling her fingers, and opened the door. "Welcome, ladies."

The women *oohed* and *ahhed* as they entered the shop and looked around.

"Help yourselves to refreshments and feel free to browse. I can take any last-minute donations here and Susan—who is near the dressing rooms out back—will explain the pricing. All our volunteers are dressed as flappers tonight, so if you have any questions or would like us to re-hang something for you, just let us know. Enjoy your evening."

"Oh, we plan to!" said a stout brunette with a wide smile.

One of her friends squealed and rushed over to admire a beaded pastel sweater set on the end of the rack Rachel had just brought in.

Kate bit her lip and watched them go. She nodded to Mr. Larson to begin the trumpet piece he'd been dying to play.

Half an hour later, she carried a roll of paper towels through the crowd of laughing, chattering women. She squatted down to mop up someone's spilled drink and nearly got knocked into the puddle when Grace called their attention and the women surged forward, plastic champagne flutes sloshing with mocktails from the beverage fountain. Kate sat back on her heels. At least they were enjoying themselves.

Grace waved and waited for Mr. Larson and the band to sit. "Good evening! Thank you all for coming!

"Before we start, I'd like to thank Ms. Lydia Sweet for loaning us the use of her fabulous shop, my very own grandmother, Ruth Pearson, for generously providing all the delicious nibbles and treats—donations are accepted—our volunteers, Susan, Ellen and Rachel, for sorting all the clothes and transforming this place into a roaring twenties speakeasy overnight, the Sugar Falls Jazz Ensemble for providing our live entertainment this evening... And last but not least... Kate Mitchell for having the brilliant idea of hosting this event and pulling together a million details in an inhumanly short timeframe."

Kate nodded and waved her roll of paper towels.

"As you've heard, we're raising money for the Gifts for the Greater Good tonight—50% of all sales of vintage items from the shop and 100% of all sales from donated clothing will go toward the food pantry renovation fund, so mingle, shop and most of all *have fun!* The runway show will begin at eight o'clock, so be ready to strut your stuff, ladies!"

Everyone clapped and Mr. Larson hit an excruciatingly high note on his trumpet before launching into an enthusiastic if not well-rehearsed swing number. The crowd didn't seem to care. The hum of excited voices filled the room as the women dispersed again to browse the racks and tables as if it were a Filene's Basement sale and they were searching for wedding gowns. Kate took a deep breath and pointed a woman loaded with items and shrugging out of her top toward the dressing rooms set up in the back of the store.

Grace arrived at her elbow. "I can't believe this crowd. You're amazing."

"The power of social media. Seems you have a reputation of hosting great parties."

Grace shrugged elegantly and smiled. "It's a gift."

There were close to fifty or sixty women there with a few stragglers still coming in. Thankfully, they'd encouraged people to drop off donations throughout the day for pre-sorting. Some still came laden with bags at the last minute, but it was quick work to sort it out. All was flowing smoothly.

"Great party," a woman enthused as Kate loaded a tray of drinks for the musicians. Again. Mr. Larson had hinted he'd like more food, too, but seeing as they'd only been playing fifteen minutes since their last break, Kate hoped she could get a little more entertainment out of them before they decimated the refreshments table. Mr. Larson was not a small man.

"Thank you," Kate replied.

The woman grinned broadly and took a healthy swig from her glass. "How often do you have these?"

"This is the first."

"*So* much fun."

"I'm glad you're enjoying yourself." Kate nodded and lifted the tray of drinks.

It all seemed to happen in slow motion: The woman lifting her hand to wave goodbye... Plastic champagne flutes of white grape juice and seltzer flying up off the surface of the tray toward Kate's chest... The gasps of those around them as they lurched out of the way, hands flying to their mouths...

"Ohmigod! I'm so *sorry!"*

The tray clattered noisily to the floor as it slipped from Kate's fingers and the band came to a screeching, awkward halt. In the stunned silence that followed, she tried to take a breath as cool, sticky liquid slid down her neck and into her dress. A trickle of liquid slid down her calf and into her shoe as the woman grabbed a paper napkin and mopped clumsily at Kate's chest.

"It's okay," she said. "It was an accident. Mr. Larson?"

The band picked up where they'd left off, and Rachel rushed forward to take over clean-up. Kate reassured the woman she'd be all right, then pasted a smile on her face and made her way to the dressing rooms to collect her regular clothes, swiping mocktail off her bare arms and trying to be thankful it hadn't gotten her hair. Much. Oh God. Her bra was *squishy*.

The dressing rooms were scenes of cheerful chaos as dozens of women, standing in various states of undress, gave fashion advice and tossed clothing around. Kate slipped in and tried to find the bag she'd stashed her day clothes in. It wasn't where she'd left it. "Susan? Have you seen my clothes? There's been a little accident. They were in a blue bag in this corner."

Susan shook her head and gasped when she saw Kate's situation. "Try the other room, maybe. I hope we haven't sold them!"

"Not funny."

Kate stepped into the hall and pulled off her shoes. She turned one upside down and watched a small puddle form on the floor.

A woman stopped and put a commiserating hand on Kate's arm. "Oh, honey. You're in the right place. I think you could use a drink." She pointed behind her to the second dressing room. "Winter White Sangria is on the left and the pony keg is on your right."

Kate blinked. "Pardon me?" But she didn't wait for a reply as she pushed through into the room. Women crowded around laughing and

207

drinking… and Nana stood behind a giant punch bowl ladling liquid into champagne flutes. Kate elbowed her way to the front.

"Nana?"

"Oh, hi honey. Phew! Quite the crowd, huh? I think we're a hit!"

"What are you doing?"

"Serving refreshments."

"Nana, you can't sell alcohol here! You need a permit for that!"

"Oh, I'm not *selling* it, honey. It's free." She winked and pointed toward a donations jar with a red bra strapped around the middle. Someone dropped a few bills and spare change in, Nana rang a little silver bell and everyone called out *ringy-dingy!* in cheerful imitation.

Gah! So this is what apoplectic felt like! "This is so irresponsible I don't even know where to begin! How are these women going to get home? Have you thought of the liability?"

"Oh, relax. I don't serve anyone unless they surrender their car keys, see?" Nana pointed to another jar with the matching panties around it. A key chain with a pink rhinestone high heel was poking out the top. *Oh God. This was wrong on so many levels…* "I've got it all taken care of. Now stop fussing and go clean yourself up. You look awful. What happened to you anyway?"

"A *drunk* woman dumped a tray of drinks on me, and I've lost my clothes!"

"Tsk. Tsk. I'm sorry to hear that. I'm sure they'll turn up…"

"*Nana…*"

"Are you in line?" someone asked from behind her.

"No." Kate heaved a sigh and gave her grandmother a 'we'll talk later' look, then pushed her way back out, the tinkling of the bell and a chorus of *ringy-dingy!* following her into the hall.

After ditching her soaked shoes in a storage closet, she found a bathroom, pulled out a wad of paper towels and turned on the faucet.

Rachel poked her head around the door. "There you are!" She pushed into the tiny room and shut the door. "Susan told me what happened. I couldn't find your blue bag, so I tried to find something I thought would fit." She held up a hanger with clothes on it. "It's a zoo out there."

Kate stared at the outfit. "Seriously?"

Rachel shrugged. "It was either this or a track suit that smelled like mouse pee. I threw that out."

"Um, thanks."

"By the way, it's quarter to eight. Do you think we should get people ready for the show?"

"It's nearly eight? Yes. Just give me a minute to wash up and... change."

"No problem."

Five minutes later, Kate poked her head out of the bathroom, praying 'the girls' didn't hop out the top of her bustier as she made her way out front again. Good grief. Did it have to be so... pointy? She sucked in a careful, shallow breath and stepped up to the microphone. "Good evening. Ladies? Hello. Hi. If I could have your attention, please? It's almost eight o'clock, so, um, it looks like the band will be taking another break. We invite you to make your final choices before we hold our fashion show. Again, thank you so much for coming. Ten minutes!"

The din of voices rose again as Kate stepped away from the microphone. She dimmed the lights, turned the accent lighting to 'twinkle' and pressed 'play' on the pre-recorded jazz music she'd downloaded from iTunes.

She tried not to dwell on what she must be stepping in with her bare feet as Mr. Larson approached. His plate was piled with food. Again. "Miss Mitchell, may I have a word with you?"

"Of course."

Mr. Larson's beady eyes frowned down at Kate's twin torpedoes. "It has come to my attention that you are serving alcohol."

Kate crossed her arms over her chest. "Well, actually—"

"I do not approve."

Kate's eyebrows rose. "I assure you, it wasn't my ide—"

"We'll be leaving now."

Her arms dropped. "*Leaving?* But the fashion show is about to begin!"

His eyes scanned her cleavage once more as if he hadn't gotten enough information the first time, and his considerable barrel-chest puffed indignantly. "It's clear this—*event*—isn't the kind of fundraiser we care to support." He turned to go then paused. "But if you could pack up a few of those little dessert puffs while we put our instruments away, that'd be great."

"Thank you for your time, Mr. Larson, but I wouldn't dream of keeping you any longer than necessary."

He harrumphed and mumbled something about the influence of *Fifty Shades* on impressionable women and waddled back to his trumpet case.

Kate poured herself another mocktail from the drink fountain— noticeably underutilized now that everyone had discovered dressing room #2—and sank onto a chair.

Rachel plopped down beside her. "Are we having fun yet?"

Kate gave a snort. She scooted her chair forward as a group of women burst into laughter behind them and took a sip of her drink. "So, has Doug heard about the job?"

"Yes! He got it!" Rachel flashed an ultra-wide smile. "Isn't that great? It's a real step up for him. For *us*, I mean."

"Congratulations. That's wonderful."

"Oh, it is. It is! *Wonderful*..." She nodded vigorously. "First the baby, now his job... Sometimes I have to pinch myself to believe it's true!" Rachel stabbed an olive with a toothpick, shoved it in her mouth and chewed rapidly.

"Sounds like everything is falling into place."

"Just like I've always dreamed."

Kate leaned forward and frowned. "Are you okay?"

"Okay? Of course! I'm fine. Just *fine*," she insisted, her smile stiff and slightly manic. "Everything's perfect!"

"It doesn't look perfect."

Rachel stabbed another olive with the toothpick, but when she looked at Kate again, her smile was gone, her eyes awash with tears. "Oh God, I can't do this anymore."

"The fashion show?"

Rachel shook her head, the tears starting to overspill. She looked around miserably then blinked at the ceiling. Swallowed. "I can't do *this*. I can't—" She began to fan herself with a limp hand, her chin starting to wobble.

Kate grabbed Rachel's hand and pulled her to her feet. "Come on. You need some air." She led Rachel toward the back of the shop, avoiding the crowded dressing rooms in favor of a rear door she hoped was a back entrance. It was a service hallway. It felt close and hot and smelled of moldy carpet but at least it was private.

Rachel didn't seem to notice. She leaned against the wall, tears sliding down her face.

Kate rummaged in the pockets of the prairie skirt and produced a crumpled tissue. It looked clean, so she handed it over.

"I'm sorry," Rachel mumbled through the tissue. "I'm doing it again. I don't know what's wrong with me lately."

"Hormones?"

Rachel smiled weakly and worried the tissue in her fingers. "I wish it were that simple."

"Do you, ah, want me to get Grace?"

"*No!*" Rachel grabbed Kate's arm and pulled her away from the door. "No. Please, don't. You know how she is." She waved her hand. "I don't want to upset her. Especially tonight."

"Of course. Do you want me to leave you... alone?"

Rachel shook her head.

"Do you want to talk about it?"

She shook her head again.

"Okaaaay. We can just... wait here. Until you're ready. No hurry." She chewed her bottom lip and focused on a stain on the hallway carpet, trying not to notice the tissue dissolving into shreds in Rachel's fingers.

"I don't even know what's wrong with me," Rachel muttered. "It just feels like life has, I don't know, *taken over*. Like everything I always wanted is coming true, but all at once. Doug has his new job, we have to find a place to live, I have to pack and move... Then there's the baby..."

"I'm sure everything will work out."

"How? How can you be sure? I think I've been wanting this for so long, or *thought* I wanted it, now that it's happening..." She let her voice trail off.

Kate forced a reassuring smile. "It just sounds like jitters to me. Happens to everyone. It's a lot to take in."

Rachel stared down the hall vacantly. "It's just... I know now a part of my life is over, you know? Unlike most of those women in there, I'll never be that carefree swinging single again. I'll be a.... a... *mother*!" she cried suddenly, weeping anew into her tissue.

"Hey. It's okay. Being a mother isn't so... bad."

Okay, maybe not the world's most ringing endorsement for motherhood, but she wasn't prepared. And, hey, it wasn't as if people became mothers for the glamour of it all! Sometimes it just... happened.

"I know. I know." Rachel said, raising her head again. "I *want* to be a mother. I do! But, I feel like I'm finally getting everything I've always wanted, and... I don't deserve it." She ended on a whisper.

"That's crazy. Of course you do. This is just the hormones talking."

Rachel took a deep breath and straightened her shoulders a little. "Right. Hormones. Why else would I be bawling like this? I mean, we've tried to get pregnant for months. Doug is *so* excited."

"It's overwhelming sometimes even to get good news."

Rachel nodded. "Yeah. Yeah. You're right." Then her face dropped to her hands. "Who am I kidding? It has nothing to do with hormones!"

Kate had a sinking, hot sensation in her gut. She tried not to glance at her watch. "What has nothing to do with hormones?"

Rachel stared at the floor. "*I saw him.*"

Kate didn't ask who. "When?"

211

"This afternoon."

"Oh, Rachel..."

"I know! Why? Why would I do it? Why would I risk everything I've always wanted—a good husband, home, *family*... It was just coffee. Like he said. *Nothing* happened. We just talked."

"*Just* talked?"

Rachel nodded. "I told him about how I was... expecting. He offered his congratulations, wished Doug luck in his new job. But I feel so guilty, Kate. We didn't even talk about old times or anything about us. Or..." She hiccupped and looked away again. "God. What's wrong with me? Why would I do this to Doug? He doesn't deserve this!"

"Do you plan to see Je— this guy again?"

Rachel shook her head. "I don't even know what I was looking for, you know? I know what we had was nothing that would have lasted, but I can't help *thinking* about it..." She raised red-rimmed eyes to Kate. "What if one of us slips? What if we make a mistake somewhere down the line? You have no idea the people who would be hurt by this if they knew..."

"Maybe if you tell Doug and get it out in the open—"

"I couldn't!"

"Okay. Then if this guy and you agree what happened is ancient history, maybe that's it. It seems to me that can be the end of it."

Rachel nodded. "Sure. Yeah." She blotted her nose and gave a watery smile. "I'm sorry. To blubber all over you like that. Again."

"Hey, cleaning up messes is my specialty."

Rachel dabbed her eyes and pocketed the tissue. She took a cleansing breath. "I can't believe how much I'm crying lately. I don't remember it being like this when... Anyway, do I look okay?"

"You look fine. I wouldn't know you'd been crying unless I'd been standing here with you."

Rachel rested a grateful hand on Kate's sleeve. "Thanks."

"Last call for refreshments before we start the show!" Kate pushed open the door in time to hear Grace's announcement. Grace stood at the microphone and caught Kate's eye with a questioning, worried look, but Kate gave what she hoped was a reassuring smile.

"Just needed a little fresh air," she said as she and Rachel made their way back to their seats.

Rachel picked up her plate. "I think I'll get more of that antipasto before it's gone. Food will do me good. And Kate?" Kate glanced up. "Thanks for being such a good friend."

Kate smiled, nodded, as Rachel turned toward the refreshments table and everyone readied themselves for the fashion show.

A buzz of anticipation filled the air. Despite the illegal bar in the back room, the juice-soaked costume and a mediocre and morally-sensitive band, the evening seemed to be a success. It felt good to be out and amongst other women—real women she might actually have something in common with. She missed having girlfriends. Not that she *didn't* have friends. She was friendly with lots of people. It just felt good to relax and not worry about whether she was making friends with the *right* people, was the thing.

Wait a minute. Had she just thought that? Where had that even come from?

Kate chewed her lip and grimaced. Stupid question. She knew exactly where that came from. The truth was, she'd never felt free to make friends simply because she *liked* someone. At first, it had been her mother who subtly implied certain acquaintances would be more beneficial—or not. Then it was Randy who monopolized her, left no room for anything but him and his needs.

How easily she'd given up her freedom to choose! How easily she'd given up herself. Was she really the world's biggest doormat?

She didn't have time to dwell on that depressing thought as a thumping bass beat filled the room. Someone turned on a disco ball, and the first 'model' strode down the runway to cheers, laughter and the flash of cell phone cameras.

Kate moved to the door to help Rachel check out those who wanted to pay for their purchases before the Naughty Nightie event, and Nana and Claire set out desserts.

Kate thanked a woman for her generous donation, and the next half hour flew by in awhirlwind as they commented on the various outfits and tallied and bagged purchases.

Suddenly the music changed again and a slinky striptease number filled the air. Grace stepped to the microphone wearing a red teddy, boa and bunny ears, looking impossibly chic for such a ridiculous ensemble. "Put away those cell phones, ladies, and get ready for our Naughty Nightie party! Whether you're looking to kick back in uber-comfy organic all-cotton pj's or wanting to add a little silk and spice to the bedroom, Belinda here has something for you! So grab a piece of paper and pencil from the basket that's making the rounds, because we're going to start with a little game. Let the fun begin!"

Nana leaned over to Kate. "I think that's our cue to leave."

"Leave? You can't leave! What about the food, the car keys...the *keg?*"

"Oh, we ran out of that a while ago. It was only a little one. Anyway, don't worry, I've got the boys lined up to taxi people home, Rachel will pack up the food, and as long as you lock up the cash in the safe before you leave, we're done." She yawned. "It's past my bed time."

Kate narrowed her eyes. "It's not even nine o'clock."

Just then someone cranked the music. The base beat thumped with Kate's heart, as Belinda invited the women to write on their piece of paper the most unusual place they'd ever had sex.

Good God. Kate's face flamed above her bustier. "Can I come with you?"

KATE RESCUED A FEW MORE discarded nighties from the mess on the makeshift runway and hung them on the garment rack, feeling more than a little exhausted. Their Naughty-Nightie consultant for the evening, Belinda Seamans, was as cheerfully plastered as many of the other guests and had insisted Kate continue to try on assorted samples as she and Grace sipped sangria and giggled uproariously at their creations long after the majority of guests had gathered themselves to leave.

Not surprisingly, Jim chose that moment—as Kate stood wearing a ridiculous ensemble consisting of the prairie skirt, a red Naughty Nightie merry widow bustier and Grace's feather boa—to enter the shop.

His eyebrows shot toward his hairline.

Kate could feel her skin turning the color of the satin bustier Grace and Belinda had decided was the perfect replacement for the 1950's torpedo top. "They sold my clothes," she explained. "And I can't find my shoes."

"These things happen," he said, his lips twitching. "Hey, Belinda. good party?"

Belinda smiled broadly, her short brown hair bobbing happily as she rolled her half-filled garment cart toward the door. "Fabulous! Absolutely... fabulous!" She frowned, raising on tiptoes to peer outside. "Is my Teddy here?"

"He's in the parking lot." Jim grabbed Belinda's elbow as she stumbled briefly on her stout legs, then recovered. "Need help getting this outside?"

She waved him away with a cheerful hand and pushed her cart out the door. "All set!"

Carter was next to step inside the shop. "Okay, ladies. I hear I'm here for Susan, Lauren, Kelly and Diane. Ready?"

"Who am I taking?" Jim looked around.

Kate pulled the boa strategically across her chest, sure her face was beyond scarlet by now. "Carter is taking everyone that lives out by Miller Brook, and I figured I'd get lost on all these back roads, so Rachel borrowed my car and took anyone that couldn't fit in with Ted and Belinda. She promised to drop my car off tomorrow if you don't mind giving me a ride home tonight."

"Oh. Sure." Jim's eyes skidded down her body, sending a fresh wave of heat across her bare skin. Good Lord, she probably looked like some bizarre cross between a Playboy centerfold and a Lawrence Welk singer.

"Oh, pooh!" Grace said as she stepped from the dressing room. "Everyone's leaving?"

Jim turned off the twinkle lights. "It's late, Grace. Party's over."

"I suppose." She stepped around a pile of clothes on the floor and shook her head at a forgotten plate of food someone had clearly stepped in.

Belinda poked her head around the door. "Grace, you coming? Teddy's waiting."

"Oops! That's my ride. Gotta go! Tomorrow is soon enough for clean up."

The door chimed behind her, then they were alone.

Jim cleared his throat. "Ready?"

Kate picked up the pile of clothes from the floor and set them on a chair. "As soon as I find my shoes..."

Jim dumped some plates in a trash bin. "What did they look like?"

"White." Kate looked around with a sinking heart at the chaos around them. Surely they wouldn't have sold them!

"Tell you what. I'll take you home, and we can look more tomorrow. After Grace has a chance to find the floor again."

"I hate to leave it all to—"

"Grace can take care of it, Kate. It's late."

Kate repositioned the boa, feeling excessively exposed despite the fact that it covered as much as the average tank top.

"Here." Jim unbuttoned his shirt, his bare chest gloriously familiar. Kate's mouth went dry as he passed her his shirt. "Unless you like what you're wearing?"

Without another word, she got rid of the boa and wriggled her arms into the sleeves of his shirt.

She followed him to his truck, the warm summer night making her glad she'd not yet buttoned his shirt. The boning of the bustier dug into her side, but she ignored the discomfort. She never should have listened to Grace and Belinda. Made for her? The bustier probably wouldn't even fit by the time she was done paying for it. The thought was more than slightly depressing.

She leaned against his truck waiting for him to unlock it. "No shirt. No shoes. I'm a mess. Thanks for the loaner." She fingered the edges of the button-down.

"Forget about it. You're a cute mess."

"Randy was never cute."

"Yeah, well, that was different." Jim yanked open the passenger door.

"I thought he was cute. At first. Then I wondered when he'd ever grow up." She gripped Jim's forearm, hating the idea that she'd become the Randy she'd always resented. "I hope you don't feel that way toward me."

"Relax. I like you."

She waved a dismissive hand. "You don't have to say that."

He helped her up onto the seat. "I mean it. What's not to like?"

The fact that I'm a big fat liar? Oh, yeah. You don't know that yet.

Jim shut the door.

"Why *do* you like me?" she wondered aloud as the truck left the parking lot.

Jim glanced over as if startled. "I don't know. Lots of reasons."

She raised a brow. "Name one."

He shifted down at the corner. A streetlight shining through the windshield glinted off his tanned arm. He had gorgeous forearms, lean and muscular all at the same time. "Okay. I like your nail polish. It makes me think of popsicles. Which are sweet. Like you."

She tried to keep her gaze casual, fighting the urge to give his shirt back so she'd stop drooling over his naked torso. "You can't like my toes."

"Why not? You forget. I've kissed your toes. They're... cute."

She mock-slapped him in the shoulder. "Stop saying that! Who wants to be cute? I hate that word."

He glanced at her and chuckled. "In that outfit, honey, you'll have to settle for cute."

"Is *this* cute?" she asked, defiantly pulling his shirt off her shoulders. Lord only knew what made her do it. Maybe it had something to do with the fact that all too soon her breasts would morph into giant, tender balloons, her love life would be shot for the next decade at least, and this, the second and last man she'd ever had sex with, only thought she was *cute?* Yeah, maybe that was it.

Jim stared at her cleavage. "Put the shirt back on, Kate."

"Why?"

"You know why."

Yeah, but would it kill him to tell her? She shrugged back into it and stared out the window.

A few minutes later, they pulled into his drive. "We're home," he said into the silence. He slid out and slammed his door.

He yanked open the passenger door.

She slid to the gravel drive. "What else?"

"Else what?"

"My nail polish? Seriously? That's all you can say to me?"

"This is ridiculous." He turned toward the cottage.

"What's ridiculous is that we've slept together, more than once, and you can't be honest enough to tell me what you really feel. What are you afraid of?"

"I'm not afraid of anything."

"Then it won't hurt to tell me," she said, trailing after him, the sharp stones of the drive nipping at her feet.

He stopped, his back to her. "Fine. I like how friendly and easy-going you are. *Usually.*"

"See, that wasn't so hard," she said, ignoring the jibe. "But it does make me sound boring."

"Boring?" He spun around. "What are you talking about? What's *with* you tonight?" He shook his head. "Never mind. This is a pointless conversation. You're clearly in a mood."

Kate ran up the porch steps ahead of him and turned her back to the door, effectively blocking the doorknob. "Is that all?"

He glanced down. She followed his gaze to see one of her breasts nearly bursting free of its confines, a dusky crescent just coming into view.

"Well?" she asked, purposely inhaling. The boning dug in again, causing another sharp stab in her side, but she didn't care.

His throat worked, and then he looked back at her face. "As a matter of fact, you do have other... features... I admire."

"Thank God," she said, sagging against her front door. "Or I would have just wasted fifty bucks on this thing."

He caught his bottom lip in his teeth. "Definitely not wasted." Kate's heart lurched as she stared at him, waiting, wondering if he'd try to kiss her.

Her breath caught as he leaned toward her, his fingers brushing her ribs through her shirt—until he pulled the sides of the button-down closed over her chest. "Well. Time to get you into bed. I mean, in the house." He reached for the doorknob. Wiggled it. "Is this *locked?*"

Kate stared at the knob, still trying to process this unexpected turn of events. "Oh. Yeah."

"You locked the door?"

"I always lock it."

"Where's the key?"

"My purse." She looked around as if it might be hanging from a nearby bush. No such luck.

He closed his eyes on a groan. "Your purse is at the shop, isn't it?"

"What do we do now?"

"Well, I'm certainly not driving back into town at this hour even if I knew who had the key. I guess you can stay at my place tonight."

"Are you sure?"

"No."

"I didn't plan for this to happen, you know."

"For what?"

She spread her hands, fighting off a sudden, overwhelming urge to cry. Why couldn't anything work out? "Any of this. *Everything*."

He ran a hand through his hair. "It's not a big deal. We'll pick up your purse tomorrow."

She stepped off the porch. "Forget it."

"What the—? Kate." He caught up to her on the path. "Are you crying?"

"You know, I do *try* to do things right. I don't set out to make stupid choices. I don't intend to wander aimlessly from one screw up to the next..."

"You're not a screw-up."

She whirled on him. "Would someone with her life all planned out be standing here in this get-up thinking things she has no right to think?"

His eyes seemed to grow darker in the half-light of the night sky. "What kind of things?"

"Things like..." Her pulse thudded in her ears, and she licked her lips, unable to make the truth flow over them even then. "... like I think I'm falling... in lust with you."

"Very funny."

She looked at him again. "I wasn't trying to be."

"Kate, you don't know what you feel. You've just lost your husband. You're making huge life changes. You—"

"I know it makes no sense! We barely know each other. But just because you're not willing to be honest with yourself, just because you can't admit what *you* feel, I—"

"*Don't*."

218

"Don't what?"

"Jesus, Kate." He ran his hand over his face wearily. "What do you want me to say?"

Kate stilled, her blood simultaneously flooding her head and making it throb morbidly. Her stomach heaved. "Nothing," she choked. "Don't say a thing." She practically ran past him toward his house, wishing she could magically disappear, or a giant, merciful wave would swarm from the lake and swallow her.

Instead, she stood, heart pounding, misery coursing through her every vein, at his back door, waiting for the earth to do the job the lake was apparently unwilling to do for her in her time of need.

"Kate."

Despite the entreaty in his voice, she ignored him, the sweat of humiliation beading on her brow. She felt dizzy with it. Why couldn't she just shut up? Why did she have to push it? Why couldn't she let things stay light and easy between them? Now, look!

Her stomach clenched and roiled.

"I feel sick," she said.

"*Kate*." His voice had that gentle tone again. "Don't do this to yourself."

"I can't talk about this anymore!"

She grappled with the hooks on the back of the bustier, struggling against his damned, blasted shirt. If only she could breathe!

"Stop," he bit out, trying to still her frantic movements. "Fine. You want to know how I feel? Will that satisfy you?" She finally unhooked the top of her bustier and sucked in a swift lungful of air. "As stupid as it sounds, and as much as you've told me to take a hike with one breath and flirted with me with the next... if it makes you feel any better... I think—"

"Oh God..."

"—I'm falling in lust with you, too. Satisfied?"

She nodded—once—then promptly vomited at his feet.

"HI," KATE SAID, hovering in the doorway.

"Hi." Jim kept his back to her. Kate's eyes slid down the thin sweats he'd changed into and tried not to notice how nicely they skimmed over his rear. Chances were good he wasn't in a frisky mood after she'd thrown up on his shoes.

"Better now?" he asked.

Kate nodded even though he wasn't looking. She slid onto one of the chairs at the kitchen table and fingered the hem of his button-down. The bustier was somewhere in the bushes by his back door. He'd obviously taken a quick shower. She didn't blame him. "I'm sorry. I think it was just too much mocktail on an empty stomach."

Liar.

Jim nodded and brought over a plate of cheese and crackers. He sat across from her, his shoulders rigid.

She chewed and swallowed a cracker and glanced up at him again. "I'm so sorry."

"No need to keep apologizing," he said, his voice weary.

"Right." Kate ate another cracker and reached for her glass of water.

The kitchen was nice. *Attractive and functional without being too fussy*, she thought, trying to distract herself from the uncomfortable silence.

Jim looked at her. He blew out a long breath. "There's something I think I should tell you."

"Yes?" Her stomach tightened again.

"I like you, Kate. I do. But... when I went to the Artisan's Fair... it was with a woman. Another woman. On a date."

Her hand shook as she set her water down. "I see."

"She's a client of mine. Or was." He ran a hand through his hair. "Nothing happened."

"Jim, you don't have to ex—"

"She wanted to—have something happen, that is—"

"Please. You don't have to—"

"She wanted something I couldn't give her, Kate," he said, talking over her. "She wanted me to be someone I wasn't. What I'm saying is— I've said the words you wanted me to say tonight and... I can't do that again."

"I'm not asking you to."

"Yes, you are. Just by being you, you are." He sighed, compassion filling his hazel eyes. "What I'm trying to say is: you've had a lot of tough stuff happen to you the last few months. And maybe you are ready to move on to the next step. If so, that's great. But, I can't be that next step. I can't be anything more than a friend. I'm sorry."

"It's okay. You're right. Things have gotten too intense too fast— you know—between us."

"I'm glad you understand."

Her stomach threatened to revolt a second time that evening but she swallowed her disappointment and forced a half smile to her lips. "I understand."

CHAPTER THIRTY-SIX

TWO WEEKS. TWO WEEKS since he'd looked into Kate's baby blues… and lied to her.

Hell, he didn't know what he felt or what to call it, but 'friends' wasn't it.

Jim shrugged out of his jacket and hung it on a hook by the back door. Cathy was out of town, thank God, and he was back to dealing with Wilson. At least he still had the job. Never again would he date a client. Ever.

He knew there was one last cold beer in his fridge, and it had his name on it.

He pushed open the door at the top of the basement stairs and frowned at the sound of movement in his kitchen. It was unlikely to be a wild animal or intruder. Unless, of course, you considered your own family intrusive.

Which at this moment, he did.

He heaved an audible sigh when he saw Grace at the stove. "Grace, what are you doing?"

She turned, as if she stood over a steaming pot in his kitchen every Friday night. He made a mental note to hide the spare key in a new place. "I'm making dinner," she said with some annoyance, as if his question was distracting her from the complicated task of boiling water.

"Why?"

She finally gave up peering at the box of pasta and poured it all into the pot, then gave it a stir.

"So we can eat," she said matter-of-factly as she tore open a bag of lettuce and searched loudly in his cupboards, he guessed for something to put it in.

"'We' who?"

"What do you mean, 'we who?' *Us!* Didn't Carter tell you?"

"Would I be asking if he had?" All he wanted was a cold beer and some peace and quiet for God's sake. Instead, he got twenty questions with a cranky Julia Child.

"Sorry we're late!" The front door slammed as Rachel and Doug let themselves in. Doug soon appeared holding a large white bakery box.

"What's going on?" Jim asked again.

"Didn't Carter tell you?" Rachel asked.

"No," Grace called from the stove. "Put the cake over there." She pointed to the counter under the window. "I'm almost done with the pasta. Could you finish the salad?"

"Sure." Rachel bustled in to offer a hand as Doug set the bakery box by the window.

"Where's Carter?" Grace asked as she stirred the pasta. "He was supposed to take care of getting her here."

"Would someone *please* tell me what the hell is going on?" Jim finally demanded.

Three sets of eyes turned as the front door opened and shut. "How's operation surprise party coming along?" Carter called down the hall.

"*Party?*" Jim said.

"Yeah," Carter affirmed as he slapped his cousin on the back on his way to the fridge. "For Kate. You know, her birthday."

"No," Jim ground out, "I didn't know. Apparently it was your job to tell me?"

"Was it?" Carter looked around at the others. "Geez. Forgot. Well, it's her birthday today and the girls wanted to throw a little surprise for her, seeing as she's all alone and new in town."

Jim closed his eyes on a bid for patience. It did little to calm him as he heard the distinctive sound of his cousin opening *his* beer. "You're throwing her a party. Here. Tonight."

"Right." Carter checked his watch. "In twenty minutes. Or as soon as I pick her up. I drove her by a job site this morning so she wouldn't have her car today." He tapped his temple with the neck of the bottle. "Ahead thinking I was."

Jim stared at the beer in his cousin's hand, alternately wishing it was in his own and wishing Carter would choke on its contents. "You plan to drive after downing that?"

"It's just one."

"I'll get her," Jim said, not really wanting any part of the whole thing. Worst case, he'd stop at the package store.

"Oh," Rachel said. "That won't work. She'll suspect something if it's you."

"Seeing as I'm as surprised as anybody that I'm throwing a party in my house tonight, I don't think I'll let on." He stood up to leave then thought to ask, "Are we expecting any more people, or should I let that be a surprise, too?"

"Don't be snippy just because Carter forgot to tell you. It's for Kate!"

He wasn't being snippy, he grumbled to himself. But even if he was—which he wasn't—didn't he have a right to feel put out if someone planned a surprise party to be held *in his house* without notifying him to see if he even wanted to be a part of it?

"Oh, crap!" Grace exclaimed. "If you didn't know about the party, then we don't have a gift!"

"I was supposed to get a gift?" Jim asked.

"It's okay," Rachel cajoled. "We'll do without. Though it would have been nice—"

"What was I supposed to get her?"

"I don't know," Rachel said unhelpfully. "Although, I had thought something from that little gift shop on the corner of Maple Street—you know the one with crafts and stuff from local artists?—might have been nice. Something that'd make her think of Sugar Falls or this summer."

"Right," Jim nodded. "But seeing as it's six o'clock on a Friday night, how likely is it they'll be open?"

"That's a great idea," Grace chimed in, as if either of them had said anything at all constructive. "How about one of those old decoys you and Gramps used to make? Is there one you don't like as much?"

"Real generous of you," said Carter wandering over to peer into the bakery box. "Take some dusty cast-off from Jim's shelf as a gift? I think she'd prefer the cake."

"I think it's a terrific idea! If Jim doesn't mind," Rachel added.

All eyes turned toward Jim.

Like he was going to say, no, they were too meaningful to him and look like a selfish jerk? But which one?

He walked to the living room and stood in front of the shelves. *Would she even want one?* Granted, she'd complimented him on them that first night, but maybe she'd just been being nice. Anyway, he couldn't give Gramps' decoys away, that didn't feel right. Even though he had them in his possession for now, they should stay in the family.

That left his to choose from.

Jim studied the shelf of decoys. They'd improved over the years. His early attempts were more rustic. Once he'd improved his carving technique he'd gone through a period of experimenting with different tinted stains and paints. Some weren't quite good enough to his eye; some he didn't think were right. Finally he picked one from the back of the shelf.

"Here," he said to Grace as she stood in the doorway.

"This one?" she asked with some surprise.

"Yeah. Something wrong with it?"

"No."

"Then dust it off before you wrap it. I'll be back in twenty minutes."

August 7
Expectations. I'm entirely against them. They only set you up for
disappointment. On the other hand, I'm all for Pleasant Surprises. In
fact, I'm expecting one any day now...

CHAPTER THIRTY-SEVEN

"I SHOULD TELL HIM."

Kate sat back on her heels—not sure where that particular thought had come from—and surveyed the piles of paperwork surrounding her. Carter had asked her to sort through a few boxes of paperwork he'd pulled from a closet to see what needed keeping and what could be safely tossed. It might seem a tedious process to some, but it felt liberating to Kate. Plus she was getting paid for the effort. She was more than happy to oblige.

Except now she had entirely too much time to think. About life. And relationships. And how she was deceiving the man she'd rapidly become much too fond of. As a friend, of course.

It had been two weeks since the Naughty Nightie party. And aside from a few brief exchanges while helping Liam take care of Smudge, she hadn't spoken to Jim—not that she knew what she could say.

Kate bit her lip. She didn't want to ruin their friendship, but now more than ever it mattered what he thought. She pulled at her waistband hoping to gain a little breathing room and recognized the futility. Pretty soon she'd have no choice but to come clean.

With everybody.

Not that she had any idea how she *would* tell him. *Oh, I'm just mailing my health insurance payment. I'd switch, but I have to keep it up for nine months to avoid being denied on a new policy for a pre-existing condition.*

Or how about...

Beer and pizza for dinner? Oh, can't have the beer, because it's not good for the baby.

Or even better...

I'm pregnant, but don't worry. It's not yours...

225

That last one made her pause. If only it *were* Jim's, she wouldn't have so much getting in the way of a future with him. She'd have more binding them together than a tentative friendship and way too much sexual attraction.

Kate closed the drawer of the filing cabinet and surveyed the small room. It had taken a few days, but she'd not only gotten to the bottom of the piles, she'd set up organizational systems even Carter could follow. At least, in theory. He seemed perfectly happy letting her take care of the office work.

And that was good news. For at least the time being they'd decided she would continue to work a couple afternoons a week. So far, she'd done simple bookkeeping, filing, and supplies ordering.

She tidied the desktop and wondered when Carter might be back to drive her home.

Home. Funny how quickly she'd come to think of the little white cottage by the lake as home. She'd yet to work up the courage to ask Ruth Pearson about renting at the end of the summer. *Which ended in two weeks.*

Oh God. She *had* to call Nancy.

Kate stood and brushed the thought away. Today was her birthday. Not that she had any big plans. Susan Lamont had called earlier in the week asking if Liam would be interested in a play date with the twins. Apparently it was the anniversary of the day they had come home from the NICU, and Susan was taking them to the pizza and games center for an evening of revelry.

Kate had been about to offer to tag along when Susan had told her in no uncertain terms to enjoy her night of freedom.

As if being alone was what she most wanted in life.

Maybe she'd run to the grocery store, pick up a pint of Ben & Jerry's and a romance novel and spend her birthday indulging in herself. Maybe she'd even have time to paint her nails.

All of them.

Kate smiled, pleased with her plan, as the door to the apartment swung open. *"Oh!"* she said.

"Hey." Jim waved. "You ready?"

Why was *he* here? She hadn't seen him for days. "Where's Carter?" she blurted before her thoughts could wander any further.

Jim held the door for her as she picked up her sweater and purse. "He forgot something and asked me to give you a ride."

"Oh. I see. Well, thanks."

"Sure."

They walked in silence to Jim's truck. He wore the same khaki carpenter pants and plain tee he'd had on the first time they'd met, though he had on a pair of dark, weathered work-boots which made her think of sexy rural men and hay barns.

Hay barns? A vague recollection of a story someone told at the Naughty Nightie party came to mind, but she couldn't remember the details. All she could remember is picturing Jim Pearson as the hero of the narrative. Her cheeks grew hot in the cooling air.

"Something funny?"

Kate glanced up. "No. Why?"

"You were smiling."

She folded her sweater over her arm. "Just remembering something from the swap and shop night is all."

"*Mmm.*" He unlocked her door and stood aside while she climbed onto the bench seat. She waited as he shut it after her and walked around the front of the truck, his sun-streaked hair tousled and unkempt. He slid into the cab and started the engine.

"So," he said to the distant horizon. "You better now? Fully recovered?"

"What? Oh. Yes. Thank you."

Kate bunched her sweater in her lap and stared out the side window, at the trees going by in a blur. A few were already starting to change color. Fall would be here soon. Another season of change.

She sighed silently and pushed the strap of her purse back up her shoulder.

"Things going okay with Carter and the bookkeeping and such?"

Kate nodded even though Jim's eyes were still glued to the road. "Great. I also helped Lydia re-organize some of her inventory at the store. I've been thinking maybe I should try to start up my own business. Odd jobs and such. See what happens."

"Sure. Sounds great." She watched his fingers curl around the gear-shifter as he approached an intersection. "Glad everything's working out for you."

"Me, too."

Kate bit her lip and glanced out the window again, the awkward conversation sitting like lead between them. Nothing like ignoring the elephant in the room. *We've had sex together but now we're trying to pretend we're just friends and all along I've kept from you the fact that I'm pregnant with my dead husband's baby.*

Gah!

This had to stop. For one thing, the jeans she was wearing were getting snug in the waist. In another few weeks she'd be wearing elastic waistbands. She couldn't keep it a secret forever. They rode in silence for a few miles before she mustered the courage to speak. "There's something I've been meaning to tell you."

I'm pregnant. Yeah. Just like that. Spit it out.

Jim ran a hand over his face. "Let me guess. Is this about Cathy?"

Cathy? Is that the name of the bimbo you almost slept with?

"No. It's not about... her. But, in the spirit of full disclosure..." *I'm pregnant.* "What I mean is, what I said the other night, the night of the swap and shop, it wasn't the whole truth—"

They pulled into his driveway and rolled to a stop. "Don't sweat it, Kate. We both said things we didn't mean." He flung open his door and slammed it closed behind him.

"I'm saying," she plowed on, body-blocking him as they both reached the back of his truck. "*I* shouldn't have said what *I* said not because I didn't mean it, but because—"

He stepped around her and starting walking toward the cottage. "Your life is complicated right now. It's okay. I get it."

She ran after him and stepped in front of him. "But you don't. *Nobody* gets it. That's what I'm trying to tell you. If you'd just stop and listen!"

She might have screamed the truth in his face, right then and there, but he reached out and steadied her with a reassuring, comforting grip that completely sapped her of the will to be brutally honest. "But first," she found herself saying, "I want you to know how much I appreciate how nice you've been to me. And, I value your... friendship." She took a breath. *Stop beating around the bush! Say it already!* "I hope, no matter what, you don't feel I've taken advantage of you."

(And, by the way, I'm pregnant.)

He frowned. "Of course not. Do you feel that way about me?"

"Why would I?"

"You know," he said, shrugging. "The sex thing and all."

Her cheeks grew warm. "Oh, *that*. That was—"

"I know. A mistake."

"I was going to say incredible."

He toed the ground with one of his boots and met her eyes. "Well. That's all behind us now."

"I guess so."

He tilted his head and she realized he'd let go of her elbow, because his hand was running through his hair distractingly, drawing her attention to all those yummy highlights. He cleared his throat and looked out over the lake. "I thought we agreed to keep things casual, Kate. Just friends."

"I know. But I never said I was against a... friendly friendship." Her stomach flip-flopped as he pressed his lips together and slanted his eyes toward her.

"A *friendly* friendship?"

"Yeah, you know..." She forgot the rest of her sentence as his tongue darted out to moisten his lips.

She smiled shyly.

He smiled back.

"Yeah, I know," he said. Then he shook his head and sighed. "Out of curiosity, just how friendly a friendship are we talking? Theoretically speaking."

Kate sucked in his words, tasting them on her tongue. Savoring them. "Very friendly?" she ventured, a warm spiral of hope and desire spinning through her despite all her best intentions to be noble and forthright.

He grinned. She could see it in his eyes as they crinkled at the corners. "I'm not even gonna try to figure that one out." Then he leaned forward and pressed his lips, warm and sweet, against hers, sliding them softly until she parted hers on a sigh. Oh, sweet heaven.

They finally broke for a breath, his mouth trailing kisses along her jaw, up to her ear. "I'm probably the biggest fool in the world for even thinking this," he murmured into her hair, "but does this mean we get to have friendly sex? No pressure. Just asking."

She sagged into his arms as his tongue danced along her earlobe. "God, I hope so."

He laughed, but before she could elaborate on that thought, she caught something out of the corner of her eye. "Jim?" she ventured, really not wanting to disturb him, as he was doing a fabulous job of being, well, *friendly*.

"*Jim?*" she tried again more forcefully.

"Hmm?" He paused, his lips hovering over her collarbone as she struggled to blink herself back to the present.

"Is someone at your house? I thought I saw movement at the window."

"*What?*" He thrust her away.

Kate stumbled, the heavy haze of desire making it difficult to do anything but blink gracelessly. "What is it?"

"Did they see us?" He whirled and peered up at his house, nervously smoothing his clothes and running his fingers through his hair, as if that would right it.

229

"Did *who* see us?" She peered over his shoulder. The house was quiet, though now that she looked, there were a couple cars on the road that weren't normally there. "Is that Carter's truck?"

"Probably. You made me forget all about it." Jim bit his lip and looked down at his pants ruefully. "You have a way of doing that."

"You have a way of making me feel... *friendly*, too." She grinned, pleased, hoping they could keep up with the easy banter. This was how she wanted to remember their time together. Light, fun and flirty. Tomorrow was soon enough for complete honesty.

His eyes crinkled again, and her heart did a little happy leap in her chest. "Speaking of friendly, why don't you come over for a little while?" He pulled on her hand and glanced through the trees at his house again. "Unless you've got other plans..."

"Actually, no. Liam's with Susan—"

"Good."

Instead of the back door, as she'd expected, he pulled her up around the house to the front. She'd never been in from this side, and the street façade surprised her. A simple covered porch wrapped around from the front corner to the side with doors to both the living room and kitchen. It was mostly empty now, but Kate couldn't help but picture a bench or pair of rockers and some potted mums to dress it up. It definitely had potential. Lord, she had to stop looking at this place as if—

"Why are we going—"

"Surprise!"

The door swung open. Stunned, Kate looked over her shoulder first, then back at the small grinning group before her.

"We would have invited more people," Rachel was saying, "but we didn't know how you felt about surprise parties, so it's just us."

"But that doesn't mean we can't have a good time!" Grace said.

"Happy birthday." Kate looked up at Jim as he stood over her, his shoulder just brushing hers. He looked nervous and sweet and she longed to grab his cheeks and give him a birthday kiss they'd both remember.

"Can we eat soon?" Carter's voice piped up from the rear. "I'm starved."

"What *is* for dinner?" Jim asked as he pushed Kate through the door into the kitchen. Unlike the last time she was in this room, now cluttered with friendly faces, it felt warm and festive. A handful of decorations hung from the cabinets and doorways. Kate's chest filled with emotion.

"Did we surprise you?" Rachel wanted to know. "Doug was keeping an eye out for you, but he wouldn't let us go near the windows, because he thought we'd give ourselves away."

"You surprised me," Kate assured them. She caught some silent exchange between Jim and Doug then turned toward the stove. "What smells so delicious?"

"Fettuccine alfredo with garlic bread and tossed salad!" Grace announced. "And it's ready. So, let's eat!"

They crowded around Jim's kitchen table, the quarters tight, but no one seemed concerned that elbows were bumped or napkins mixed up as they eagerly consumed the simple meal. Laughter soon flowed as easily as wine, and Kate found herself caught up in the relaxed camaraderie of Jim's family.

If only it could last.

"Hey." Jim bumped her with his elbow, and Kate watched him swallow his bite of bread. "What's with the long face? We're doing something wrong if you're not enjoying your party."

"Actually, I was thinking I was sorry it couldn't last."

"You think this is all we've got? I know it doesn't look like much, but you get presents, too."

"Presents?"

"Well, present, actually. But it is wrapped. I think." Jim looked around, nudged his sister on his other side. "Where's the gift?"

"I thought we'd do cake first," she whispered.

"No," he said. "Let's do the gift."

Kate pretended not to hear the exchange and made a point of drinking her iced tea as Rachel excused herself from the table and went to the other room. She soon returned with a medium-sized box wrapped in what looked suspiciously like a brown grocery bag turned inside out.

"Why didn't you put it in wrapping paper?" Jim murmured to his sister.

"I couldn't find any," she mumbled back. "I know it doesn't look like much, but it's made by a local artisan." She smiled mysteriously at Kate. "We hope you like it."

Kate took the box, excitedly tore off the paper and pried open the cardboard box within. Pushing aside the crumbled newspaper, she pulled out her gift. It sat warm and heavy in her palm, the smooth wood silken against her skin. She looked up. "I don't know what to say."

"Don't you like it?" Jim asked.

"It's... exquisite." And it was. The carver had caught the delicate detailing of the bird entirely through his own skill. Unpainted, carved from a single wood burl, the patterning and irregularities of the wood caused the finished piece to seem more natural—more alive—than anything she'd ever seen. She didn't have to ask. She knew—intimately—the hands of the artisan who'd made it.

"This is one of yours." She met Jim's eyes, searching for some meaning behind the gift. He only nodded. "It's beautiful. Truly. But it's too generous." She made as if to hand it back, although if he'd gone to take it, he would have found her grip tight on the smooth wood.

"I want you to have it."

She smiled and hugged it to her chest feeling her eyes moisten with emotion. "Thank you."

"Time for cake!" Grace announced, scraping back her chair.

"We'll clear the dishes." Rachel and Doug began to gather plates noisily. Carter wandered over to help with the cake.

Kate clutched the bird as she and Jim stood in the corner of the room. His eyes were beautiful, unreadable, upon her. "Are you really sure?" she asked. "I love it, but I don't want you to regret giving it away."

"It suits you." He gave a small, uncertain smile that made him look so vulnerable, she held her breath. "I guess you make me think of that burl. Difficult to figure out, but worthwhile once you do."

She could feel tears burning the backs of her eyes, but didn't want to make more of it than it was.

"I hope that doesn't change," she whispered back, conscious of every nerve cell straining to read him—his posture, his eyes, his expression.

He shrugged his shoulders and his lips tilted in a half smile. "Why should it?"

Kate pretended to study the carving as she blinked away tears.

"It's a mourning dove," Rachel chimed in as she walked by with the salad bowl. "They mate for life. I think his choice was very romantic."

"I don't know that that's true—" Jim began.

"I'm sure you never meant—" Kate murmured.

"*Happy Birthday to...*" Grace and Carter began to sing as they started forward with the cake, Rachel and Doug joining in. Jim was silent, watching her.

"Blow out your candles!" Grace urged.

"Make a wish!" Rachel added.

Kate held the dove tight to her chest and glanced at Jim. He was smiling, his cheeks still lightly pink, his eyes bright, and in that moment—*she knew*. She knew with a certainty and clarity that might have taken her breath away if she hadn't already had it held tight in her chest.

She didn't just lust Jim.

She was head over heels in love with him.

Kate let her breath go in one long sweeping exhale—and blew out every candle.

CHAPTER THIRTY-EIGHT

———————————

"THANK YOU. THE PARTY was a wonderful surprise." Kate cradled her gift in her hands as she walked back to the cottage, Jim strolling at her side.

"It was mostly the girls' idea, but you're welcome."

She walked slowly, savoring. Soon Susan would pull in the driveway with Liam loaded up with sugar and excitement. Soon Kate would have to tell Jim why her life was so complicated, why she was the *last* woman on Earth he should get involved with—casually or otherwise.

But now...

Now she had the quiet sounds of evening floating over the water, the faint light of the fading day like a lover's breath in the sky, and a feeling in her breast she had never known existed.

Until Jim.

She paused, looked at the sky and wondered why she couldn't have met Jim first. Things would have been so different. So much better. Easier. She wouldn't have a box of dead husband sitting on her dresser, for one thing.

"Penny for your thoughts."

She glanced up to see a half-smile hovering about his lips. "I don't think they're worth that much."

"I wish you wouldn't do that." The smile was gone now. "I wish you wouldn't shut me out like that."

"Do I?"

"Yes, you do. You make a joke, change the subject—or feed me some line about your life being too complicated. I'm a big boy, Kate. I want you to be straight with me."

She nodded and looked out over the dark water. "I want that, too."

"Then why shut me out? I'm trained to handle burning buildings and explosive accident scenes. I think I can handle whatever you were thinking."

She took a breath and clutched the dove tight in her palms. "I don't want to scare you away."

"Do you see me going anywhere?"

"Not yet."

"Then tell me."

She licked her lips, as if that might let the words slide over them more easily. She didn't want to mess this up, but the more she tried not to, the worse it felt.

"I was thinking... I wish I'd met you first," she finally said.

He was silent, and she blinked away the tears swarming the backs of her eyes. She turned toward the water, not daring to look at the pity she'd surely see on his face.

She was a fool! A fool to let herself fall in love. Nothing could come of it. It was too late. She'd had her chance with Randy. Now she had to forget the fairy tale fantasies and live in the real world.

"Why?" Jim's question cut through her thoughts, his voice soft.

Why? She couldn't stop it now as a tear slid in a silent stream down her cheek. "Because he deserved better than I could give him."

"Are you kidding? Why would you say that?"

"Because I should have loved him. *Really* loved him. But I didn't. Not the way I should have. If I had... maybe—*oh God!*—maybe he'd still be alive."

"Kate. Oh, sweetheart..." He turned her then, pressing her face into the soft material of his shirt, and a few silent tears soaked into the fabric as he wrapped her in a hug so kind it made her want to weep even harder.

"I thought I did. At first," she mumbled into his shirt. "I was so flattered. He was very charming."

She pulled back then and swiped impatiently at her tears. "I was young and infatuated. People tried to warn me. He's wild, they said. Not dependable." She swallowed a sob. "I thought I knew better. We were a good match, I told myself. *I* was dependable. *I* was responsible. Opposites attract, right?"

She dared a peek at Jim through her lashes. He stared at her, his expression unreadable. She plowed on. "He got a job at a luxury car dealership, and like a fool, I dropped out of college to move in with him. He had big plans, and I was his right-hand gal."

She shook her head at the memory. "*Stupid.* I had one semester left to earn my bachelors. One semester, and I threw it away, thinking I was smart enough to change his bad habits...

"But he changed *me.*" She stepped away and stared out over the lake. "And I let him. I let him take over until there was almost nothing of me left."

"You left him." Jim didn't touch her, but Kate closed her eyes and leaned into the sound of his voice. "You left him. The real you was always inside."

She whirled then. "But I let him consume a decade of my life! A decade of my life I'll never get back."

"You make it sound like it was wasted."

"It *was* wasted!"

"You wouldn't be who you are without him. Liam wouldn't *be*."

"I thought I could change him."

"I've made that mistake myself," Jim murmured.

A wry smile played about his lips, and Kate longed to touch them, as if some of that sweetness could flow into the empty places inside and make her whole again.

"Well I should know better. I've watched Oprah."

He smiled at her weak joke then pulled her into his arms. She didn't resist but stayed there, still, breathing in his quiet reassurance as his lips brushed her hair.

"So," he asked, a smile in his voice, "is that the deep dark secret you've been trying to warn me about all this time? You didn't love your imperfect ex-husband perfectly? 'Cause I'm thinking I can handle it."

Kate swallowed and squeezed her eyes shut. *There would never be a better time.*

"No." She bit her lip. "There's something else. Something I should have told you sooner, but I—I didn't know how."

He brushed the hair away from her cheek. "I'm sure it's not all that—"

"I'm pregnant," she whispered.

"*Pregnant?*" His hand dropped.

"It's Randy's."

His eyes skittered to her waist.

"I know this is a surprise."

"You could say that." He passed a hand over his face then pinned her with his eyes. "Pregnant?"

"I should have said something."

"*You think?*"

"I didn't want to ruin what we had."

"By being *honest*? Where would you get the idea that would ruin it?"

"Please, don't be angry. I know it was selfish, but I can't undo it. I—I didn't intend to…" She raised a hand in a helpless gesture. "I never *planned* for this… *for us*. But you were so… And you made me feel—

Oh God! I knew I was on borrowed time. I knew it couldn't last. But every time I told myself I'd come clean with you, I'd only end up falling deeper...

"I know. That's not an excuse. I *have* no excuse. But *please*, know that I never, ever meant to hurt you. I'm *so* sorry." Her voice caught, and she moved to step past him, but he grabbed her arm.

"Wait. You can't drop a bomb like that and then walk away."

"I know it's a lot to take in—"

"Yeah, it's a lot to take in," he said harshly, but then he ran a hand through his hair and looked out over the water, blowing out a long, ragged breath. He took several more deep lungfuls of air as he stared into the distance, the silence drawing out between them. Finally, he looked at her.

His brow furrowed. "What do you mean, 'falling deeper'?"

"Nothing."

"Tell me."

"It doesn't matter now..."

"*Tell me.* I think you've kept enough from me."

She squirmed under his gaze, wishing she weren't the cause of the confusion and hurt and anger she saw there. It couldn't hurt any worse than this, could it? When she told him *everything*, when he walked away because she came with more responsibilities and baggage than any man would sign up for—friend or not—the humiliation of having bared her soul, too, couldn't hurt more than knowing she'd lied to this man from the beginning, right?

"Please know that I— I don't expect anything from you. Especially now." She blew out a breath. "But what I said the other night... it wasn't a lie. And I know you have no reason to believe me, and I wouldn't blame you if you didn't, but..." She swallowed and met his gaze. "I'm... I've fallen in love with you."

He went still. "You're in love with me?"

"I know it sounds crazy. I mean, we've only known each other a short time..."

She let her words trail off and sucked in a shaky breath.

He stared at her.

She watched his chest rise and fall.

The blood pounded in her ears.

"Kate. I'm..." He cleared his throat. "I'm flattered."

"Flattered," she repeated dully.

"It's..." His eyes were so unspeakably kind she wanted to die. *Flattered??* Oh God! "You know I have feelings for you..." She nodded, reflexively, and forced a smile to her lips despite the fact that her heart was squeezing so tightly in her chest she wondered if it would ever beat again. "But I've said those words too easily in the past. I don't even know what they mean anymore. I don't trust myself to know what they mean. And now…"

"It's okay," she lied, and her lungs, like her heart, clenched tight in her chest. She knew the feeling, knew she was *this close* to completely and utterly losing it.

"Kate. A woman like you… after all you've been through… You deserve more than empty words."

"It's okay. *Really.* I understand.*"*

She tried to step away as tears swarmed her eyes and threatened to prove her a liar, but he gripped her cheeks in his palms and tilted her head gently to kiss her brow and a few traitorous tears spilled over onto his fingers.

"I do care about you," he whispered.

She nodded once, not trusting her voice. It was better this way. Better that he didn't love her, too. Then only one of them would leave heartbroken.

He sighed against her forehead. "You tried to tell me. Earlier. You tried to warn me you were pregnant."

"Yes."

He pulled back, and his mouth hitched up on one side, not quite a smile. "I wasn't listening very well."

Her heart beat heavy in her chest. "No."

He nodded and sighed again, his palm stroking down her arm to squeeze her hand. "A lot of things make sense now. You were right; it's complicated. But it's okay. It's okay. We can get through this."

"*We?*" She stepped back. "No. Jim, that's not why I told you. This is *my* problem. Not yours. I'll take care of it. I'll take care of… them." She looked at her belly, placed her hand over it, as if it were already visible. The baby was still too small to see, but such a large force already.

He stared at her incredulously. "*How?* You're virtually unemployed. Virtually unemployable—"

"Just because I don't have a degree doesn't mean—"

"I meant because you're pregnant, but there is that. I know you've been doing odd jobs here and there, but have you even thought about how you'll get by long term?"

"Thought about it?" It was her turn to be incredulous. "I've spent my entire summer thinking about it!"

"Of course you have. Of course." He stepped away, pacing. "Do you have much set aside? Life insurance? Savings?"

"Some, but—"

"You look about as far along as Rachel, maybe you could share babysitting once the babies are born. That'll help."

"I... I suppose..."

"You'll need a place to live. Any chance your folks are in a position to help out?"

"I don't think—"

"I'll bet Grams can let you stay a bit longer here at the cottage. Your Nana would probably let you stay with her until you got on your feet, too, if needed."

"Could you stop—?"

"Then again, if you got married that could—"

"*Married?* To whom?" She gestured toward herself. "What man in their right mind would want *this?!*"

He shrugged and cocked one eyebrow.

"This isn't a joke."

"Maybe I'm not joking," he said, his face taking on an odd expression. "Okay, yes, I'm not thrilled you weren't straight with me from the beginning, but I understand. I get it now. But that doesn't negate the fact that you're an amazing, desirable woman any guy would be lucky to have."

"Amazing and desirable but not someone you fall in love with."

"Hey," he touched her chin and his lips tilted softly. "I've fallen in serious like if that makes you feel any better. And even you have to admit we're very—how should I put it?— compatible."

"Nana said marriage is more than good sex."

"No offense to your Nana, but it's a good start." He let his hand drop. "Besides, there are plenty of practical reasons to consider it. What about health insurance? Adding you to my policy may cost less than insuring ourselves individually. It at least bears looking into..."

"Do you even hear yourself? I'll figure this out on my own. This is crazy..."

"It's not as crazy as believing a solution is going to fall from the sky out of wishful thinking! How's that worked for you? Huh?" He stopped and shook his head. "I'm sorry." He rested his hands on her shoulders. "Look. You said you loved me. I at least care about what happens to you. It's a more solid foundation than the starry-eyed romantic notions most couples start with. We've both tried that route and failed. Who's to say this wouldn't work? Let's at least discuss it. I hate to see you struggle when—"

She threw her hands up. *"No!* I'm not going to discuss marriage just because you have some overblown sense of responsibility. This is my *life!* You can't take over like some macho superhero!"

"I'm not trying to be anyone's hero, Kate. I'm suggesting a solu—"

"But I deserve more than that!" She said, the blasted tears welling up and overflowing again. "I may not have a solid plan of what I'm doing or where I'm headed or how in hell I'm going to make it all work, but I at least know *that!"*

"Kate, I didn't mean…"

"Don't," she said. "Please, don't." Her hand was shaking as she brought it up to dash away her tears, and she felt brittle and hopeless and cheated all at the same time. She couldn't do this. She couldn't let him sacrifice his future for her mistakes. And she couldn't give up on that tiny ember of hope of finding someone who could love her, utterly and completely. "I need what you can't give me. And I won't settle for less... ever again."

He blew out a defeated breath. "I *do* care about you."

"I know." Her chest felt tight, her lungs aching, like she was trapped in a box and running out of oxygen. But the knowledge that he cared wasn't enough, not *nearly* enough to live on for the rest of her life.

"Friends?" he asked.

He reached forward then, wrapping her in an all-too-brief hug, and in that moment, she knew. With sickening clarity she knew *this* would be the moment she'd remember. The pitying regret in his eyes as he pulled away again. The pulsing frustration deep in her gut. The scents of Jim and resignation and summer melding improbably, heart-wrenchingly together.

She shook her head.

"No, not friends," she said, her voice breaking. "Never just friends."

August 15
I know the sound of a heart breaking. Silence.

CHAPTER THIRTY-NINE

KATE BRUSHED LIAM'S HAIR from his forehead and pulled up the thin sheet. The room was warm despite the open windows, but she couldn't bring herself to turn on the air conditioning. Somehow, artificial air felt wrong. Out of place.

Just like her.

Kate swallowed the lump in her throat, straightened and headed back to the dimly lit living room. Maybe she'd made a mistake running back to Connecticut. Once she'd gotten on the road, she'd made half the drive on adrenaline alone, the remainder had been spent, tears streaming down her face, wondering if she should turn around.

But she hadn't, because despite the almost overwhelming urge to rush back to Jim and take whatever he could offer, the salient fact remained: She loved him. He was a good man. He deserved to start fresh—not be handed some screw-up's leftover wife and children. Taking him up on his offer—however well-meaning it was—would be a mistake for both of them.

She nearly jumped out of her skin when the doorbell rang. Peeking around the sidelight, she threw the door wide. "Ma?"

"I wish you wouldn't call me that. It makes you sound like Laura Ingalls. Here, open the door a little more. I can't fit the carrier through."

"What the—?"

"I need you to take Sandy." Her mother thrust the dog carrier forward and shut the door with her foot. "I'm at my wit's end. I'm having anxiety attacks from worrying about her. *Feel.*" She grabbed Kate's hand and held it to her chest. "Do you feel that? Feel how irregular that is? I'm a wreck! I've tried everything, but it's no use!"

Kate peered in the carrier. Sandy whimpered pityingly.

"We've balanced her chakras, switched to two different special diets, I've had her tested, massaged and aroma-therapied. But she just lolls around. Listless. Lifeless. It's breaking my heart! Do you have any decaf tea?"

"In the cupboard."

"Good. Maybe that will help calm my nerves." Her mother bustled into the kitchen and started the water boiling. "Your father is no help. He won't listen anymore. Just hobbles around and complains about his gout and stomach cramps."

"Stomach cramps? What's wrong with his stomach?"

"He's stubborn, that's what. Refused to take my advice. That colchi-whatever gout medicine is doing a number on him. Serves him right for pooh-poohing me. He's getting a cleansing, all right, but not the pleasant kind."

Kate reached up for cups. "So why is Sandy here?"

"I need you to take her. A few days at most. Tell me if a different environment is healing to her. I'm still not convinced it's not that new carpet, but your father refuses to listen when I suggest replacing it."

Kate looked around at the half-filled boxes and stacks of belongings around the room. "I'm packing. *Moving.* I can't possibly take—"

Her mother clutched a hand to her heart. "Not even for your own sister?"

Kate fought not to roll her eyes. "She's not my sister, Ma. She's a dog."

"I can't believe you'd say that. I love her like my own baby. If you won't do it for her, then at least would you do it for the sake of my heart?"

Kate pulled a box of tea out of the cupboard.

"One day. That's all. Please? It'll give me time to have the carpets properly cleaned. It's all organic cleansers, but I still don't want her in the house breathing in any vapors. She's fragile enough as it is."

"I don't have any food for her."

"I brought a bag in my trunk. You can keep it for when you watch her next week. And her ceramic dish. You know plastic isn't good. Allergies. And phthalates. Very bad for them. You shouldn't use plastic either."

Kate sighed. "Fine. One night." She approached the carrier and crouched down. Frowned. "*This* is Sandy?"

"Oh, yes. I know. She looks a little rough around the edges nowadays, but I stopped having her trimmed months ago. It's more work for Rosaria to keep her groomed, but Ahmed has said all along shaving her was denying her the right to be what nature intended. I tell you, that man is *so* intuitive.

"Anyway," she continued, giving Kate a brief hug and walking toward the door, "I need to get going. It's late, and I'm sure you'll want some girl time before bed. Far be it for me to interfere with that!"

"Wh—? Don't you even want your tea?"

"I don't think so. I only drink organic these days. My heart, you know. But thanks just the same. See you tomorrow?"

"Sure."

After her mother left, Kate poured herself some non-organic decaf tea then went and crouched down in front of the carrier. Sandy peered through the crate's bars—and the shag of fur that now covered her eyes. "So. What's wrong with you?" Kate asked, opening the door. Sandy lumbered up onto her legs and padded out. Looked around. Or at least appeared to. "I don't suppose you can tell me the last time you went out?"

After spending an inordinate amount of time sniffing around the back yard, Sandy did her business and slowly made her way up the steps and into the house again. Kate sighed and patted the couch next to her. Poor thing. They both needed help.

Before she knew it, they were asleep.

"MOM! *MOM!*"

Kate awoke to the sounds of heavy breathing and excited giggles. The former coming from Sandy and the latter from Liam as the dog practically wet herself in excitement at being near a three-year-old.

Kate rolled over on a groan. No doubt the dog's sudden active nature could only mean one thing. "Oh, crud! How late is it? We need to get Sandy outside. Where's her leash?" Kate patted around the end of the couch, blinking rapidly to lubricate her cursed contacts. Why didn't she just get Lasik surgery already? Oh, right, that cost money.

"Aha! Got it!" Kate turned in triumph, the leash in hand, and nearly choked in disbelief at what she saw.

"Ohmigod! Liam! What have you done?"

Sandy scampered happily around the boy, her shaggy doggy bangs replaced by short, uneven clumps of fur.

"I give her a haircut!" Liam said proudly, the little blue safety scissors in his hand still sporting a tuft of fur.

"You gave her— but honey! You can't do that! *Look at her!*"

"She can see now!"

"But..." But, nothing. He was right. The dog that had slowly stumbled around her living room the night before was now trotting about joyfully, licking Liam like the savior he obviously was.

243

"Oh, for God's sake," Kate said, a giggle bubbling up inside of her at the absurdity of it all. "Wait until I tell Ma."

Kate tilted her head. Sandy tilted hers back.

Kate reached for the safety scissors. She'd tell Ma the good news of Sandy's miraculous recovery... just as soon as they evened things up a bit.

CHAPTER FORTY

IN THE DAYS THAT FOLLOWED, Kate threw herself into packing. She felt unmoored. For the first time in years, she faced a future without a steady job, a husband, or a home... She pushed aside a box and sank onto the couch. No, unmoored wasn't the right word. She felt... unfettered. It was as if life could go in a million directions. She only had to make the right choice.

She closed her eyes, fatigue washing over her.

Choices had never been her strong suit. Hadn't she chosen Randy? Hadn't she chosen to spend ten long years as nothing more than a glorified secretary?

What *was* her passion?

An image of kind, hazel eyes flashed in her mind's eye.

No. There was a difference between sexual passion and being passionate about life. She knew that now. Okay, a simpler question. What made her feel good?

Brilliant purple pansies bobbing their heads in neatly ordered flower beds came to mind. Then other memories flooded her: Carter's shocked expression the first afternoon she'd worked on his office. Grace's gratitude for reorganizing her closets. Mrs. Pearson's joy once the ice chest and dessert plates were cleaned and put into place. The sense of pride when they'd tallied the proceeds of the swap and shop event.

Maybe that was enough. Maybe a passion didn't have to feel overwhelming. Maybe, sometimes, it could just feel good—like putting things to right.

Kate ran a hand over her face and fought the tears she'd thought she'd already spent. That was all well and good, but discovering what she was good at, even enjoyed, didn't fill the void in her heart.

Kate tossed a glance at her laptop case. She hadn't logged on for days. But she'd made a commitment to Mrs. Pearson. The entries had steadily trickled in, surprising Kate with the number of bachelors Sugar Falls could boast. And even though most were considerably younger—

which she defined as anyone younger than twenty-five—it had proved a not unpleasant diversion from REAL LIFE.

I could use some diversion, she decided, pulling the laptop from its case.

Forty minutes later, a chat window popped open on her screen. Kate's stomach did a flip-flop.

Jim: *Hi. Long time no chat.*

Liz: *Out of town.*

Jim: *And they don't have computers in...?*

Kate couldn't help but smile, even though the ache in her chest throbbed anew. If only she could start over. Do it right this time.

Liz: *Nice try. I've been busy. How are you?*

There was a pause and then a reply appeared.

Jim: *Okay. Tough week. Missed chatting with you.*

Her heart lurched in her chest until she realized it was only a light-hearted comment on his part. He didn't know who she was.

Liz: *Sure you did.*

Jim: *No, really. I did.*

Liz: *Why?*

Jim: *Maybe I like your sense of humor. I've been a little shy of that lately.*

She hadn't given him much to laugh about had she? Kate bit her lip. Typed.

Liz: *That's all?*

Jim: *I don't know. I might like your sense of style, too, but that's yet to be determined.*

Liz: *You'd hate it. Way out there. I'm SO not your type.*

Jim: *Is that so?*

Liz: *For starters, I've got wild hair...*

Jim: *Maybe I like wild.*

Liz: *...streaked with pink?*

Jim: *Pink can be very feminine.*

Liz: *...and multiple body piercings. Did I mention that? Even a belly button ring...*

Jim: *I'm intrigued.*

Liz: *...and PURPLE toenails!*

Kate stared at the screen. *Purple toenails? Sh—!* Where was the delete key?! *Where was the blasted delete key?!*

Jim: *Kate?*

Kate's pulse thudded behind her ears, her heart taking a hard skittering thump in her chest as she stared at her name on the screen. *Her name* on the screen. The jig was up.

Liz: *Yes?*

It was probably only a few moments, but it seemed like hours before a reply flashed onto her screen.

Jim: *I know it's you.*

Liz: *I was going to tell you.*

Jim: *Of course you were, but let me guess... it was complicated.*

Liz: *I guess I deserve that.*

She stared at the screen, waiting for... what? It was over. They both knew it. This only made it official. The last nail in the coffin. She'd lied to this man from the moment they'd met. How could you form any lasting relationship on lies?

Liz: *I'm sorry.*

Jim: *Doesn't change the fact that running away with Liz just got a whole lot more impractical.*

Kate felt a half-smile form despite the urge to cry. Lord, he was still Jim. And she loved him despite all the... complications.

Liz: *I'm sorry.*

Jim: *Quit saying that.*

Liz: *I don't know what else to say. I know you're angry with me. I don't blame you.*

Jim: *No, Kate. Not angry. Disappointed. I thought we had something together.*

Liz: *Who? You and me or you and 'Liz?'*

Jim: *There never was a Liz. We both know that.*

Hot tears slid noiselessly down her face as she typed her reply.

Liz: *Well, you deserve better than an imaginary woman. Or me.*

Jim: *Does it matter? I can't have either.*

CHAPTER FORTY-ONE

JIM LOGGED OFF THE INTERNET. Five o'clock. Too early to think about bed. Too late to do anything else. It was almost a relief when the call came over the scanner... *multiple vehicle accident... intersection Miller Brook and Route 6...*

Jim grabbed his keys and headed for the door, the dispassionate familiarity of the routine calming. This, at least, he knew how to do. They'd call out an engine in case of a fuel spill, direct traffic, wait for the wreckers. Not too exciting, but better than sitting at home.

He sped the mile down Route 6 toward town and, hearing that Engine 2 was already on its way, headed directly to the scene.

He pulled to the side of the road just short of the intersection, behind the traffic already backing up. Engine 2 was just arriving, sirens blaring. Jim leapt from the cab of his truck.

Nothing could have prepared him for what he saw next.

"*Jesus.*" They'd need more than a wrecker for this one.

He quickly assessed the scene with a practiced eye: SUV, driver's side mangled around a telephone pole, a pickup's front end crushed, obviously having impacted the passenger side of the SUV.

T-boned. Christ. It had fatality written all over it. He pulled a pair of plastic gloves from his glove box.

The smell of gasoline stung his eyes. A handful of people milled around already, stunned, murmuring in hushed tones. He and three other responders hurried forward. They knew what to do. Check for injuries. Assist the paramedics. Contain the fuel spill. Direct traffic. Clear the scene.

Ted Seamans stood at the pickup, assessing the driver's condition. Jim watched his eyes go flat. He knew then and there the news wasn't good.

One fatality.

Jim turned and stepped off the curb toward the SUV and stumbled. On the back window there was a maroon and white Sugar Falls Wildcats sticker. A US Marine Corps emblem just below that. The vanity plate read *Futball*.

Shit. Tommy. Tommy Daniels.

He moved quickly around the SUV and through the tinted glass saw the faint outline of a booster seat in the back—a small limp body still in it. His chest constricted as he helped wrench open the front passenger door.

The smells of blood and death hit him in a wave. Tommy's airbag had deployed, the fine white powder still floating in the air around him. Jim averted his eyes, not so much in deference, but because there was nothing to be done there. Meg, his wife, sat in the passenger seat, her neck angled oddly to the side, honey-colored hair matted with blood. Jim felt for her pulse. Weak, but there. He swung around and barked out a call for paramedics.

Motioning for back-up, he turned toward the back seat. Tommy and Meg's daughter, Amy, sat slumped over a stuffed toy, her father's blood, or maybe her own, spattered across her pink pants like dots of paint. Someone opened the back door. More sirens sounded in the distance. He watched as Roy reached in to feel the child's neck, saw the look of surprise on his face when he found her pulse. Alive. She was alive. The air in Jim's lungs came out in a huff—he hadn't even realized he'd been holding it—as they swung back around, back to the blur and chaotic order of moving bodies. Vehicles. Voices.

After that, time had no meaning. He moved, acted, responded, and yet it all seemed to be happening to someone else. The little details stood out. The smell of French fries from the local fast food restaurant as it hung in the air. The discordant laugh of a toddler somewhere nearby. The heart-shaped charm that dangled from Meg's wrist as he helped load her onto the stretcher for airlifting. It read #1 Mom.

It seemed an eternity before they were ready to load Amy for transport. As Jim helped pass her small body to the awaiting paramedics, he blinked. Paused. His hand was shaking. Jesus. His hands never shook.

Swallowing, he buried it. Time for that later. Much later. And with the chopper's deafening roar pounding his eardrums, he turned back to the grisly task of dealing with the dead.

HOURS LATER, TOO SHAKEN to drive home, Jim sat on a barstool in a dark corner of Lucky's nursing a beer. He felt numb. Or wished to hell he did.

Jesus. Tommy Daniels. Dead. Old Man Richards. Dead.

Tommy was his age. Coach of the Wildcats football team. They went to Boy Scout camp together when they were ten. Snuck cigarettes under the bleachers in high school. And Meg. She'd been in the same class as Rachel. Loved to help teach kids to ice skate on the green when the Rec. Department flooded it each winter. Owned a hair dressing salon in town. Old Man Richards used to plow their driveway. Went bird hunting every October with Dad. Had a thing for pork pies and raspberry iced tea.

Jim drank and listened, in shared disbelief, as patrons and employees recounted the events of the evening, shared the same stories over and over. As if, in the retelling, they could somehow make sense of it all. Why there? Why them? Why?

He was ordering a second round when Jeff slid onto a neighboring stool. "Mind if I join you? I've got a ton of paperwork, but I saw your truck outside..."

"Sure." Jim spun his drink mat on the bar.

"Makes you want to run home and tell your family how much you love 'em, doesn't it?" the bartender asked a nearby patron.

Jim nodded in silent agreement even though he knew the bartender wasn't speaking to him.

Jeff got his cola.

They drank in silence for a long while.

"I must've driven through that intersection a thousand times in my life," Jim finally said. "Never gave it a second thought."

Jeff nodded, picked up his cola and took a long pull.

"What the hell happened?"

Jeff shrugged. "Best guess is Richards had a stroke or heart attack at the wheel. Ran the light." He shrugged again. "Doesn't make much difference now."

"Suppose not. Any word on Meg? Amy?"

"Both critical. That's all I know."

Jim stared down the neck of his bottle and tried to understand what cosmic lesson the universe was trying to teach them all. All he could see was a man—his peer—cut down in the prime of life leaving behind a wife and child. If they even made it through the night.

"It could have been any of us," Jim said. "It could have been you. Or me." *Or Kate.* A flash of honey-colored hair came to mind, blurring momentarily with Meg's, matted with blood. *It could have been Kate.* "Just like that. Everything we love. *Gone.*" Jim took another drink, and set the bottle down, his hand shaking again as he realized what he'd just said.

"Jesus."

"I know," Jeff said.

Love. He loved her. He loved Kate.

Jim let out a huff of disbelief and looked around, feeling bizarrely, morbidly elated. "I could be dead. *Dead.* Just like Tommy. And Kate would never know how I feel about her." He swiped a hand down his face. "How could I be such an idiot? What am I even doing here?"

"Getting quietly soused?"

Jim shook his head. "No! I mean *here.* In Sugar Falls. Without her. How could I let her leave?"

"Is this a rhetorical question?"

"Want to hear something really crazy?"

"Sure."

"I think I believed letting her go wouldn't hurt so much if I never told her. But you know what? It hurts more." His gut clenched. "Not that it matters. She's gone now. I fucked up and now she's gone."

Jeff didn't answer, just glanced Jim a look of sympathy. He took another sip of soda. "Sorry to hear that. Anything I can do?"

Jim studied the rows of glasses overhead. "You got a magic potion to make a woman come back to you when you don't deserve a second chance?"

"If I did, I would have used it already."

They sat quietly for a while longer, lost in their own thoughts.

"What about Justine? Is that really over, or are you still in love with her, too?"

Jim startled at the question, turning it over in his mind, the parts that weren't numb yet, that is. "No."

And it was true. Sure, he'd been stunned, blind-sided by her decision to reunite with her husband, had experienced an almost visceral need to find some explanation for how and why.

But that was gone now. Spent. A memory already fading.

"I don't know if I ever was," he admitted as much to himself as his friend. Jim pushed away from the bar and threw some bills on the bar top. "Well," he said, "it's been a rough night, I think I'll call it a—"

"I'll drive you home."

"Nah. I'm okay." Jeff slid him a look that said he'd be a cop again if he had to. For a friend. "Fine," Jim nodded. "All right."

Jeff held the door for him. "Tell you what," he said, cracking a rare half-smile, "if you don't play with the radio, I'll let you sit up front."

CHAPTER FORTY-TWO

SHE WAS LONG OVERDUE for it. She knew this, but somehow the act of buying the pregnancy test seemed too final—as if by acknowledging the fact that this would confirm she was pregnant she also acknowledged a small part of her still held out hope it would turn up negative.

It didn't even take the full three minutes.

There it was. Two tiny little pink lines. Positive. She was pregnant all right.

Kate sank onto the toilet seat and stared at the little white wand, tears welling in her eyes. Crap.

She couldn't pretend any longer. And the damned ass that had done this to her was right this moment sitting neatly in a box in her living room awaiting—what? What the hell was she going to do with him?

Kate threw the wand into the trash, walked back to the living room—and nearly fainted.

"Sandy! Ohmigod! No! *No!*"

Not knowing what else to do, Kate grabbed the dog and shoved her into her crate, a fine trail of gray particles spattering the carpet in her wake. Tiny little doggie prints ran into the kitchen and back to the living room. And Randy's FedEx box lay sprawled and emptied across the living room floor.

Kate stared at the carnage in horror, her breath coming in shallow little hiccups. Dear God. Dear God in heaven.

She sank to the floor, desperately trying to gather the ashes into a semblance of a pile, but it was no use. They were everywhere. Clinging to the fibers of the carpet. Floating like everyday dust motes in the sun. A single tear hit the carpet beneath her, turning the ash dark.

"How did this happen?" she whispered.

"I sorry, Mommy." Liam stepped out from behind the sofa, his little head hung low. "I want to see inside." He stepped forward again and gave a little hopeful grin. "You want the vacuum?" Kate stared at her son, the urge to weep—or laugh hysterically—nearly overwhelming.

"Liam, I can't vacuum up your—" She'd been about to say 'father' but then realized how incredibly odd that would sound to a boy who wouldn't understand what the pile of dust meant. She looked around, the fine particles still floating like snow around them. Oh Lord. How else was she going to clean it up?

Blinking back tears and fighting the bubbles of morbid laughter forming in her throat, she pulled Sandy out of her crate and clipped on her leash. "Looks like I have some clean-up to do. Can you take Sandy to play out back for a few minutes?"

Liam nodded eagerly and grabbed the little dog. "Mommy?" he asked, tilting his head. "Why you have that box of dirt?"

"I don't know. I should do something about that, shouldn't I?"

Right after I clean up this one last mess.

After shooing Liam and Sandy out the back door, Kate pulled the vacuum from the hall closet, and in deference to the dearly departed, installed a fresh vacuum cleaner bag.

"I TOLD YOU TO TAKE care of those ashes."

"Nana, I didn't call to get a lecture," Kate sighed. "I'm doing something about it now. I only wanted to ask if you've heard from Mrs. Pearson about whether she's willing to rent the cottage to me for a little while."

"No. She's been out straight baking and such for the funerals."

"What funerals?"

"You didn't hear? Terrible tragedy. An accident downtown at the lights. Two people dead, a mother and child still in the hospital. No one's sure if either will make it." Nana *tsk, tsked.* "Terrible."

"I'm sorry. I hadn't heard."

"Anyway, I'll try to see if she's made a decision. I did hear that maybe Rachel and Doug were thinking of staying at the cottage for a while now that he got that job, but between the funeral preparations and the auction on Saturday, I'm not sure if anything's decided yet."

"Sure. I understand."

"But you and Liam are welcome to bunk with me until you get on your feet. You know that."

Gratitude welled up in Kate's chest. "Thank you. But I'm hoping to stand on my own two feet. In fact, I'm heading out right now. I'm bringing Randy's ashes to his father. I know they haven't spoken in years, but I'm thinking this way maybe he'll have a lot to say, like what I should do with the ashes, for starters."

"If you're sure. I thought he was too sick to even come to the funeral."

"I know, but I need closure, Nana. I need to move on."

"Good luck, Sweetie."

"Thanks."

Kate flipped her phone shut, buckled her seatbelt and checked the rear-view mirror. She hadn't seen her father-in-law since the day she and Randy had announced they were getting married. Randy had had some heated conversation in the other room and stormed out, fire in his eyes, as he'd grabbed her hand. "I don't need anyone's fucking blessing," was all he'd said.

And they hadn't spoken since.

She'd thought the whole incident was proof Randy loved her. She thought it was romantic like Romeo and Juliet, but now she saw it for what it was—Randy hating the fact that someone else might dare tell him what to do.

It hadn't been about love at all. The realization was sobering. And depressing. Was she somehow inherently unlovable? Why did she keep getting involved with men who couldn't bring themselves to say those three simple words?

An hour and a half later, Kate pulled to the curb in front of the house.

It looked smaller somehow, the years unkind. A thin layer of road dirt clung to the siding, the paint peeling, dandelions gone to seed the only sign of life in the parched front yard. She looked down the row of nearly identical houses, like a line of weary workers waiting for their big break. The one that would never come.

Checking the number on the mailbox again—just to be sure she was at the right place—she sucked in a breath. She probably should have called first. Checked to see if he was even home.

Too late for that. She was here. She turned to the back seat.

"Okay," she said, shooting for cheerful, "we're here!"

Liam looked doubtfully out the window.

"Now your Grandpa has been very sick for a long time. That's why we've never met him. So, I want you on your best behavior. Understand? He's probably got some little tubes in his nose to help him breathe, and he may be in a special chair. I don't know. But he was your daddy's daddy, so we need to be polite. If you're good, I'll get ice cream after, okay?"

Liam brightened. "A medium?"

"Sure."

All too soon, they stood on the tiny concrete stoop. Kate wiped her palm on her pant leg, clutched Liam's hand with the other, and pressed the doorbell. The electric chiming seemed inordinately loud, making her want to run, but then, eventually, she heard shuffling behind the door.

The door opened a crack. "Yeah?"

"Mr. Mitchell? It's Kate. Kate Mitchell."

The door opened only fractionally wider. "What do you want?"

"I'd just like to talk with you. I have Liam here. Your grandson."

The door opened wider still, Mr. Mitchell's watery dark eyes taking in the boy he'd never met.

"Only a few minutes. *Please.*"

"Suit yourself," he said.

The inner door swung open, and her father-in-law turned and began shuffling away. Kate gingerly pulled open the screen door and pushed Liam ahead of her.

The room was dim. The furniture care-worn. Newspapers and dirty dishes lay scattered on every available horizontal surface.

Mr. Mitchell hunched over the couch, shoving debris aside, wheezing despite the oxygen tank at his side. "Wasn't expecting visitors."

"I'm sorry. I would have called, but I wasn't sure you'd see me. Here," she rushed forward to help, "don't trouble yourself. We're fine." Quickly clearing a seat cushion, she motioned for Liam to sit with her and waited while Mr. Mitchell lowered himself into a tired brown recliner.

"You're probably wondering why I've come."

The older man shrugged. He couldn't have been more than his mid-fifties, and yet he appeared twenty years older. "You want somethin'."

Kate grabbed Liam's hand as he reached toward some unknown pile of pills on the coffee table. "Don't touch your grandfather's vitamins, honey." She pasted a smile on her face. "I came to seek your input on what you'd like me to do with Randy's ashes. As his closest living relative—"

"Whatever the hell you want."

Nonplussed, Kate tried again. "Surely you—"

"Look," he cut her off, his dark eyes fixed on her, "Randy told me ten years ago he didn't want my input. Can't imagine... he'd want it now."

"Sir, I don't know what happened that day. I've never known. But, surely, now that he's gone, whatever objections you had about me—"

"*You?*" He choked, coughing into his sleeve. He shook his head. "You were the best thing ever happened to that boy. Any fool could see that."

"Then...?"

"He had some fool idea about marrying you and living over the garage. Said if I'd loan him the money, he'd pay me back with his race winnings."

"Gambling?"

"No, stock car. Over to the track. Always went on about how he was going to be some big NASCAR driver and if only I'd help him out, it'd be his big break. Stupid idea. Told him he'd get himself killed."

"I never knew."

He passed a hand over his face. "He was always thinking about himself. One crazy plan after another. I told him he needed to settle down. Think about his wife. What did she think of his hair-brained idea?"

He shook his head wearily. "He didn't want my advice then, don't see any reason he'd want it now. You do what you want with his ashes. He's been dead to me ten years already."

Kate looked to Liam. "Would you like us to come again?"

Mr. Mitchell looked over at his grandson, pursed his lips then shook his head once. No.

She nodded, rose unsteadily to her feet, bid her father-in-law goodbye and left.

Kate blinked against the early fall sunshine, turning toward the balmy breeze that lifted a few tiny dandelion tufts and carried them away, and came to a decision.

She finally knew what to do with Randy's ashes.

IT WAS A SMALL MATTER to get directions, and after stopping for a quick bite to eat and gassing up the car, they headed up the highway, to the hill on the far side of town, to Randy's final resting place.

The road jostled and bumped the car as Kate negotiated the final bend. And then she stopped at the padlocked gates. A faded sign on rusted metal posts stood to the left: King's Speedway. She turned off the engine and stepped out. This was it. This was Randy's passion. His dream. This is where he belonged.

Opening the trunk, she pulled out the vacuum cleaner bag with his ashes, took Liam's hand, and started walking the perimeter of the fence.

"What we doing?" Liam asked.

"I wanted to find a special place for this... dirt."

"Why?"

"I'll tell you when you're older."

"When I four?"

Kate smiled. "A little older than that."

The sun was warm on her cheeks, the breeze calming. The leaves, still lush with summer foliage, swayed in the trees overhead. They hiked that way, up around the track, past the aged bleachers, through the knee-high grass to a point high above it all.

"Waz that?" Liam asked in wonder when they finally crested the berm at the end of the track.

"A race track."

"Wow."

"Your daddy wanted to race here someday. That was his dream."

"I like cars!"

"I know, honey. He did, too."

Kate blinked back the tears. Now wasn't a time to cry. Now was a time to make things right.

"It's time to let this dirt go now. You want to help me?"

Liam nodded eagerly. Searching for some way to rip open the bag, Kate pulled out her keychain, and with a slight hiccup over the irony of it all, tore the bag open with her car key.

Liam grabbed one side and shook, Randy's ashes billowing out onto the breeze. Kate struggled to let them go neatly and then gave up, shaking the bag with Liam, watching the growing cloud get carried long by the wind over the racetrack like a giant exhaust plume. They watched it for a while, as it whirled and floated, slowly fading into the distance.

There. It was done. Finally over.

Swiping a tear from her cheek, she turned toward Liam.

"Hug you, Mamma," he said quietly. "I sorry 'bout the dirt."

"It's okay. I shouldn't have left it in that box so long." She knelt beside him, tugging him close. "I love you, too, Pumpkin."

His little arms gave her a returning squeeze and the ache in her heart eased just a little.

No, she wasn't unlovable. *Liam* loved her.

And even though he hadn't loved her perfectly, Randy had loved her, too. She knew that now.

Her breath caught as loss washed over her.

She'd told Jim she'd wasted ten years, but she knew now that wasn't true. She'd lived them as imperfectly as she'd loved, because that's just how life was. Life was messy. Love was messy.

Kate watched Randy's ashes dissipate in the wind, aching for what might have been had they only been honest with each other.

257

She took a shaky breath and slowly let it go.

It was time. Time to forgive them both—Randy and herself—for having loved imperfectly, recklessly and, yes, even selfishly. Time to let go of past mistakes and what might have been and take the next step.

She stood and took Liam's hand in hers. "Time for ice cream."

August 27
It turns out, I'm not perfect. I know this isn't exactly a newsflash, but I've been hypocritical enough to point fingers at others' imperfections while ignoring my own. I'm trying to fix that though. So now, in the interest of moving forward, I just want to say: I'm sorry. I tried my best to make things right. And wherever you are—my first love—I wish you checkered flags. R.I.P.

CHAPTER FORTY-THREE

A WEEK LATER, KATE stared at the poster of Greece taped to the ceiling in her gynecologist's office. "I've done a pregnancy test and been trying to take my vitamins, but this pregnancy has been pretty easy. I hardly had any notable symptoms until the last few weeks, so I didn't see any reason to rush in."

Dr. Nichols snapped her rubber gloves on. "Generally, unless we think there might be complications, it's perfectly safe to wait till you're near the end of the first trimester. Any idea the date of conception?"

Kate nodded. "Mid April. April twenty-first to be exact."

Her obstetrician looked up. "That's pretty exact," she said with a smile.

"It was the last time my husband and I were together. He was killed in a car accident shortly after that."

"I'm so sorry."

"We were separated." Of course, that bit of information was probably only more confusing. What woman got pregnant with her husband when they were separated for heaven's sake? It seemed a lifetime ago now—the night Randy had kissed her at his apartment. A bittersweet longing for the old magic that had once sparked between them had welled up within her, and she'd clutched at it—they both had. But as soon as it was over, she'd known the magic was gone, like smoke spiraling into thin air.

Kate stared out the window as the doctor palpated her abdomen.

"*Hmm,*" murmured the doctor.

"What?"

"I think I'd like to do an ultrasound if that's all right with you."

"Why?"

"Routine. We'll verify the age of the fetus, check to be sure it's developing normally. Anyway, I had a cancellation, so if you have time, we can do it now."

Kate agreed and lay on the exam table as the doctor squirted gel onto the receiver device. Nervous tingles fluttered in her belly. She knew it wasn't the baby yet, but soon she'd see it. Soon, it would be more than a heavy fullness in her breasts, a dizzy moment when she stood up. She wouldn't have chosen this path for herself, but as she lay on the table, waiting, she felt a peculiar sense of *rightness* about it. Life would go on.

Just let things happen...

"Let's get started, shall we?"

Kate nodded again, and the doctor turned on the ultrasound machine. She tilted the screen to give Kate a better view and moments later, an image, blurry and indistinct, came onto the monitor. A moment after that, the baby's heartbeat filled the room.

"Hear that?" the doctor said turning up the volume—as if any mother-to-be could mistake the first sound of her baby's life. It caused Kate's own heart to pound faster, stronger. "A good regular heartbeat. Here's the baby. The heart." The doctor pointed to the monitor, indicating each in turn. "Everything seems to be developing normally."

Normally? Kate smiled numbly and stared at the monitor, trying to make sense of the image. Even though the heartbeat was strong, there was something wrong. Doctor Nichols didn't seem to notice, or maybe she was well-trained not to overreact to any possible deformity, but...

Kate couldn't hold it in. "Where are its arms and legs?" she demanded. *Its fingers? _Toes?* She'd seen all of that with Liam at this stage! What was wrong with *this* baby?!

"It's too soon for that. Give it another month or two. Let me take some quick measures and we'll be all set."

Kate frowned at the monitor. *Month or two?* "Wh—? What do you mean you can't see the arms and legs *yet?"*

The doctor moved the computer mouse, clicked some keys on the console and looked up. "We won't see the arms and legs until the fetus is about twelve to sixteen weeks. I judge yours to be about seven, Kate."

The room was closing in on her. Her chest was tight. She couldn't have heard that correctly. "That can't be right."

"Don't worry. Your baby looks perfectly normal."

"No." Kate needed to get through to her, needed to make sense of this. There was something wrong with the computer, something that

would explain this. "I conceived on April twenty-first. *April* twenty-first. This baby is four months old!"

Dr. Nichols paused and tilted her head in that detached sympathetic posture they must teach in medical school. "I'm sorry, but I would put the date of conception closer to early July. When did you say your husband passed away?"

Kate swallowed, already knowing but dreading what was to come. "April."

"Is there any possibility this baby is not your late husband's?"

Kate nodded. *Jim's.*

The doctor didn't press for a reply as she continued clicking keys and moving the computer mouse. Kate stared blindly out the window, the sound of the baby's heartbeat still filling the room.

Jim's baby.

Oh. Dear. Lord. What have I done?

"I get the feeling this is unexpected news," the doctor said as she pulled the sheet over Kate again.

"Very," was all Kate could breathe.

"You can get dressed now. I'll come back in a moment and we can talk. Okay?"

Kate nodded numbly and pushed herself off the exam table.

I'm pregnant with Jim's baby. Jim's baby. The baby is Jim's.

As many times as she told herself, she couldn't seem to get it to register. Her hands shook as she pulled on her jeans, slid her tee over her head.

After a quiet knock, the doctor reentered and waited for Kate to look up.

Kate sat in the chair by the door feeling like an unwed teenager. "*How can this be?*" she blurted. "I haven't had my period since before my husband died!"

The doctor sat at her desk, a reassuring, professional expression of sympathy on her face. "Amenorrhea is not uncommon in women who are under extreme physical or mental stress."

"Amenor-what?"

"Amenorrhea. In layman's terms it means the absence of your menses or period."

"But I've always been so regular! You could set a clock by me!"

"That may have been true under normal circumstances, but I'm guessing the last few months have been anything but normal. Amenorrhea is quite common among athletes in training or women who are experiencing a particularly emotional time in their life—such as a death in the family."

"But—"

"Often the body will simply delay ovulation until it's under less stress. For you, I would guess that occurred sometime in early July."

Kate nodded. *July second to be exact.*

"Am I correct in guessing you have an idea whom the father is?"

"Yes." Kate fought not to cry.

"Any concerns you'd like to talk about?"

"None that you could fix."

"I'm sorry if this is unwelcome news. Let me reassure you, your baby appears quite healthy and is developing perfectly normally." She stood as she checked her watch. "So, keep up with the folic acid supplements and multivitamins, eat well and we'll see you in four weeks. Okay?"

Kate nodded again, took her visit slip from the doctor and walked to the scheduling assistant in a haze. With her appointment card in hand she stumbled into the bright September sunshine.

Pregnant.

With Jim's baby.

What in the world was she going to do *now?*

September 4
You know those days when life just walks up and blind-sides you? Takes
the wind out of your sails? Strands you up the creek without a paddle, life
vest or flare, to gnaw on your own shoe for sustenance?
I wish it were one of those days.

CHAPTER FORTY-FOUR

IT WAS AFTER SEVEN by the time Kate pulled into her grandmother's
driveway. She almost wished she hadn't committed to participate in the
Gifts for the Greater Good auction the next day, but she had to keep
moving despite the haze of disbelief still clouding her brain. Since she'd
officially submitted her resignation to Nancy, she had no choice but to
follow through with her plans. Between part-time office work for Carter
and a few hours helping Lydia at her shop each week, Kate figured she'd
earn enough to get by until she got her business off the ground.

She turned. Liam was asleep in his car seat, his head slumped
awkwardly to the side. She resisted the urge to prop him up, knowing it
would wake him. Better to unload first.

Pulling the few bags she'd packed from the trunk, she carried them
to the front door. The door was thrown wide before she even had a
chance to knock.

"Kate!" Nana cried. "You're early! I didn't expect you until eight!"

"Traffic was light." Kate stepped into the small foyer and lowered
her bags to the floor. She hadn't gone into a lot of detail on the phone but
knew Nana would understand. It wasn't until she straightened that she got
her first look into the living room beyond—where two elderly women
stared back at her with keen interest.

"Nana?" Kate muttered out of the side of her mouth. "Why are your
friends here?"

"They are here," Nana replied, as she shut the door firmly behind
Kate, "because you need help."

"So you set up an ambush?" Kate muttered back.

"Think of it as an intervention," Lydia Sweet offered helpfully as
she bobbed what looked like a Starburst in her cocktail.

Another woman with a sour expression elbowed Lydia. "I wouldn't use that word."

"What word?"

"*Intervention*," the sourpuss murmured back. "Remember? Her ex-husband was a lush. You know, *the dead one*."

"*Claire!*" Nana admonished as Kate continued to stand disbelievingly on the doormat. Were they really intending to discuss her private life? *Here?*

"I know you wouldn't have wanted me to invite them if I'd asked you," Nana was explaining as she pulled Kate further into the living room. "But think of it this way, each of us has nearly fifty years of experience with dating and marriage. That's nearly two hundred collective years of female wisdom at your disposal."

"Over two hundred...? But there are only three of you."

Just then the door to the kitchen thumped open and Ruth Pearson stepped through with a plate of hors d'oeuvres.

"Ruth Pearson?" Kate hissed into Nana's ear. "You invited *Ruth Pearson?*"

"Of course," Nana replied with utterly annoying aplomb. "Why, in heaven's name, wouldn't I?"

Kate turned her back on the other 'ladies' and pinned her grandmother with what she hoped was a meaningful look. "Nana, have you *any* idea what I wanted to talk to you about?"

"Well, I thought I... Isn't this about you carrying Jim's baby?"

Okay, audience or not, she had to sit down.

"You *knew?*" Kate felt for the edge of the sofa as Lydia shuffled eagerly to the side. "But... *how?*" Did she have some sort of neon sign above her head with an arrow saying: Jim's baby on board? How could they possibly know? *She* had just found out!

"Lydia guessed," explained Ruth as she held the tray out to Kate who shook her head numbly. "Lydia's always had a knack for that. Usually knew when we were pregnant before we did. Freaked your grandmother here out to no end."

"It *was* awfully surreal," Nana agreed as she took a selection from the tray and popped it in her mouth. "Just once I wish she could have let me figure it out for myself."

Lydia shrugged and bobbed her dissolving candy. "It's a gift."

"But, I thought it was Randy's," Kate mumbled before she had the sense to censor herself.

"*Randy's?*" Nana nearly choked on her ham and cheese roll up. "Couldn't possibly be his."

"Definitely not Randy's," Ruth agreed.

This was getting out of hand. "I think I know what's possible and what's not possible. You forget I already have one child." She jumped up, and her hand flew to her mouth. "Liam! I almost forgot! He's still in the car. If he wakes up alone, he'll have a fit!"

"Don't worry," Ruth said as she calmly swiped port wine cheese onto a cracker. "Rachel said she'd take him for a few hours."

"Rachel... knows?"

"Oh, heavens, no, she doesn't know," Ruth assured her. "We just said we needed a hand tonight and she agreed to help. No questions asked. She'd a good one, that one."

As if on cue, the doorbell rang. Nana scurried to answer it and talked in hushed tones to what Kate could only assume was Rachel. Moments later, a sleepy Liam stepped through the door and said Auntie Rachel was going to take him to the park and would that be okay?

Kate nodded, not knowing what else to do, and then Liam was swept through the door again.

"I said she could use your car," Nana said as she sat down. "So she wouldn't have to transfer the car seat."

Kate nodded again, her mind in a blur. She sat on the sofa.

They knew. They all *knew*.

"Have a beef roll up. They're good." Kate blinked up at the gruff woman—Claire was it?—who held out the tray of food. "You look like you could use a little red meat right now."

Kate took a roll-up obediently. "I... I don't know what to say. Until this morning, I thought it was Randy's."

Claire rolled her eyes. "June, your granddaughter needs a drink."

"She can't have alcohol!" Lydia interrupted. "It's bad for the baby!"

"Would you relax? I just meant water or something. She's not thinking straight. How could it possibly be the dead husband's? That was months ago!" Claire pointed at Kate with the end of a frilly toothpick. "Have you seen her stomach? She's not even showing! And we all know baby number two pops almost as soon as the pregnancy test comes back positive..."

"But..." Kate began.

"That's true," Ruth cut in. "I remember when she first came how skinny she looked in her little bikini. She would have been at least two months then if it had been her husband's. Plus, she mixed raw hamburger without gagging. I could never touch raw meat at all for the first trimester with any of my pregnancies. I'd be running for the bathroom every time."

"But..." Kate tried again.

"Me, either," Nana interrupted. "Plus, I would be so darn tired. You're absolutely right. It *must* be Jim's baby."

"*But we only slept together once!*" Kate cried as she leapt from the couch. *Make that twice. Okay, technically, three times. But still...*

Claire chortled into her on-the-rocks tumbler. "Once is all it takes."

"But..."

"*Walter.*"

"*James.*"

"*Anne.*"

The ladies spoke in near unison.

"*What?*" Kate turned to her Nana who'd spoken last. "*Mom?* Are you telling me Ma was a mistake?"

Nana blushed as she shrugged. "We always told people she came a month early, but she was actually two weeks past my due date."

Claire snorted. "It didn't help you any she was a whopping eight-pounder, either."

"But..." Kate looked around the group of women. It seemed she was having a singular inability to utter anything but that one word this evening. "Are you all telling me your first-born were all *mistakes?* How is that possible?"

Lydia took Kate's hand and settled her back on the couch beside her. "Honey, you have to understand. We were teenagers at a time when the world was going crazy. We didn't know if there'd be a tomorrow—or if our men would even be here tomorrow."

"What are you talking about?"

"You know, the war and all..." Lydia trailed off meaningfully.

Kate knew she was frowning, but it was difficult to concentrate on calculating when you were being fed a line of bull. "That makes no sense. Nana, you were *born* during World War II."

"Okay, so war had nothing to do with it," Lydia allowed. "I just think it makes it sound so much more romantic, don't you?"

"Makes *what* sound romantic?" Kate asked exasperatedly.

"Not waiting," Ruth said.

"I imagine it was like it was during the war," Lydia said. "The urgency and all. It felt like it to me, at any rate."

"Would you cut it out about the war?" Claire demanded. "We need to get to the point."

"Which is?" Kate was afraid to ask.

"That we decided we'd do it together," Ruth said.

"Together."

"Lose our virginity," Nana clarified helpfully.

"*Oh God,*" Kate groaned. This was not something she needed to hear.

"Now before you go thinking something scandalous, I have to explain: we didn't want to be a bunch of silly brides who didn't know what to expect on their wedding night. I mean, what if our men were duds? We'd be stuck with them for the rest of our lives! So, we agreed that as moral support for each other we'd go all the way on the same night."

"*D-I-Day,*" Lydia cut in meaningfully.

"D-I-Day?" Kate echoed doubtfully.

"*Do-It-Day*," the ladies said together.

"And we did!" Lydia said happily, her eyes going soft and dreamy.

"Six weeks later rabbits were dropping like flies, if you know what I mean," Claire cut in.

"Is that why you all got married the same summer?" Kate asked, comprehension finally dawning. She turned to Lydia. "You did, too, didn't you? Get married then? But you never..."

"No, we never did have any children," Lydia cut in with a bittersweet smile. "But I was so scared I *might* be pregnant, I convinced my Stu we should get married just in case! And I already knew he was a keeper—if you know what I mean!"

Kate looked around at the group. She had more in common with these women that she would have ever imagined. Except they had taken charge of their lives and Kate's was a runaway train. There was another difference, too. In their day, an unplanned pregnancy meant one solution: marriage.

Things weren't that simple any more.

"The thing is," she began, "Jim doesn't know yet and... I don't know that I'm ready to tell him."

"You'll start showing soon," Claire advised around a mouthful of roast beef. "Mark my words. It doesn't matter how many sit-ups you do, you'll start showing. You need to tell him sooner or later."

"I know... I mean, that's not the point." Kate frowned. "Telling him isn't the solution."

"It's a step in the right direction," Ruth said. "He can't make this right if he doesn't know."

"I know that. It's just... what do you mean 'make this right?' What do you expect him to do? Marry me?" She laughed then, a short, choked sound.

Four sets of eyes blinked at Kate over their bifocal lenses.

"You do, don't you? You expect that once he hears I'm having his baby he'll ask me to marry him and everything will be fine, don't you?"

"Well... yes," Nana said.

Kate stood and set her untouched hors d'oeuvre on the coffee table. "It doesn't work like that nowadays." She was shaking, she realized numbly. She needed air. She didn't even want to tell them he'd already proposed without even knowing the baby was his.

Ruth stood, too. "James is a good boy, Kate. He won't shirk his responsibility."

Kate's mouth gaped, she knew, but she was too upset now to worry about it as tears of frustration burned the back of her eyes. "You don't get it. I don't *want* Jim to marry me because I'm having his baby! I want him to marry me *because he loves me!*" She stopped then, her hand flying to her mouth. "I didn't mean that! What I meant was—"

"You're having his love child!" Lydia clapped her hands gleefully, a reaction that seemed bizarrely inappropriate to Kate. "This is wonderful!"

Wonderful? What was wonderful about carrying the unwanted child of a man—

Kate caught herself short. *Unwanted?* Dear heaven, nothing could be farther from the truth! Since she'd learned she was carrying Jim's child, she couldn't think of anything more exciting.

It thrilled her. Amazed her.

This child had been conceived in passion. In joy. In wonder.

In lies.

Kate sat heavily on the edge of a chair and hung her head in her hands. He'd asked her point blank, *you're covered?* And she'd said, *yes.*

"Kate?" Nana asked. "What's wrong?"

Kate looked at the group of concerned faces before her. "What's wrong? You even have to ask? I'm about to have the unplanned baby of a man who has no idea this is coming and you even have to *ask?*"

"He must have known there were risks, as it were," Ruth said. "It's not as if you young folks don't learn these things."

"Yes, he knew there were risks," Kate murmured feebly.

"Didn't you take precautions?" Claire demanded. "It's not as if you don't have access to contraception these days."

"No," Kate murmured even more feebly, "we didn't. I... I didn't think we needed to."

"I'm shocked!" Ruth spoke now. "I thought Jim was more responsible than that!"

"He is. *He was!*" Kate was beyond embarrassed, but she couldn't let Jim's own grandmother think ill of him. "I... I implied I was on the pill."

"You what?!" It was her own Nana who turned on her now.

"I thought I was already pregnant, all right?! He... I... Anyway, it didn't seem like a big deal at the time!"

"I guess you were wrong about that," Claire mumbled.

Nana shot her friend a quelling look.

"I know this is a mess. I know it is. But it's *my* mess." Kate stood on legs more than a little shaky now. "You all mean well, but you can't fix this. I'll figure it out. *On my own.*"

"He'll do the right thing," Lydia murmured encouragingly as Kate walked to the door. "I know he will. It'll work out."

Kate didn't have the heart or will to contradict her. She didn't want Jim to 'do the right thing.' She knew with utter certainty that he would propose again the moment he knew she was carrying his child. And that was the problem. She'd just be another responsibility he'd 'take care of,' because that's what Jim did. It was the kind of man he was. But it wouldn't be a marriage. At least, not any Kate wanted a part of.

"I'm going for a walk," she said dully.

The ladies nodded in unison, for once, blessedly silent.

HOW COULD SHE HAVE been so *stupid?* How could she have been so out of touch with her own body not to have realized she wasn't pregnant but *ovulating?*

Kate's strides lengthened in the shadows by the edge of the road. She had no one to fix this. No one to turn to but herself.

She barely paid attention as the car slowed beside her, the glow of headlights confirming what she already knew—it was time to turn around. Then she heard the window slide down, and her heart slammed in her chest. She didn't dare look. Because if it was *him*...

"Kate, what are you doing out here?"

Kate blew out a slow breath and didn't even try to hide the raw emotion in her eyes. "I was just..." but she couldn't finish, couldn't even begin to formulate the rest of the sentence, as Rachel threw open the driver's door and ran to wrap Kate in her arms.

"Oh, honey, what's wrong?"

Kate looked over Rachel's shoulder at the empty rear seat.

"Before you ask, Liam's with my dad. Grams wouldn't tell me why you needed help tonight, but I knew it must be something major. I'm sorry. I couldn't stay away. We've been so worried. Susan and Grace are on high alert waiting for my call."

Kate bit her trembling lip and looked at the sky, willing her flooded eyes to dry up. She'd caused these good people so much trouble. "I never meant to worry you."

"I thought that's what friends were for."

Friends. The tightness in Kate's heart eased a little.

"So," Rachel said, stepping back. "I'm guessing the ladies gave you a hundred pieces of advice, drove you crazy in the process, and you've come out here to work it out on your own."

Kate gave a wobbly smile. "Something like that."

"How about we go gather the girls and you tell us what's going on?"

"It's complicated," Kate warned.

"Trust me. We're good with complicated," Rachel assured her as she held open the passenger door.

CHAPTER FORTY-FIVE

———————

"I'VE GOT A PROBLEM."

Jim tried not to roll his eyes as Doug sank pitiably onto his couch. Sure, no one wanted his help until he was knee deep in crap himself. He took a long slug of his beer and sat across from his brother-in-law.

"Join the club. So what's the problem?"

Doug stared at his shoes. "I think my wife is having an affair."

"*What?!*" Jim spewed beer across the rug. *Great.* One more mess to clean up. "What makes you think Rachel's having an affair?"

Doug sighed. "Not an *affair* affair. At least, not yet." He sighed again, reminding Jim of a sad, lost puppy.

"Doug—"

"She's been talking to an old boyfriend."

"Old boyfriend? What are you talking about? *You're* her only boyfriend!"

Doug sat up again, leaned his elbows on his knees. "Except for Jeff. She doesn't know I know about him, but I do."

"What the hell are you talking about? Who the hell is Jeff?"

"*Jeff.* Jeff. She had this *fling* with him back when I was in college. I thought it was long over, but I ran into him at the gas station today and he mentioned," Doug took another breath, "*he mentioned he and Rachel met for coffee last week.*"

Jim sank onto the couch. "Wait a minute. Jeff *Dayton* Jeff? But he and Grace..."

"Weren't together at the time. It was after graduation when they'd split up."

"Jesus."

"Yeah."

"But that was years ago, Doug. Meeting for coffee is no big deal. Especially seeing as he didn't lie about it. I'm sure it's ancient history. For both of them."

"If it's ancient history, why didn't she tell me? But she hasn't. Not one word! She's gone and had coffee with some old flame and doesn't tell me? Don't you think that's a little suspicious?" Doug was on his feet now, his hands gesturing almost comically.

"You actually think Rachel would cheat on you? Are you kidding?"

"No, I'm not kidding! She's been acting weird lately. Restless. *Moody...*"

"She's pregnant!"

"It's more than that. I tell you, I think she's thinking about having an affair with him!"

"Talk to her."

"I can't."

"You will!"

"I won't!" Doug plopped back onto the couch defiantly.

Jim's legs ate up the distance to the kitchen. Of all the stubborn, stupid, ridiculous...! He had *real* problems to deal with, not some made up, imaginary— "Call her!" he insisted, thrusting his phone toward his brother-in-law.

"She won't admit it."

Jim rolled his eyes and punched in Rachel's number. "Hey, Rachel? It's Jim. Doug's here. Yeah. Hey, the reason I'm calling is Doug thinks you're having an affair. Uh-huh. I told him he's crazy, but he's got some— Rach?"

Jim dropped his arm. "Lost her. Must have gone out of range."

Doug scowled and took a swig of Jim's beer. "Isn't that convenient?"

Jim sighed. "Oh, snap out of it. She's *not*, I repeat, *not* having an affair with Jeff."

"Maybe not yet, but she's thinking about it."

"Then get her thinking about something else!"

Doug raised his eyebrows. "Like?"

Jim grabbed his beer back and became intensely focused on pulling the label off his bottle. "You know. Spice things up a little."

"Uh-uh. Rachel doesn't like things too crazy if you know what I mean."

Jim closed his eyes on a bid for strength. Where was Carter when you needed a guy with no verbal filter to say what needed to be said? He winced. "You sure about that? I mean... just asking."

Doug peered up at him. Jim avoided eye contact. "Are you suggesting what I think you're suggesting?"

Jim cleared his throat. "If you're thinking what I'm thinking, then, yes."

Doug frowned. "I've always held Rachel on such a pedestal. She's a wonderful woman."

"Yes. Yes, she is," Jim agreed.

"She deserves to be treated well. With respect."

"Yes. Yes, she does."

"And she came back to me, you know? She didn't want him after all. I swore then and there I wasn't going to do anything, ever, that might remind her about, you know, *him*... Maybe that was a mistake."

"Maybe."

"And, hey, your sister's a beautiful woman. Who wouldn't want to—you know?"

"Nothing more needs to be said, I'm thinking."

"You're right." Doug bounded from the couch. "You're right! I just hope it's not too late!" He clasped Jim in an awkward hug. "Thank you! I'm so glad we had this conversation!"

Jim grimaced and took a step back. "Me, too."

CHAPTER FORTY-SIX

"DO-IT-DAY?" RACHEL let out an indelicate whoop of laughter. "Wait till Mom hears about this!"

"Rachel, I don't know if they want it to be common knowledge."

"I don't know, sounds to me like they're kind of proud of it," Grace interjected, pushing aside her iced tea. "Think about it! They're rebels, all of them. Nobody had sex before marriage back then."

Kate bobbed her straw in her lemonade and smiled wryly. "Apparently they did."

"I guess you're right." Rachel grabbed an onion ring from the basket in the center of the table. "I can't believe how good these taste. If I don't eat when I get hungry—" She cut herself off abruptly and stuffed an onion ring into her mouth.

Kate nodded. "No problem." The smell of the onion rings wasn't doing great things for her own stomach, but she'd been so grateful when Rachel had stopped the car, she hadn't quibbled about where they were going.

"So," said Rachel, "you weren't crying and walking aimlessly in the dark because our grandmothers had premarital sex, so how about you tell us the real reason we're here?"

Kate grimaced and bobbed her straw again, glanced around the diner. "You get right to it, don't you?"

"I have a feeling we have a limited amount of time till Dad runs out of entertainment for Liam and calls for reinforcements."

"Right." Kate sipped her drink. "Do you want the short version or the long one?"

"Quit stalling," said Grace. "Give us the short and we'll probe for details."

"Right." Kate played with her straw. "The thing is... I'm..." She blew out a long breath. "This is harder than I thought it would be."

"We could say it for you, but I think it's good for you to say it first," said Rachel.

"I'm sorry?"

"You need the practice. You know, for when you tell the father. So go ahead, tell us."

"You know I'm pregnant?!"

Rachel took another hearty bite of onion ring. "Well, duh. I think we kind of got the hint when you opened with the premarital sex story. Plus, you go a little green around the gills every time I bite into an onion ring. Why didn't you just say something? I could have ordered something else."

Kate blinked her surprise at the three other women around the table. What was it with these people? Was she that much of an open book? "I don't know what to say."

"Why don't you say the words? As I said, good practice."

"Okay." She took a breath. "I'm pregnant."

"See? It gets easier every time you say it. I know. First few times it feels so unreal, and I actually thought I *wanted* to get pregnant."

Grace turned abruptly. "Thought you wanted? What's that supposed to mean? Of course, you want to be pregnant!"

"You're pregnant?" Susan gasped.

Rachel blushed, nodded. "Eleven weeks."

"Congratulations!"

"Thanks."

"What do you mean, 'thought you wanted?'" Grace said again.

Rachel frowned. "We're not talking about me. We're here for Kate. Kate needs to be able to say the words."

"I don't know how—" Kate began.

"Yes, you do," Rachel insisted. "I know it's scary, because every time you say the words, 'I'm pregnant' it makes it more real. Like you're one step closer to that delivery room."

Susan frowned delicately. "I don't remember it feeling like—"

"What do you mean, 'thought you wanted?'" Grace persisted.

"She's right," Kate replied shakily. "It's true." She buried her face in her hands.

"Okay," said Susan, "she's pregnant. The next logical question is: who's the father?"

"Doug, of course!" Grace gasped.

"What?!" Rachel cried.

Kate held up a hand in silent plea. "Are we talking about me or not?"

"We're talking about you," Susan assured her, giving her friends a quelling look. "So, who's the father?"

"You don't know?" asked Kate.

"Oh," said Rachel, "we have a hunch, but let's pretend we have no idea."

Kate blanched as Rachel stuffed another onion ring in her mouth. "The ironic thing is, I thought the baby was Randy's, my late husband's..."

"Mmm." Susan frowned. "I'm thinking that's not a good opener. For telling the father. It's not a good way to start. I mean, you don't want him to remember who else has been in the picture, because we all know it's irrelevant. I wouldn't open with that."

Kate sat back, nonplussed. "I'm sorry. I don't know if I can do this. This is too weird. You... our grandmothers... no one is reacting... *normally*."

"You mean we're not freaking out?" Rachel said.

"Well, yes. I mean you are, but not about *this*." She waved a hand toward her belly.

Grace reached across and touched Kate's hand on the table. "Don't you get it? It's because *this* is not a tragedy. *This* is a miracle!"

"A miracle?"

"Yes! Life doesn't always go according to plan. I mean, it rarely does. But it works out. So what if you're pregnant with Jim's baby? We know it might not be the order you'd like things in, but it doesn't make it bad—"

"Wh—? How do you know I'm carrying *Jim's* baby?"

Grace blanched this time. *"Ohmigod!* Are you saying it's *not* Jim's?"

"No! I mean, yes! It's Jim's."

"Phew! You had me freaking for a moment there."

"Sorry."

"It's okay." Grace dabbed her forehead with her napkin and took a few deep breaths as if to calm herself. "So. Now what?"

"Yeah," Rachel said. "When are you going to tell him?"

"I don't know," Kate replied. "I'm afraid of how he'll react."

"Jim? Why would you be afraid of him? You must know he'll do the right thing."

Kate sighed. "Why does everyone keep saying that? Don't you understand that's the *last* thing I want him to do?"

Grace frowned. "No, I don't understand. Don't you care about him?"

"Of course, I do! Too much."

"Then what's the problem?" Rachel asked.

"I don't want to be another person Jim is responsible for! I don't want to be another person he 'saves!'"

"Seems to me those are just words," Susan said.

"But they're important words!"

"Really? Are they so important you would push him away because of them? And what about the baby? Doesn't he or she deserve a father? A father—I might add—who would be more than willing to be a part of its life?"

"I'm not saying I'll keep him out of the baby's life. I'm just saying I don't know if now is the time to tell him. Up until this morning, this wasn't even a possibility I'd considered. I need to get my head around it. I need to think things through."

"Well time's a ticking," Susan gently added.

Kate let out another sigh. "I know."

"Don't you love him?" Rachel asked.

Kate bit her bottom lip to keep it from trembling, nodded.

"Then what are you afraid of?"

"Everything," she whispered, tears welling. "I've made so many mistakes. So many wrong choices, and Jim is such a good guy. He deserves somebody who's not so confused. I'm afraid..." She gulped and took a stabilizing breath, looked up at them again. "I'm afraid he'll end up resenting me. I screwed up..."

Rachel met her gaze, her own eyes welling with tears. "But you love him," she whispered, "and if he really loves you, the mistakes you've made won't change that. You have to believe that."

"I don't know..." Kate began.

"*No!*" Rachel insisted. "You *have* to believe that! You have to!" Then she buried her face in her hands and began to weep.

The other three women blinked at each other in surprise.

"Are we still talking about Kate?" Susan asked.

"What *did* you mean, 'thought you wanted?'" Grace asked again, more gently this time.

"I can't talk about this now!" Rachel sobbed into her hands. "We're here to help Kate!"

Kate reached across the table and rested a hand on Rachel's shoulder as it shook under her palm. "Tell them, Rachel. It'll help. Truly. It'll help."

They all waited as Rachel visibly pulled herself together. She took a couple last shuddering breaths then pinned Kate with tear-filled eyes. "You're right. I *know* you're right. But it's not them I need to tell—it's Doug."

"*What* do you need to tell Doug?" Grace wanted to know.

"And *you*," Rachel said more firmly, pointing at Kate, "need to tell *Jim.*"

She nodded. Rachel was right.

"If you'll tell Doug, I'll tell Jim, but *you*," Kate turned to Grace, "*have* to tell Jeff how you feel."

Grace paled.

"You have to," Kate insisted. "He deserves to know. And you won't be happy until you've come clean. You've run from it long enough." She looked around the table. "We all have."

Grace turned expectantly to Susan.

"What?" Susan asked, looking at the others. "I'm apparently the only one here not keeping secrets!"

September 5
Wish me luck. After years of drifting, flirting around the edges, dreaming,
I'm stepping off the cliff to see if I can fly. I've got a crazy get-up for the
occasion and an even crazier group of new friends to cheer me on. Want
to know the weird thing? It doesn't scare me. Much. Not stepping off
scares me more. It's time. I'm ready. And as a wise 'Tibetan' monk once
told my mother, "Bonsai!" ☺

CHAPTER FORTY-SEVEN

KATE BIT HER LIP AND TUGGED at the edge of her sequined top,
feeling decidedly conspicuous in the crowded parking lot by the high
school gym. "I wish it came down a little further."

"It's supposed to bare your belly," Rachel assured her. "That's the
point. Now stay still. I've almost got your hair fixed." She pulled a bobby
pin from her lips and tucked another strand into the elaborate up-do she'd
crafted back at the house.

Kate wrapped her arms around her middle, knowing it did nothing to
hide the gauzy turquoise harem pants she wore, or the fringe of beads
dangling against her bare midriff where the matching cropped jacket left
off.

"Stop worrying. It's the perfect costume to get attention for your
new business."

"I still can't believe how you guys pulled this all together so
quickly."

"Well, you can thank Susan and the Sugar Falls Community Theatre
for the get-up, but the rest is all you. You, Kate, are The Clutter Genie
who will—"

"—make chaos magically disappear," Kate finished on a laugh. "It
sounded so good last night, but now... You don't think it's over the top?"

"Maybe a little, but that's okay. It's catchy! Memorable. You'll
make a splash tonight, and before long, the clients will be lining up
outside your door. You'll see."

"I hope you're right."

"I know I'm right. There." Rachel stepped back. "I think I'm done.
You look perfect."

"Thanks. I owe you."

"No you don't, just help me adjust this bustier. It's shifted again."

Kate worried her lip as she tugged the bustier back into position for Rachel. "Rach, I know you and Doug are trying to work things out, but are you sure this is a good idea?"

Rachel tugged the red bustier higher then poked her arms into a gauzy white overshirt. "I need to do this. We had a long talk after I got home last night. I'll never be happy if I think I've settled or missed out, Kate. Despite everything that's going right in my life, I still need to explore... see if this is right for me."

"If you're sure."

"I'm sure." Rachel swept back her honey-blonde hair and shielded her eyes from the late afternoon sun.

"But... riding a motorcycle... in your condition?" Kate asked hesitantly.

"We're not going far." Rachel reached over and gripped her hand. "Oh, I know you think it's crazy, but—pregnant or not—I *want* to do this. I have to see if I've been romanticizing things all these years. Maybe it'll feel silly, even wrong, but I don't want to spend the rest of my life wondering."

They stood near the edge of the parking lot and waited, the crickets chirping in the nearby athletic fields.

Moments later a motorcycle rumbled toward them. Its lone rider wore all black, his leather jacket supple with age.

He stopped.

Rachel took a breath and stepped forward with a tentative smile.

The rider smiled back from behind his visor, then pulled his helmet off.

"Ready?" Doug asked.

Rachel nodded, unstrapped the second helmet from the seat and slid into place behind her husband. "Where are we going?" she asked.

He slid his helmet back on and revved the engine, only his brilliant smile visible. "Anywhere, Gorgeous. So long as it's with you."

CHAPTER FORTY-EIGHT

"HOLY COW, RUTH HAS outdone herself. Can you believe the turnout for this thing?" Nana peeked around the curtain at the auction in progress for the umpteenth time that evening. They were halfway through the program, and Kate was desperately trying to calm the fluttering in her belly. Between her splashy debut at the auction and the flyers tucked into every program advertising her new business, she prayed she would woo plenty of clients to earn a decent income. She had to.

"Okay the school band is almost done with their intermission piece. You're up next. Ready?"

Kate nodded—what else was she going to do?—and stepped onto the stage. Hundreds of eyes turned to her. She swallowed hard.

Grace winked from the podium. "Our next item up for bid will be in hot demand. The Clutter Genie will make chaos magically disappear! As you see in your program, we're taking bids on one full room reorganization tonight. Not just a closet. Not just your junk drawer, we're talking *one full room*. I've seen the organizational magic this lady can perform, from home offices to fundraisers, so don't be shy. How about we start the bidding at fifty dollars tonight? Do I hear fifty?"

Kate smiled and waved as a gentleman in the back made the first bid.

"Now this is a valuable service, so we'll be increasing the bids in twenty-five dollar increments. Do I hear seventy-five?"

As the bidding rose above $125, Kate flushed with excitement. She smiled and waved again.

"$150. I'm looking for $150. Do I hear $150?"

"Two hundred."

Kate caught her breath as Jim walked down the aisle toward the stage, his eyes boring into hers. His lips tilted in that half-smile that had her heart skipping a beat. "But I want to know if she'll wear the outfit for me, too." He was wearing a navy suit, no doubt for the announcement of the calendar voting results at the end of the auction. He'd never looked more appealing.

"I'm sorry, sir, the outfit is for promotional purposes only, but I can assure you she's worth every penny. I've seen her work magic on a kitchen reorganization—"

"Two twenty-five!" someone yelled from the back row.

"Two fifty," another voice called out.

"*Five hundred*," said Jim, standing just below Kate now. The room grew quiet. "But I wonder if the lady will entertain other proposals?"

"*Jim*," Grace scolded, her palm over the microphone, "this is a charity auction. We have to keep this family-friendly."

"I'm all for family-friendly. I was just wondering if the lady would entertain a proposal of marriage."

An excited murmur rippled through the crowd.

Kate's knees buckled. She struggled to breathe. "I don't—"

"Five twenty-five!" yelled a voice from the crowd.

Jim whirled. "*Grams?* I'm trying to propose here! Don't bid *against* me!"

"It's for charity," she replied, palming something to him. "Sweeten the pot for her, James."

Jim turned back to Kate with a smile. "Okay. I'll sweeten the pot. Five fifty—if you also let me adopt Liam as my own son."

The room fell silent as Kate stared at him in shock.

"The lady drives a hard bargain," he said into the silence. "Okay. Five seventy-five—if you'll also let me be the father of your future children."

Kate couldn't hold it in. The single tear slid onto her cheek. In an instant, Jim took the three steps onto the stage and was beside her, wiping it away.

"How'd you guess?" she whispered.

His eyes held hers. Intent. Searching. "Guess?"

In an unconscious movement, her hand found the soft swell of her belly and his eyes followed, then his lips curved in a disbelieving smile. "Kate," he breathed, "are you saying... I already am a father?"

She nodded, unable to form the words.

His lips brushed her forehead. "Why didn't you tell me?" he whispered.

"I didn't know. I don't want to be saved," she murmured.

"Did it ever occur to you maybe *I* do?" he asked, pulling back so she could see his face. "I've got this hero complex I need help with."

Despite the ghost of a smile his joke elicited, she sighed. She glanced out at the rapt crowd then back again. "And I don't want you to marry me... just because I'm pregnant."

"Okay, I won't," he assured her. Then his face broke into a beautiful, crooked grin. "But, can I marry you because I'm crazy about you and want to spend the rest of my life with you?"

She trembled, hope bursting in her heart like fireworks in July.

"Come on, Kate. Paint your fingernails purple. Marry me."

She wanted, desperately, to accept but shook her head instead. It wasn't enough.

"What more do you want?" he rasped. "I— *oh.*" He cleared his throat. Swallowed. "You need to hear it, don't you?"

She nodded.

He took a deep breath. Grinned. "I. Love. You." The words whispered over her, a balm and caress soothing away the pain of the past, hinting at the promise for the future. "Marry me, so I can get used to how it feels to say that—and mean it—over and over for the rest of our lives."

"Are you sure?" she breathed.

"As sure as I am we're keeping this outfit of yours."

"Rachel has first dibs," she laughed, relief and joy bubbling through her. "She already called them. But... you're really sure?"

He nodded.

Kate stared in wonder at the sapphire and diamond ring he held out. She knew its history. Knew it wasn't new. But that made it all the more perfect. It was a thing of beauty and promise that was being given a second chance to shine.

Just like her.

"Yes," she said tearfully, brilliantly. "*Yes!* I *will* marry you!"

Jim slid the ring on her finger then whirled to the crowd. "*One thousand!*" he shouted.

And then he swept her into his arms to share a smoldering kiss— blissfully unaware of the roaring applause, their grandmothers' self-satisfied grins or Grace pounding the gavel as she exuberantly declared, "*Sold!*"

EPILOGUE

IN THE END, SHE WORE pale blue—a long, simple sundress she'd discovered at Lydia's shop. It skimmed her toes as she walked toward him, the flowing fabric conforming to her legs as the breeze blew in off the lake. She'd insisted she didn't want to wear white—she'd done the fancy-gown/church-wedding before. She wanted this wedding to be different—to be simpler and less fussy.

He'd never seen her more beautiful.

His chest felt full, as if the joy inside him would burst the confines of his body at any moment. It had been less than a month since he'd proposed, and Grams and Nana had pitched a fit about not being given enough time to pull together a proper wedding, but he hadn't wanted to wait another minute to start life with his new family—and the woman he loved.

Thank goodness Kate was as impatient as he was; although, now that she was nearly three months along, that might have something to do with wanting to be married sooner than later.

Kate held a bouquet of wildflowers tied with a long satin ribbon and smiled that soft, sweet, hopeful smile he knew he'd never grow tired of. Liam, looking smart in his baby blue suit, held her hand as they made their way down the dock to where he stood, waiting, with the Justice of the Peace.

He'd been skeptical of getting married on the dock, but Kate had pointed out the futility of finding any other venue on such short notice. Besides, she'd said, the lake was where their love story began. He wasn't sure if she meant chicken raft, the photo shoot... or the skinny dipping... but it didn't matter. She was right.

Kate passed her bouquet to Grace who stood to one side with Liam and Rachel. Doug and Carter and Ian stood opposite. Kate met Jim near the end of the dock, and he took her hands in his. Her hands trembled slightly, or maybe that was him, but they felt warm and soft and *right* in his own. He ran his thumb over her fingers and smiled at the sparkling pale blue polish she wore.

"I love you," he said, just for her, although it felt easy and natural now after a month of practice.

"I love you, too."

"What do you say we do this?"

She smiled and nodded, overcome with emotion, and by the end of the ceremony, he couldn't have told you what they'd said even though he'd agonized over the vows for days. All he remembered was Kate's smile, Liam solemnly handing over the rings, the elation of hearing the words *husband and wife* and being given permission to kiss his bride.

He'd done so with gusto, hoisting Kate into a high hug and twirling her in a sweeping exuberant circle.

He'd never meant to knock Carter in. Honestly.

Carter landed with an inelegant splash in the cooling late-September lake water and no one laughed as hard as Grace as she generously leaned down to give him a hand back up... until he pulled her—wedding attire, bouquet and all—into the lake beside him.

Jim felt laughter bubble up inside him as Grace sputtered to the surface.

They hadn't meant for it to happen. They hadn't planned for things to end up the way they had, but sometimes, he figured, you have to accept the hand life deals you. True, maybe it's the luck of the draw whether you win or lose, but he was more than happy to play this hand out.

He looked Kate in the eye and knew she felt the same way.

He turned to the side and winked at Liam. "What do you say we get this party started?"

Liam nodded and took his hand, his blue suit already splattered with lake water. He didn't seem to mind. Over the past few weeks, he'd taken to swimming like a fish.

Jim turned to his new wife.

"I love you," he whispered.

And without another word, he reached out and took her hand, and they ran, as a family, off the dock and leaped, laughing, into the water.

Cheri Allan

Dear Reader,

I hope you enjoyed falling in love with Jim and Kate as much as I enjoyed writing their story! I have a special place in my heart for everyday heroes, and Jim is that all-around good guy that *should* get the girl in the end, don't you think? So, any guesses of whether it will be a boy or a girl? ☺

If you enjoyed meeting Carter in *Luck of the Draw* you won't want to miss my next 'Betting on Romance' novel, *Stacking the Deck,* where Carter finds his own happily ever after.

Also, be sure to sign up for my mailing list at www.cheriallan.com to receive invites to exclusive contests and info on new releases! It's easy and free and you may well win cool stuff from beautiful New England! What's not to love about that?

Sweet regards from Sugar Falls!

~ Cheri

About the Author

Cheri writes kissing books about love and other shenanigans from her charming fixer-upper in rural New Hampshire. She is often distracted by social media, reality television, and a menagerie of cats and dogs. If you find her whizzing down the slopes at the nearby mountain with her family or inadvertently killing perennials in her garden, bring her coffee. She will gratefully provide the conversation and chocolate.

Cheri loves to hear from readers!
E-mail her at cheri@cheriallan.com.
Friend her at facebook.com/cheriallanauthor.
Or, visit her website and blog at www.cheriallan.com.

If you enjoyed this book, please consider telling other readers by writing and sharing a review.

Cheri continues her 'Betting on Romance' series with *Stacking the Deck* because—after all—every woman deserves to get lucky.

Book Two 'Betting On Romance' Series:

STACKING THE DECK

Our match-making grandmothers are at it again...
Stacking the Deck in Sugar Falls!

Liz Beacon has life all planned out—prioritized, color-coded *and* cross-referenced. She long ago traded in the geeky high school nickname, teenage pounds and dysfunctional family for a fab career, killer abs and a man every woman would envy. Okay, so her sex life is non-existent and her almost-fiancé is technically a coworker. Life, if not perfect, is still on track. But then, Liz is called home to Sugar Falls, NH, to prepare her childhood home for sale. She's spent ten years denying her insecurities and hokey lawn-ornament roots. There's nothing she'd rather do less than face all she happily left behind, including her embarrassingly one-sided high school crush.

Carter McIntyre has sailed through life on his winsome smile... and by the skin of his teeth. A college drop-out with ADHD, he's learned it's safer to play the carefree charmer than step up and take over his uncle's landscaping business. But then his class valedictorian returns to Sugar Falls and hires him for some home improvements. Now Carter's wondering if it's too late— to grow up, take a chance and win over the only girl who ever believed in him...

www.ingramcontent.com/pod-product-compliance
Lightning Source LLC
Chambersburg PA
CBHW071301170626
46809CB00001B/311